THE ISIS
IMMIGRATION
SECRETARY

Harry DeMell

authorHOUSE®

AuthorHouse™
1663 Liberty Drive
Bloomington, IN 47403
www.authorhouse.com
Phone: 1 (800) 839-8640

Published by AuthorHouse 07/25/2017

ISBN: 978-1-5462-0062-8 (sc)
ISBN: 978-1-5462-0061-1 (hc)
ISBN: 978-1-5462-0063-5 (e)

Library of Congress Control Number: 2017911263

Print information available on the last page.

Any people depicted in stock imagery provided by Thinkstock are models, and such images are being used for illustrative purposes only. Certain stock imagery © Thinkstock.

This book is printed on acid-free paper.

ONE

Ali checked his guns as he watched the sun come up over the desert. He had seen deserts before. He had fought in them, killed men in them. He felt at home in them. As Ali held his guns he felt in control. He had used many guns before, and he felt strong when he touched them.

It was early, but the morning cold was quickly giving way to the heat of the day. His shirt stuck to the seat of the jeep, but the heat didn't bother him. It would be almost a hundred degrees that day. Where he was from it was often much hotter. He couldn't waste gas to run the air conditioner. He couldn't be sure how long he needed to wait.

Ali passed the time by reciting Koranic verses. He took an old tee shirt and wiped clean the revolver and the automatic for the third time. Each bullet was individually wiped to be sure that there were no prints to be found. He placed the automatic directly underneath his seat where he could get it quickly if needed. He placed the revolver just beside him.

There wasn't much to see or do. Ali sat in the jeep with the windows open and looked at the sand and shrubs. Every so often he took out his binoculars to see if anyone was coming. He checked his cell phone for the twentieth time, but there still was no reception in this remote place. You could drive for two hours through this part of Texas without reception. By some miracle the GPS worked. He looked and waited.

Ali finished another bottle of water, and tossed it onto the back seat. All garbage would remain in the car. He didn't want to leave anything that could be used to trace him no matter how unlikely that was. He fished through his pocket for a candy bar and everything fell out. He cursed as he gathered his money, some receipts and some loose M&Ms. He kicked the last few M&Ms and some lose receipts under the seat. He held a Starbucks cash receipt, crumbled it up and tossed it under his seat.

He adjusted his revolver, re-crossed his legs and then took a deep breath. He was happy to wait in the service of Allah but was nervous. There wasn't a doubt in his mind that what he was doing was in the service of God as he understood it.

Ali was a dark-skinned man with large aviator sunglasses and a Yankee baseball cap. His two-day beard made him look fierce. As he sat there he thought about his family in Jordan and wondered if he would ever see them again. It had been a long time since he came to the United States. He could not go back.

Right on time. He could see the pickup truck as it drove through the dry wash to avoid detection by the border patrol. It came in and out of sight as it went over the sand. They needed to be careful this close to the border. Texas was big, but a random patrol could cause them trouble. The truck disappeared around some rocks and shrubs before coming up to the crest of the small hill.

There was little security by the border in this part in Texas. It was just too remote. There was too much desert this close to the Rio Grande. No one in his right mind would try to cross here, yet many did. Bodies of aliens trying to enter the United States were regularly found here. Most died of thirst.

Inland immigration stops made the ride dangerous but Ali had instructions how to avoid detection. He had good information from the coyote that the patrols missed this area. He also knew that the Border Patrol had a schedule that he could count on to avoid detection. Nevertheless, he made sure that no one would spot his jeep. He knew exactly what he was doing.

"*Figanerru.*" *Finally*, he said aloud to himself in Arabic. "I'll take care of this."

As the pickup truck pulled up behind some brush, Ali picked up his binoculars. He looked around before getting out of the Jeep. Two men came out of the pickup. The driver was Mexican, short, stout and nervous. The other looked Middle Eastern with his closely cropped beard but could have been mistaken for Mexican. He was tall and fit and stood at attention as he looked at Ali with his dark, piercing eyes. They both wore jeans and tee shirts. The Mexican wore a straw cowboy hat and the other man a baseball cap.

The driver came over to the jeep. In a heavy Mexican accent he said, "There you go, John. Got him here just like I said."

"Good. Were you spotted?"

"Never. I've done this a hundred times before. If you listened to me you should have had no problems either. Do you have the second half of my money?"

"Yes. I have it right here." Ali handed the driver a brown paper bag and then he took a step back.

As the Mexican looked into the bag, Ali pulled the revolver from the back of his waist.

"Mierda! You don't have to do this." The Mexican looked stunned as Ali pumped three bullets into his chest at close range. Ali took out a knife and was about to cut off the driver's head when the passenger said, "Don't. They will find out who we are when we are ready. Not yet."

As the passenger straightened his baseball cap, Ali saluted him. "Yes, Captain." Ali stood at attention. He took the old tee shirt from the jeep. "We need to wipe down the truck."

"Sure. Don't salute me again. People will ask questions." The passenger turned towards the truck. "There's another person in the back of the truck." Ali handed the passenger the gun. The passenger walked to the back of the truck. As he did a small, dark-skinned woman jumped out and started to run. The passenger slowly aimed and shot her three times in her back. She fell in the sand. He wiped the empty revolver clean and tossed it aside. Ali took out one small joint sealed in a plastic bag, went over to the truck and spread the weed around the inside of the cab.

"Good to see you, Naib. Let's get the package."

The men went to the truck where a wooden box was wrapped in a large duffel bag. The box was the size of a small coffin. It weighed as though someone was in it. The two men could barely lift it as they loaded it into the Jeep. Ali noticed the Korean markings on one corner of the box.

Ali and Naib got into the jeep. They took off quickly.

"I can't believe you got this here all the way from Pakistan."

"We'll talk later."

"They will blame this on the drug gangs," Ali said. "It's a long ride to New York. Once we're there, we'll file a few papers with immigration, you'll get an ID and a work card, and the pressure will be off. I have the

3

law firm picked and ready. They even have an Iraqi secretary who will assist you."

"Allah will protect us."

* * *

The court smelled like a high school locker room as Tony Sorrelli looked at the list of cases posted by the entrance. There were no windows and the air was stale. The room was packed.

It was master calendar day at the New York Immigration Court, and every one of the dark wood benches were filled. Nervous people were standing in the isles and in the back. There was a small crowd outside the entrance listening for their names to be called.

The judge sat in the front of the court on a raised platform and in his black robe. Once in a while he would adjust his glasses or wipe back the sweat on his receding salt and pepper hairline as he examined information on his computer. In front of the judge sat the prosecutor with a shopping cart filled with files. She was a young woman dressed in a black suit with large rimmed glasses and her hair conservatively cut short. She was an attractive woman hiding in business attire. In front of her sat an open laptop. At the adjoining table was an attorney, his client and an interpreter. There were small microphones by their faces. Papers were spread out on the tables.

Behind the judge was a large round seal of the U.S. Department of Justice. The seal also said 'Executive Office of Immigration Review.' There was a clock to one side and a large computer screen at an angle so only the judge could see it. The judge was constantly staring at both. To the other side there was a bookshelf filled with too many books and with plants covering the top.

About half of the forty scheduled cases would show up. Those who didn't would be ordered deported without a hearing. They call it *in absencia*. It would be difficult for the judge to handle even twenty cases that morning.

Master calendars were where the judges did most of the case processing. You could feel the tension at these hearings as determinations were made as to whether people could remain in the United States and whether families would be separated. Testimony was rarely taken, but it was a place where pleadings were taken, documents were exchanged and cases moved along until a real trial would be needed. Agreements were made to allow some aliens to leave on their own and to order some deported as a matter of law. A few cases were dismissed. Most cases were disposed of in these ways.

The courtroom looked like a miniature United Nations. People looked as though they came from all parts of the world, were different races and wore different dress. There was a Buddhist monk with a shaved head next to an African wearing a long flowered shirt. Several Central American Indians were mixed about. Mothers were trying to control their children. One was breast-feeding a child. One bench was filled with Chinese. An orthodox Jewish man sat just behind them with his black hat and coat. Next to him, an overweight Catholic priest was sweating and fanning himself with a newspaper.

The majority of people, though, were dressed to look as American as possible wearing *I love NY* tee shirts or something similar. Some were dressed as though they were going to a ball game. Jeans and tee shirts and short skirts were common. There were several men wearing baseball caps with American flags on them. Their attempt to look American made them conspicuously not. There was just one woman, standing in the back, dressed to the nines in high stiletto heels, an expensive low-cut dress and a fringed leather jacket buttoned to accentuate her ample breasts.

Tony Sorrelli impatiently waited his turn. He stood just inside the courtroom door so he could just hear as the judge tapped his desk with his fingers. He looked over at the woman's cleavage and smiled. She ignored him like an expert.

Tony had been practicing law for fifteen years, almost all of it in immigration, visa and nationality law, and he stood there in judgment of everyone present. Next to him stood another man in a gray suit carrying a file. The man looked stressed and began looking up and down each row in order to find his client. He then walked down the aisles and whispered loudly, "Mr. Chang?" No one answered.

Tony smiled at him. "Good morning, Harold."

"Hey, Tony. What do you have on today?"

"W. T. A waste of time. Don't you know who your client is?"

Harold Peters, an immigration and criminal attorney and a longtime friend of Tony's, answered, "No. It's a new case for the office, and I haven't met him yet."

Harold Peters stood there in his three-piece gray suit, black loafers and wide tie. He stroked his beard as he looked around the room.

"Should you be here if you haven't prepared your client?"

Harold looked at Tony from the corners of his eyes and ignored the question. He understood how judgmental Tony could be. "Stop the crap. I have something for you."

"What?"

"I was asked to do a TV spot on a talk show late tomorrow afternoon. I can't go. Wanna fill in for me?"

"Immigration policy? Manhattan?"

"Yeah."

"Email me the info. I'll do it."

Tony slicked back his dark hair and checked to be sure his tie was on correctly, as he stood tall and straight. He buttoned his dark blue double-breasted sport jacket that he wore over a yellow shirt with a red-striped tie and tan slacks. He had a red handkerchief showing in his breast pocket. The light shined off of his polished wing tip shoes. He looked around at the other lawyers, some dressed corporate and some disheveled.

Lawyers in the hall were giving their clients last minute instructions. Some took money or hastily filled out notices of appearance to identify them as their lawyers. There was a small line of lawyers reporting to the judge's clerk. Each seemed to be fumbling through papers. One was filling out a blue form as quickly as she could. To the left of the judge was a stack of files representing cases waiting to be called. As each lawyer checked in, the clerk took a file from his pile and put it in the back of the judge's stack.

A lawyer was sitting there and took out a small computer and began to open it.

The judge talked to the lawyer sitting before him. "Counselor, you are not allowed to use your computer in the courtroom."

"I thought because the government attorney had one…?"

"You are not allowed. Please put it away."

"Yes, your honor."

"How do you plead on your client's behalf?"

The lawyer seemed nervous. "My client does not fully understand the charges and the pleadings. We need more time to discuss this matter. Can we have an adjournment?"

The judge had a look of disgust on his face. "For what? Just answer the charging document. Is he an American citizen? Is he a native of India? Did he enter the United States on October 22, 2008 on a visitor's visa and stay longer than permitted? If you don't know these things how can you take on this case?"

"Well. I was just retained and I need more time."

"The court notes that your notice of appearance is dated ten days ago, but I'll grant your request. My clerk will give you a hearing notice four weeks from today. You must know I would have entertained a short written motion for more time had you filed one."

"Oh."

Tony laughed. As the lawyer walked past him, he turned to Harold. "He shouldn't be here if he doesn't know what's going on with his own case." Harold gave Tony a displeased look. Tony thought that a lawyer had no business being in that court if he couldn't competently and zealously represent his client. Tony noticed that the lawyer's shirt looked like it wasn't properly ironed. Tony wanted to lecture him on law and dress but turned to the matter at hand.

The judge's clerk called the next case.

"Rodriguez. 251." The numbers were the last three digits of the alien's file number, just in case there was more than one Rodriguez, and there often were.

Tony looked at his client and waved him along. "That's us."

Tony and his client pushed past a man and woman who could have been linebackers and took seats at the table on the right. The prosecutor didn't look up from her file. The judge pressed a button on his computer to begin recording. "This is Judge McCormick on this fifteenth day of June at the Immigration Court in New York City. Will counsel for the respondent introduce himself?"

"Tony Sorrelli for the firm of Zalmanski and Sorrelli, New York City."

"And for the government."

"Sandra Peterson, Assistant District Counsel."

Tony smiled. "Good morning, Judge, and good morning Ms. Peterson."

The judge looked at Mr. Rodriguez. "Mr. Carlos Rodriguez. Please stand up. Do you swear to tell the truth and nothing but the truth?"

"Yes."

Does Mr. Sorrelli speak on your behalf?"

"Yes, sir."

"Is English your best language?"

"No, Spanish is, but my English is very good."

"Do you want an interpreter, Mr. Rodriguez?"

"No, sir."

"Do you still live at the address on the notice?"

"Yes, sir."

"Mr. Sorrelli. Has your client received a copy of the notice to appear in this matter?"

"Yes, your honor."

How do you plead to the allegations one through six?"

"We admit them."

"So you admit that your client is removable from the United States."

"Yes."

Does your client designate a country if removal becomes necessary?"

"The Dominican Republic."

"How did this case come before this court?"

Tony leaned forward in his chair. "My client applied for naturalization. He has a fourteen-year-old conviction for marijuana possession. He served no jail time. He's been clean since. The law says that he needs five years of good moral character for naturalization, but he has almost three times that. Instead of granting citizenship, the government started this proceeding. They didn't even give him the time to file an administrative appeal, which my office filed after the notice to appear was issued. He has a right to have the appeal heard. This is a waste of the court's time. This man has a long-term job for a valet parking service, supports three United States citizen children, has been paying taxes and has no other blemishes other than this possession charge that occurred when he was twenty years old. He is a prime candidate for discretionary relief by this court. I am requesting that these proceedings be administratively closed and this matter remanded to CIS to allow Mr. Rodriguez to complete the administrative appeal on his naturalization." CIS is Citizen and Immigration Services, also known as immigration.

"What's the government's position?"

"The government opposes administrative closure and wishes to proceed with this matter on the merits. I have discussed this with my supervisor. Mr. Rodriguez has several arrests for grand theft and minor drug possession."

"Your honor, those several theft arrests were all dismissed. This is the United States of America, and a person is innocent until proven guilty. We have one conviction on a minor drug possession charge. This was an old conviction and my client can apply for relief. The government knows that this is a waste of the court's time and their time too."

"You know, counselor, I cannot close this matter without the consent of the government. What relief are you asking for?"

"We are asking for cancellation of removal." Cancellation of removal is relief that an immigration judge could grant to a worthy legal permanent resident alien who had committed some offense.

"Do you have your applications filed, Mr. Sorrelli?"

"No, but we'll have it all completed before the adjourn date."

The judge tilted his head and gave Tony a look with the sides of his eyes. "I see that Mr. Rodriguez has been a client with your office for some time. I'll give you an adjourn date two years and three months from now. That's the earliest date I have. You have a call-up date for the applications and evidence in sixty days. Is sixty days adequate?"

"Yes."

"Wait for my clerk to provide you with the notice."

Tony and his client got up. Tony went to the clerk's desk in the corner past the judge to wait for the adjourn date notice. As Rodriguez left the courtroom, the two linebackers followed him. As Tony waited for the notice, he noticed there was some commotion just outside the courtroom. He looked closely and saw the linebackers had put their Immigration and Customs Enforcement badges around their necks and were in the process of handcuffing Rodriguez.

Tony rushed over. "What's going on here?"

One of them took his ICE badge and flashed it in Tony's face. "Stand back, counselor. We're taking your client into custody. You can talk to him on the ninth floor later."

Tony knew that it was useless to argue with these deportation officers. He went back into the courtroom where the next case was going on.

"Your honor. I need to interrupt."

The judge turned to the parties sitting in front of him. "Counsel. Please wait in back for a moment so I can address Mr. Sorrelli." The other case got up and went behind the barricade. The government attorney remained. The judge turned the computer and sound recording to the Rodriguez case.

"Your honor, my client was just arrested by ICE agents. I demand an immediate bond determination hearing. I want an order releasing him on his own recognizance immediately." ICE stood for Immigration and Customs Enforcement.

Judge McCormick turned to Ms. Peterson. "What's the government's position on this?"

"The government opposes any such order. Mr. Rodriguez is subject to mandatory detention because of his crime, and we already have an adjourn date for a hearing where counsel can further argue this."

"That adjourn date is more than two years away. If my client isn't released he will lose his job and his children will have to go on public assistance. He will lose his apartment."

"The law says that he is subject to mandatory detention, counselor," the judge said.

"This is ridiculous. That just means that he can be put under an order of supervision as in the case of someone paroled."

"Mandatory detention means detention," Ms. Peterson added.

"No. In every other area of American law, an order substitutes as detention. In habeas corpus the order would be enough to get us into federal court even without physical detention."

The judge picked up his hand as if to stop them. "I cannot do that without the consent of the government."

"The rules have to have some flexibility. That's justice," Tony said.

"We are a country of laws, and the laws have very little flexibility," the judge said. "I have to follow the words of the law and the regulations."

"Who's in charge of this court? The prosecutor? I'm asking you to take charge of this case and do justice. This is the Department of Justice. You work for the Department of Justice, and I expect you to take that seriously. You're a judge. You have to administer justice, damn it. I expect you to use some judgment and administer justice. You cannot allow the prosecutor to run this court!" Tony got louder and louder.

"You've made your point, counselor!"

There was complete silence in the room.

Tony turned to the prosecutor. "Sandra, how can you let this happen and look at yourself in the mirror?"

Ms. Peterson did not look at Tony and did not respond.

The judge ended it. "Mr. Sorrelli. If I give you the order you want, the government will immediately appeal it to the Board of Immigration Appeals, and they will reverse the order."

"Give me the order. It's the right thing to do."

"My verbal order is to deny a bond hearing. Now, Mr. Sorrelli, you have your decision and I have to get back to the next case."

"This is the only area of American law where the prosecutor runs the court. It feels like Soviet Russia or Iran," Tony said.

"Enough, Mr. Sorrelli. You are well known to this court, so I am giving you some space, but you can take this too far. You have your decision."

"And it is not fair to allow the prosecutor to use her computer and deny that right to the lawyers."

The judge crossed his arms. "Mr. Sorrelli?"

As Tony left the courtroom the attractive woman dressed to the nines stopped him. He could smell her perfume ten feet before he passed her. "Are you a lawyer?" She had a thick Russian accent.

"Why do you think I'm here? Drama class?"

"Can I ask you a few questions about my case?"

Tony handed her a card. "Call my office for an appointment. If you have problems today, ask the judge for time to get a lawyer. He'll give you a few weeks. He's a decent judge."

"You say that after what happened?"

Tony left without answering her and went to see his client to explain what would happen next. Rodriguez was eligible to ask the court to be forgiven. He could prove legal residence for seven years and reformation and hardship to his family. It was very likely that his client would win, but at what cost? Tony took his client's valuables and promised to call his wife.

Supervisor Gomez's office was at the corner of the floor. He sipped coffee as he read the *New York Post*.

Tony entered a door that read "Do not enter." He went to Gomez's door, knocked and pushed it open before he received a response. "I want my client released."

"I want a million bucks. Goodbye, counselor."

"You can set a bond."

Gomez stood up. "I don't even know which case you're talking about, and by the way, never come into my office again without being invited."

Tony left, went to the clerk and asked to see his client. The woman behind the counter was sitting so low he could only see the top of her head. "Counselor, your client is being processed. You will have to wait until we're finished." She spoke in a very low voice.

"And how long do you estimate that will take?"

"Anywhere from one to four hours."

Tony did not answer and returned to his office.

* * *

Tony's office was three blocks from the Immigration Court. It was in an old run down office building that was about a hundred years old. The lobby and elevators had been redone in a modern style and didn't quite fit the rest of the building. There was construction of a new building just next door to it. The dirt and dust got onto everyone's shoes as they entered the building. The noise made it difficult to think, and Tony walked fast to pass it. The new modern building just next door would make Tony's building seem older still.

Tony was too stressed to wait for the elevator, so he ran up the two flights of stairs. He entered the suite past the sign over the entrance "Zalmanski and Sorrelli P.C.".

Tony passed through the waiting area. There were old metal chairs around a worn gray carpet. A messy coffee table with magazines took up most of one corner. On the wall opposite the entrance there was a framed map of the world, and several countries were worn out from touching, including the Dominican Republic, Jamaica, China, and Mexico. Many other countries were worn somewhat less.

Maria, the receptionist, sat behind a window and greeted the clients who were separated from the rest of the suite by a door. She was a small Mexican looking woman with oversized glasses, a streak of purple in her hair and a large cross around her neck. Her desk was crowded with pictures of a small girl and several statues of Catholic saints.

Several people were sitting in the waiting area.

Tony walked through a second door into the office area without acknowledging the clients. He walked up to Maria's desk from behind. "Do I need to know anything, Maria?"

"No. Just a couple of voicemails."

As Tony went down the hall to his office he heard Zalmanski. "Tony. Come in."

Tony entered Zalmanski's office and sat down.

Bill Zalmanski was the senior member of the firm and a veteran of many years in the business. His face and receding hairline had the look of wear and tear. It showed years of stress and experience. Bill was wearing a worn brown tweed jacket over a wrinkled shirt. His tie was a little too wide and a little undone. The top button of his shirt was askew. Overweight and in his late sixties, he hated to leave the office and rarely went to court. He saw clients only occasionally and thought that his responsibility was to make sure that the office ran smoothly.

Bill's dark wood antique desk was covered with mugs of all sizes, shapes, colors, and materials. Behind him was a matching credenza with an old cassette-dictating machine. Next to it was a small bronze statue of three soldiers in battle gear, holding guns with the inscription 'Semter Fi'. Next to it was a pile of magazines and newspapers. There was a warn leather couch on one side. Bill had his feet and hands crossed as he looked out over Broadway towards City Hall.

Zalmanski continued to look out at the street. "How'd it go?"

Tony explained what happened and banged his hand down on the desk. "Bill! They had no right to arrest him. The detention law is unconstitutional and needs to be challenged. McCormick has no balls and can't even pick his nose without the prosecutor's permission. Not a lot of justice in that courtroom."

Bill barely looked up. "You did what you could, Tony. We have other work to do."

"These people are exploited by the system. If we don't help them, who will?"

"Calm down."

"It's hard to concentrate right now. I'm steaming. I'd like to go to federal court and file a habeas. They get away with this over and over again. We're not worth our salt if we let this go. They push us around with impunity."

13

"We won't be paid for it, and if you lose you'll just make it worse."

"We've got to do something. We're lawyers. We can't let them shit all over us. He was referred by Bueno. That man refers a lot of business to us. He'll be pissed off."

"Don't be hotheaded. This is when you make a mistake. We've got to be practical. It's a money loser and a waste of time. You knew there were problems with this. You've got to look at it from both sides."

"We need to go to federal court."

"There's little chance of winning. Leave the case alone for a couple of hours. You'll see it clearer if you put off any action. I'll explain it to Bueno. He'll understand. Let's discuss it in the morning. If he wants to foot the bill, you can take an appeal."

Tony took a deep breath. "Do you have any interviews for the new associate?"

"Not today."

* * *

Zalmanski picked up a resume and read through it.

"My dream is to practice immigration law and help the poor and needy realize the American dream. I want to use my skills to change the world for the better."

Bill tossed the resume into the garbage.

He picked up a second resume. He read.

"Career goals: practice law in a professional environment."

Zalmanski picked up his phone and dialed. A voice answered. "Hello."

"Is this Chinese Ryan?"

"What?"

"I said. Is this Chinese Ryan?

"Well, my name's Ryan but I'm not Chinese. I'm Ryan Goldberg. Who is this?"

"I'm Bill Zalmanski. I understand you're looking for a job."

"Yes, I am."

"I got your resume from the bar association and see you speak some Chinese and Spanish."

"Some."

"Come to my office tomorrow. I may have some work for you. Have you ever done immigration work?"

"No. My experience is in real estate."

"Fine. How about 10:00 a.m. tomorrow?"

The plans were made.

* * *

Adara Aden was the office manager. An attractive Iraqi-American woman in her thirties, Adara had the stature of a leader and everybody was afraid of her, especially men. They were afraid that, like a preying mantis, she would have sex with them, tell them they weren't good enough and then bite their heads off. She was slim and tall with dark long hair, large dark eyes and large breasts. She dressed to accentuate them. Her face was not classically beautiful but was rugged and sensuous. She had a sexuality about her that was intimidating. She knew how to entice men when she had to. She treated women with authority and contempt. When she looked at you, you could feel her dark piercing eyes judging you. Only a hint of crow's feet gave away her true age. Her slight Arabic accent gave her an additional air of authority.

Adara's office was at the end of the secretarial pool where she was able to watch everyone through a large glass window. Without staring she managed to watch everything that went on. If a secretary spent more than a minute on some personal matter, she would intervene.

Her desk was immaculate. Only one item at a time was opened. When a call came in she would close what she was working on, put it aside and take out what she needed for the call. On the side of her desk was a yellow pad with the date written on top and a list of things that needed to be done that day. As she handled each item, she would cross it out or place a note on another day's list if it required more attention.

Adara walked into Tony's office, her high heels clicking after giving the weakest knock possible and without waiting for a response. She had on a tight dress with a slit that went a little too far up the side of one leg. She sat down opposite him, crossing her legs so that one was thigh was exposed. "How did it go today?"

Tony explained the situation.

"You did what you could. Take Bill's advice. I need you to get beyond this so you can go on to the next case. Understand?"

Tony nodded.

She leaned forward. "Feel better. I'll call his wife and explain what happened. We have many other cases that need your attention. If you want to talk more about this just come in."

Adara went into Bill's office. She sat with her legs straight ahead and behind the desk. "Have you found a new attorney yet?"

Bill tried not to stare at her. "I have someone coming tomorrow morning. We'll see."

"That new girl we hired isn't working out. I'm going to fire her on Friday."

"She's only been here three days. How can you tell?"

"She's not working fast enough. She doesn't understand the work, and she doesn't ask the right questions. When they don't know and try to hide it, they make mistakes. That is just unacceptable."

"Don't you want to give her some more time? She seems pleasant enough. I'm sure she's eager to learn. You know, you started out as a receptionist."

"If she asked for instructions, I would give them to her. She's trying to hide the fact that she doesn't know what she's doing. That shows her personality, and I can't live with that."

"I know you're right. Okay."

As Adara walked out of the office Bill looked at her ass straining to bust out of her tight skirt. He took a deep breath and picked up a mug and took a sip of coffee.

TWO

Sheriff Kelly drove up to the truck. It was not unusual to find illegals dead in this remote area near the border. Usually they die from dehydration. He fixed his aviator sunglasses and his Stetson hat.

There were already several police on the scene with their dogs. They were talking to two hikers. Kelly looked at the two bodies as the police looked for evidence. The bodies had been partly eaten by small animals and were already drying and mummifying in the hot dry desert air. One of the police came over to him.

"Good morning, sheriff."

"Good morning, officer. Call me J.K."

"The hikers found the scene and called it in, J.K. They had to hike eight miles to get to a phone. We lost some valuable time there. The victims were each shot three times in a triangle pattern. One was shot execution style and the other, a woman, in the back, probably while trying to escape. We estimate they've been here probably about a day and a half, maybe two. The coroner will decide. The dog found evidence of marijuana in the cabin but no ashes, and the car wasn't disassembled. Either it was there for personal use or as a distraction. This was not a drug matter. Probably alien smuggling gone bad."

"Not this bad. This looks like an execution. Keep looking. Any prints?"

"No J.K. The truck was wiped clean. Professionally done. There were tire tracks nearby. The size indicates a four-wheel-drive vehicle. Probably an SUV. Around here that tells us nothing."

"Weapons?"

"We have the murder weapon. An old revolver with the numbers filed off. We'll test it to be sure. Also wiped off. Even the bullet casings were wiped. Very professional."

"Not good. It would sound usual for a drug assassination. Unusual for this to happen after alien smuggling. Maybe someone eliminated some competition. Pass the information on. See if there have been any other murders carried out the same way. Maybe it will lead to something. I'll call the FBI to see if they have any similar crimes."

Kelly put on rubber gloves and went to the back of the victim's truck. He noticed scratches on the rear bed. "Officer. These scratches look fresh. They look like something was recently dragged over them. Have you tested the back for drugs?"

"The dog didn't pick anything up there. We'll check for other substances. Could be arms. The scratches look like a heavy box. Could be tools. That might mean something. We'll follow up."

"There are too many people walking around here. The footprints are being screwed up."

"No sir. We photographed the footprints. Eliminating the hikers, it seems that only one person got out of the other car and that one went from the pickup to the jeep and was taken away. There was no attempt to hide the footprints. If it's alien smuggling it's only about one alien."

"It doesn't work that way, son. It looks like they brought one person here and that the smugglers were shot to shut them up. He must be someone important."

"Yes, Sheriff Kelly."

"This smells bad. Which way did they go?

"The tire tracts head north towards US 10. That also tells us nothing. In a day or two they might have gone eight hundred miles. Maybe more."

"We're going to need help. I'll contact Homeland Security. This isn't alien smuggling or drugs. Have them bring in a team to take every test possible.

* * *

At the end of the day Adara walked to the subway and took the local train to the 23d Street stop. She went upstairs to the El Quiote restaurant. She walked over to a tall redheaded woman. "Viviana. Good to see you. Busy day today. I need a drink."

Viviana wore a skintight black dress that covered her neck and arms and went down to her ankles. No clothes were visible underneath. She took a sip of wine as Adara smiled at the bartender and pointed to her drink. He brought a glass for her.

"Why can't I use my father's business to get a green card? I know we discussed this before, but explain it again."

Viviana was looking beyond Adara at some of the men at the bar.

Adara took Viviana's chin in her hand and directed it towards her. "Please focus. You are here on an L-1 visa. We have already extended it and after the next one, your time is up. You can't get a green card because you need to show that you are a manager or an executive."

"I am."

"Not according to the immigration laws. An L visa is for a businessperson who works abroad to come here and operate a branch or related company. You have to show that you employ managers who manage other people, abroad and here. You don't. The operation is just too small."

Two attractive men with business suits came and stood next to them. One placed a Gucci briefcase by his feet.

Viviana took a sip of wine. "We're a sales office for my father's winery. I don't need a big staff. I give orders to the main company and they fill it. We then handle any problems, but there aren't many."

"The rules are what they are. You take orders and oversee problems. I get it, but the operation here doesn't lend itself to this type of visa. You need a bigger operation to make this work. We'll change your visa and find a way to keep you here."

"I want a green card."

"Plan B."

"I can't do plan B."

"Viviana. You are my closest friend. We are not getting any younger. You need a husband. Tell me that there isn't one American man you want to build a life with."

The attractive man with the Gucci briefcase turned to Adara. He looked like an athlete in a two thousand dollar suit. His friend, equally well dressed, stood a step behind. "You sound like you know a lot about business visas?"

Adara whipped out a card and handed it to him. "Call and make an appointment if you have any questions."

"Can we buy you two drinks?"

"No."

He read the card. "You don't look like Bill Zalmanski to me. What's your name?"

Adara took Viviana's arm and led her to another place at the bar.

The maître d' called Viviana's name and escorted them to a table and handed them menus. "I recommend the pulled pork today. It's especially good."

"Thank you," Adara said.

They ordered.

"I can find someone. I can pay."

"I see that every day. Some people get their green cards that way but many fail. You have to prove the marriage is good now and again two years later. It's not easy. They want documentation. If you show bank accounts together, they will see if only one of you is signing the checks. I see blackmail. If you fail, the law says you will be barred for life from getting a green card. Your clock is ticking."

"So is yours."

"We're talking about you now."

"And you. What's going on with that lawyer in your office?"

"Tony? Forget about him. I need a man. He's an immature boy and isn't interested in a relationship. I don't have time for anyone like that. If it was going to work, it would have a long time ago."

"Sometimes I think you really are interested in him."

"Me? No."

"So why do you talk about him so much?"

"It's just office talk. Tonight we talk about you."

"My father has plans for me. He would like to arrange a marriage with the son of one of his friends in the industry. Once I return to Argentina, he'll put the pressure on."

"Is that so bad? You said he has a few rich, handsome boys for you to choose from."

"You said it. Boys."

"I'm sure you can find a good man among them."

"I want to find my perfect man."

"Good luck with that."

"I'm trying."

"You're telling me in a city where there are at least a hundred thousand men who are possibilities you can't find one?"

"Adara. You can't either. Your clock is ticking too."

"I'm a citizen. Less pressure."

The waiter showed up with a glass of the same wine for each of them. Adara held up her palm. "We didn't order these."

"Those men did." He said. The two men waved and smiled.

Adara turned just enough to give them the message that they wasted the price of two drinks. The men started to survey the other eligible women at the bar.

The meal came and they asked for extra plates so they could split the two meals and try each other's. Adara took a bite. "We need to go out more. I need some time, but maybe you should go online."

The waiter came over. "How's the pulled pork?"

Adara smiled. "Good."

Viviana sighed. "I don't know if that's me."

"What do you have to lose?"

"Dignity?"

Adara took some of Viviana's food. "Have you gone online?"

"Yes. The last guy was at least ten years older than his photo. He apologized and told me he didn't have a more recent picture. If I have to do that again, I'll slit my wrists."

Adara removed Viviana's steak knife from the table.

* * *

The plains of North Texas seemed endless as Naib was driving. They hadn't seen another car for the past half hour. Ali was in the back seat napping when Naib noticed the lights on the car behind them begin to flash. A quick look at the dashboard showed he was going over ninety miles an hour. A moment later Ali looked over and told him to pull to the side.

21

The policeman stepped out of the car with his hand on his gun as he walked over to the car and asked Naib to produce his driver's license and step out.

"Just do it," Ali said.

As Naib stepped out, the policeman again asked him for his driver's license.

"No speak English," Naib said in broken English.

Ali got out of the car. "Officer, I have what you need."

As the officer turned to look, Ali quickly pulled his gun and pumped three bullets into him. Naib dragged the policeman's body into the tall grass beside the road. They went to the police car and ripped the dash camera off, got into their car and took off.

"What now?" Naib asked.

"First, I'll drive. Next, we need a new car."

* * *

Tony looked at the email printout in his hand and found the address in an industrial building on the west side of Manhattan. The only indication that it was a television studio was a small name on the directory. He was on time with a few minutes to spare. He looked at his reflection in the blackened windows and smiled. He wore a dark business suit with a red tie that contained the flags of many nations.

He entered and went to the fifth floor where he was buzzed into a busy office. The receptionist looked at him. She brushed back her hair and smiled. "You must be Tony Sorrelli, the immigration lawyer. Thank you for coming. Have you watched the Thomas Miller Johnson show before?"

"Sure. Many times. Thank you for having me."

"Please see Martha over there for makeup and our manager Mr. Frederick will explain how the show works."

"I don't need makeup."

She stood up a head taller than Tony and pointed firmly. "Over there, please."

Tony sat down in Martha's barber chair. "I don't need makeup."

She bent down and eyeballed Tony. She smiled very widely. "Let me do my job."

"I look fine."

Martha just did her job. When Tony was done he looked as though he was sunburned. His eyelashes were a bit pronounced. She showed him a mirror and he was not pleased.

A large man with his sleeves rolled up and his tie loosened and tucked into his shirt came over. He was a fast talker. "Thank you for coming on the Thomas Miller Johnson Show. We're doing one fifteen-minute segment that will be aired later tonight. Please talk only when a question is directed to you and try not to be too detailed."

"But what if I need to explain some details?"

"Don't. There will be two other guests. You will be talking about refugee policy. One man is a former immigration agent and the other is the director of the Christian Immigrant Assistance Society."

"I have the details. I know them both."

"Ok. Short answers. Few details and don't ask Mr. Johnson any questions. OK?"

"OK."

"You're up. Let's go."

Tony entered the room and put out his hand but Johnson pointed to the chair. Tony sat and an assistant came over and asked him if he wanted something to drink. Tony asked for water and the assistant placed a mug of water before him.

Johnson looked at a monitor between Tony and the other guests. "Good evening. I'm Thomas Miller Johnson, and this is the Thomas Miller Johnson Show. Tonight we are going to discuss refugee policy in the United States. This is a hot button topic. As you know, the conflicts in the Middle East have created hundreds of thousands of refugees. The president has promised to take at least ninety thousand this year alone, and this promises to be an important issue in the next election cycle. We have today Frank Bolan, a retired border control officer and supervisor who is a frequent guest on this show. His thirty-five years of experience will give us insight into the workings of the system. We also have Jasper Goodman, Director of the Christian Immigrant Aid Society. That organization has been assisting refugees for over one hundred years. We also have Tony Sorrelli, an immigration attorney. Tony has assisted thousands of immigrants during his career."

They each nodded for the camera in turn.

Johnson rustled some papers and then read from the monitor. "Mr. Bolan. It seems that millions of people have been displaced by the wars in the Middle East, especially because of the Syrian civil war. Don't you think it's America's duty to accept these people?"

Bolan was a man in his late sixties with a mountain man's beard—big, bushy and gray. He wore a shirt with the top two buttons opened revealing a large gold cross. Bolan looked purposefully with his thick-rimmed glasses into the camera. He pointed as he talked. "It's our government's first duty to protect America. By bringing these people into the United States we are endangering the welfare of the American people. These people are coming here to perform jihad and that means violence against America."

"Wow!" Tony raised his hands. "Most of these people are good people who only want to be part of the American dream. Are you telling us that because of a few bad eggs you'll throw out all the good ones?"

"What city or town would accept one hundred refugees if they knew that one would perform jihad and that means a mass killing? None."

Tony turned towards Bolan. "You don't know if that's true."

"Yes we do. What do you think is happening right now, and not just in America?"

"We have home grown extremists who do these things. Any refugees we bring in can't be worse. They are overwhelmingly good people."

Bolan had a look of anger on his face. "Listen Tony. We have to deal with Americans who screw up. Why the hell would we want to import more screw-ups?"

"These people are suffering and are true refugees. What about our pledge to take the huddled masses yearning to breathe free? We need to help these people."

"Need? We need to help these people?" Bolan took a handkerchief and wiped his forehead. "We don't need to do anything except what's good for America. These people want to destroy our way of life. You need clients. America needs security."

"They are suffering refugees and we can help them. In every generation we have taken in people who turned out to be good Americans and helped make us stronger. We have a responsibility to take in refugees. And by the way; we have plenty of clients."

Bolan banged his fist on the table. "First of all these people are not refugees."

"Of course they are."

"They have to come under the legal definition of refugee first." Bolan reached down and pulled up a paperback book. "Want me to read you the definition of refugee?"

Johnson interrupted. "I don't understand. It seems these people are typical refugees in the plain English sense."

Bolan raised the book. "We're talking about the law. The law! Let Mr. Sorrelli tell you what it says."

"Refugee is a legal definition that says a refugee has to be singled out and have a well-founded fear of persecution on certain grounds. These refugees meet that criteria."

Bolan had the look of fire in his eyes as he waved the book high above his head. "Singled out means not everyone. You people want us to take everyone. We can't. No country can take the whole of another country. They have to be persecuted. There is no requirement that we have to take Muslims."

Goodman interceded. "There is no religious test for refugee."

Tony put his hands on his head and had that "oh no" look come over him.

Bolan had that "got ya" look come over him. "Ah ha! You are a director of a Christian aid group and you don't even know the definition of refugee." Bolan opened to book to a clipped page. "Here it is. It specifically says "religious persecution" as one of the enumerated grounds. You haven't even read it."

Tony came to Goodman's aid. "America is a country of compassion. Surely we can be generous enough to bring suffering people into our country in their time of need. Before World War Two we refused entry to thousands of Jews. We don't want to do the same thing now."

"The Jews didn't want to destroy America. Would you say the same thing if thousands of Nazis had wanted refugee status?"

Johnson raised his hand. "We allowed tens of thousands of Nazis into the U.S after the war. How do you feel about that, Mr. Sorrelli?"

"That was a mistake."

Bolan was spitting as he spoke. "I'll say that these Muslims are just Nazis who pray. They would put Jews and Christians in the ovens if they could, all in the name of the Koran."

25

"That is so racist," Tony said.

"Wrong." By this time Bolan was pounding on the table again. "I'm not saying we should deny anyone because of their race. Just their religion if you can cal it that. I call it an ideology of conquest and submission that uses god as a cover."

"Mr. Goodman. What do you think about this?" Johnson said.

"Well. We don't distinguish between people in need when we decide to help refugees. People are suffering and we have a religious and moral duty to help them."

"What about the 'Christian' in your organization's name?"

"We don't go there. Many in our organization would consider that racist. We believe helping people is the Christian thing to do."

"Give me a break," Bolan said. "The Middle East Christians are the ones being exterminated. These and several other minority religions are being exterminated. Those are the ones that need help."

"Muslims are being persecuted by other Muslims," Tony said.

"Are you saying Mr. Sorrelli that all Muslims qualify as refugees?" Johnson asked.

"Yes. We are here to help these people become part of the American experience."

Bolan looked at Tony and mumbled under his breath, "Idiot." The microphone picked it up. Tony returned with an angry look.

"It would be racist for us to exclude Muslims," Goodman said.

Bolan banged his mug, and water went flying all over the set. "Racist? Are you insane? Since when is this about race?"

"Arabs are of a certain skin color and type."

"No Mr. *Good Man*. Muslims can be of any racial type. Christians and other religions can be of any racial type too. Don't play that card."

"Do you have an opinion about this, Mr. Sorrelli?" Johnson asked.

"It would not be American to start separating people by their ethnic, racial or religious backgrounds," Tony said.

"What the hell do you liberals do every time you separate people for different treatment because of all kinds affirmative action?" Bolan shouted.

"I thought we are discussing refugee policy," Johnson added.

"Don't get me started," Bolan replied.

Johnson put up his palm to stop the debate. "Time for a commercial break. We will be back in a few moments. Stick with Johnson!"

They stood up and shook hands as the commercial ran on the monitor. Tony noticed that it was for a food-slicing device and that they would throw in a second one free if you just paid separate shipping and handling.

They sat down and continued.

Johnson began again. "You are back with the Thomas Miller Johnson Show." He turned to Tony. "Mr. Sorrelli, why should we take any refugees if we are afraid that some might be violent?"

"These refugees are fully vetted. We have a rigorous system to check each one."

"Whoa!" Bolan had both hands in the air. "Give me a break. There is no system to check these people. We simply put out the information to see if INTERPOL or other law enforcement agencies have any information on these people. Most of the time we don't even know if their names or other information is even correct. Goodman's organization doesn't want to know."

"Our organization is concerned with helping people in need. These people are in trouble but…"

"No freaking buts. You wouldn't bring a rabid dog into your home. Not if your children were there. You would be careful to fully check each one."

"These people are not rabid dogs. They are human beings that are in real danger."

"So protect them over there. If you want to bring a rabid dog into your home, do it, but you're bringing these people into mine."

Tony interrupted. "There are ways to fix this. Better procedures would be a good first step."

"Yeah! Like what?" Bolan asked.

"Like better checks. Fingerprint checks."

"Isn't that being done now?" Johnson asked.

"Yes," Tony said.

"That's right," Bolan continued. "And it proves useless."

"By your standards we would never take in any refugees," Tony said to Bolan.

"Each situation is different. When we took in refuges from Communism we didn't have this issue."

"Would you like a last word, Mr. Sorrelli?" Johnson asked.

"Sure. America has always been a compassionate nation. We are a beacon of tolerance and reason for the world. Those countries that emulate us have changed the world for the better. We need to continue to be that bright star in the sky."

"And you, Mr. Bolan?"

"Let enough of these people in and we'll be a footnote in history. Let's worry about preserving what we have. The best way to help the world it to be sure that we are safe and strong."

"Mr. Goodman?"

"Anyone wishing to donate to our organization should go to our website. All contributions are tax deductible."

* * *

Adara came to the office early the next morning carrying her breakfast. Mohammad Hamid was already waiting by the door for the office to open. They entered together.

"Are you here to see Mr. Sorrelli?" she asked.

"Yes. He told me to come early to go over my case before we go to court. Can I talk to you?"

"Yes. Come in."

They went into her office as Zalmanski entered. Adara felt relieved that she was not alone. As Bill passed she said, "Good Morning, Bill."

Bill stuck his head in and said hello to both of them.

She opened up her coffee and took out a small cookie. She looked at the calendar on the computer. "Your appointment isn't until 10:00. Tony will surely be here by then. He'll help you."

Hamid was a large man, dark skinned with a beard. He was out of breath after walking up the stairs. Adara noticed his Che Guevara tee shirt, the torn jeans and the yellow sneakers. "Is this the way Tony told you to dress for a hearing?"

"I want you to make sure that Tony does a good job today, sister. You know that I rely on you to make sure these Americans take my case seriously. We have to stick together, sister."

"You're in good hands. Have a seat in the waiting room so I can get to work."

"I trust in you and Allah. I know both of you won't let me down."

"We will do right by you because it's the right thing to do. Pray to Allah but listen to Tony's advice."

"These Americans don't care about us. All they care about is money, like the Jews."

Adara stared at him expressionless for a moment. "I will see to it you are treated with justice."

Hamid leaned forward and whispered. "It would not be good for this firm if my case failed. I trust you know that already."

Adara stood up. "Don't threaten me. Please wait outside for Mr. Sorrelli."

"I would never do that. I meant your reputation."

"Why did you come to us in the first place?"

Hamid picked up his hands, palm forward to Adara. "You were recommended by a friend."

"And why would that friend recommend us?"

"He said you did a great job with his case."

"Then don't threaten us." She pointed to the waiting room, and Hamid took a deep breath. "We hope that when your case is done you will recommend us to others."

"Are you trying to throw me out of your office?"

Adara stood up. "I need to get on with my work. If you have anything else to discuss, I am here to assist you."

Hamid was expressionless as he left.

Adara put her hand on her chest.

As Tony arrived, Bill stood by his desk, sipping coffee and reading the newspaper spread out over his desk.

"Tony, come on in."

"What's up?" Tony sat down, pushed aside some mugs and opened his paper container of coffee.

"You've got Mohammed Hamid's political asylum today. He owes money, and I want you to get it before you go. I don't trust him."

"That's two of us. The interview isn't until 10:00. I'll get it."

"I mean not only because of the money. I just don't trust him. Anyway, we have to be better at collecting fees. If we don't have the money a month in advance, we need to file a motion and get out of the case. This happens too often."

"I know. It's not always easy to keep on top of these things."

"If you don't pay your rent, see how long it takes for the landlord to keep on top of it."

Tony changed the subject. "I hear Adara's going to let the new girl go. Is that a good idea? We should wait until we get a replacement."

"She's in charge of that. I'm going to leave it alone. We have a busy morning."

"Ah hum."

"By the way. You were good on the Johnson show last night."

"Thanks."

"You should acknowledge when you opponent is correct."

"You mean Bolan?"

"Yes."

"He's never correct."

"Are you that sure?"

"I'll get going."

* * *

Tony finished his coffee and was working on a file when his intercom buzzed. Maria, the receptionist, didn't wait for Tony's answer. "Your first appointment. Mohammed Hamid's been waiting for you. He's been here a long time."

"He's early. I took the on-time consultation first, Maria. I'll be right out."

Tony pulled Hamid's file and reviewed it. Today was the day of the hearing, and he would have to appear whether or not the client paid the fee. The judge couldn't care less whether lawyers were paid. Tony got up and walked to the waiting area. "Good morning." Tony stretched out his hand.

Hamid got up and limply shook Tony's hand. They went to Tony's office and sat. "I told you to dress with a tie and sport jacket today. You need to show respect for the court."

"This is what I have."

"Did you bring the balance of the fee?"

"I have a postdated check. The money was transferred from my friend's account yesterday. You need to wait until Monday to deposit it."

"You know our policy is payment before the final hearing."

"This is the best I can do. I assure you the check is good. I'm a religious man. You can trust me."

Tony knew that once a client said that he could be trusted, the client could never be. "Do you want me to do my best or do you want me to win? Never mind. Buy a new shirt and clean pants at least. Any shirt is better than that."

"Am I going to win?"

"One of several things can happen. You can lose and we'll appeal. You can be granted political asylum, which will lead to a green card. That is in the judge's discretion. If the judge chooses to, he can grant withholding of removal. That is if he feels that you're in danger if you return but you are not worthy of asylum. It means no green card but you can stay here and work and maybe even travel."

"That's enough."

Tony spent the next half hour going over the questions and discussed how Hamid should answer and when to say he didn't understand or know the answer.

At the end they both got up. "I'll meet you in the courtroom at 1:00. Be on time."

"OK."

On the way out Adara stopped Hamid. "Did you give the balance of the fee to Mr. Sorrelli?"

"Yes. Make sure he does a good job. You know that you are my sister. We have to stick together."

"I told you that you're in good hands," Adara said.

"It would be unfortunate for this firm if we were to fail. I came here because of your reputation."

"I heard you the last time. You should not threaten us."

"I did not mean to threaten you."

"If you do not trust us, please find another law firm. Just be on time for the hearing."

She walked Hamid to the door and returned to Tony's office. "Don't trust that client. I have a bad feeling about him."

"I'm sure the check will be good."

"Oh really? You think so?"

* * *

Maria walked into Bill's room. His desk was covered in mugs. "There's a Mr. Ryan Goldberg here to see you."

"Bring him in."

Ryan walked down the hall. A young man of medium height and weight entered with a big smile. He showed up in a gray three-piece suit, wingtip shoes and a shiny new tie.

As Ryan entered Zalmanski's office he noticed a crumpled paper on the floor just in from the door. He bent and picked it up with his left hand, entered the room and held out his right hand. Bill shook it, pointed to the trashcan where Ryan threw the paper, and they both sat down.

"Here's a copy of my resume." He pulled an envelope from his jacket pocket and put it down on the desk. Bill didn't look at it.

"I saw your resume on the bar association website and printed it out. I also graduated from The Manhattan Law School, 37 years before you."

"I can tell you about my experience."

Bill looked out the window. "Where did you learn Spanish and Chinese?"

"I took Spanish in high school and Chinese in college."

"You are probably wondering what I'm doing with all these mugs."

Ryan just smiled.

"Well, I'm going to invent the perfect mug. I'm studying sizes, shapes, what they're made from. No one takes this seriously."

"I see."

"No one takes the time to get things right. I'm going to get this right."

"Uh hum."

"What do you know about immigration law?"

"Nothing. But I'm a fast learner."

"Some mugs are made to look good and others to keep coffee warm, some to be unbreakable and some that won't easily tip over. I'm going to make one that does all these things."

"That's interesting."

"You see that couple sitting in the waiting room? The Hispanic ones."

"Yes."

"They have a 245 interview today. Take them and I'll pay you $250."

"But I have no idea what a 245 interview is."

"Easy. He's Mendez. Came with a tourist visa. She's an American citizen and they're married. You take them to the 8th floor at immigration, just three blocks away. Check in with the receptionist and wait until you're called. Read through the file while you're waiting. They've been prepared. Don't talk too much."

"Shouldn't I go with you a couple of times to learn the ropes before I go alone?"

"Nah. I never go anymore. What kind of Jew names his son Ryan? Are your parents trying to be Irish?"

"Huh?"

"Do you think there's an Irish family somewhere with a son named Moshe?"

"Huh?"

"I also have an idea for a new airplane. You see the pilot can't really see where he's going. He needs to be able to look down, so my plane will have the cockpit in a glass bubble on the bottom."

"That's interesting. What if the plane bottoms out? The pilot could get killed."

"Then the pilot will have to pay attention to what he's doing."

"I see."

"Here's the file. The officer will ask to see their originals and they're in this part of the file. He'll ask a few questions to determine if the marriage is real. Piece of cake."

Ryan took the file, introduced himself to Mr. and Mrs. Mendez and they went off to the Federal Building.

* * *

When Tony got to court, the judge and the prosecutor were waiting for him. Mohammed Hamid was sitting in the back with a new New York Yankees tee shirt. He held a small bag with what Tony assumed was the

Che Guevara shirt. The rest of his clothes were unchanged. Tony looked at the yellow sneakers and sighed.

Judge McKormick went through the documentation for the record. He asked Hamid if everything in the application was correct and Hamid answered that it was. He then went through the evidence item by item and gave them exhibit numbers.

"Mr. Sorelli, is your client ready to proceed with direct testimony?"

"Yes."

"And the government?"

"Ready," Sandra Peterson replied.

In a deportation case, the government had to prove deportability. Once that was done, they could get to the political asylum case. The person asking for asylum had the burden to prove he was eligible for it.

The judge looked at Mr. Hamid. "Please stand up. Listen to the translator before you give your answer. Do you swear to tell the truth?"

"Okay."

"I'll take that for a yes. Proceed, Mr. Sorrelli."

Tony leaned back in his chair, crossed his hands in front of his chest and looked at Hamid. "Mr. Hamid, please explain to the court why you left Jordan."

"Well. I was a member of a religious organization called *The Righteous*. At least that's the way I think it should be translated. The government was arresting members and I was afraid that before long I would be arrested."

"How long were you a member of this organization?"

"About four years."

"How did you come to join?"

"Well, modern Jordan has failed to represent the values of the average man and we feel that a new government is necessary."

"I am holding up a document. What is this?"

"It's a record of arrest. I was arrested during a protest in Amman and held for a week. That was a year before I left."

"I would like to submit this and its translation into evidence. May I approach the bench?" Tony rose.

The judge waved him forward. "Give a copy to Ms. Peterson. Continue, Mr. Sorrelli. Any objection, Ms. Peterson?"

"For the record, counsel for the respondent is required to submit evidence to my office 30 days before a hearing, but in this case we'll waive it. No objection, your honor."

Tony continued. "Mr. Hamid. How many people were at this protest?"

"About 200."

"And what was the reason for this protest?"

"Well. We felt that the government was not sensitive to the people's need for fairer laws."

"Was the protest at all times peaceful?"

"Yes."

"So why were you arrested?"

"The government in Jordan doesn't like opposition."

"How long were you held?"

"About three days."

"And how were you treated?"

"Badly. They roughed us up and asked a lot of questions about the organization and the members. They threatened our families."

"But you didn't leave until one year later. Why was that?"

"When I heard that the government was picking up our members I left as soon as I could."

"How did you hear this?"

"Several people I knew were arrested. The father of a friend told me what happened to his son, and I thought that I could be next."

"How did you get a United States visa?"

"I got it from a member of the organization. They took someone's passport and switched photos. That got me to Kennedy Airport where I told the man at immigration the truth."

Hamid explained in detail his life in Jordan. The questioning went on for more than an hour.

When Tony finished, the judge asked, "Do you have any questions, Ms. Peterson?"

"Yes, Mr. Hamid. Isn't it true that the mission of The Righteous is to overthrow the democratically elected government in Jordan and establish an Islamic state that will allow no other religions nor elections?"

"Well, Jordan has a king and well…some members have that idea but I believe in democracy."

"Isn't it true that Jordan has truly democratic elections for its parliament?"

"I don't believe that."

"Isn't it true Mr. Hamid that you were quoted as saying that there should be violent overthrow of the government and all Americans should be deported from Jordan because they bring anti-Islamic ideas into that society?"

"No, I don't remember saying that. Why do you ask me that?"

"First of all, we ask the questions and you answer them. Second: take a look at Exhibit M from your original political asylum application. The article from the Amman Record is in Arabic and you have submitted an English summary. We did our own translation and it seems that you left out much of the article. On the second page you are quoted as saying that the elected government should be overthrown and that Islamic law will replace democracy."

"Well. I believe in democracy."

"Is that quote correct?"

"I don't remember saying that."

"So you are saying that the article was wrong."

"Yes."

"Why would some reporter lie, Mr. Hamid?"

"Maybe the government wanted to use that to jail me."

"Are you that important?"

"You know, the government just looks for ways to suppress the people."

"Isn't it true that the spiritual leader of your organization, Mohammed Aziz Mohammad Abdul, is constantly quoted as calling for worldwide jihad?"

"No. You have him mixed up with Mohammed Abdul Aziz Mohammed. The names are similar, and you may have made a mistake."

The judge interrupted. "I'm looking at Exhibit R and it contains a report by Aziz Mohammed Mohammed Abdul. Isn't he a member of the parliament in Amman?"

"No. Mohammed Mohammed Aziz Abdul does speak out for democracy."

"So you agree with me," Ms. Peterson added.

"I'm sorry," Hamid said. "Now I'm getting the names mixed up. Are you asking me about Aziz Aziz Mohammed Abdul or Mohammed Aziz Mohammed Abdul? He has nothing to do with this."

"He who?"

"Aren't we talking about Mohammed Aziz Mohammed Abdul?"

"We ask the questions Mr. Hamid."

"I'm sorry. I don't understand."

Peterson addressed the Court. "I got this name from The U.S. State Department Country Reports for last year where they describe Mohammed Aziz Mohammed Abdul as a threat to democracy in Jordan. I would like to present a copy into evidence. Here's a copy, Mr. Sorrelli."

"No objection."

"Mr. Hamid. It states on page 47 of the report that many members of The Righteous are wanted by the Jordanian government and some have fled to Syria to fight with ISIS. Do you know that?"

"I know that some are wanted by Jordan, but I know nothing about ISIS."

Ms. Peterson continued. "Mr. Hamid, didn't you ask for political asylum at the airport?"

"Yes."

"Why did you do this?"

"Well, I want to be legal."

"So you planned from the beginning to come here."

"Yes."

"Who paid for your passport?"

"The Righteous."

"Why would they do that?"

"Because they knew I was in danger and they wanted to help me out."

"How long were you arrested for?"

"Several days?"

"Didn't you say a week at your initial asylum interview?"

"Yes. It was a week."

"You also said in your application that it was three days."

"Well, between three days and a week."

"You don't remember exactly?'

Hamid looked at Peterson menacingly. "No, not exactly."

"Are you telling the Court that you don't remember how long you were in jail?"

"I remember. It was three or four days. Maybe a week."

"No other questions at this time."

Judge Richards turned to Ms. Peterson. "Have the background checks cleared yet?"

"Not yet."

Background checks determine whether there is a record in the U.S. or abroad about an alien. The judge cannot make a decision unless they're completed.

The judge looked at his watch. "I have another case on for this afternoon that I need to finish today. We need to complete this at another time. My clerk will give you an adjournment notice for about three months. I will fit you in on a day when we have a canceled case. You can continue cross then. I have several openings around that time. Please see my clerk and work it out."

Hamid leaned over to Tony and whispered into his ear, "Well, do you think we won?"

"You did fine today."

When Tony returned to the office Bill stopped him and asked what happened. Tony explained.

"Good, Tony. At least we'll know if his check clears."

* * *

Ryan escorted Mr. and Mrs. Mendez to the federal building. They went through security where they had to take off belts, shoes, jackets, and all metal objects.

Ryan put on his belt and spoke to a guard. "Is security always like this?"

"Yeh, but with the Imam's trial coming, everyone is more careful than usual. Expect more security during the trial, counselor."

On the eighth floor they were stopped by a guard who asked to see their appointment notice. They entered a large, crowded waiting room. A fan was circulating the stale air, and half the people in the room looked as though they were about to fall asleep. Ryan went to the counter to hand in the appointment notice.

The clerk did not look up from her desk. "Are your clients here?"

"Yes. About how long do you think we will need to wait?"

"I can't tell you that. Have a seat." She took the notice and walked away slowly without looking at him at all.

The eighth floor is reserved for green card appointments for family and employment cases. Family cases include marriage cases.

Ryan sat down next to Mr. and Mrs. Mendez and started to look through the file. It was organized and made sense. The first sleeve had correspondence, notices and appointment letters. The second had the applications and copies of all evidence. The third had originals and additional items like tax returns and the fourth had the retainer agreements, bills and receipts. Notes were written on the file folder.

Ryan read the file and waited to be called. He waited a long time. He noticed several attorneys reading newspapers and paperback books. Their clients all seemed to be nervous. One woman was breast-feeding a baby, another changing a diaper.

Each time someone left the room and returned for any reason, the guard asked to see their appointment notices. As one heavy woman was stopped she said in a loud voice, "What the hell do you think I'm here for? My health?"

About two hours later Ryan heard, "Mendez family to the side door."

The side door opened and standing there was a man about thirty years old, shirt, tie, pants, belt, and shoes all in black. Only the oversized silver watch and silver chain hanging from his belt to his trucker's wallet added contrast. His black hair was slicked up and looked dyed. His powdered face gave him a ghostlike appearance.

"My name is Officer Lukens. Follow me."

Ryan followed as Officer Lukens walked femininely down the hall to his cubicle. Ryan noticed Lukens's spider tattoo on the back of his neck. Lukens sat down on one side of the desk and the others sat opposite him. Lukens swore the Mendezes to tell the truth, and he asked Ryan to hand him all originals, including current job letters and passports.

Lukens scanned the documents. "You're new. I've never seen you before."

"Yes I am."

"I never see Zalmanski here anymore, but Tony is such a sweetheart. Tell him I said hello."

"Sure."

"He's the best dressed lawyer, you know."

"Uh hum."

"Most of the lawyers are poor dressers. Tony always looks stunning."

"Uh huh."

"You look good too. You could be a banker in that suit."

"Thanks," Ryan said incredulously.

Lukens turned to Mr. Mendez. "Do you swear everything on this application is correct?"

"Yes."

"Were you ever a member of the Communist party?"

"No."

"Were you ever arrested?"

"No."

"Did you ever tell anyone that you are a United States Citizen or vote in an American election or accept public assistance?"

"No."

"Do you have any proof that you reside with your wife? Let's see it."

Mrs. Mendez took a shopping bag and took out stacks of bills, bank statements and photos. Lukens took the stack of photos and started to look through them. Ryan could see the photos clearly. The first photo showed the Mendezes sitting side by side on a couch. During the next twenty or so photos they were increasingly disrobing then kissing. In the final two photos she was performing oral sex on her husband. Ryan's mouth was open. Lukens didn't seem to be surprised at all.

"Who took these photos?" Lukens asked.

"My brother," she answered.

A drop of saliva ran off of Ryan's tongue onto his lap. Lukens showed no surprise.

"I see why you married him." Lukens took the two final photos and skimmed through the other items. "I'll approve this case. Have your clients wait outside. You can wait here for the passport. It will take thirty days for us to mail the card to them. I need to stamp it with the temporary proof of legal residence."

Ryan waited and was afraid to say a word. His mouth was wide open.

Lukens finished the paperwork and turned to Ryan. "You should close your mouth unless you want someone to put something in it. I'm just the man to do it." Lukens laughed. "When you have this job, you see everything. I took two of those photos for my collection." He showed Ryan the last two pictures in the pile and then he pulled a stack of at least a hundred photos from his drawer. "Look at these."

Ryan couldn't believe his eyes. They were all pornographic. There were pictures of naked people in bed, in showers, feeling each other and often with other people in the room. Every race and ethnic group seemed to be represented. One photo had what looked like a nude couple holding a sheet up together with what seemed to be a bloodstain in the middle. Lukens pointed to it.

"That's interesting."

"Interesting! You learn more about people in this job than any other. There's an education in that pile. I've collected these photos over just the last four years. Imagine how many I'll have by the time I retire." He added the new photos to his collection.

Ryan took the passport and got out of there as fast as he could.

THREE

Sheriff Kelly arrived at the Airport in Amarillo, Texas and drove two hours to the scene. When he arrived at the morgue he examined the body. He turned to the coroner. "This is the same style of execution we had at the border. I'm sure it's the same killer. Have you found any evidence?"

The local policeman drove him to where the body was found and walked him around the scene. "These are tire tracts of a car flooring it. The tire belongs to a four-wheel drive. Might be a jeep or some other SUV."

"Looks like the same tracts we have. We'll need a forensic match."

"Hard to be sure, sheriff. There are a million cars with the same tires."

"Looks like they're headed out-of-state."

"What about the dash cam?"

"Gone. Probably taken by the killer. We haven't found it yet. The GPS wasn't working in this spot and neither was the dash cam backup."

Kelly got on the computer and posted a report on an FBI lookout site.

* * *

Hamid was on his way to work when he stopped next to a free newspaper box to light a cigarette. Another man with Middle Eastern features stopped and opened the box, then placed a small package into the box as he took a newspaper.

He whispered to Hamid. "The messenger has arrived. He's on the way."

Hamid opened the box and folded a newspaper over the package and took both with him. He immediately walked the few blocks to work.

Hamid began his shift at the Irving Avenue News and Tobacco Shop at 8:00 AM. He entered the store and lit a cigarette. Mo, a teenager who had just completed the night shift, noticed the package and asked him, "How did it go in court?"

"You know. I tell them what they want to hear. I have to go back in three months. We'll need to put some cash in the checking account or I'll have trouble with the lawyers. Take this to the bank and deposit it into my account." He took a handful of money from a drawer behind the counter and made out a deposit slip. He then went into the back room where he placed the package into a locked file cabinet.

"Do you think you might get it?"

"The judge looked like he was going to grant it. We'll see. If not the lawyer will appeal and we'll buy some more time. I'll be here long enough to finish the work."

"I'll be happy when we get rid of that package."

"It's perfectly safe so long as you don't drop it."

Mo smiled, put on his jacket and left.

* * *

Tony threw down the tax return and leaned over to the client. "You don't understand. If you don't pay taxes, we cannot complete the case. Your boss is sponsoring you for a green card based upon employment. He has to show that the company earns enough money to pay your salary. Without the proper taxes, you won't be able to do this."

"*You* don't understand," the client said in a thick Irish brogue. "This is a bar. We get tips and cash. My boss doesn't want to show the money. He doesn't want to pay sales tax or employment taxes. Half the workers are illegal and off the books and the other half get paid half in cash. All bars operate this way. He can't show squat."

"Shawn, I told you from the beginning that we would have to show this. Now we are in the middle of the case and the government wants the taxes. We have to show that the company has the ability to pay the wage they offered you when we began this case. How do you think we're going to do it without your taxes?"

"I'm paying you to figure that out."

"I don't care about his business. I'm not his business lawyer. I'm his and your immigration lawyer. I'm like a doctor who tells a patient that he has to take his medicine. A year later the patient comes back sicker than ever and explains that he didn't like the taste so he didn't take the medicine. The doctor tells him he's going to die. *Next patient.*"

"I paid you good money when we started this case and you told me it could be done."

"You didn't take your medicine. I gave you instructions to follow and you didn't."

After a few more minutes of this, the client left and Tony dictated a letter. He buzzed Maria and told her to send a "cover my ass" letter to that client's boss. That's a letter to inform a client of something you are sure they are not doing or doing wrong in case they claim later that they didn't know what needed to be done.

Bill walked into Tony's office. "How many times have I told you not to let this become personal?"

"I told Maria to do a letter."

"Tell the clients, write them letters, but don't get into arguments with them. At the end of the day all they'll remember is how they feel."

"But they need to have the truth knocked into them."

"New business comes from clients who feel good about us. If you argue with them, even if they do the right thing all they'll remember is the argument."

* * *

Somewhere near Amarillo, Texas, deep into a dirt road Naib sat in the jeep as Ali returned with a stolen SUV. They dragged the heavy box into the new car and Ali started to cover the jeep with brush.

"Where did you get the car?" Naib asked.

"As a strip mall down the road. Nobody saw me."

"There are security cameras in many of the stores in these malls," Naib said. "You were probably picked up by some of the cameras."

"How can they find me? I'm wearing a baseball cap and I have a two-day beard. I could be anyone."

"Whose car is it?"

"I saw an old lady get out and go into a store."

"She'll report it to the police a soon as she gets out. You should have looked for one from one of the employees. They wouldn't have noticed it gone till work ended. This was not a good choice."

"If we hadn't shot the policeman…"

"You should have been more careful. Why couldn't you just take a car from someone's driveway? Even that would have been better. We'll need another car in a few hours."

"The mall was busy. Nobody even noticed. I had to do this."

"I understand," Naib replied.

"I can't take another day in the motel. This car will do."

"We'll drive out of the state. It'll be some time before they'll be looking for us in Oklahoma. If we're lucky they'll look in Chicago or somewhere. Let's go."

* * *

The next morning, just as J.K. was checking out of his motel room, a police car pulled up and waved him in. They drove about twenty miles north where several police cars were taking evidence from a beat-up white Jeep Grand Cherokee.

"This seems to be the same car from the shooting. It's been wiped really clean. Haven't found any prints yet, but they left in a hurry. Even the empty water bottles were wiped clean. We'll send them out for any DNA evidence. There's garbage and we still might find something." The policeman took J.K. to one side of the car where another policeman was using tweezers to remove some assorted coins and M&Ms from the cracks in the seats. He pulled out an old tissue and a few receipts.

"What's that," J.K. asked.

"There's a cash receipt for a Starbucks at Newark Airport, several days old. Another one for some article of clothes there. Also cash."

"We can use these to see if any security cameras picked up the transactions. That might lead somewhere."

"Could be nothing. This car was rented at the Kansas City airport. I bet the paperwork they used was bogus. We'll check. They might have come from the New Jersey or New York area, flew to Kansas City and rented the car there. I betya this is where they're going."

"Too speculative for us. Could be a prior renter. If you want to try, go for it."

With that, J.K. called up the FBI in New York City. "Please put me through to Mark Auburn."

* * *

Bill stood over his desk with several newspapers spread out. With his left hand he slowly turned the pages. With his right he held a box cutter and once in a while cut out an article and put it on the side.

Bill picked up the intercom and called Ryan. "Come on in."

Ryan came in.

"I'm having dinner tomorrow tonight with Tony and some immigration attorney friends. I'd like you to join us."

"Sure." Ryan took the information. "What are you doing?"

"I'm cutting out articles that are important. I'm going to photocopy them and give them out."

"You should download them and email them to everyone. It's more efficient."

"Do you have any computer savvy? I'm useless."

"Sure. In fact you'll find that I can do a lot around here. You need to update your website. You haven't touched it for over two years. Everyone uses their personal emails. We should have office emails."

"We...huh. Okay."

"In the meantime, I'll scan these articles and get an email list so everyone gets a copy."

"Thanks."

"Do we have a scanner?"

"Buy one on the office account. Adara has the account info."

"Consider it done. Also, we can set their smart phones so that you can track everyone with GPS, if they don't mind. That way if, for example, Tony or someone is at immigration you will know it."

"Never heard about it."

"It's called 'Stingray' technology. Very new but the police are using it."

"Some of the staff will mind."

"I'll ask everyone if it's okay with you. Adara likes the idea. We've discussed it."

"She would. Very controlling."

"Later we might want to computerize the office further and have passwords for each of us so we can enter the office system from anywhere. Makes it easy to work from home. The system we have is ancient in computer years."

"Stop short of that. I don't even have a computer at home. The last one I had was an Osbourne. I want to discuss this with Tony and Adara first."

"Adara's on board."

"Where'd you learn all this?"

"School and on my own. My generation's good at these things."

"Mine isn't. Lets go step by step and see how it works out."

"Fine."

"Start with the articles and see who's okay with the cell phone thing."

"You got it, boss."

"Don't call me boss. Save that for Adara."

"Okay."

"We'll discuss updating the website next."

As Ryan left, Bill called Adara on the intercom. "We may have hired a monster."

When Adara heard the story, she laughed. "Let's see what he does. We're twenty years behind the times anyway."

* * *

At the end of the day Tony went around the office to turn off the lights and lock up. Adara was working late, and he noticed an attractive woman sitting in the waiting area.

Tony approached her. "Can I help you?"

"No. I'm waiting for Adara to finish. I'm her friend and we're going out for dinner."

"Oh. Where are you going?"

"Don't know. We'll have a drink and decide."

Just then Adara came in with her jacket over her arm. "I see that you two met, Tony. This is my friend Viviana. She's from Argentina."

47

Tony took Viviana's hand and gave it a small kiss. He turned to Adara. "Where have you been hiding such a beautiful friend?"

Adara took Viviana's arm. "We have to go."

Viviana stood up. She was just a bit shorter than Tony and was slim with curly red hair, tight jeans and a red blouse with the top two buttons undone to reveal what was a very skimpy lace bra underneath. Both women looked like they were on the make. When she smiled, Viviana parted her lips just a bit and licked her bottom lip. "It's a pleasure to meet you, Tony."

Tony volunteered. "I can recommend a nice bar near the office where you can enjoy the New York ambiance."

"Why don't you join us?" Viviana said.

Adara stepped in between them. "Tony had a long day and I'm sure he wants to go home."

"I'd love to go. I couldn't allow such beautiful women to drink alone. This is New York after all. You need a man to protect you." He turned to Viviana. "Did I tell you how beautiful I think redheaded women are?"

"No, but please do."

"And sexy."

"Tell me more."

"How wonderful," Adara sighed.

Tony took Adara and Viviana to the Cuban Fiesta restaurant at the South Street Seaport. They sat at a table overlooking the East River. They watched the boats and the lights and had mojitos and then started on wine. They stayed for diner.

Tony went to the men's room and Viviana turned to Adara. "Are you sure you're not interested in him? He's delicious."

"You know how I feel about him."

"I would feel terrible if I stepped on your toes."

"Go slow with him. He's not the serious type."

Tony returned and turned to Viviana. "What are you doing in the United States?"

"My father owns a vineyard in Argentina and I am here representing his company. We produce some of the best wines in Argentina."

"You are probably doing very well here."

"Yes. Our wine is in demand."

"You must be too."

"We also represent other vineyards in the northwest and in Chile."

"It must be beautiful there." Tony leaned towards Viviana.

Adara was getting upset. "Don't forget I'm here too."

"Oh, Adara! Tony's just trying to be nice."

"He succeeds too often."

"I want to hear about the company. I love good wine," Tony said.

"Is that so?"

"Yes. I've taken some courses and you'd be surprised what I know."

"I bet I would. I think it's very important for a man to know what he's doing."

"If I don't, I'm sure you could teach me."

"We have some good offerings."

Adara sighed. "Yes. Tony seems interested in what you have to offer."

Tony leaned towards Viviana. "I know that wine is an aphrodisiac. You have to be careful how much you drink. It would be terrible if you lost your self control."

Viviana giggled. "You can be sure I won't let that happen. I know what I'm doing. Let's order another bottle of wine."

"Oy vey," Adara said.

Viviana picked a bottle of Argentine red and they each had a glass.

"Do you like this wine?" Viviana asked.

"Yes. It is smooth and has a hint of cherry," Tony said. "It makes me want more."

"Are we still talking about the wine?" Adara asked.

"And what about you?" Viviana said to Tony. "You shouldn't drink too much. It's very important for a man to be in control at all times. It would be just terrible if, for example, you let a woman get control over you."

"Maybe that's what I need, a woman in control."

"You have Adara. I know her well and she likes to be in control."

"I don't know if I'm strong enough to have two women in control. The thought excites me."

"Please give me your glasses? Both of you. Now!" Adara reached for Viviana's wine. Viviana pulled her glass away. Tony pulled his out of her reach. "You two have had enough."

"I can handle this," Viviana said. "I was brought up with wine and I know when to stop."

"Yes, but you weren't brought up with Tony."

"I was brought up with my three brothers and I know how to handle myself around strong men. I can handle Tony. He's a pussy cat."

"I'm just the man who needs to be handled. I need a woman in control. Adara bosses me around."

"I might be too much for you. I might be dangerous."

"If I die, I die."

"Tony," Adara said. "Tomorrow is a workday. We all need to get home at a reasonable time to get ready for work tomorrow."

"What's your rush?" Viviana said. "I haven't asked Tony what he likes in a woman yet."

"I like a strong woman who knows what she wants and isn't afraid to take it. You both look like that type of woman."

"You should only know," Viviana said.

"No, he shouldn't. We need to get home before you have too much to drink."

"Oh come now, Adara. It's already too late. I'm just a simple woman who's enjoying a conversation with a strong, determined man."

"No. You're a lamb sticking your head in the lion's mouth," Adara said.

"No, Adara. Tony should be afraid of sticking his head or anything else in my mouth, or something like that. I might bite it off." Tony and Viviana laughed. Adara sighed.

Adara asked for the check put the tab on the office account. On the way out she turned to Tony. "Goodnight. It was nice of you to join us."

Tony turned to Viviana. "Where do you live?"

"On Fourteenth Street and Seventh Avenue."

"That's in my direction. Adara lives in Queens and she's going in another direction."

"Don't worry, Tony. I'll take Viviana home."

"No. I wouldn't hear of it. It's on my way."

"You needn't bother."

Viviana stopped it. "It's late and if he's going the same way, I'll be fine. I can take care of myself. I won't let Tony do anything improper. I'm a big girl."

Adara looked a bit upset but hailed a taxi and went on her way. Tony and Viviana took a taxi in the opposite direction.

The taxi passed through Chinatown and turned onto Fourteenth Street. As Tony bent over to kiss Viviana she grabbed his head and stuck her tongue into his mouth. The driver saw this in the rear view mirror and almost rear ended the car in front.

"Do you want to come up for a while?"

"Sure."

They were kissing in the elevator while Viviana was fumbling for the keys. Once in the apartment Tony took her blouse and bra off in record time. Viviana helped.

As Tony started to kiss her breasts, she grabbed his arm and took him into her bedroom. She sat on the bed and pulled down his pants.

"Oh my! Look at *you*, you show off! You're ready." She opened a drawer and pulled out a condom and put it on him in record time.

"I love when a woman is prepared."

"I love it when a man is ready."

She had a dark wood four-poster bed. On the wall above the headboard was a large cross with a plastic Jesus hanging from it. Tony started to kiss her from head to toe.

"I'm ready too," Viviana said.

Tony took her into his arms. As they were having sex, Tony was looking into Jesus's face. He thought that his mother would not approve, but that wasn't enough to stop him. He thought to himself, "Forgive me, Rosa."

Viviana shouted into Tony's ear, "Faster!" Tony looked at Jesus and tried to go faster.

A few seconds later she shouted again: "FASTER!"

Tony went faster.

Then louder again: "*FASTER! FASTER!*" She yelled it again and again. Tony wondered what the neighbors thought. The neighbors would be right. He tried to go as fast as he could, but it seemed that it wasn't fast enough. He knew the condom wouldn't last.

"*FASTER*, damn it!" she insisted as she grabbed his ass and pulled him violently inside. He could feel the condom shred to pieces.

Tony looked at Jesus and whispered "Jesus help me."

Tony couldn't do it any faster, and the harder he tried the more he was afraid that he would lose his erection. The pressure kept Tony going, but when it was over he wondered whether he met her standards. She melted into his arms and Tony felt good.

Later as they rested, Viviana explained that she had known Adara for several years and that they were very close. Tony was surprised that he didn't know about her since he had worked with Adara for more than ten years and thought he knew everything about her. He explained to Viviana how he had met Adara when she was a receptionist and how she had taken on more and more responsibility until she ran the office. Now Adara was a partner in everything but the name.

Viviana wanted more sex and Tony barely complied. During the second go, he wondered where the nearest emergency room was. He was sorry that he hadn't brought oxygen and digitalis.

In the morning Tony staggered out very early, before Viviana could demand more, and took a taxi home to get ready for work.

FOUR

Mario's of Fourteenth Street is a small Italian restaurant that is never empty, has not been redecorated for several generations, and has an old New York atmosphere that invites you to sit and enjoy a hearty meal. The tin ceiling and the blue and white ceramic tiled floors are a breath of old New York. The old wood tables with the red and white checked tablecloths and the old photos of famous patrons on the walls attest to the authenticity of this establishment. The food is good, the portions are large, and the atmosphere is intimate.

You could walk by the restaurant a hundred times and never notice it.

Jack Martin was the first to arrive with Harold Peters. Jack had dropped the ez from his name to sound more American. Their office was just down the block from Mario's. Martin was a man of about sixty and had been in the business almost as long as Zalmanski. Tall and young-looking for a man of his age, he had the air of a former athlete. Jack had his tie off and the top two buttons of his shirt undone. His hair was impeccable, and he smelled as though he had just shaved.

Peters was ready to challenge whatever was said that could be in any way incorrect. Like Tony, Harold enjoyed challenging the system and putting the world right.

They took the two steps down from the street to the restaurant and Mario, or the latest descendant to call himself that, saw to it that they had their reserved table of choice.

Zalmanski came with Sorrelli and Goldberg. They had a table in the corner, but half the seats backed up against the other tables. Last to show up was Jeff Pounders. Jeff was a large African-American with a bit of a

Caribbean accent. He huffed and puffed as he hurried so as not to keep the others waiting.

"You can't eat here," Bill said to Jeff. "Too fattening for you."

"Look at the pot calling the kettle black. No diet tonight. Never at Mario's."

Without asking, the waiters placed a bottle of red wine and garlic bread made from Jewish challah on the table. Within a few seconds the bread and wine were gone and a waiter brought more.

Tony turned to Harold. "Ever find your client?"

Harold frowned.

As Jeff sat down Jack said, "We can eat now. Idi Amin is here."

"So is Poncho Villa."

Each poured himself some more wine and took some more bread. After some small talk the discussion got down to business.

Harold pulled out some notes. "Last time we discussed the new case that ruled that sugarcane was not an agricultural product for farm worker visas. I wanted to find a similar case to litigate in the Southern District of New York, but no one here had any cases that I could use as a test. Jack discussed the problems he was having with his new client ID cards and promised to bring us up to snuff at this dinner. Tony said he would bring us up to date about his lawsuit against the government when he climbed aboard the immigration detention bus and the guards threw him to the ground. Zalmanski wanted to continue his rant about the exclusion laws and why they didn't make sense."

Zalmanski continued. "I want to introduce Ryan Goldberg. He's new in our office and I wanted him to meet the boys."

They all shook his hands.

Zalmanski turned to Jack. "Jack. Ryan's a Jew with an Irish name."

"Yeah. And you're a Polack with a Polack name," Jack said.

"Don't answer that," Jeff said to stop that discussion. He turned to Bill. "What's happening with your son?"

"Don't talk about it." Bill turned to Ryan. "He's thirty-eight, working on his second PhD and has never worked at a paying job a day in his life. He lives at home with my ex and I'm supporting them both. At this rate I'll never be able to retire."

"Why don't you cut the umbilical cord? Stop funding this nonsense?" Harold asked.

"How can I? His mother has a retail job at Barnes & Noble and barely makes enough for rent."

Harold continued. "You know, they usually grow up by the time they're forty-eight."

"Thanks for that."

They adjusted their seats as the restaurant filled up and the surrounding guests came in close.

"How do you like the hot office manager?" Jack asked.

"Adara?"

"Of course. Bill and Tony's hot Arab taskmaster."

"She runs an efficient office." Ryan said.

Jack laughed. "Efficient? I'd steal her away from your firm if I could. She's more than efficient. The clients love her because they know she cares about the work and gets it done right. She also brings in the men who want to look at her." He turned to Tony. "And you? Tell me you don't look at her."

"Our relationship is purely professional."

Jack made an incredulous face. "If I were twenty years younger I'd marry her and run away to Tahiti. Why the hell don't you, Tony?"

Tony ignored the comment.

Harold turned to Goldberg. "What in heaven's name made you want to get into immigration law?"

"Bill offered me a job."

"At least you're honest. If someone offered you gonorrhea for free, would you take it?"

"That's what I call a ringing endorsement of the profession. I'm glad you're not one of those bleeding hearts who are in this business to save the illegals, like Tony is," Harold said.

"And why not!" Tony said. "First of all, Harold, you're a bleeding heart too. Second, they're not illegal; they're undocumented. These people have the right to a piece of the American dream. They come from places where there are no human rights and they have no future. These people have been exploited and come her for a chance at freedom."

Bill spread out his arms and held up his palms to stop the talking. "I'd love to agree, Tony, but they're illegals. Try to do what they're doing in their countries and see how you would be treated. *And* if enough of them come here, there'll be no future here either." Bill turned to Ryan again. "Tony and Harold want to make all the illegals citizens. That's a good way to encourage another thirty million to come here illegally."

Jack turned to Tony. "I saw you on the Johnson show. Do you really believe all that crap, or are you playing to the paying customers?"

Harold immediately stood up for Tony. "Listen, bro."

Jack laughed. "Bro?"

"Tony's correct. The right thing to do is to take these refugees in."

Bill bottomed his glass. "Charity begins at home, boys. Let in a few hundred thousand foreigners and we're making it harder for our people to get jobs and compete. The big winners are the employers."

"Like you when you hired Adara?" Jack asked.

"We do it because these are basically good people trying to start new lives and become part of the American dream, but many of them would poison us if they could."

"You're going to poison the kid's mind," Jack said.

Bill laughed. "I have a joke."

"Oh no!" Jack said.

"God asked the Chinese if they wanted a commandment, and they said no. Then he asked the Africans if they wanted one, and they said no. He asked Moses if the Jews wanted one, and Moses asked him how much they cost. When God said they were free, Moses said he would take ten."

No one else laughed.

"This is a real good way to start with your Jewish associate," Jack said.

"I want to practice law. This is starting out more interesting than I thought. I'm looking at a whole world of law that I didn't know existed two weeks ago," Ryan said.

Bill smiled and patted Ryan on the back. "It existed, son."

Jeff continued the conversation. "So, Jack. Have you resolved the problem with your ID cards?"

Jack Martin decided that it was a good marketing tool to produce client identification cards that looked very much like immigration green cards. It took a second look to see that instead of the usual government information, the card stated that the alien was a "legal permanent resident *applicant*" and that the *"card was issued by the Law Firm of Jack Martin for identity purposes only."* The Department of Homeland Security did not think this was funny and pulled every one of his firm's cases and stopped work under the excuse that they would need to conduct an investigation and that they would conduct the investigation until they had all the cards returned and destroyed. This was no small matter.

"We have almost all of the cards. This is killing me. As long as our cases are not being processed we can't bill, and if the feds don't lighten up soon we'll have to lay off the staff."

"You can't lay them off. Good people are hard to find and train. You have to hang in there," Bill said.

"Tell me about it," Jack said.

"You above all should know how difficult it is to fight the government," Bill said. "Just the cost of defending against them can cripple you. They have unlimited resources."

Harold Peters interrupted. "We have more to discuss. Let me tell you what I know. First, Renee Curtwright is heading the new task force prosecuting the Imam. The U.S. Attorney's office wants publicity." He looked at Tony. "How do you like that, Tony?"

"Oh no! She's been the U.S. attorney on several of my cases and she's one tough son of a bitch. She always threatens you with sanctions for filing a frivolous case. She likes to intimidate you and show she has the biggest dick in the room," Harold said.

"She must be a dyke," Jack said.

Harold laughed. "I don't think so. Tony use to bang her."

"Maybe that turned her around."

"It's been a long time since we've dated," Tony added. "That was just after I got into this business. Old news. My dealings with her since have been purely professional."

"Bullshit," Harold said. "She loved you and you broke her heart."

"I never promised her the sun, the moon and the stars."

"For someone who thinks he knows women, you don't have a clue."

"I think I do."

"Let me tell you the way it works," Bill continued. "Women get attached to a man easily. You must have missed what was going on. One by one you're getting on every New York woman's shit list. Sometimes the woman you need is right under your nose."

"You mean like Adara?" Jack asked.

"Thank you, Bill, for that lecture on romantic relationships," Harold said. "Now let me continue. Word from the street is that Renee's boss, U.S. Attorney Hite, is running for the Senate and wants to make this a high profile matter. She wants her boss's job. He goes to Washington, and she's first in line for the U.S. Attorney job. She's very connected. They're also going after notarios."

Jack Martin continued. "That last part is going to be good for business. It will scare the public from these fly-by-night storefront-would-be-immigration lawyers."

"You know that some of these notarios are better than some lawyers. How many jack-of-all-trade lawyers have you seen fuck up cases?" Harold said.

Tony said, "You know what they say. Ninety-nine per cent of the lawyers give the rest of us a bad name."

Bill took a long drink of wine. "We're trying to manage a practice, build a future and help people, and the government is trying to do whatever it can to screw us."

"No. They're trying to make us accountable to the public," Tony said.

Jeff Pounders banged down his fork and knife. "No. No. They're trying to further their own careers. They don't give a damn about the aliens we represent. In fact, if they had their way, they would deport them all: us too. The U.S. Attorney just wants publicity. Hite couldn't care less about them. Just another prosecutor looking for headlines."

Harold turned to Tony. "How's your lawsuit going, Tony?"

Tony climbed aboard an immigration bus after Immigration and Customs Enforcement (ICE) agents arrested his client. As the bus was in motion, he climbed onto the front bumper and demanded his client be released or he would not get off. The bus went thirty miles an hour down Broadway, slammed on the brakes and Tony went flying. He sued the government.

"I can't talk about it anymore. ICE might settle, and one condition is that I don't discuss the settlement."

Several dishes were put down. There were two salad dishes, a calamari, and a mozzarella and tomato salad. Each dish was enough to be shared several ways. For a few minutes there was silence. More dishes came, including enough lasagna to feed the Yankees. It disappeared in about four seconds.

Jack turned to Pounders. "What's happening with the Chinese restaurant?"

Pounders turned to Ryan. "You need some background. I have a Chinese restaurant from China. They have several restaurants there and are doing well. They want to open a restaurant on the Jersey shore. They transferred about four hundred thousand dollars here, opened a corporation, rented property, contracted to build the place out and well you got it."

"I'm listening," Ryan said.

"Now I want to transfer the chef and the owner here on work visas to run the place, and immigration is giving me a hard time. They're documenting me to death."

"You should have just snuck them in and applied for political asylum," Bill said. "That way they would have gotten permission to work and stay here for years while their cases were going on. You just did it wrong."

They ate dinner and drank wine and discussed all manner of unimportant items.

Harold got back to the main subject. "We were talking about excludable offences last month. Tony was talking about homosexuality as an excludable offence."

Bill downed his third glass of wine and continued a little too loud. "It's nobody's business who I have sex with. I like to fuck twelve-year-old girls and it's nobody's business but my own."

Everyone at the surrounding tables heard and the room became quiet. Ryan slithered down and put his hand in front of his face.

Martin put his hand on Bill's. "A little louder please, so they can hear you in New Jersey."

"Same sex marriage is legal now," Ryan said.

"That has little to do with it. The immigration laws still exclude homos," Bill said.

"You mean gays and lesbians, don't you Bill?" Tony said. He turned to Ryan. "Since the Supreme Court threw out the defense of marriage act, it's legal to marry and sponsor someone of the same sex but they can still be excluded because of their homosexuality."

"Don't you mean 'their gay or lesbian sexual orientation' Tony?" Martin said.

"They can't even run their cafeteria right, and they have the nerve to tell me who I can fuck," Bill said loudly.

Martin put his finger in front of his lip. "Keep it down, Bill. I'll keep a look out for one of my Korean clients for you."

"Women are more trouble than they're worth."

"It's getting late. Time to go home," Martin said. "Where's the check?"

* * *

After dinner, Tony and Harold left the restaurant together and began to walk. Everyone else took taxis.

Tony took off his tie and opened up his collar button. Harold left his bow tie alone.

"It's not late. Let's go to Sounds of Brazil for a drink and see if we can find some women?" Harold asked.

"Not tonight. I have plans. I'll take a rain check."

"Wow. Secret pal, huh?"

"Just visiting a friend."

"At 9:30? Sounds like a booty call."

They walked and talked for several blocks and then Peter took a taxi. Tony went to a nearby brownstone and rang the third floor walkup apartment. A woman's voice asked who it was and buzzed him in. She opened the door wearing only a robe with a towel over her hair.

"Hello, Tony."

"Hello, Sandra."

Sandra Peterson closed the door and let the robe fall open to reveal nothing underneath. Tony pushed the towel off her head, pulled back her hair and began kissing her neck as she melted into his chest.

* * *

Ryan was setting up the new office he shared with Carmen as she handed him a copy of a memo on filing immigration forms. They both read the memo.

"Well, you've got your first memo." Carmen took a copy of the memo and thumbtacked it to a board with dozens of other memos all overlapping each other so that this one was the only one that could be read. "You should save this so you can refer to it until the next memo comes along and countermands this one."

"Where is this from?"

"Immigration. We get these all the time."

"I don't have a clue about what this means," Ryan said.

"Don't worry. I've been in this business my whole life and I don't have a clue either. One thing's for sure: when you try to file something at CIS someone will cite this memo as the reason why you can't do it."

"So how will this help me?"

"You can waive this and bluff. Say you understand it and it allows you to do what you want to. It might work."

Carmen had grown up in the immigration business. Her mother was Jack Martin's secretary and now was his second wife. Zalmanski hired Carmen as a favor to Jack when Jack couldn't have his stepdaughter around anymore. It was difficult giving her orders. He traded her for a secretary who Adara was having difficulty with. It was a good decision for them both.

"So how do I know where to file applications?"

"Ask someone here. The government makes it so difficult to get it right it's crazy. They say that you don't need a lawyer, and then they set up a system that's almost impossible to get through. You miss a deadline and you're out. The killer is, if you make a mistake you end up being deported, and the system wants you to make a mistake."

"I'm glad Bill offered me this job, but I'm afraid I won't get it right."

"You will."

"People's lives are in my hands. I don't want to mess up."

"You won't."

Zalmanski was walking by and came in and sat down. "I heard that."

"You seem to hear everything," Carmen said.

Bill put on a big smile. "Well, not everything." He turned to Ryan, "Let me tell you something. You are already more competent than 90 percent of the people in this business. You don't have a clue what's out there. You'll discover that most of the government doesn't know what's going on at the next table let alone have an idea of how the system works. All they want to do is to get to 5:00, deny a few cases and go home. They don't give a shit about their jobs. You'll see that most of the lawyers can only start cases and have no idea what to do once there's a problem. They just fill out forms and collect money. They're shit throwers. They throw shit against the wall to see what sticks."

"But I'm new. I'm happy to have the job and I want to learn more, but…"

"No buts. Don't be a schmuck. I see the way you handle these matters. You want to do a good job. That already puts you ahead of the crowd. I saw you pick up that paper that first day when I met you. Almost anybody else would have left it on the floor. That got you the job even if you had two heads. You've handled several other things for me well. Tony is about to dump a lot of work on your desk. Even Adara likes you and she's demanding, very hard to please. I'm glad I'm not married to her. She'd kill me. If you want to learn more, we have the books. We buy CDs with immigration lectures you can listen to, and you can join the Immigration Lawyers Bar Association. They have all sorts of useful programs. We'll pay your dues."

"Thank you."

"Just don't get a swelled head and ask for more money." Bill walked out.   Carmen smiled. "Don't worry. I've got your back."

"I'll scan and email the memo to everyone. It'll take a minute."

"Ask Bill for more money."

* * *

Mark Auburn sat in his office early that morning and reviewed several emails. As head of the FBI legal department in New York City, his responsibilities were substantial. He was over six feet tall with light brown hair and looked athletically fit. At 49 he looked a long way from middle age. He dressed in a gray business suit and a white shirt. If you looked up the term "WASP" in the dictionary, his picture would be there.

He got up and went into a small conference room where a large board covered with notes and strings from note to note hung against one wall. He turned it around.

Several people came into the conference room. Renee Curtwright and Charles Robinson sat on the side. Robinson was wearing a charcoal gray pin-stripped three-piece suit with a collar pin and cufflinks, and well-shined black oxford shoes. He was tall, young and had had a recent haircut. His blonde hair was meticulously groomed. Ms. Curtwright was about ten years his senior and her body language said that she was the boss. Everyone made sure to say "hello" to her first. She was wearing a black man-tailored suit with patent leather high-heeled shoes and a gold chain with a heart. Robinson especially noticed how the gold contrasted with her dark brown skin. They both exuded attitude.

Across from him sat Oscar Gomez, a supervisor at immigration. He sat there wearing a corduroy jacket and, as he folded one leg over the other, his white socks shown beneath his trousers. As they sat and chatted, deportation inspectors Stan Piertowsky and Harry Wong came in.

Gomez pointed to two seats next to him. "Sit down. We have an assignment we need to talk to you about."

Piertowsky and Wong were wearing jeans and athletic shoes. Piertowsky was wearing a Yankee sweatshirt and Wong was wearing a plaid button-down shirt. They sat down.

Auburn spoke first. "The U.S Attorney's office has applied for an order to tap and investigate some immigration lawyers based upon a lead. It's unusual to do this, but Assistant U.S. Attorney Curtwright seems to think this should be made a priority. It seems that some suspects may be using this law firm to help them to stay in the U.S. while they plan certain terrorist crimes. We need to be sure to know that the lawyers are knowingly supporting terrorism. We've asked to tap their phones and their email and to check their files. We expect to look at all their Middle Eastern clients."

"What are we looking for?" Wong asked.

"Any contact with people of Middle Eastern or Muslim origin, but especially any coming northeast from Mexico who may be planning some terrorist act. With the Imam's trial coming up, there is some chatter that someone has been sent here to perform a disruptive act."

"What act?"

"We're not sure."

"How can we be sure of anything?"

"You can't, but look for patterns. How do the clients know each other? Can you use their cell phone records to see if they are calling the same third persons? Are they calling Mexico? You get it. See what you can come up with."

"Who are the lawyers?"

"Zalmanski and Sorrelli. Just a couple of blocks from here."

Piertowsky looked puzzled. "Those are the good guys. We know them. They may not be the sharpest tools in the shed, but they do a competent job and care about their clients. They seem very vanilla. Are you sure?"

Curtwright stood up and went over to Piertowsky. "They are bad. They have clients that they know must be terrorists and they help them anyway. They are more interested in a buck than they are in protecting this country. They are knowingly abetting criminal activity. We're going to find out what's going on and stop them."

"We can't listen to every call. It would take too long."

"No, but you will check out their Middle Eastern clients and get their telephone numbers. Search their immigration files. See who these people are talking to and who they are getting calls from, especially numbers between Mexico, the border and here. See where it leads. Report to Mr. Auburn here. Got it?"

Wong and Piertowsky looked at her and nodded.

"Get started immediately. I'll have the court order in a day or two."

"Can we ask why this firm is being targeted?" Wong asked.

"Several of their clients may have ISIS connections. It seems unusual that they should all use one law firm. There might be something to this. We need to know what's going on," Auburn replied. "Here's a list of the clients we suspect. This is just a start: Ali Raman and Mohammed Hamid and several more. They have a diverse client base, but we want all the clients with Muslim backgrounds checked."

"We're not supposed to target people this way," Piertowsky said. "Isn't that racial profiling?"

"What do you want to do, check all the Chinese grandmothers?" Curtwright asked.

Wong and Piertowsky looked at the list. Wong looked at Auburn. "We'll do it. You know, Sorrelli is just a flaming liberal who likes challenging the government. I don't think he'd even jaywalk. We haven't seen Zalmanski for a few years. He doesn't want to get involved too much in any case."

"Maybe, but the fact that they seem to be lawyer central for our suspects is reason enough to take a look at this," Auburn said.

Curtwright got up and went directly to Wong and eyeballed him. "We're trying to prevent a terrorist act in connection with the Imam's trial. If you don't do your jobs and someone dies as a result, you will be the cause."

"Yes, ma'am."

"And if that happens because you two slack off, you'll spend the rest of your careers at the public help desk downstairs."

"We got it. You can count on us."

Curtwright stood up. "You're dismissed. We have other things to discuss. Please stay, Officer Gomez."

Wong and Piertowsky got up and left without another word and without looking anyone else in the face.

When they were gone, Auburn turned to Curtwright. "What are we up to with the warrant?"

"The judge said she would sign it if everything was in order. I'm not worried." She turned to Gomez. "Please monitor them."

He nodded.

"We know who a few of the suspects are, but let's see where this takes us. Until we have more, they have a right to have their political asylum applications adjudicated." He nodded again. "Can you trust those two?"

"Yes. I'll keep you informed from time to time. No emails, of course."

"Humor me," Gomez said. "How did we get to this firm?"

Auburn walked up to the board and turned it rightside forward. "We got a tip from a sheriff in Texas. Border Patrol found a dead coyote and civilian near the border by Marfa, Texas. Later a patrolman was shot in what seemed like a routine traffic stop. They got the likely car that was rented at the airport in Kansas City and driven all the way west of Big Bend National Park in Texas. We checked with the rental company, and it was taken with stolen papers. The security cameras yielded a photo of the man." He pointed to the photo. "We also found a credit card receipt in the car from a Starbucks from the airport in Newark with that man's photo from another security camera. That transaction was in the man's real name. That led us to an airline ticket. TSA matched it to Ali Raman. He has a political asylum case pending with Zalmanski's office. They're handling another political asylum case, Mohammed Hamid. Both have Interpol watches on them as possible ISIS operatives. They're both being monitored separately from this investigation. They have some related cases."

"But is that enough to get us to go after the firm?" Gomez asked.

"Hell yes!" Curtwright replied. "They have several more Middle East political asylum cases that look suspicious. They have an Iraqi secretary that is managing these cases. I know these lawyers, and they would take dangerous cases without regard to the safety of the United States."

"I got it. I'll let you know what I know."

"I want Piertowsky and Wong to report directly to me," Curtwright said.

"No. They report to me and I promise to keep you in the loop," Auburn said.

Curtwright tapped her fingers on the table a bit, and they all nodded as Gomez left.

After he left, they closed the door. Curtwright walked over to the board and began to look carefully. "This board looks like a mess to me. Please explain again what's going on."

Auburn walked to the board. "We have several things going on, and the connections are not always clear."

"Please explain."

"We get so many leads that it's impossible to follow them all. Zalmanski and Sorrelli have a couple of bad eggs and possibly a few more. I'm hoping that the fact that they're all using the same firm is a meaningful connection, but it might not be."

"Go on," Curtwright said.

"We have similar investigations going on here and in other cities, but it's impossible to properly follow them all. Ali's trip to the border and his possible connection with three murders makes this case stand out. Also the sheriff thinks that there might be some arms transport going on. That's a guess. With the Imam's trial getting underway, we're worried about an incident."

"Why would they transport arms into the U.S?"

"It's very unusual, but they may want to keep a very low profile and not deal with arms dealers at all."

"Doesn't sound right to me. What else could it be?" Curtwright pointed to one note on the board. "What's the Pakistan connection?"

"Let me make this clear. We have no confirmation on the Pakistan problem or any arms smuggling. This is speculation, but we're investigating. The Pakistan military has not been able to confirm or deny reports of missing weapons. Many of their weapons have surfaced among ISIS forces. Some of those weapons have surfaced in Europe and even Nigeria. It's entirely possible that they may be smuggling arms or missiles across the border into the U.S. We're watching this."

"But they can buy weapons here," Robinson said. "Almost anything. At least guns."

"Of course they can. That makes it more troublesome. It must be something special."

"Like what?"

"Anti-aircraft missiles are always a possibility."

"How would they get those into Mexico?" Robinson asked.

"The same way they would get them into the U.S. Shipping."

"But aren't the ships regularly checked?"

"As in the U.S., only a small percent are actually checked. Between that and the corrupt nature of the system in Mexico, it's possible to bring in almost anything."

"Like a bomb?" Robinson asked.

"Yes, Charlie. And that's what we're most worried about."

"Could it be a nuclear weapon?"

Auburn paced a bit. "Not likely. There would be some chatter or at least some problem with a missing one. We don't have any intel on that."

"What are you doing about it?" Renee asked.

"Everything, but we don't want to go crazy either. It might be nothing. Interpol and several nations are monitoring the situation. The CIA has been following up in several cities where these men might have been. We have to worry about our piece of the puzzle."

"What's the worse that can happen?" Robinson asked.

"I hate that question. It's like asking a doctor what's the worse that can happen. He'll tell you that you can get cancer and can it spreads throughout your body. You'll die. The worse case here is a bomb."

"Like atomic?"

"That is a leap."

"No," Curtwright said. "You should be checking every angle."

"As a matter of fact we are," Auburn said. "Pakistan cannot do anything with their nuclear arsenal without the approval of North Korea and Saudi Arabia. One has helped them with the technology and the other has paid for it. There is no other place to look."

"Iran."

"Too closely monitored."

"Are you sure those two countries are on top of it?"

"We have requested that Pakistani military intelligence look into it. I have no authority to go beyond that. I don't have the resources either. I can tell you that Pakistan is not reliable. Individual officers have loyalties outside of the government, and the government is not all on the same playing field." Robinson pulled out a pile of charts from a draw. "This will show you the path of some arms we can trace. We intercepted a shipment of weapons to ISIS disguised as area rugs made in China. A shipment such as that one could make it into Mexico and be smuggled here. Hell, it could be shipped directly here, and there is only a one in ten chance we would pick it up. We need more resources."

Curtwright got up, sat next to Robinson and looked closely at the charts. "What's this one?"

"Back to Charlie's question. It's a list of Pakistan's nuclear arsenals with locations and chains of authority."

"Is it accurate?"

"Military intelligence says yes."

"Can we trust the military?"

"I hope so."

"So the answer is no," Robinson said.

"Don't get too carried away with this. The first possibility is we're dealing with an alien smuggling and that nothing dangerous was brought in. Second that they want to make a statement about the Imam's trial and have either some high-powered rifles or some conventional explosives. The two Zalmanski clients work in a tobacco store on Fourteenth Street. We're monitoring it. If they come here, we'll know about it."

"Shouldn't we assume the worst?" Robinson asked.

Curtwright laughed. "We are."

FIVE

Naib sat behind the counter at the gas station in Paducah, Kentucky. The Lucite box surrounded him like a cage. He was clean-shaven and now had a crew cut and wore a new Ralph Lauren polo shirt with a blue cable-knit sweater thrown over his shoulders.

A policeman came in and one took some soda and candy and placed a twenty-dollar bill on the counter. Naib made change.

"You look new here," the policeman said.

Naib glanced down to the shotgun just under the counter. The gun was placed so that it could blow away a robber or anyone else standing in front of the window. He placed his left hand on it and slowly clicked off the safety. "Yes, sir. I'm here helping my cousin for a few days."

"You're a relative of Farzard?"

"Yes. I'm visiting, and he asked me to man the counter while he runs some errands." Naib gave the policeman his change.

"Farzard helps us. A good man, and he contributes to the local PBA."

"I am proud of my cousin."

"I detect a British accent."

"Yes, sir. I'm here from London for a couple of more days."

"Good to meet you. Enjoy Kentucky." With that the policeman left.

Naib picked up his cell phone and called Ali. "Get me out of here."

"Take it easy. You're in a safe house. I'll talk to Hamid and arrange something in the next few days."

"I need to get to New York now. People ask questions here."

"Just country people trying to be friendly. Nothing to worry about. It's more important to be safe than fast. Trust me. You are in a safe place.

We'll talk about it in person tonight. The Farzard family is in deep cover. They're considered honored members of this community. They will never be questioned. Let's do this right and take our time."

"No. It's more important to complete my mission before something goes wrong."

"It's important that we talk face to face. Destroy the phone. We'll use the other disposable one."

"Don't be long."

* * *

Maria showed up that morning with her daughter Pepita. She put her daughter in the conference room with some paper and pencils to draw.

Maria went into Bill's office. "Mr. Zalmanski. I had to bring my daughter today. Is it O.K? My mother couldn't watch her today."

"What about your boyfriend?"

"He disappeared."

"Have you told Adara?"

"I'm afraid."

"I'll smooth it with Adara."

Ryan went into Zalmanski's office and sat down. "You wanted to see me, sir?"

"Stop that 'sir' stuff. Save it for someone who appreciates it. Call me Bill."

"Okay, Bill."

Zalmanski picked up a thick file. "Take this and file a petition for review with the U.S. Court of Appeals for the Second Circuit."

"You want me to do what?"

"This is the Li case. Judge Richards denied this case and we appealed it to the Board of Immigration Appeals. That's a kangaroo court. They upheld the judge in a one-line decision. We have thirty days to file the Petition for Review with the Court of Appeals, and we've already wasted two weeks."

"I don't know what to do."

"Figure it out. It's easy. The issue here is the judge's discretion. He refused to grant a case where the alien had been here for more than ten years and needed to show a very high level of hardship to his family. The judge said he didn't show enough."

Ryan leaned forward. "Isn't that a discretionary decision, and isn't that type of decision unreviewable on appeal?"

"Shit! You're actually learning something. You're right, but we get around it by claiming it's a factual issue and the judge improperly weighed the facts. We can't win on appeal. The Circuit Court won't impose its judgment over the finder of fact, but we'll buy the client some time to do something else, and sometimes we can make a deal with the U.S. Attorney's office to settle the case in a way that benefits the client. We need to buy time. There's a lot of hardship here. He has two United States citizen children, owns a restaurant that employs ten people—three on the books—and one of his children has asthma. Li pays the kids' health insurance. The guy files real taxes. You don't see much of that in this business. There's a lot of sympathy in this case. For now you have to file the petition with the court, serve the U.S. Attorney's office and DHS and add a couple of paragraphs of explanation to the papers. It's a win if they send it back to the immigration judge to reevaluate the facts."

"What if I need help with this?"

"See Tony."

"Tony gave me another case to work on."

"What case is that?"

"Rodriguez. Tony appealed a bond decision and has me working on a habeus. He said if you ask I should tell you that a Mr. Bueno guaranteed the fee. We're also asking to have Rodriguez's citizenship completed in federal court. Tony gave me another similar file to learn from."

"It looks like you're carrying some heavy weight."

"I hope I know what I'm doing. Tony goes over everything."

"If you acted like you knew everything, I'd be worried."

* * *

Adara wore a particularly low-cut blouse that day. The lace bra underneath was obvious. She needed to wear a bra. Two upper buttons were undone as Carmen stared at her breasts. She came into Adara's office, bent over her desk and asked her to review a file. She forgot what she came in for as she stared at Adara's cleavage.

"Carmen, why are you showing this to me? Finish it and leave it on my desk. Put Post-its by anything you want to discuss."

"I just wanted to make sure I was preparing this the way you want it."

Adara got up without responding and went into Tony's office. She sat down without being asked and leaned forward. "What do you think about this Jewish kid Zalmanski hired?"

"You mean Ryan? I thought you liked him."

"I do. I just want your opinion."

"He's fine. He's trying to learn the work and he's not afraid to ask a question or admit when he doesn't know something. Good sign. I saw he bought a book, *Spanish for Deportation Officers*, from the government printing office, so I know he's serious. He passed Bill's garbage-on-the-floor test. I vote that he stays, at least for awhile."

Adara left the room and then buttoned her blouse up.

As Adara left Tony's office she heard some sounds from the conference room. A four-year old girl was sitting, drawing and talking to herself.

"And who are you?" Adara asked.

"I'm Pepita. My mommy is Maria. Hello."

"Is anyone watching you?"

"My mommy is."

"That's fine."

Adara asked Maria to come to her office. "You must know it's improper to bring children to work."

"I'm sorry, Adara. It just became impossible today. I would tell you this won't happen again, but the truth is that this was just a bad day when everything went wrong. It will rarely happen. I told Bill."

"Most would say that it won't happen again. Well, you're honest at least. What about her father?"

"He disappeared a year ago. He doesn't send a dime or even call. I depend on my mother, but today she couldn't help."

"We have an office to run."

"Mr. Zalmanski said it was okay."

"Of course he would."

"It won't interfere with my work."

"Of course it will. Try not to let it happen again."

* * *

Maria looked at two men coming to her window. "Can I help you, Mr. Hamid?"

"My friend's name is Arafat and we want to see Ms. Adara."

"Is this his first visit?"

"Yes. Please ask Adara to see us."

"Please fill out this paper so we have some basic facts. You will be charged a two hundred dollar consultation fee that will be applied to your case if we begin."

Arafat was an overweight man in his sixties, bald and in desperate need of a good periodontist. The more he smiled the more obvious it became, and he smiled a lot.

Maria took the completed form to Adara. Adara decided to come to the door. "Mr. Arafat, it's unusual for me to conduct a preliminary interview. I'll have one of the attorneys talk to you soon."

"We want to talk to you first, sister. I know you will want to take good care of our friend. We work together, and I want him to get the best lawyer possible. That's why we came here," Hamid said.

She took him into her office and they talked in Arabic. Arafat explained that he needed to apply for political asylum and that he could only trust someone from his part of the world.

"You understand, Mr. Arafat, that I am an American citizen."

"Yes, but we have this bond that we can't have with real Americans. Our people need to stick together. These Americans won't understand me the way you can."

"I'll make sure your case gets the care and attention it deserves."

"Thank you, sister," Hamid added.

Adara looked over the questionnaire. "You have a similar political asylum claim as Hamid does."

"Yes, similar."

"It says you work in a warehouse in Newark. I thought you worked with Hamid."

"Well, the warehouse supplies the stores and food carts around the area."

"Okay."

Adara set up the retainer, took a deposit and gave Arafat a receipt.

"Please wait outside until one of the lawyers can begin a workup on your case."

When Ryan returned to the office a few minutes later, Maria stopped him at the door. "Adara wants you to take Mr. Arafat to your office and do a political asylum workup. Everyone's busy."

"But I haven't done one."

"It's easy. Here's his friend Hamid's file. Take a copy of the application and get all the information. I started that process. She wants you to look at his friend's affidavit and get enough of his story to prepare a similar affidavit; just change the story to reflect his facts. Take ten minutes to read it over. That's all you need. You then need to see what documentation he can get to back up his story. Ask about witnesses. See if we can get statements from them and if they'll come to court. Tony will go over it and make a to-do list for his next visit."

Ryan took the file to his desk in the office he shared with Carmen and started to read it over. He wondered how the firm could trust him with all this work when only a couple of months before he hadn't even considered looking for a job in this area. He went to the waiting room and called Arafat in.

Carmen got up and pressed a button on her intercom. "I'll be right back." She went into Adara's office, and Adara listened.

After every few questions Hamid and Arafat began to talk in Arabic.

After about fifteen minutes Ryan realized that the information he was taking was almost exactly the same as Hamid's. "This is almost the same story as your friend Hamid's."

They spoke some more in Arabic and then turned to Ryan and continued in English. "You know we came to this country for the same reasons." Adara listened and laughed.

As they spoke, a worried look came over Adara. She did nothing as Maria came in to tell her someone was waiting to see her. Carmen went back to her desk and quietly worked on another file as she listened.

"Maybe so, but I want *your* story. I can't repeat your friend's," Ryan said.

"You're Jewish, aren't you?" Arafat said. "Goldberg is a Jewish name. That makes us brothers from the same part of the world. We must stick together. These American Christians don't understand us."

"I'm American."

They ignored Carmen.

"Other people don't understand the cultural bonds we share. Our peoples are outsiders in this country. As brothers we need to help each other. Just because our peoples have some issues… I know you'll understand what needs to be done so I can stay in the U.S. legally."

"That doesn't change anything. Do you have a story, or are you just using your friend's?"

"You have the story and it's true," Arafat said. "I wouldn't lie to you, my brother."

"Listen," Hamid said as he leaned in and pointed directly at Goldberg's face. "You know your job. Take this information. Start the paperwork and take our money. That is your job. Let us worry about the outcome."

"That's not the way this works. I need to be sure we have a real case."

Hamid dropped an envelope on Ryan's desk. He looked at it and saw it was filled with hundred dollar bills. "Take this money and do what you have to. You would not want to piss me off." Hamid cracked a big smile. His teeth were in better shape than Arafat's.

Ryan gave them a receipt for two thousand dollars.

"How did you enter the United States Mr. Arafat?"

"With a visitor's visa. I have been living and working in Belgium on a work visa."

"It's usually hard to get a visa to come here."

"Yes, I left my wife and teenage son there. I also left a house and a good job."

"You will be asked why you didn't apply for political asylum there. Your case could fail on that issue."

"Let us worry about that," Hamid said. He gave Ryan a threatening look.

"If they see he was in a country where he could have applied for asylum and didn't, they will just deport him to there."

"Do your job."

Ryan's throat dried up as he turned towards the computer and started to type.

After another hour, Ryan had a draft affidavit typed on the computer and gave it to Arafat to review. "Come back next week and we'll work on this affidavit. Once I file it, it will be difficult to change the story. I printed it triple-spaced, so make notes on the pages about what we can add to it to make it as complete as possible. It needs to be as complete and honest as possible. If you are not sure of something, tell me. Get as much of the evidence as you can. Don't wait until you have everything. We'll make a list of things we need to do and start doing them. We need to file this before you're in the United States for more than one year."

"Why is that?"

"Because the standards by which these applications are approved become more difficult after one year. It's in the law. They believe that if you have a real case, you will file it quickly. We can file the application now so you get permission to work and you might even get permission to travel. Before we submit the affidavit and evidence, we better get it right."

"Can I travel back to Jordan?"

"No. Let me explain. You are going to ask for political asylum from that country. If you go back there, you are telling the government that you are not afraid to return. It will kill your case."

"If I can get permission to travel, I can fly to Egypt and fly into Jordan on another passport. The government here won't know."

"If you want political asylum, you won't try to do that."

"Can I visit my family in Belgium?"

"Only if you get permission to travel first. If you travel without permission you won't be allowed back."

"We will be back next week, brother." Arafat smiled and showed Ryan several gaps in his teeth. Hamid stood up and sneered.

After Hamid and Arafat left, Ryan looked at Carmen.

Adara hit the intercom and explained that Hamid told Arafat what to say.

Adara came in and brought Tony with her. "How'd it go with Arafat?" Tony asked.

Carmen laughed. "He's full of shit. He told Ryan whatever he thinks will work because he thinks his friend will get political asylum. Adara listened and Hamid told him what to say. They threatened Ryan to just do his job. It's all bullshit."

"He called me his brother because I'm Jewish. That 'brother' business bothered me. He's trying to manipulate me, and he's lying. They're both lying. It's so obvious."

Tony sat forward. "This man has a right to make this application. These people come to this country because of real persecution abroad. They don't completely trust us because of their history dealing with governments in their own countries. It's our duty to establish trust and help them. This is the profession we chose."

"I sat and listened to most of Ryan's interview with this guy. Everything in my gut tells me he's full a shit. Adara listened to their Arabic and Hamid was telling Arafat what to say," Carmen said.

"He's entitled to his day in court and we're going to give him the best chance we can. It's not up to us to determine whether it's true or not. That is what the court is for."

"He can't wait to go back to Jordan. He's not interested in asylum. He just wants to work here and come and go. I don't think we should file this if we know it's false," Ryan said.

"Do it. It's not false just because his friend helped him, and it's not a bad case because he wants to see what rights he can take advantage of." Tony got up quickly and left the room.

Adara sat quietly and now spoke up. "I listened. I agree with Ryan. They don't want political asylum. They just want to stay here legally for some time, to get some money until they take care of some matter. I don't now what that is, but it worries me."

Carmen and Ryan looked at each other and laughed.

Adara went into Zalmanski's office. "We have this new asylum case, and I think they are lying and might commit a crime."

"What crime?"

"I'm not sure. They need to stay here legally until they can finish some job. They spoke in Arabic and I listened on the intercom. They're more interested in work and travel than in asylum. I think they have some project they're working on and plan to leave afterward. I think the only reason Arafat is here is because he speaks passable English. They may be waiting for some person to get to New York."

"Speculation. All clients lie. The question is how much. It's possible that they're just trying to save money for some business venture."

"I don't think so. I have a bad feeling."

"A feeling is not enough. Did you hear anything specific?"

"Not really."

"What do you mean 'not really'?"

"They seem to be waiting for someone to come here and take care of some business. It didn't sound like they were interested in making a profit. I would be all right with that. They seem to need money to complete some work and then leave."

"Exactly what did they say?"

"I'm not sure. I couldn't hear well and missed some words here and there. They're definitely working on some project and seem worried."

"Unless you're sure about a crime, we have an ethical duty to keep it to ourselves. Let the boys handle it."

* * *

At the end of the day, Viviana showed up and asked to see Adara. As she entered Adara's office, she saw Adara sitting with a little girl. Spread out on her desk were papers, crayons, scissors, paste and colored papers cut to different shapes. Adara was helping Pepita make some art.

Viviana sat in Adara's office and they talked and waited for the staff to leave. Maria came in for Pepita and thanked Adara.

"Thank you, Adara."

"She was no problem. She's such a joy. In the future you need to have a backup plan."

"Yes. I hope someday you have children. You were so good with Pepita," Maria said.

"Adara put on her jacket and stuck her head into Bill's office. Jack Martin was sitting with Bill and they both had their feet up on the desk sipping Scotch.

"Hello, Jack."

"Adara. If you ever get tired of this old guy, just call me."

"You're cute. I'll keep that in mind, but you know I'm happy here."

"You can't blame me for trying. You have the same name as my third wife."

"I thought you were only married twice."

Jack and Bill laughed.

As Viviana and Adara were leaving, Tony walked by and saw them.

"Good to see you, Viviana."

"I just came to say hello to Adara. What a surprise to see you."

"It shouldn't be much of a surprise. I'm here every day."

Viviana laughed. "How are you doing? You're looking good."

Tony took her hand and kissed it. "Not a fraction as good as you."

"Oh my god!" Adara said.

"I'm still waiting for your call," Viviana said.

"Good luck with that," Adara said.

"You won't have to wait very long. It's been busy here."

Adara took Viviana by the arm and dragged her to the door. "I'm sorry, Tony. Viviana and I just need to talk tonight. Alone."

SIX

Ryan met Tony at 8:00 a.m. the next morning at the cafeteria in the Federal Building where the immigration offices are. When Ryan got there, Tony was sitting and talking to a well-dressed man. Ryan bought a coffee and sat with them. "Ryan. I want you to meet Mark Auburn. Mark is chief attorney for the FBI upstairs."

Mark stood up and turned to Ryan. "Good to meet you."

Ryan noticed Auburn's strong grip and the handgun on his belt.

"Mark and I have been at different ends of a few cases over the years. He's always handled his side fair and professionally."

"Tony has too. When he's not saving the world, you will find his knowledge of immigration law deep. You can learn a lot from him. He knows immigration law, and he has a unique twist on policy," Auburn said.

"What do you do for the FBI?" Ryan asked.

"I supervise cases. I'm the chief legal officer for the New York District. That's all I can discuss about my work."

Ryan noticed that Mark had an Arabic language book. "I see you're into languages."

"Arabic is an interest of mine. I listen to language tapes when I commute. It beats the small talk on the railroad."

"I grew up in Great Neck. There are many Iraqi Jews there. They left Iraq because of religious persecution and would be an asset if you need native Arabic speakers," Ryan said. "They'd love to help the U.S. government."

"Thanks, but we have all the help we need with this language. It's just my hobby."

"From what I hear, the FBI needs Arabic speakers. I have the perfect place to find them. My father's synagogue."

Auburn ended that line of conversation. He turned to Tony. "Speaking of Arabic speakers, how's Adara doing?"

"Fine. She holds up the fort."

"Tony, if I weren't married I'd steal her away from you."

"She's not mine to steal."

"I don't know about that. Don't let her slip away. What do you boys have on today?"

"We have a naturalization appeal where the applicant has a fourteen-year-old conviction for marijuana possession." Tony said.

"Surely CIS won't hold that against him after all this time," Mark said.

"Well, they probably will. We have to show good moral character for five years, but the government usually denies the cases for any reason they find. This is a reason," Tony said.

"So he won't be a citizen. He'll still have a green card."

"No. We got him released from immigration detention based on this appeal. He would have to go back if we fail. He'll be in detention until the immigration judge can finish the case. That could go on for months. The first appeal is a waste of time. It's an agency appeal, and they almost always rubber stamp CIS's result. If we really want to win, we need to go to federal court. We can win there, but the case has to be completely clean. It's expensive for the clients, and they usually just give up. That's what CIS wants."

Ryan listened and soaked up the information. "I'm observing today."

"You've got a good teacher," Auburn finished.

Tony looked at his watch, nodded and went with Ryan to the seventh floor waiting room to meet Mr. Rodriguez. At the entrance the guard made a point of warning them to turn off their cell phones and then insisting on inspecting each one.

Tony handed in the appointment letter and they sat down. "This is Mr. Goldberg. He's new to our office and I want him to sit in and observe the citizenship interview."

"Sure."

Tony looked at Rodriguez. "Remember. Answer the questions in as few words as possible. Tell the truth, but make it short. If you don't know an answer, don't make it up."

"Got it."

"Did you memorize the questions about government and history?"

"I graduated high school here. I got it. I'm ready."

"That's not what I asked."

"Don't worry. I can handle it."

After about an hour, they heard over the loudspeaker, "Mr. Rodriguez to door number one."

When they got to the door, a mousey-looking woman was standing there. She looked as though she had slept on her right side and combed her hair only on the left that morning. She walked bent a bit to her right side and didn't look at anyone directly in the face. "Mr. Carlos Rodriguez? Come with me. Who is that, Mr. Sorelli?"

"He's new at the office, and I want to break him in."

"Okay. He can't speak though."

They walked around several banks of cubicles and into a small windowless office near the back. The officer asked Rodriguez to stand and be sworn in.

"You can sit now. I'm Officer Miller. Please give me your passports and taxes. I'm going to ask you a few questions. What is your current address?"

She went through the application, never once looking at any of them directly. She finally got to the key question. "Have you ever been arrested?"

"Yes. Just once."

Tony pulled out a paper from his file. "Here is the disposition of arrest."

Officer Miller turned to the client. "Have you ever committed any crimes for which you weren't arrested?"

"Well, I was arrested a bunch of times over a year, but this was the only one I was convicted on. It was a rough time in my life. I was a stupid kid and it was just a mistake."

Tony kicked the client's foot and leaned forward. "That's not correct. He plead guilty to one count to cover all the charges. That's the way these things work. It's only one crime and one conviction and here's the disposition."

"Mr. Sorrelli. Let your client speak for himself."

"He doesn't understand what a conviction is and what it covers. That's a legal question and he can only answer factual ones."

"Well, he did."

She went on to ask additional questions. She asked if he was a member of the Communist or Nazi parties. "Are you or have you ever been a terrorist or a member of any terrorist organizations?"

"I'm Dominican."

"That's not what I asked."

"Listen to the question and answer the question. Tell Officer Miller if you don't understand," Tony said.

"No."

"Counselor. You cannot tell your client how to answer." She turned to Costello. "Do you owe any arrears for child support?

"I live with my children."

"What are the three branches of government, Mr. Rodriguez?"

"Congress, the Senate, and the House."

"Name one U.S. Senator from New York State."

"I can't remember. I guess I'm a little nervous."

"It's all right. You need to get eight out of ten right. Tell me. Name three of the original thirteen states."

"Om. Texas, Philadelphia and Maine."

"What's the highest court in the land?"

"The Supreme Court."

"Good. Finally. How many members does that court have?"

"Uh. Six?"

"Mr. Sorrelli. I will need dispositions for the other crimes."

They left and proceeded to the hallway. The three immediately turned on their phones.

Tony looked at Rodriguez. "What didn't you understand about answering the questions in as few words as possible? Now we have to get your complete criminal record and I need to prepare a memo of law on the subject of one conviction covering several acts.

"Wait a minute. I paid for this application and I shouldn't have to pay more."

"Listen. If you go to a restaurant and order lunch and you don't finish it and you come back the next day and order lunch again, don't you expect to pay again?"

"It's not the same."

"Make an appointment next week and we'll discuss it further."

On the way back to the office Ryan asked Tony. "Why did you want him to make an appointment next week?"

"To cool him off. It's always the ones who think they're smart that fuck up."

About thirty seconds later Tony said to Ryan. "I need you to do the memo."

* * *

Officer Miller picked up the telephone. "Yes, Officer Gomez. He just left....No. The alien was Dominican, not Muslim....No. I understand what you're looking for and I don't think this is useful....Yes. I will call you if I have anything to add to your investigation."

SEVEN

Charles Robinson walked across the Brooklyn Bridge from his apartment in Brooklyn Heights to his office in Manhattan. The United States Attorney's office was in a modern building attached to a federal prison at the foot of the bridge. He walked into the cold stone gray building through security down the hall and up a flight of stairs to his office and past the pictures of past U.S. Attorneys each standing with famous people, some of them United States presidents. He sat down, took off his sneakers, and put on his wing tip work shoes. He took a rag and went over the shoes quickly to make sure they shined.

Renee Curtwright walked by.

"Let's go, Charles. You're just in time."

They walked together to the conference room on the third floor where coffee and donuts were waiting. There were several other people from their office.

Charles sat down next to Mark Auburn. Mark turned to him "How you doing, kid?"

"Fine, Mr. Auburn. You must have your hands full with security for the Imam's trial."

"We have the best team on it. The NYPD is handling the grunt work."

United States Attorney Hite, a man in his fifties who was well dressed and well groomed, entered the room. Robinson tried not to look at his hair plugs or the powder on his face. Auburn wondered how a government employee could afford a suit that easily cost five thousand dollars.

Curtwright was close to the door. "Good morning, Mr. Hite."

"Please sit down," Hite replied. They all did. Renee Curtwright sat directly next to him. "Although you all know the situation, we need to discuss my plans. As you know, nothing leaves this room." They all nodded. "I want to discuss the details about the future of this office. As you have suspected, I have established a committee to raise money for my upcoming campaign for the U.S. Senate."

Auburn held in a laugh. The whole world knew he had a committee and was raising money to run for the United States Senate. He was only interested in the publicity that high profile cases brought him. He hadn't spent ten minutes doing his job since he had made the decision to run two years earlier. It was a wonder that he knew anything about what was going on in that office.

Hite continued. "Once the campaign gets going, I'll have to resign as United States Attorney. There will be issues with succession, investigations, and prosecutions that our office is handling. We will need to continue all the work we've been handling, and it's of special importance to me that this work be handled properly and cleanly during the transition and after I leave because your work will reflect upon me and my campaign."

Auburn was not surprised that he forgot to say "because it is the right thing to do."

"You know you can count on us," Charles said.

"I know I can, but there are things in process that need to proceed on time. Bluntly, I need the publicity of the several high profile cases we're working on to proceed so that the press will pick these items up before and just after I leave this office to run for the Senate. I'm counting on you to do this. Even after I leave, we will still be a team and I want everyone in this room to understand that our bond will continue, even after I'm elected."

"We are all proud to be part of your team," Renee said. They applauded.

"With this said, I need to review several items. The Imam's trial is ready to go. The press will pick this up and it's the centerpiece of our activities."

"And what about security for the trial of the Imam?"

Auburn spoke up. "Everything is in place for the trial. We have been conducting sweeps of the area every few days to make sure that no one disrupts the trial. During the trial we will provide ample protection along with the NYPD and the U.S. Marshal's Service."

"The FBI is handling further investigations into this and security is high," Renee said. "The FBI has some information that there might be a homegrown plot to disrupt the Imam's trial. They are looking into this. In any event, the trial should proceed within the next few months unless the defense has some tricks to postpone it further. We'll see to it that the trial begins while you're on the job."

"We have an informant, out of state, that gave us information that with other information leads us to believe there might be a plan to disrupt the trial. We're not sure about the details. We're monitoring it carefully," Mark said. "As part of this we're also looking into the possibility that an assassin has been brought into the United States as part of that plan. We have assigned security accordingly. We are working with local law enforcement in several jurisdictions to prevent that."

Renee couldn't wait for Auburn to finish. "As part of that investigation it seems that the possible assassin or assassins are connected to a law firm in New York. We're familiar with that firm and I can personally attest that they're bad immigration lawyers. We're on it."

"We obtained an order for a search and tap from Judge Croyden and we're on it. If they communicate with the assassins, we'll know about it. We are selectively tapping their calls and emails and checking their clients from selected countries," Robinson said.

"Muslim countries?"

"Countries where ISIS or other terrorists might be conducting business."

"Good to put it that way. It sounds better."

"It seems the firm of Zalmanski and Sorrelli might be assisting these terrorists. Once we can prove this, we will prosecute them," Renee added.

"Good to know," Hite said without looking up from his notes. "It would be good publicity for us if this started before I left this office."

Auburn wanted to roll his eyes. "We're on thin ice here. We may be gathering info that won't be admissible in court and might conflict with attorney-client privilege."

"Just do what you have to. I want the credit for any arrests and prosecution before the election."

They discussed several other items. On the way out, Auburn walked Robinson to his office. Charles leaned over and softly said, "I wanna vomit. He cares more about his career then the United States of America."

"Don't worry, kid. We'll make up for it."

* * *

Hamid opened the pantry and showed Arafat a small box. "This small device is a detonator. Hard to believe that this thing can do so much damage."

"I'm very nervous about keeping this in the store."

"Nervous about what? The device is harmless until it's connected to a power source. Don't worry. When the trial starts, we will show them."

"What if we're robbed or if there's a fire?"

"Do you really believe that Allah would allow that to happen?"

* * *

Ali and Naib were driving for about four hours when they arrived in Chambersburg, Pennsylvania. They now had an old Chevy and pulled off of Route 81 and several minutes later into a service station where they waved to the man behind the counter. The man waved back.

Ali parked the car behind the station and went in. The man behind the counter told a blond teenage girl who worked there to take his position at the counter and she did.

"Ali, good to see you. Come with me."

Ali followed him around the back and opened his trunk. They took the box and put it into the back of another car. The man took another small but heavy bag and added it to the package. Ali opened the bag to see the tip of two rifles. He looked a little harder to see that scopes were attached to the guns.

A young man appeared. They did not shake hands. He looked at Naib. "I am Ahmed. My father owns the station. Good to meet you. You know how to use these, don't you?"

"I was a major in the Jordanian army and I won an award at Sandhurst for marksmanship. There's no one better than me with these weapons."

"Take it. Do you have the package?"

"We have it," Ali said. "It's better not to ask questions."

"You need some coffee, maybe some food or something else?" Ahmed said.

"We need a good night's sleep and then we will go."

The owner came over. "I'm glad that you have met my son Ahmed. Where did you get that car?"

"We stole it yesterday morning near an office building in Kentucky. I'll show you on the map." Ali pulled out the map and gave him the approximate location. "It needs to be left in that area."

"We know what to do. It's good you're changing cars. I will see to it that the car is left somewhere near where it was taken." He pointed to the late model sedan.

Naib smiled possibly for the first time. "This is good."

"Take some food and use the bathroom if you have to. Get a good night's sleep if you want and then when you are ready, you can move on."

"Yes."

"You will take Ahmed with you. You can trust him completely. He was born here and has no accent. He will come in handy and you can trust him with your lives. He knows our friends in the area and where to get help if you need it. He will drop you off and return, so there will be no question about cars."

The next morning as Ahmed drove through the rural back roads of Pennsylvania with Naib and Ali, he looked at the well-kept houses, the churches, and the beautiful countryside. They spoke in Arabic.

As they passed an adult bookshop Naib said, "These Americans are not just immoral, they shove it in your face. We will punish them."

They stopped at the adult shop and Naib asked, "Why are we stopping here?"

"We have a friend who owns this. He will give us cash and we might need it. He makes contributions to our 'charity,' and my father thinks you need that contribution now."

"If you say so."

"I think it's a good idea."

Ahmed quickly returned to the car and showed some cash before he gave it to Ali. "You understand how it works. They just contributed to our charity."

"Don't get too used to this country," Naib said. "This is the place of Satan. These people only care about their little temporary pleasures and don't have any morals they live up to. They are godless people who think they understand god. They are more interested in their petit possessions and conveniences than in making the world better. We'll do our jobs and leave."

* * *

Auburn picked up the intercom in his office. "Yes."

"The Pennsylvania State Police lost the tail, but we know the direction he went and we believe he'll be coming east. He changed cars and picked up another passenger—a young man. You know who. We have his store watched."

"If they pick us up, we'll blow the investigation. Just watch from afar to see where he goes. Track the kid's cell. Keep me up to date."

* * *

The next morning there was a woman waiting at the door when Bill and Tony arrived. They immediately knew who she was and that this was a real crisis. Her husband, Carlos Rodriguez, was in deportation proceedings and his citizenship case was not going well.

Tony took her into his office. "How can I help you, Mrs. Rodriguez?"

"Immigration came to my home at 5:00 this morning and arrested my husband and now I don't know where he is. I'm afraid they'll send him back to the Dominican Republic."

"Mrs. Rodriguez."

"Oh please, call me Angela."

"Angela. This means they denied the citizenship appeal. I thought they'd give us a chance to complete it. They agreed to release him pending the naturalization. That is over."

"What can we do?"

"There are two things that we can do here. We can allow him to remain in immigration custody and try to complete his deportation case, or we can make a request for a naturalization hearing before a federal court."

"I thought they denied the citizenship."

"Well, it was denied at the administrative agency level. We have another shot in federal court."

If Carlos were to be deported, he would be barred from returning to the U.S. for ten years. His wife would have to make a new green card application—basically start from scratch.

"What if he's deported and he just comes back?"

"First it's a crime to return without permission after being deported. If he's caught, he'll probably get two years in prison and be barred from legal status here for life. If you try to get him a new green card, it will be denied based on the deportation and the conviction. Both require special applications to waive the ten-year penalties. There would have to be an application for each reason, and it was possible that one or both would fail."

"So it's possible."

"It's possible, but we'll file applications to have him forgiven. We need to show hardship to you and the two children. It could fail."

"It's three soon."

"Three then. Hardship needs to be based on several factors. Financial hardship requires a showing that he's supporting the family. Do you have his taxes?"

"We're not making a lot, but we're doing fine. He manages valet parking and works mostly for cash, and we don't have to file for the cash."

"You *do* have to file. Everyone who earns money in this country has to file. Without taxes it's unlikely that he would get the waivers. We can't say he's committing a crime by not filing taxes and then claim he's earning the money to support his kids. He would have to file back taxes for several years."

"Won't that cost us money?"

"Yes."

"I can't do that."

"Are the children healthy?"

"The little one was premature and has asthma problems."

"Do you have health insurance?"

"The State of New York pays."

"Well, that doesn't help us. Do you get health coverage as part of some public assistance?"

"Yes."

"That weakens your hardship claim since the children will get the same assistance whether he is here or not."

"Oh!" she said.

"Does he have other family here?"

"No. They're all in the Dominican Republic. His brother was deported and his parents are gone."

"I'm like a chef," Tony said. "You want me to make a stew without any meat. It will be thin. I need some meat for this or we can't get going."

"Do we have to do both?"

"No. It's either fight the deportation or the citizenship or both. We should fight both, but at some point we'll be able to drop one and continue with the other. One is in Immigration Court and the other in Federal Court. You're not paying us to lie down dead."

"Isn't the immigration court a federal court?"

"Yes it is, but it's a different kind of court with different powers. The immigration court can forgive his deportation or not based on the facts and with the judge's discretion. That means if the judge feels he's a good man, he is."

"And the other court?"

"The other court has the power to make him a citizen despite the conviction based upon his many clean years. That would be faster, but it would cost you much more."

"We already paid you."

"We have gone way beyond the original agreement."

"I'm a poor woman. You have to help me. Please."

"If we go to federal court, I cannot proceed until we are paid. I have a partner who would object. Either way it will get costly. There's a good chance that if he remains in detention they'll transfer him out of New York. We might have to send a lawyer to assist him. That costs."

"I would be appreciative if you helped me."

"I'm sure you would, but we need to be paid. I'm sure Bueno will help him."

"Bueno has helped us already. I'm not sure I can go to him for help any more. You're a good-looking man. I cannot pay you with money, but I can show my appreciation other ways."

"Let's get back to the case. If we do not go back to…"

"I'm a good-looking woman. I know how to please a man and I would be very appreciative of anyone helping my children's father."

"This is not going to happen. I would never go near any client or anyone I work with. It's not ethical."

"Make an exception."

Tony got up. "I'll be right back." Tony went into Carmen's office and whispered something into her ear.

Carmen got up, went into Tony's office and sat in his seat. "Mr. Sorrelli just got an emergency call. He will finish the conversation with you at a later date." Carmen just sat there and stared at Mrs. Rodriguez. After a very long two minutes, she left.

Tony went into Bill's office as he stood there with newspapers all over his desk and a paper cutter in his hand.

"Sit down, Tony. Why do you look so sad?"

"I just can't help this one."

"Grow up. He lied, cheated on his taxes, never paid us fully on the last case, and you're not god. Take a sip of coffee and get on with it. We have another twelve hundred files that need work." Bill got up and took the cutouts to Ryan's office before Tony could answer.

EIGHT

Bill was the first into the office that day as he spread out the *New York Times on* his desk and opened his container of coffee. The article about the Imam's trial caught his attention. There were all sorts of questions going through his mind about how the trial would impact the practice.

He went through several letters that Adara had left for him. One was a letter from the firm of *Carlin and Kaminsky* informing him that they were retained by the Rodriguez family and would need the file.

Tony and Adara came in and sat down in Bill's office. Tony opened his coffee and said, "Morning Bill. Another exciting day begins."

Zalmanski threw the letter in front of Tony. "Have Carmen take care of this today. I don't want them to claim we held things up even for a day. Remember how loyal clients can be."

Adara laughed. "You care more about these clients than they care about themselves. Wasn't she here last week? She knew she was changing lawyers."

"These are the guys who advertise in the subway," Tony said. "They charge high fees and don't fight. Talk about going from the frying pan into the fire. Yes, she was here just a few days ago. She probably hired them just after she came to discuss the case."

"They did us a favor. Rodriguez didn't trust us any more. They weren't going to pay for a fight and whatever the outcome, we would have lost," Adara said.

"I wanted to finish this. Bueno guaranteed part of the fee and we did a lot of work based on that. I've already started a motion for a hearing on the rearrest and a request for a bond. The paperwork appealing the denial of citizenship is ready for federal court."

"It's dead. Bury it," Bill said.

Tony couldn't look Bill in the eye. "Too late. I filed a motion with the Board of Immigration Appeals on Judge McCormick's denial of his stay and his rearrest. I also filed a habeas with the U.S. District Court."

"In one week?"

"I filed it the day after she came in. I've already discussed this with Robinson at the U.S. Attorney's office to try to resolve it. He knows the case and he's reasonable. They may release him and allow him out to complete the natz in federal court if we file immediately."

"Has Bueno actually paid?"

"No. It's on my own dime."

"You see how they appreciate it? Let's see if they pay now. Carlin and Kaminsky could have never done this."

"I'll send copies of the papers to the wife and to Kaminsky. They might release him any day, and I want the credit."

"No loyalty in this business. We need to discuss how we're going to get things done with the Imam's trial going on just two blocks from this office. It's just a few weeks away, and we'll have problems just going across the street. Our clients will see police all around, and they'll be afraid to come here. We'll need paper to do anything at immigration."

"Our clients have a right to walk the streets, and the police have no right to question them without probable cause."

"Be real, Tony. Our clients don't want to know about rights. They're afraid of the authorities and won't come here if they're too many police around. The trial could last several months, possibly even past the elections. We'll be screwed through the summer at least."

"I understand. We'll instruct the clients not to talk to anyone, and it's no problem but we will have some issues to deal with," Adara said.

Bill continued. "Adara will be in charge of scheduling. We'll have to be very careful how we handle this. Mistakes could cause us problems."

"We won't let that happen," Adara said.

* * *

Later that day Bill went into Ryan's office. "You gotta have lunch. Any plans today?"

"None," Ryan said.

"Good. Join me."

Bill and Ryan walked down Chambers Street towards the Brooklyn Bridge. As they walked past Tweeds Courthouse, Bill explained that they were going to *The Metropolitan*, a pub-type restaurant that was behind the courthouses and just south of Chinatown. It was a place where many of the judges from the several courts would often have lunch and a place where the lawyers would come when they wanted to run into them. The dark wood atmosphere and the high-backed booths of dark wood and leather provided a measure of privacy and quiet.

As they entered they passed Judge McCormick, who was sitting together with another immigration judge having coffee. They nodded to Bill.

Bill then caught the eye of Oliver Totten sitting with Federal Judge Cathy Croydon. Justice Totten also nodded a slight hello.

They walked over to Justice Totten. "You slumming again?" Bill said.

"It's not proper to converse with one side of a case during major litigation," Totten said.

"He's right," Ryan said to Bill.

Zalmanski and Totten looked at each other for a brief moment and started to laugh.

Oliver nodded towards Judge Croydon. "This is Bill Zalseski and his associate Ryan Goldberg. Bill and I are old friends, and Ryan is new to Bill's firm."

Judge Croydon made no effort to shake their hands and simply said, "Good to meet you."

In another direction they saw Mark Auburn with Charles Robinson, huddled and talking. Bill went over and said hello to Auburn and held out his hand.

"How you doing, Mark?"

Auburn stood up. "I want you to meet Charles Robinson, assistant United States Attorney. And this is the famous Bill Zalmanski."

Bill laughed. "I don't know about that. I want you to meet Ryan Goldberg, our new associate. I thought I'd initiate him into the world of judges and high class lawyers."

Robinson stood and shook Bill and Ryan's hands. "I know Mr. Sorrelli from your office. We were involved in a couple of cases together."

"I'll let Tony handle those." Bill turned to Mark. "This is where the legal profession meets."

"You will find some judges here," Auburn asked.

"What about some high class lawyers?" Bill asked.

"The real question should be: is there such a thing as a high class lawyer?"

"The legal system is in trouble," Bill chuckled.

"If you wanted a little class, you should have brought Adara," Auburn said.

"Well, you're here so there is at least one high class lawyer here," Bill replied.

Mark turned to Ryan. "So you're still doing immigration law. Sorrelli and this old fart haven't scared you away yet, huh?"

"Not yet. I'm learning and I'm getting into it. There's so much to know."

"My advice is to learn from Adara. She's the class act. She's the balance between the mechanic and the dreamer. You need to juggle that every day."

"I'll tell her you spoke highly of her."

"Good. How did that naturalization go?"

"The client didn't do his homework and we have to go back."

"Oh well. That happens," Robinson continued. "You're learning a lot, I'm sure. Soon you'll be an expert."

"After I'd been practicing a few years, I told my supervisor that it felt great being an expert in criminal prosecution," Auburn said. "She laughed and didn't respond. That was many years ago, and I now realize even today with many more years under my belt how far I still have to go before I will really be an expert. The learning never ends."

"If it ended, it would become boring," Ryan said.

"That's the attitude we look for when we hire at FBI."

"Ryan's the best associate I've had since I hired Tony," Bill said.

Mark smiled. "Wow. That's high praise. The last time we met, I got that impression."

Bill and Ryan sat at a different part of the restaurant, and Mark resumed the conversation with Robinson.

"That's Zalmanski. The kid's new and shouldn't get caught up in this. Our suspects are using that firm. It's probably a waste of time but...my hands are tied."

"Mine too. I did the paperwork on the search. Renee is pushing this, and it's tying up several people. If it gets out that we're tapping a law office, there might be hell to pay. We might not be able to use any evidence we get from it. I don't understand why she has such a hard-on for these people."

"She used to date Sorrelli."

"That explains a lot. We need a meeting to discuss any evidence you've collected."

"Too soon. The evidence I've seen doesn't prove anything yet."

"If we prevent an assassination, it would be worth it."

"If? We're getting nothing from that firm that can help us here."

Judge Croydon asked Justice Totten how he knew Zalmanski.

"An old friend from the army and law school, Bill Zalmanski. We were in Nam together. When bullets are flying around you get very close."

"I know that name. I signed warrants on them some time ago. You should stay away from them."

"Bill? It can't be right. He may not run a class operation, but he's not a criminal. Warrants for what?"

"I can't go into details. Do you have any cases with him?"

"Just one, a matrimonial."

"Recuse yourself. All I can tell you is the U.S. Attorney's office is investigating them."

"That's hard to believe. They run a paper mill. His partner is an idealist, and I can't imagine that they would do anything intentionally wrong."

"Recuse yourself. I'm talking too much already. I'm telling you as a friend and in my capacity as judge. They are being watched as part of an investigation into a plot to disrupt the Imam's trial. They're bad lawyers. I shouldn't tell you this, but they might be representing ISIS terrorists."

"Them? Bad? ISIS? You gotta be kidding. They are not bad lawyers. A little quirky maybe, but honest and well intentioned. Bill and I also went to law school together. Our ex wives were friends. Still are. There isn't much I don't know about him, and I know he's an honest guy. I'd be very surprised if he were doing anything funny."

"You can find a violation of the law against anyone if you want to. You know that. I'm afraid they're going down."

"That doesn't make it right." Totten took a sip of coffee and just stared. "I'm the judge in a matrimonial case. It's been going on for years. Actually it's between his ex-wife and him. From time to time they have disputes, and I act more like a marriage counselor. It allows them to blow off steam."

"Get rid of it. If the investigators get wind of the fact that you have a relationship with him and you're the judge on his case, you'll have a difficult time explaining yourself. Cover your ass."

"Damn it. They don't deserve it."

Bill and Ryan ordered lunch. "One rule about this place. You shouldn't discuss individual cases with the judges," Bill said.

"Got it," said Ryan.

Robinson got the check and split it with Auburn.

As they walked out, Auburn said, "Thank god I only have one more year until I vest my retirement."

"Can you hold out that long?"

"We'll see."

"What are you going to do after you retire?'

"At my age? I'm too young to really retire. I needed to do my twenty and one to vest. I'll probably go into criminal defense. With what I learned in the FBI, I can name my fee. I hope to make some real money then. I'll secure my pension and then the fun begins."

"You could stay with the FBI."

"That ship has sailed. I wanted to, but I didn't get the promotions I deserved. Just wasn't political enough. It was a good run and I loved the job, but you have to know when to get off the horse."

"How does your wife feel about your working after you retire?"

"The kids are out of the house, and it's just a matter of time for the lawyers to finish their work. Almost over."

"Sorry. I didn't know."

"I tried to fix it and it didn't work. My father had a saying: *If it's dead, bury it.* Time to bury it."

"I may put in for your job."

"You may not have the seniority to get it. We have several people who might beat you to it, but you can be sure I'll give you the best recco possible. Aren't you in line to take Renee's job?"

"I'm not happy there. Too much politics and not enough justice."

* * *

Ahmed was in the driver's seat. Naib and Ali sat in the passenger seats when they entered the truck stop. They drove to a far corner between the tractor-trailers and some forest. Naib got out and lit a cigarette.

A few minutes later a black Chevy Impala drove up, and a slim young black man got out.

"Are you Tyrone?" Ahmed said to the driver.

"Yes. You Chris?"

"Yes," Ahmed said.

"Give me the money and we'll change vehicles. This car was taken from the airport near Newark. I watched the owner park it. He left the ticket in the car. He probably went away for several days. It was in the long-term lot. It won't be reported stolen at least till then."

Ali gave Tyrone an envelope with ten one hundred dollar bills in it. Tyrone looked at it briefly and pocketed it.

"Good. Help us transfer a box to the Chevy," Ali said.

"No problem, bro."

The four men went to the back of the car. They struggled to move the box to the other car.

"What do you have in here, lead?" Tyrone asked.

"Don't ask questions. Just help us move this and we'll be on our way."

They struggled for a few minutes. Tyrone went back to the first car and took the bag with the guns. He felt the package, and Naib could tell that Tyrone knew exactly what he was holding. He transferred it to the Impala. The trunk closed with plenty of room and they got in.

"Those felt like a couple of nice rifles."

"Just do your job."

"Should I get rid of the other car?"

"No," Ali said. "Just leave the car. I'll come back for it."

"But our plan was…"

"New plan," Ali said. "Leave the car. I'll take it." He drove toward home.

"Can you drop me off in town?" Tyrone said to Ali.

"No, too dangerous. We'll drop you off on the road about a mile from town. No one will see us there."

"Fine."

They drove about a mile and turned down a dirt road and down about a hundred yards until Ali was sure no one could see him. "Get out here."

As Tyrone got out, Naib pulled out his handgun.

Tyrone put up his hands. "Hey man! What are you doing? You don't have to do this."

Naib shot him three times point blank.

Ali took the envelope with the hundred dollar bills.

* * *

Viviana came into the office and asked Maria if Adara was there. Adara came out and looked hurried. "This is a bad time to talk. I've got a desk full of work and people waiting. Call me tonight and we'll catch up."

"Okay."

When Adara went back to her office, Viviana turned back to Maria. "Is Tony in?"

Maria took Viviana into Tony's office without clearing it with him.

"Bad timing, Viviana. When we work we work, but I'm glad to see you."

"I didn't hear from you and was wondering how you're doing. It's been quite a while."

"I'm sorry that I didn't get back to you. It's been so busy here. Let's talk in a few days and maybe we can make some plans."

"That would be nice. I thought we had such a good time. I was surprised that you didn't call."

"You mean that I didn't call yet."

"I was worried that you didn't like me. I thought we had such a good time."

"We'll definitely talk."

"When?"

"Soon."

"How soon?"

"Just as soon as I can."

"I have a special bottle of wine that I'm saving just for you, one of our best. Let's plan a dinner together."

"Not right now. We'll talk."

"Tonight?"

"If I can."

From just around the corner, Adara listened and clenched her fist.

* * *

Sherriff Kelly sat at his home computer. He opened a bottle of beer and began surfing crime reports around the nation. He filtered the reports and looked for people shot three times. He came upon the report of a young black male shot three times in a triangular pattern outside of Lancaster, Pennsylvania.

He picked up his telephone and called Mark Auburn.

NINE

Mark Auburn arrived at the U.S. Attorney's office about two minutes late. The receptionist gave him a dirty look and told him to go right in.

"Sorry I'm late, Mt. Hite. I'll blame it on traffic." The offices were only one block apart.

Renee Curtwright sat silently next to Hite.

"Hello, Renee."

"Hello," Renee said without looking at him. "I wanted an update on the Naib investigation."

"Our people have tracked him through Mexico and into Texas. There was a murder of a coyote southeast of El Paso, and it's possible his group was involved. Not enough evidence to be sure so we're just guessing here. Too many of these happen, so we can't be sure it's our boy but the time and the place are consistent with our surveillance and with the info we have. A Sherriff Kelly called it in to D.C. and then to me because he thought it looked unusual. He matched it to a policeman's murder near Amarillo."

"Why did he call you?"

"There is a possibility that someone involved in that shooting has New York connections. Based on this tip we may have tracked him to a known sleeper in Kentucky and then to Pennsylvania but lost him. Kelly called me last night and alerted me to a similar shooting near Lancaster, Pennsylvania. The victim has a minor criminal record for car theft, and the people Kelly is trying to track down abandoned a car. I'm looking into this. We have an ID on one suspect and we have him using that law firm in Manhattan. There are several other persons of interest using that firm to stay in the U.S. They each file applications for political asylum.

All have similar stories. This allows them to stay here, get permission to work, get a social security number, the works. The process can go on for years, and they can operate freely during that time. We're watching the firm to see if our new suspect goes there. We've tapped their phones and emails on an order from Judge Croyden. He might be coming to New York, but we're not sure if that's correct or what will happen then. If he does, we'll be ready."

"And what are you doing to see to it that he doesn't assassinate someone here?'

"This is not an easy man to track. Our lead in Mexico referred him to the coyote who was killed. That's why we think there's a connection. We would have lost him if he hadn't contacted the sleeper in Kentucky, but we're not even completely sure where he's headed. In fact, we might be following different people. His surveillance photo seems to match the one from the Jordanian Mukhabarat. New York is the probability. He's now clean-shaven and dresses like anyone else. He has several passports and we're trying to use facial recognition to keep track."

"What else makes you think that there's a connection?" Hite asked.

"There have been several murders with the same M.O. Three shots in a triangular pattern—two to the chest and a finish to the head. We have four victims in three states. We hope to pick them up and stop any future activity."

"I've seen that before. It's not enough. It could be from someone he's with. Was that his M.O. before coming here?"

"Not in the records."

"I'm running for the United States Senate, and any activity by Naib might be construed as my failure to manage the situation. Things are especially sensitive with the Imam's trial coming up. I want him caught. Do you understand?"

"Yes."

"I want credit to go to our office no matter where he goes."

"He hasn't done anything in the United States we can pin on him for sure yet except an illegal entry. The murders may or may not pan out. We can arrest him on that and prosecute him, but he won't get much. We can deport him to Jordan. If we prosecute him here, we have to prove the case. That takes resources. Then he get's the publicity of a trial and we have to deal with his incarceration or execution. If we deport him to Jordon, they'll see that he disappears. They will probably try to extradite him. His government and several others in the Middle East want him, including Saudi Arabia. It's certain that there are ISIS connections here and this guy has made at least one contact."

Hite held up his hand. "I want him arrested and charged with conspiracy to commit a terrorist act. I want it done in the Southern District of New York. I want it done before I have to leave and begin my Senate campaign. We get the credit. Understand?"

"The only thing we're sure of right now is that someone's here illegally and there are several executions that might or might not match up to him."

"Stop playing games. Find him and then we'll charge him. I need to do it while I'm still the U.S. Attorney. If it's dismissed later, the press will give it light treatment. In the meantime we might just stop a terrorist act."

"We're working with FBI office in Philadelphia right now."

Hite banged his fist onto the table. "Listen carefully. I don't want anyone else involved. Our office must do this. Let him come to New York so we can make the tag here."

"We will coordinate it as best as we can, *but* our offices in New Jersey and Pennsylvania may have their own opinions about this. They'll want to grab him as soon as possible."

"I don't care. Find him and make the arrest here. I want the credit for this."

"Yes sir. Is that all?"

Hite looked down at the papers on his desk and waved Auburn off.

When Auburn left, Hite turned to Renee. "Well?"

"There's more than one of them and they're headed here. I'm sure of it. They plan to disrupt the Imam's trial. I don't know how, but I feel it. I'm guessing that once they're here they'll go to that law firm and file for political asylum. That will allow them to stay here legally while their applications are processed."

"That sounds plausible."

"I know those lawyers, Zalmanski and Sorrelli," Renee said. "They're bad lawyers. *Bad lawyers.* They would knowingly help terrorists. I know Tony Sorrelli. He'd convince himself they were well meaning even if they showed up in his office and beheaded someone. We'll watch them and get them when the time's right."

"That firm might just not know what's going down."

"They know and don't care. They just want the money. Let me make the call on that. They would represent known terrorists."

"Even known terrorists are entitled to a lawyer in America," Robinson said.

"We're going to take the lawyers down."

"Are you sure this isn't personal, Renee?" Hite asked

"No, strictly professional. Tony Sorrelli is dirt and deserves what's coming."

* * *

Naib looked at the miles of farms and cows along the highways without taking much. They drove past some Amish men with their beards and in their traditional dress.

Ahmed drove and sat next to Naib while Ali slept in the back.

"So tell me about you, Naib. I understand that you were an officer in the Jordanian army. Why are you doing this?" Ahmed asked.

"You have lived in America many years. Is this not so?"

"Yes. I was born here."

"And you are involved in this county. Are you not?"

"That's true. What do you have in back?"

"You shouldn't ask these questions. The less you know the less someone can get out of you. You know but you are not 100 percent sure. If you were a stranger, just knowing that much would be a problem for us."

"Sorry. Just wanted to make conversation," Ahmed said.

"You can never tell anyone what we are doing. Better not tell your father."

"Doesn't he know?"

"He thinks he does, but he doesn't. You can tell no one."

"You can bet on it."

"An American expression. Not ours. Are you a God-fearing man?"

"Of course."

"How old are you?"

"Twenty seven."

"You American Muslims don't understand what's going on. You have your luxuries and legal rights, but when you leave here everything changes.

You are nothing and life is worthless. Only our goals are important. Our goal is to build a Muslim caliphate. We have begun. We will also punish and eventually change America."

"The caliphate is losing ground."

"We are having temporary setbacks. It's Allah's way of testing our resolve. What we do here will turn things around. Pious Muslims from all over the world will rush to be part of our great struggle once our mission is completed. Muslims like you who have never suffered, never felt the lash of the Western whip, will be committed fighters in our cause."

"You think I never suffered? You think I haven't felt discrimination?"

"What you suffered here is nothing. You grew up in America and you were sheltered your whole life. Are you going to tell me that someone called you a name or you could not get a job? No one in America is suffering except the righteous. America makes others suffer."

"We have problems in America."

"Like what?"

"There were girls who wouldn't date me because of my religion. I've had friends who shunned me after nine-eleven, and I was passed over for jobs too."

"Don't make me laugh. I've seen death on a scale you can't imagine. People all over the world are afraid for their lives every day. Governments kill people at will, so don't tell me about your suffering. People die from lack of care or food as governments look the other way."

"I'm sorry."

"I've been to parts of Syria where there are thousands of bodies rotting in the sand."

"Wow."

"Americans think that if the price of gas goes up a few cents or if some policeman stops and questions them, they are suffering. I've seen whole families killed as a warning to others. Wives and children killed for something the husband did just to make sure that everyone knows to be careful, just to make sure that everyone lives in fear. America supports the governments that are responsible for this suffering. We must punish America."

"You were an officer. You might have done more in the army."

"I will tell you. My brother was an officer in the Jordanian army too. He fired at the Zionists from Jordan into Eilat. The Jordanians shot him for his efforts. I have allowed the Jordanian army to train me. I waited until I got everything out of them that I could. After I complete this mission, I will take revenge against Jordan. I have dedicated myself to the Islamic State. If I live through this, I will help bring Jordon into the caliphate and the king will be beheaded."

"You don't think 'two wrongs make a right,' do you?"

"You have much to learn. That is an American concept. It takes strong action to stop your enemy. You kill for the greater good. America does it all over the world, except they do it for their own good. We do it for Allah. It happens in war all the time. Do you think America hasn't killed in the name of some good?"

"America is an evil and racist society," Ahmed said.

"How much education do you have?"

"I finished college with a degree in sociology. I haven't been able to find a job yet, so I work with my father."

"Sociology? This is bullshit. Did you really think you could find meaningful work with this?"

"Sure."

"What kind of work?"

"I'm not sure."

"You're not sure? And your father allowed you to study this. Even the righteous make mistakes. Who paid for this?"

"I went to a state school. We only paid a small part."

"They call it an education. I call it indoctrination. Your time and effort would have been better spent in the madrassa. These people will turn on you sooner or later. The only reason they don't is because they fear taking us all on at once."

"Many Americans are good people."

"They will turn on you. You think because the so-called 'liberals' say they are our friends that they won't turn. You will see. Their niceness comes from their fear. We will see that they have more of that than they can take."

The car got off the New Jersey Turnpike near Newark, New Jersey and drove through the side streets. Ali drove around a bit to make sure that they weren't being followed.

They arrived at the warehouse. It was an attached brick bulding on a mixed-use block. Ali texted someone, a garage door opened and the car pulled into a large garage. The garage had boxes of soda, water and other drinks stored on one side. Near that there were boxes of candy, snacks and other supplies. He pulled past several food carts that all said "Halal" on the side. They waited a few seconds, and another man emerged from a back and closed the garage door.

On the back of the floor were food carts in various states of repair. Next to them were carts ready to be taken out. They went into the basement through a door under the main steps. Once through the door, they walked down to a second formidable steel door with three types of locks. As they entered, they turned off the light-activated security camera in the corner. There were bars on the several basement windows, and there was wood behind them. Anyone trying to get in would have to tunnel through concrete.

The basement was filled with more boxes of tobacco products, candy, soda and many other things that could be sold at their store or in the carts. There were two glass display cases that were similar to the ones in the Irving Avenue store.

The top floor was occupied by a family of illegal Mexicans. The rear of the main floor behind the carts was an unoccupied apartment partially under renovation. The renovation looked like it had been going on for some time and would never end. They wanted it that way. The family gave the house some cover, and they knew that if the family suspected anything they would be afraid to go to the law. The family, including their two children, came and went and discouraged squatters from coming into the house. In case they became a problem, the whole family could be eliminated and would not be missed.

There were two other men working on a food cart. The man who closed the door waved them away, and they put on their sweatshirts and left quietly.

The same man who opened the door came to the car helped them remove the box from the car and put it on a dolly to bring it into the house. Together they took the box into the basement and into a side room with a steel door. "Good to see you, Captain."

"Good to see you, Hamid. We'll talk later."

They opened the door and turned on the light. The room was an arsenal filled with all sorts of weapons on one side and what looked like ninety-pound bags of sand.

"I will take the car to Philadelphia and return home," Ahmed said as the others nodded.

They thanked Ahmed as he drove off.

Without another word, Naib and Hamid took the rifles and got into another car. "Just drive, Hamid."

The car went through the Holland Tunnel past the tobacco shop. Naib looked in the window as they drove past and turned to the Hamid. "Is it safe to go in?"

"Yes. That big German stein in the window is the signal. If there's an issue, it will be removed. We'll park the car and go for a pizza across the street to make sure anyway."

"No. Forget pizza. You drive about a mile away and come back. If that mug is still in the window, we'll unload the car," Naib said.

Auburn entered the pizza place, bought a slice and a soda and sat near a scruffy looking woman. He opened the *New York Post* and looked into it. "See anything?"

"There's a car that's passed a few times. It slows down each time. Otherwise, nothing happening. We've got the camera set up. Anything important happens, we'll know it."

* * *

Maria called Zalmanski on the intercom. "A Ms. Choe here to see you."

"Bring her in."

Ms. Choe was a small Korean woman in her fifties, very young looking for her age and simply but conservatively well dressed. She walked slowly behind Maria and politely said hello to Zalmanski as she sat opposite him.

"Mr. Jack Martin sent me."

"He told me a lot about you. What kind of work are you doing for him?"

"I'm assisting him with taking information from Korean clients and completing forms."

"And before that?"

"I worked in a nail salon."

"Did you work in a massage parlor before that? That's usually the pattern."

"Yes."

"I assume you have no papers, and he pays you cash."

"Yes."

"Why did you leave his employ?"

"His wife seemed to object to me. Also, his firm is having some problems with their green ID cards. He fired several people and said it was better for me if I left."

"Let's talk awhile…"

* * *

Tony arrived at the United States courthouse in Brooklyn for the 9:30 a.m. hearing. It was a modern building of light stone, and its stainless steel elevators had a reassuring look. These were the halls where mafioso were prosecuted, where major cases were litigated, and where news was made. He entered the courtroom and signed in. His client, Mr. Rodriguez, was already waiting. He sat between two guards and wore an orange jumpsuit with his hands in shackles. He could not scratch his head.

Jose Bueno was sitting in the back row when he noticed Tony. Bueno was a big man, at least two hundred and fifty pounds and six-foot-three. He had a scar on his forehead almost to his eye. You wouldn't want this guy following you on a dark night.

Bueno was dressed all in black—black jeans, a black shirt and sports jacket and a black string tie with a gold dollar sign clasp. He carried a black cowboy hat as he squeezed his paunch out of the seat and came huffing and puffing to the hall. On either side of him were two angry-looking men also dressed in black.

Tony walked up, and one of the men moved away. Tony sat and looked at Bueno's black alligator cowboy boots and up to his slicked black hair. "Didn't we explain how to dress for this?"

"Carmen told me to dress business-like. This is how I dress for business. Isn't this right?"

His men nodded.

"It's right for a mafioso hit man or maybe Wild Bill Hickok."

"I don't know what they look like but this ain't it."

"Okay. You'll be fine for today."

"Carlos says we owe you money."

"That's right."

"Don't worry about it."

As Tony approached, Rodriguez stood up and reached out the several inches his shackles would allow, took Tony's hand and shook it too much. "Thank you, Mr. Sorrelli. You don't know how important it was for me. I would have lost my job, my apartment and maybe even my wife. I'll pay you for the work. I promise. If we can get my money back from Carlin and Kaminski, I'll bring it right to you. You know Bueno will cover this."

"Sure."

"Really."

"Let's concentrate on today's hearing. One last time. Are you sure that your taxes are in order? The U.S. attorney might go line by line questioning you about it."

"And I tell you again. It's all good. We went over this. They're real taxes."

"You're wife thinks their not."

"She doesn't handle them. I do."

"Whatever you do, don't make anything up. Just answer like we prepared. If you don't understand a question, say so."

"I get it."

"Just explain that you give all your papers to the accountant and you believe he's doing it right."

"I said I get it."

"Is that true?"

"Of course."

His opponent, Mr. Dan Stewart, entered, signed in and sat down next to him. Dan was about Tony's age with a yarmulke and a well-trimmed beard. He was heavier than Tony and dressed in J.C. Penny. He slapped Tony on the back. "How are you doing, Tony?"

"Fine. Why are you fighting so hard on this case?"

"Not just this one."

"This is a clean case. Can't we refer this matter back to CIS to finish the citizenship, with your recommendation, of course?"

"I can't do that. You know I'm reasonable."

"I do."

Judge Croyden entered, and everyone in the court stood: all three of them, the guards and Rodriguez's wife.

The bailiff stood up. "Matter of Rodriguez. Attorneys please approach the bench."

They approached the bench and the judge said, "How are you doing, Mr. Stewart? I got a lot of compliments about your little talk at my law school class last week."

"You know, your honor, it was a pleasure to be invited."

"What's this case about, Mr. Sorelli?"

"My client applied for citizenship. Some fourteen years ago he was arrested for possession of marijuana and was sentenced as a youthful offender. This conviction is not a removable offence. His naturalization application was denied for lack of good moral character because of that old arrest."

"Mr. Stewart. Do you have anything to add?"

"Yes, your honor. It is a removable offence. He can be deported for it, but the immigration judge might give him another chance. That's where this case should be. I requested that my opponent withdraw his application before this court. This case is not as clean as he would have us believe. In order to become a United States citizen, a person has to demonstrate that he is entitled to it. The applicant has to demonstrate clean hands. He has no right to citizenship. Mr. Rodriguez cannot meet that burden."

"Clean hands" was a legal term that meant his case was flawless.

"Counselors, I read the pre-trial statements and there seems little disagreement. What's the sticking point?"

"My client has six arrests for marijuana possession but one conviction covering them all. This started before his eighteenth birthday and more than nineteen years ago. The government says that this precludes good moral character. This man is working, has a U.S. wife and two U.S. children who he supports, pays his kids' tuition for Catholic school, and has taxes to prove it all. He has otherwise been an upstanding member of society. Based upon a habeas corpus before another judge, his case was administratively closed by the immigration court, so he's not subject to removal and this court has jurisdiction. If the case is denied, the removal case will be reopened by stipulation."

"For the moment," Stewart said.

"If we fail here, my client will have to proceed in immigration court."

"None of that is opposed," Stewart said.

"What about this court's jurisdiction?"

"After the government denies a citizenship case such as this, the district court has de novo jurisdiction to decide the case on its own," Sorrelli said.

"And what's the government's position on this?"

"The court has jurisdiction only when the removal case has been dismissed. Mr. Sorrelli hopes to make a motion to have that case dismissed once you grant naturalization pending the termination of that case. Right now the case has been administratively closed until you make the decision here. Mr. Sorelli should not pursue this case. We believe that there are other issues that will come up concerning Mr. Rodriguez's finances that will prejudice his case."

"How long will the questioning take?"

"My case will take just twenty minutes," Sorelli said.

"And the government?"

"About two hours."

"Proceed."

It was customary for the side requesting the benefit to go first.

Sorrelli stood up in front of the court. "I call as my first and only witness, Mr. Rodriguez."

Rodriguez was sworn in and took the stand.

Sorrelli continued. "Where were you born, Mr. Rodriguez?"

The judge interrupted. "Please skip the biographics. I can read the application."

"Okay. Mr. Rodriguez, is this a copy of your application for citizenship, and is this your signature and is everything on this application true?"

"Yes."

"Were you ever arrested by the police?"

"Yes, nine times."

"Please tell the court what happened."

"I was smoking marijuana with some friends near my home when I was a kid. Each time the police came and arrested us. All the arrests were the same. I was hanging with my friends and the police came."

"Were you ever convicted?"

"One time."

"It looks like you have nine arrests, Mr. Rodruguez."

"I believe there are nine charges. I don't understand how you count that."

"Is this a copy of the disposition of arrest?"

"Yes."

"I'd like to submit this into evidence. For the record it shows three charges for disorderly conduct, which under New York State law is not a crime but only a violation."

"No objection," Mr. Stewart replied.

Tony handed copies to Mr. Stewart and then the bailiff.

"And how old were you when this happened?"

"Sixteen, seventeen."

"Did you continue using marijuana after that?"

"Only when I was a teenager. Not after."

"Why not?"

"It was getting me into trouble and my mother moved us to another neighborhood to get away from my friends. I also started to make applications for jobs and I knew that more trouble would sink me."

"Please approach the bench," the judge said to the attorneys.

"Mr. Stewart, is this the only issue? If so I will grant this case."

"I want Mr. Sorrelli to continue."

"Continue, Mr. Sorrelli."

Tony continued. "Mr. Rodriguez, have you ever been a member of the Communist party or supported any fascist or terrorist organizations?"

"I'm a Catholic."

"Please answer the question."

"No to it all."

"What kind of work do you do?"

"I work for the Bueno Valet Car Service."

"Is all your income on the books?"

"Yes."

"Do you file your taxes every year?"

"Yes."

"I would like to submit into evidence twelve returns for the past twelve years with transcripts showing that all taxes were paid and none are owing."

"No objections, your honor."

"Do you owe any money for child support or unpaid judgments?"

"No."

"Have you traveled outside the United States since you came here as a legal permanent resident?"

Stewart stood up. "I'll stipulate that all other items are in order to move this case along."

"Fine. Mr. Sorrelli, is there anything else?"

"We rest."

"Mr. Stewart. Cross examination?"

"Yes, your honor." Stewart slowly walked up close to the witness until he could smell his breath. "You said that you were arrested multiple times for smoking marijuana but only prosecuted once. Is that correct?"

"Yes."

"You said you were arrested six times. Is that correct?"

"Yes."

"But your transcript shows nine arrests."

"I believe three times I was not charged or was charged with something that was dismissed."

"But the question was about arrests, not charges."

Tony stood up. "I object, your honor."

"Objection sustained," The judge said. "The difference isn't enough to make a difference here, Mr. Stewart."

Stewart continued. "So in effect you have multiple unsolved crimes and a history of drug use."

"No, I stopped."

"Mr. Stewart," the judge said. "We discussed this before. It is standard practice to have a defendant plead to one crime in satisfaction of several offences. Do you have anything else?"

"Not on this subject."

"Continue, Mr. Stewart."

"Mr. Rodriguez. Do you file taxes every year?"

"Yes."

"On time?"

"Yes."

"Are these taxes true and correct?"

"Yes."

"I see that two years ago you made fifty six thousand dollars gross income. About twenty per cent of that was in tips. Is that correct?"

Rodriguez looked at the tax return. "Yes. That's what I put down. I believe it's correct."

"I see here that you deducted fourteen thousand dollars in charitable contributions."

"Yes."

"And where did you make those contributions to?"

"Saint Mary the Divine Church."

"You sent documents to my office in response to our demands about this. Did you not, in the form of bills and receipts?"

"Yes."

"Are these the receipts?"

"Yes."

"I offer them into evidence."

Sorrelli stood up. "No objection."

Stewart continued. "These receipts are from Home Depot. How are these charitable contributions?"

"I bought these items to do work on the church."

"Is that so? What kind of work was that?"

"Repairs of all kinds. I'm good at these things."

"Why would you do that?"

"My daughter goes to the school there."

"You pay tuition though."

"Yeh, but it's the right thing to do."

"Give us some details about the work you did."

"Well, I painted some rooms, replaced several wooden doors, replaced a sink in one of the bathrooms, and other work."

"Isn't there a maintenance staff at the church?"

"This was in addition to what they do."

"Do you know a Father Mann?"

"Yes. He's the priest there."

"What if I told you that I have a statement from him that you did no charitable work for that year or for any other?"

Rodriguez hesitated a moment and looked ashen. "I gave all my papers to my accountant and I believe they're correct."

"What if I tell you that perjury is not only a bar to citizenship, but a crime and a deportable one at that?"

Sorrelli stood up. "I object. This is not in evidence. The best evidence would be the witness himself."

"Counselors, please approach the bench." They both came to the judge. "Don't do this, Mr. Sorrelli. If Mr. Stewart is correct, your client may be perjuring himself. Speak to him. You may not want to go there. We'll take a fifteen-minute recess so you can talk to him."

At the end of the recess the judge called the case. "We're back on the record. Have the parties discussed this matter?"

"Yes, your honor." Sorrelli said. "I had a discussion with my client and with Mr. Stewart. We would like to withdraw this case. The government will not oppose this if it's withdrawn with prejudice."

"'With prejudice' means that this application cannot be again considered. Is that correct, Mr. Stewart?"

"Yes."

"Case dismissed. Court to resume at 1:00."

Rodriguez came over to Sorrelli in the hall. "Why did you do that? I was doing fine."

"No, you weren't. You were perjuring yourself, and if you kept it up you could have been arrested."

"I'm the client. I should make that decision. Not you."

"I did you a favor. If it had gone on, you would have been hiring a criminal lawyer."

"Where am I going now?"

"Back to immigration jail. The agreement with the other judge was that if you were not granted citizenship, the old case would be reinstated."

"I spent a lot of money on this. You can't just stop it."

"Let me put this in Brooklyneze. He had you by the balls and if you continued, he would have pulled them off."

Bueno looked at Rodriguez. "Listen to your lawyer."

Rodriguez nodded as he was taken away.

* * *

When Tony arrived in the office Maria asked him if his phone was on. He took it out of his pocket.

"I turned it off in court, and I forgot to turn it on."

"There are several messages from Ryan. Please call him at once."

Tony did. "What happened?"

"I'm on the ninth floor trying to file that Rodriguez bond request, and the officer in charge won't accept it. I told her that it's time sensitive, but she said that she doesn't have the file in her unit and won't accept it."

"She has to. She can deny it, but she has to allow us to fee it in. Be assertive."

"If I'm anymore assertive, they'll throw me out."

"Who's the duty supervisor?"

"A Ms. Klein."

"Never heard of her. Wait for me on nine. I'll be right there."

Tony dropped his bag on Maria's desk and left in a huff. As he entered the federal building he ran into Harold Peters on his way to the immigration court on the twelfth floor.

"I'm steaming."

"What happened?" Harold asked.

"Ryan is stuck on the ninth floor. He's trying to file the bond request and they won't accept it."

"They have to. It's in the regs."

As they waited for the elevator, Tony started to tell the story. A middle-aged woman with a paisley dress came and the three of them got on the elevator together.

"Some asshole wouldn't let Ryan file a stay, a Ms. Klein. These losers are only interested in how little work they can get away with till five o'clock. They don't give a shit about the work or getting it done right. If they had to exist in the real world, they'd die. Bunch of fuckin' losers."

"Take it easy, Tony. You'll pop a gasket."

"How can they get up in the morning and know that they're going to do this stuff day after day? How can they look themselves in the mirror?"

"Tony, get a grip on yourself. Don't let your temper get the best of you. That's when you'll screw up."

The elevator door opened, and Sorrelli and the woman got out. He found Ryan and they went to the window. Ryan asked for the officer of the day.

"There she is. That's Ms. Klein." Ryan pointed to the woman with the paisley dress.

Sorrelli looked at her and couldn't say a word.

She handed him a slip of paper. "Fee in the motion at the bond office and bring it back. Leave it with the receptionist when you're done." She turned and walked away.

TEN

The firm of Zalmanski and Sorrelli is closed to the public on Saturday mornings, so Tony arrived wearing worn jeans, a gray tee shirt, a denim jacket and a short brimmed straw hat. He did not expect to see clients.

As he entered he saw Adara at the conference room table with the checkbook and bills spread out. She was wearing a white long-sleeved tee shirt with a black lace bra visible underneath. Tony could just notice the scars on her arm through the shirt.

"What are you doing here?" Adara asked him.

"I had a few things to catch up on. If you're around in a couple of hours, we can grab some lunch."

"Love to."

There was a knock on the door and Tony answered. It was Mrs. Rodriguez.

"We're closed. Can you come back Monday?"

"No! I came home yesterday evening and found this. It's a denial of the stay you filed. They're going to deport Carlos and he'll die. You've got to save him."

"Calm down. Come in."

"You've got to save him."

"Let me read the letter."

"We've got to stop this today. What about my children? What am I going to do?"

"Nothing is going to happen today. They don't work on the weekends and there's nothing for me to do on a Saturday. They can't deport him. He's entitled to his hearing. Let me read this."

They sat down in his office and he read the letter. She pulled a chair to the side of his desk close, so she could look over his shoulder as he read. He leaned away and she came closer.

It was clear to him that immediately after the request was filed, a form denial was issued. Tony wondered whether the officer in charge even looked at the file.

"They must have mailed this a couple of hours after we filed the request. We didn't get a copy yet. It'll probably be in the Monday mail."

She leaned down to look closely and brushed up against him. "What are you going to do?"

Tony inched his chair away from her. "I'm not sure there's anything to do."

"Not sure? You've got to help my husband. I'll do anything. Tell me what I can do. You're the only person who can help him. I'll do anything you say."

"For any amount of money, I might not be able to stop this. We'll just have to go ahead with the hearing."

"Please Mr. Sorrelli, I'll do anything you say."

"The next step would be to file another habeas corpus in federal court, but that would be expensive and is almost guaranteed to fail. I don't think we should do it."

She leaned closer to Tony and bent over him, pressing her breast against his hand as she feigned a better look at the letter. "There must be something I can do to make them stop this."

Tony pressed the intercom. "Adara, I need a copy. Please come in."

"Do it yourself, Tony. You know I'm busy."

Mrs. Rodriguez moved to look Tony in the eye and swiped a breast across his arm. "I need you to help me."

Tony could smell her breath. "Adara Get in here now."

Adara came in with an attitude and then she saw the scene and smiled. "Mr. Sorrelli. It's time for my coffee break. I'll be back in a half hour." She turned to leave, went to the front door and opened and closed it without exiting, then quietly went back to the conference room.

"You're a man who won't take no for an answer. Fight for me," she said.

Tony got up. "I need to make a copy."

He went into the conference room where Adara was laughing. "Thanks for helping me out."

"This is just what you deserve, Tony. How does it feel to have someone come on to you?"

"Don't leave me alone with her."

"Why not? You handle women so well."

"I'll get even with you for this."

Adara gave him the biggest smile as she leaned back in her chair and almost fell over.

Tony made the copy and returned to the room to find Mrs. Rodriguez standing there with her jacket off and several buttons opened on her blouse. "It's so hot in here. I guess I'm just so nervous and scared. I know you will take care of me."

"Only your immigration problems. It's time for you to go." He pointed to the door.

"Are you throwing me out?"

"No. I need to do some work, and I understand what you want from me."

"Don't throw me out."

"I'm not throwing you out. We're supposed to be closed today and I just came in to do a couple of things. I'll handle this Monday."

Mrs. Rodriguez walked up to Tony and put her arms around him. "I'm so scared. I don't think I can handle this. I'm so alone. Please hold me."

Tony broke away and sat behind his desk.

She sat down deep on the chair by his side and threw back her head. "I need to know what you're going to do for my husband."

"I need to look at the file and think about it. I cannot do this while you're here." He got up, grabbed her arm and led her to the door.

She placed her hands on her breasts and pushed them up until they were ready to pop out. "Don't throw me out!"

"We need to discuss how we're going to win Carlos's case in court. We need to file the evidence I asked you for. Call Monday for an appointment."

Mrs. Rodriguez started to cry. She sat down and spread her legs, bent down and put her hands on her face. Tony went into the conference room and asked Adara to comfort her and to ask her to leave.

As Adara went in, she told Ms. Rodriguez, "Tony and I have to get home before the babysitter leaves. Our children are expecting us and we have to leave now." With that, Adara took her by the arm and as she walked her to the door, she said, "You can rest assured that whatever can be done will be. Good day."

Adara hugged Tony's arm. "Please don't let her come between us. How would I explain it to the children?"

"Ha."

* * *

Naib and Hamid got out of the subway in Foley Square just across from the federal building. They walked to the courthouse steps and judged the distance between buildings and streets.

The food vendors were closed, but the kiosks were there. They measured the angle from the kiosks directly next to the stairs. The best angle was from the Chinese food vendor. The halal stand was at a poor angle to the action.

Hamid stood in front of the courthouse as Naib took his picture. They took turns taking pictures of themselves at different angles around the square and at different angles to the kiosks. Many of the photos failed to capture them and just contained the landscape.

"How can I shoot from that space?" Naib said. "They'll see everything. "This is not good. We should stick to the original plan."

"You bet it's not good. We *should* stick to the plan. This side show can screw it up." Hamid looked upset.

"We have our orders," Naib sighed. "Do you see any other building where we could do this? President Kennedy was shot from a window a lot further than this and with equipment far inferior to what we have."

A policeman walked over to them. "Can I help you?"

Naib walked right up to the policeman and eyeballed him. "It's a free country. I'm just taking a walk and enjoying the New York sites."

The policeman clutched his gun and looked at them from an angle as he waked away.

They walked across the street to the other courthouse and counted the steps to the building. Naib took out a paper and wrote the estimated distance. They did the same thing from different angles and Naib drew a map. Naib made note of garbage cans and newspaper boxes just in case they wanted to place a bomb in one of them. They walked from each of the food carts to the courthouse steps and made notes of the number of steps.

They went away from the building and walked past the African Burial ground to plan the escape. They walked at a medium pace to a McDonalds and then beyond McDonalds to the avenue behind it, where they discussed a possible escape.

"Forget about a car," Hamid said. "You never know what traffic will be like. This is Manhattan. We could easily get stuck. We will need to go to the subway and take a train somewhere where a car can quickly take you away."

"I can't go back to the store. You should be there though."

"The plan was for one of us to watch and report later."

Naib continued. "Too dangerous. Suicide. I do not think it is necessary." They went around the corner where they bought some coffee and fruit. Hamid took a sip of coffee. "Many people will go down into the subway and that would be the perfect getaway, but we need to stay around. We'll have to time it right."

"That's hard to do," Hamid said. "We also have to detonate a bomb in the kiosk. It might be easier to do it that way. If we do that, there won't be any need to use the guns. We should be far away when it goes off. The explosion will kill them if we do it here."

"No. Any explosion will be to mask our escape."

"If we can escape."

"If that is the will of Allah," Naib said. "We might have trouble getting out of the area. We will need a reason to be here."

"I have the perfect one. I'll make an appointment with my lawyer. You should start a case with him soon if you think that this will take more time. They have an office just a couple of blocks away. I'll take you there. Having a case will be your reason to be here. They will even give you a card with the appointment. When it happens, everyone will go to the window to see what's happening. They won't notice that you came in after. You won't need to get out of the area."

"That might work. I want to walk by the lawyer's office. This is better than a car. The problem is that if we use a car, we might be checked coming in. The car will have to be stolen. There's danger in that."

"No. We can be bringing a new food cart in. Everything we need could be in the food cart. These are never checked."

They walked back to the courthouse and past the lawyer's office just a block away.

They turned the corner just as Tony and Adara were leaving the office.

Hamid and Naib saw them and ducked into a store across the street and tried to become invisible. After a few minutes, when Tony and Adara seemed to have left, they left the store. Hamid browsed around while Naib surveyed the street. The traffic went slowly down Broadway: too slowly for a car to get away. It would be worse on a weekday. From the street they noticed a subway stop just a block away, but that seemed too near the courthouse and would be one of the first ones checked.

Tony stopped in his tracks and looked at Adara. "I forgot my appointment book."

"Do you need it during lunch?"

"I want to discuss a few things while we eat."

Tony and Adara returned to the office. Adara waited in front of the building while Tony went upstairs. After about two minutes he came down.

As Hamid left the store, they walked to the corner by the law office to estimate the view.

Adara was waiting just as Hamid and Naib were looking at the lobby. Adara walked up to Hamid. "Are you here to see us?"

Hamid had a big smile on his face. "I was just here with my friend to recommend that he use your firm for his political asylum case. I told him that your firm is the best."

"On a Saturday? You know we're closed."

"I just wanted to show him where it was. We're off today." He turned to Naib. "I want you to meet our sister Adara."

Naib took a short bow. He did not offer to shake her hand.

Tony walked over and Hamid put his big smile back on. "Tony! How wonderful to see you. Meet my friend Naib. He has a case to discuss with you."

Tony put out his hand to shake Naib's. "Good to meet you."

Naib took a second to respond and in a slight British accent said, "And good to meet you too." They shook.

"They are the best. I don't know where I would be without them," Hamid said.

Adara and Naib looked into each other's eyes. There were no smiles, nothing accepting in their stares.

"Hamid speaks very highly about your firm," Naib said.

"We are not really open today. We just came in to catch up on some work. I'd be happy to talk during the week," she said.

Tony handed Naib a card. "Call us Monday. I would be happy to discuss your problem with you."

Adara looked at Tony. "We have a lunch appointment we'll be late for." She turned to Naib. "Good to meet you."

As they turned and walked swiftly up Chambers Street, Adara said to Tony, "That guy scares me. There's something very wrong."

"Nonsense."

"It is not nonsense. Hamid was not just showing him where our office is. They looked like they were casing the joint."

"Case us? Why? There's nothing to steal. It's just their cultural differences that are getting to you. You're better than that."

"Fuck the cultural differences. I'm tired of hearing you make excuses for every client. I know these people better than you do. I can smell something dangerous here. That man is a killer and I can feel it. They are trouble."

"You can't believe that. You can't condemn everyone you meet just because of a random feeling. I admit they seem a bit suspicious, but it's a cultural thing. The vast majority of them are good, hardworking people who support our values. Don't condemn them until you have the whole story. Anyway, why would they want to hurt us? We're here to help them."

They went into Mudville, a restaurant on Chambers Street and a hangout for immigration officers. Following them from about a block away, Naib and Hamid watched.

"Do you think they suspect anything?" Naib said.

"No. He thinks all his clients are saints, and she is one of us. We can trust her."

"I'm not so sure."

"If you think they suspect anything, I'll deal with them."

"That would be a big mistake. This is not the time to draw any attention." Naib looked at the card in his pocket. "I'll call Monday for an appointment. We have to now, to dispel suspicion. It's a good idea anyway. If we're stopped anywhere, we can explain what we're doing. If you have a case on file with immigration, they won't arrest you and they'll even give you permission to work."

As Adara and Tony entered the restaurant, a waitress with about ten pounds more in her chest than her dress could handle and a couple of teeth short of a set pointed to a seat by the front window.

"Hi, Tony."

"Hello, Claire. You know Adara. She works with me."

The two women starred at each other blankly without another word.

Tony ordered a club sandwich and a Bud and Adara ordered the chicken salad with balsamic dressing on the side and a Diet Coke. As the waitress left Adara said, "We should discuss this with Auburn. Something's up and I don't like it."

"What do you think you'll say? That you don't like the way these guys look or that they're walking around Manhattan on their day off? By those standards the whole city is guilty. Besides I have an ethical duty not to say anything about a client unless I have good reason to believe that client is planning a crime."

"They're not clients yet."

"Hamid is. Doesn't matter. They spoke to me in my capacity as an attorney. I'm bound."

Claire came over with their drinks. "You still saving the world, Tony?"

"Yeah. One immigrant at a time."

"I could use some saving."

"I don't do that kind of saving, Claire."

"Too bad."

"Besides, you're too much for me."

"You don't know till you try."

"I don't think I'm strong enough for you."

"Let me worry about that."

The waitress smiled at him and walked away, shaking her ass a bit more than necessary and paying no attention to Adara.

"I can't believe that. With me sitting here."

"Listen, Adara. If you have some facts you can point to, I'm happy to discuss it, but we just can't go accusing people of I don't know what because we think they look suspicious. What are you going to tell Mark, that you don't like the guy's face?"

"I have a bad feeling about them. I listened to Hamid talk to another client he brought in some weeks ago. Carmen left the intercom on."

"You know that's very wrong. What goes on in our office is confidential. The very nature of legal representation would by destroyed if it wasn't."

"Nevertheless, they're up to no good. I just don't know what. I should listen to my instincts."

"You've been living in the U.S. since you were a child. You think like a policeman instead of a citizen."

"I'm an American and I also sympathize with my own people, but my own people are also Americans. Why are you so willing to give the benefit of the doubt to the aliens all the time?"

"I'm a lawyer. My career is dedicated to helping these people. In every generation there were immigrants who came to America who were suspected of something or another by the majority. In every case they became Americans. When my grandparents came here a hundred years ago they were referred to as *wops*. Do you know what that means?"

"Yeah. Without papers."

"Right."

"Oh please! First of all, that's not what's going on here. It's not their nationality that bothers me, it's just that I have a bad feeling about this. Second, your career is also dedicated to a just legal system. It's not just to allow them to commit a crime if we know about it."

"Discuss it with Bill. I won't before you do. Bill is usually levelheaded. You'll see it my way after stewing on it a night. If Bill sides with you, I'll go along with you."

"You say that because you know what Bill will do."

"No, I don't."

"You do. Bill will say that it's not our problem and tell me to get back to work."

"Sometimes that's good advice."

* * *

That same Saturday morning synagogue service ended a bit late and Ryan, his girlfriend Rachel and his parents went into the reception room for a luncheon. As they entered the room the rabbi took a bottle of wine, poured a glass and said a prayer. He then took the bottle and poured a bit into many small cups to give to the congregation. Each person took a cup. He said another prayer with a loaf of challah bread and after everyone had a sip of wine and a piece of bread, they lined up for a Middle Eastern-style buffet.

Ryan and his family sat down next at a table with several other people.

"Shlomo, do you know my son is now practicing immigration law?"

Shlomo was a little older than his father and a little fatter and a little balder than anyone else in the room. When he opened his mouth you could cut his accent with a knife. "Congratulations, Ryan. Do you have many Middle Eastern clients?"

"We have clients from all over the world. It's like a little United Nations. We have people who speak several languages, including Arabic."

"That's my native language."

"I know."

"I was born in Syria, but I bet there are only a few hundred Syrian Jews left there. Maybe none. Bad government there. Bad war. No one worth supporting. Are you following the Imam's trial?"

"Not really."

"You should. The American news is very different from the Arabic news online. The overseas news is adamant that what's happening to the Imam is a persecution by the United States government against some innocent clergyman, and they won't allow it. The language is clear that something will happen and it's also clear to me that our government is blind to the threat."

"Don't be so sure."

Shlomo leaned towards Ryan. "Don't be so sure this government knows what's going on. I understand the language and I listen. The American press says one thing, but the Arabic press says another. Our government seems to be clueless."

"Are you telling me that there's a threat and the U.S. government is clueless about it? I don't think so. I have confidence in our government. Anyway, how can they not know? I'm sure the government of the United States is monitoring threats against us," Ryan said.

"They missed nine-eleven. The Arabic press was full of threats."

"There are always threats. How can anyone be sure what's real or not? I think there doing much more now."

Shlomo pointed repeatedly at Ryan. "They may not be. I'm relying on comments from Muslim political leaders that say that the Imam's trial won't go unanswered. Once they make a statement like that, they are putting their reputations on the line. If they don't do anything, it would be a loss of face."

"I'm sure the government is on top of it."

"Grow up. Governments are just a bunch of people worried about how little work they can do until they go home or what they can get out of the job on the side than about what they should be doing. Their bosses are just interested in how much power they can get and how they can use that power to enrich themselves."

"That's not true. The people who work for immigration do care."

"Do you own a short wave radio?"

"Do they still make them?"

"Sure they do. You need to listen to the source. Otherwise you hear just what propaganda the news companies want to feed you."

"The news in this country is basically reliable."

"No, it's not. The news channels are all propaganda. In America you can choose the propaganda you like. You haven't been a lawyer for that long. You'll see. You just need some more seasoning."

"I have confidence."

"Have confidence in your own reasoning. Don't have confidence in the news. They're all trying to shovel their propaganda on you. You may agree with it or not, but it's propaganda. It's hard to get the facts and think about it for yourself."

"I have confidence in the U.S."

Shlomo just starred.

* * *

The apartment building on Third Avenue in the East 30s overlooked traffic coming out of the Midtown Tunnel. Zalmanski stood in his briefs as he shaved, occasionally looking out of his window at the traffic below.

"I cleaned out the left side of the dresser for you. It's empty. Just put your things where you want them."

"Uh hum," came an accented woman's voice from the other room.

"I also made space in the right closet. If it's not enough space, I'll try to make some more."

"Uh hum."

"I know you don't like all the same foods I do, so tomorrow we can go food shopping and I'll get you whatever you want. There's plenty of space in the kitchen."

"Thank you, Bill." Ms. Choe entered with a white silk robe and slippers. Her long black hair hung free over her back. She went up to Bill, opened up her robe and pressed her naked body against his back. "When you're done in the bathroom I want to get dressed."

ELEVEN

Ali showed up at the office with Naib.

"Maria, I just want to make a payment and see Mr. Sorrelli." Ali took out five one hundred dollar bills, and Maria wrote him a receipt.

"Mr. Sorrelli will be available soon if you want to wait."

"My friend here needs to start a political asylum case."

"He will need to pay a consultation fee, and I need to take some basic information." She pulled out a form with the title "intake sheet" from her desk.

Naib reached over and took it from her. In his British accent he said, "Don't waste your time. I'll fill it out while we wait. I have a pen."

As Ali paid the consultation fee, Naib silently filled out the form.

Carmen looked at the bottom of the intake sheet where it said "Referred by…" and noticed Hamid's name. She notified Adara and told Tony someone was waiting.

Tony came to the front desk, and Carmen gave him the intake sheet. Naib and Ali followed him back to his office. As he perused the intake sheet, Naib spoke.

"Good to see you again," Tony said. "I'm glad that you want us to help you."

"I never considered anyone else."

"Okay. What's your story?"

"I was a Major in the Jordanian army and was a minor player in an attempted coup. You can check everything I said. It is completely true. I assure you. Three of the leaders were quietly executed and about seventeen of us quietly disappeared. Several of the plotters are fighting with the rebels in Syria. One obtained political asylum in Sweden. I decided to come here and request political asylum."

"It says here that you are wanted by the Jordanian government. Can that be verified?"

"Yes. I assume the government will do a routine background check on me and this will show up."

"And what will they find when they check?"

"They will find that there is an Interpol hold for me for attempted murder. There was no attempted murder, only a planned coup. It might have led to violence but might not have. We had hoped to succeed without bloodshed."

"If there's an extradition order filed on you, this might be dangerous."

"There is none, I'm sure."

"If there is, we won't know for a few months."

"That's fine."

Tony stared into his stone eyes as his neurons fired warnings right and left. "It also says you entered the United States through Mexico. Did you pay a coyote to get in?"

"No. I crossed the border on foot near Allen, Texas and a friend picked me up and drove me to New York where I knew I could find work. In fact I'm staying with your client Hamid."

"Of course."

"He says very good things about you. So does Ali. I want you to handle my case. I want to speak to your secretary, Adara, who speaks Arabic. My friends trust her."

"I hope all of us will earn your trust. We want you to be happy. That's how we get new business."

"I'm sure I'll be satisfied."

Tony asked Adara over the intercom to come in.

"Do you have a passport?"

Naib handed it over. Tony looked through the pages full of visas and visa stamps. "It shows that you were in Lahore, then Dubai and then Yemen, and it seems you flew to Mexico City after a stopover in Lisbon. How were you able to get a transit visa to Lisbon?"

"I didn't. It was issued at the airport since I had my army ID and a ticket to Mexico City."

"Did you try to get an American visa?"

"No."

"Why not?"

"I was afraid that if I made any sort of application it would be reported to the Jordanian authorities and I might be picked up."

"If this is true you, may have a very strong case for asylum."

Adara came in and they nodded to each other. The men would not shake Adara's hand.

Naib stood up. "Good to see you again. It is comforting to know that there is someone here who understands our culture, someone who I can rely upon to ensure that there are no misunderstandings."

Adara smiled. "Of course. You are in the best of hands. If my brother had American immigration issues, I would bring him here."

"That's reassuring. Can I call you directly if I have any questions?"

"If Mr. Sorrelli cannot help you, I surely will." Adara went behind Tony's desk and picked up the intake sheet. "It looks like you have an interesting story. I will follow your case carefully and make sure that it is handled properly." Adara thanked them for coming and went back to her office. She pressed the intercom. "Tony, your intercom was on. I'll just turn it off."

Tony continued. "Can you document the coup? I don't remember reading anything about this in *The Economist*."

"I will get you some information. My friend in Sweden will have the documents."

Tony thought for a moment. "If you can show that your friend got asylum in Sweden, on these facts, it might go a long way towards getting asylum here."

"I'll see what I can do. I can also document that I graduated Sandhurst."

"The British military academy?"

"Yes."

"That's like graduating from West Point here."

"Exactly. I was sent there by the Jordanian military for training. They had the highest hopes for me. My loyalty was always to the people of Jordan."

Adara went to Maria's desk and asked her to have Tony come to her office.

Tony entered. "What's up?"

"Sit down a bit. I want to listen to those two."

As they sat, the men in Tony's office talked in Arabic. Adara listened.

After a minute Tony asked, "Heard enough?"

"No. They are talking about us, but I don't like them. Something's wrong."

Naib was looking around Tony's office. They spoke in Arabic. He turned to Ali. "From these windows we can see everything going on down Broadway. We can monitor the police and people fleeing."

"The conference room is even better," Ali said. "This will be the safest place for us. The police would never just walk in here. It's not the American way."

Naib stood up and walked to the window. "It might be too close to the … I'll go there from the warehouse in Newark. Why not?"

Adara leaned into the intercom and became apprehensive. She looked at Tony. "This is very bad."

Tony returned to his office. He questioned Naib slowly and allowed the men to talk in between.

Adara listened. She could pick up bits and pieces of the conversation.

"When we set it off……."

"Three… is completely safe…"

"…change the plan…not three miles…"

"…eliminate…"

"What if they figure…out?"

"Eliminate the threat."

"The explosives will…"

"…Imam…"

After they left, Adara sat down with Bill and discussed what had taken place. At the end Adara said, "I'll do it."

* * *

Curtwright and Robinson arrived early and immediately went into Hite's office with their coffees. They sat down as he studied his computer. After about two long minutes Hite turned to them. "Tell me what's happening with the Imam's trial."

"We're coming along well." Curtwright pulled out a list from her briefcase and went through it. "We're ready to go to trial ahead of schedule."

"And what about the time frame?"

"We expect Judge Croyden to schedule it in the next few weeks."

"Are you sure it's watertight?"

"Yes. Do you want to go over the details with us?"

"No. I don't have the time. I have a meeting with my campaign staff in ten minutes and that will take most of the morning. Do it. It's one thing to get an indictment and another to proceed to trial. Are you ready?"

"Of course."

"Okay. It would be an embarrassment if the case were lost before the election."

"Not a problem. Would you like us to go over the details with you?"

"I said I don't have the time."

As they walked out, Renee looked straight ahead and asked, "Anything else?"

"I think we're rushing this. Several witnesses are not ready and the FBI is still looking into others involved. We might do better waiting."

"The election is in November and Hite needs us to proceed."

"We work for the people of the United States."

Renee laughed. "Just move it along."

* * *

Ryan opened the mail and found an order from Judge Totten. He opened it and went directly into Bill's office.

Bill sat and read it. "Very strange. He's recusing himself from the matrimonial case. Why now?"

"What case."

"My divorce case. He did the divorce seventeen years ago. From time to time I return with my ex whenever we have problems that we need to resolve."

"Isn't he your friend from Viet Nam and Law School?"

"Yah."

"He should have done this seventeen years ago. He hasn't had jurisdiction for all this time. Your ex and you should never have been assigned to him in the first place."

"That's not what it's about. He must be under some administrative pressure to get rid of old cases. He knows I wouldn't have said anything. He's always been a moderating force with my ex. He talks sense into her and gives her a chance to blow off steam. It makes it easy for me to help her out without looking like it's charity. It's a little strange that it happened now."

"It will be assigned to another judge and quickly dismissed." Ryan read the order a bit more. "He could have dismissed it outright."

"He wants another judge to do that. Still strange though."

Ryan pulled out another letter and handed it to Zalmanski. "This is on the Hamid case. It seems the judge adjourned the case for six months. No reason given."

"Well that's not so strange. We can't complain much about this one since he has a weak case and might lose. He's a fucking liar. If he stays another six months, who knows, he might marry an American. We'll charge him extra."

"He might not look at it that way. He probably expects to win."

"You'll see, Ryan. Clients often become victims of their own bullshit. They talk themselves into believing that they have great cases, but they're relieved to postpone judgment day. Not just here but other types of cases also. I think this Hamid guy knows the truth, but you can never tell. Give it to Maria. She'll calendar the case and send out a letter. At least we're paid to date."

"Sure."

"Let Maria explain to you what she does. It's not just showing up at the next hearing. Every year we need to renew his fingerprints, so we have to arrange for that a few months before the next hearing. We may also have to update other evidence. New taxes have to be added. Job letters updated. These things have to be scheduled. The short story is: more work for us that we can't bill on."

"We should work this into the retainer."

"When clients pay us, part of it is like insurance. We're ahead on some cases that go through smoothly and we're behind on others. That's the business. If it gets too out of whack, we bill and the client usually complains. If we had to count hours like the big corporate firms we would be arguing every bill every month with the clients and we wouldn't get the real work done."

Ryan went to his desk and took a sip of coffee.

Carmen came in with an unlit cigarette in her mouth. "Whadda you have on today?"

"At two I have to take Mr. Pierre to deportation for an interview. He's been ordered deported, but they're not deporting Haitians because of the earthquake."

"Still? It's a waste of time. You'll wait two hours and they'll look at him and send him home. These cases are going on for years now."

"So why am I going?"

"You're hand-holding. He's afraid to go alone and he's willing to pay. If they arrest him, you can't do much about it either."

"When will they start deporting Haitians?"

"Maybe never. Once they decide they can't send 'em back to a certain country, they designate that country TPS. That stands for 'temporary protected status,' except it's not so temporary. It goes on for decades. They marry here, have kids here, and the kids get them green cards when they're twenty-one. It's almost like a little amnesty. It's a cash cow for the office. Once they're in that status, they have to come in every year to renew, so we can expect some money. They might marry or find another way to get legal. Sometimes they get arrested and we get a second deportation case."

"When the problem ends, shouldn't the status?"

"Yeah. You would think so. It should, but it becomes political. No president wants to pull the plug. It plays bad in the ethnic communities. Politicians are more concerned with what's good for their reelection chances than what's good for America. The countries where these people came from can't handle a flood of deports, so it becomes political that way too. It's easier for the government to just kick the can down the road a year or two at a time. It's like everything else with the government: once they do something, they never take it back."

"Wow."

"And they get permission to work while they're here. Temporary protected status is a political status. Once granted, they're eligible for all sorts of public benefits—the same as almost anyone else. The United States legalizes hundreds of thousands of aliens and allows them to stay and work here. That encourages them to smuggle their families here, and before you know it there are hundreds of thousands more. Some get arrested coming through the border and we get more work from that."

"What about the politicians who promise to deport them all?"

"They're just showing they know nothing about the system."

* * *

At 2:00 Ryan arrived at the ninth floor deportation office. Mr. Pierre was waiting.

"Did you check in, Mr. Pierre?"

"Just five minutes ago."

"And what did they say?" Ryan sat down next to him.

"The woman at the window told me to just sit and wait."

"I expect they'll just extend your permission to remain for another six months."

"Don't know."

Ryan took out a copy of *Interpreter Releases,* a weekly update on immigration law and policy, and began to read. A man came and sat next to him and put out his hand. "You can get most of that info online, you know. I'm Jeff Pounders. You're the kid that Zalmanski hired. We met at Mario's."

"Sure. I remember you. Good to see you." Ryan put out his hand. "I've been there a while now. This area of law is so interesting."

"You can learn much from Bill. Don't let his high fashion clothes fool you. He has really good judgment on the law. Tony knows the black and white on the pages, but Bill understands how the system really works. Are you involved in the amnesty project with Tony?"

"No. What's that?"

"The immigration lawyers association is pushing something called Comprehensive Immigration Reform. That's a code word for amnesty, giving green cards and then citizenship to all the aliens in the country. Congress won't pass it, but they might have passed a less comprehensive bill before the stock market crashed in '08. Anyway, it's impossible now. Congress says they're for it and then it's constantly torpedoed. The unions and the enforcement types gang up to kill it. The Black Congressional Caucus feels it takes jobs from African-Americans. They kill it quietly.

Tony is on the task force pushing for it. He's always trying to save the world. I'm surprised he hasn't recruited you."

"Not yet. I haven't thought about it."

"Everyone is either in the 'make them all American' or the 'kick them all out' camp. I'm going to show you that there's a third way to handle this."

"The other side wants to deport them all. I know."

"If you grant an amnesty, they'll be thirty million more coming in. If you kick them all out, you'll need a police force bigger than all the police forces we now have. The way is to...."

From behind the door they could hear someone yelling. "This is an order from the Department of Justice. Do you know what that means? Do any of you know what the word 'justice' means?"

There were some muffled voices in response.

"I said justice! I'll say it again. *Justice*!" He was getting louder and louder. By this point everyone in the waiting room was silent and listening. "There is no one here who knows what that word means. The order says justice. What you're doing is an injustice."

"This is Homeland Security," a voice with a Russian accent from behind the wall yelled.

"Department of Justice! I'm going to federal court. I'm going to sue your agency. I'm going to sue you personally. I'm going to sue your asses off. Try to explain to a federal judge why you arrested a man with a stay. That's kidnapping. It's a crime."

The door opened and Ryan could hear the man with a Russian accent. "Enough, counselor."

As the man came out, Pounders and Ryan stood up.

"This is Tony thirty years from now. The other is Piertowsky. He's enforcement and a reasonable guy," Pounders said and then he turned to the man. "Calm down, Irv. You'll have a coronary."

Irv was a short rotund man in is seventies with possibly the worst toupee in Manhattan. Irv wore a polyester leisure suit. He made Zalmanski look like a good dresser. He was a day too long on a shave and had a briefcase that should have been sold as an antique in 1964.

"Those bastards arrested my client even though I've got a stay of removal from Judge McCormick."

"That stay only stops them from sending him outside the country," Pounders said.

"I know, but that's not the same thing as doing justice. If they can't send him out, what's the point of holding him?"

"Meet Ryan. He's working for Zalmanski."

Ryan's client sat there with a look of terror on his face. He looked at the exit as Ryan patted his shoulder to reassure him.

Irv shook Ryan's hand. "You working for that old fart? You're going to get an education. I taught Bill everything he knows. Isn't that right, Jeff?"

"You know," Pounders said. "They'll get even for you giving them a hard time."

Irv turned to Ryan. "Some guys will tell you not to piss them off and some will kiss their asses. The trick is to build a reputation of being reasonable and tough at the same time. Be reasonable, but if you tell them you'll fight and you don't, they'll shit all over you."

"Are you going to file a habeas on this?" Ryan asked.

"No."

The door on the side opened up and Piertowsky came out with an angry look. "Pierre, this way please."

As Ryan turned to the door, Irv said, "That's the guy I was yelling at."

Pierre got up and went in. The officer told Pierre to sit across from him and Ryan to sit far to the side.

"I'm officer Piertowsky. Can I have your papers?"

"Are you going to extend Mr. Pierre's stay?" Ryan said.

"Am I talking to you? The last lawyer in this room used up all my good will today. You're allowed in as a courtesy. If you interfere, I will have to ask you to leave. You guys are in enough trouble already."

"Sorry. What do you mean we're in trouble?" Ryan asked.

"I'm sorry. I was thinking about someone else."

"Oh."

"Mr. Pierre, do you have an updated passport?"

"No, my embassy is not issuing them now. I asked."

"It's not my job to get documents for you. We can re-arrest you at any time. If you don't follow instructions, we will."

"But I tried. They're not issuing them now."

"My client said he tried. You can't expect him to get what he cannot."

"I told you not to speak. You lawyers are always try to make it hard for us to do our jobs." He turned to Pierre. "Are you working?"

"Yes, I'm a minister. I'm paying my taxes."

"I'm going to give you an appointment to come back in six months. I expect you to obtain a valid travel document by that time. If you can't get one from your consulate, get a letter showing that you tried and that they won't issue it. I won't accept excuses."

"But they won't, sir."

"I need it for my paperwork."

"Yes, sir."

"You don't need a lawyer."

Ryan got up and said to Pierre, "Let's go."

Ryan returned to the office and went in to see Tony.

Tony was reading something on his computer and asked Ryan without looking, "How'd it go?"

"Well. The officer gave Mr. Pierre a hard time for no reason. He was pressuring him to get a passport, but he must know Pierre can't do it."

"S.O.P," standard operating procedure, Tony said. "They're instructed to do that, but I can't tell you why. Once in a while these guys are bullied into getting some travel document and sometimes they're deported, but it rarely happens."

"So why all the fuss?"

"Shows them who's the boss. That's the same reason they bully us. We shouldn't have to take it, but you just can't fight every case. We've got to pick and choose."

"I understand. He also said something about us guys being in trouble and then he backed off."

Tony brushed it aside. "He handles maybe fifty cases a day. He couldn't have been thinking about us."

Tony turned to look at Ryan and leaned back on his swivel chair. "I need to talk to you about something. Sunday evening week after next, my mother is making dinner at her house in Bensonhurst, Brooklyn. You're invited. Bill and Adara are coming. Just show up. Don't bring anything. My mother is a fantastic cook. Anything you bring won't be as good as what she can cook. She does this about once a year for no reason. You can bring your girlfriend. Do you have a girlfriend?"

143

"Yes and yes. I also have a car. Can I at least bring a bottle of wine?"

"Nothing. She needs to be in control of the whole dinner. It's a big deal. Are you kosher?"

"Yes and no."

"What does that mean?"

"Well. I call myself hypocrite kosher. I'm kosher at home and I try to be kosher-style outside of the house. I'll order grilled fish in a diner. Like that."

"Isn't that like being a little bit pregnant? Would any rabbi call that kosher?"

"I do what I can do."

"Fair enough. My mother will have something for you to eat. There'll be a fish dish you should be fine with." Tony wrote down the address and handed the paper to Ryan. "Can you be there about four?"

"A Jewish four or a British four?"

"British."

"We'll be there." Ryan looked at the address. "No problem. I know the area and I have a GPS in my car."

"I didn't know you had a girlfriend. You don't talk much."

"You don't either, Tony. I talk to Carmen some. She talks to the girls. Everyone here seems to know everything about you. You seem to do well with the women."

"I do all right. Tell me about your girlfriend."

"Her name is Rachel. She's a law student at the Manhattan Law School. We discussed getting engaged when she graduates."

"I'm looking forward to meeting her."

"Should be fun."

As Ryan left the room, he started to wonder if he hadn't just made a big mistake.

TWELVE

Mark Auburn sat at his computer and observed the security camera recordings. They showed people come in and out, but that was exactly what you would expect. Why have a store if not for the traffic? The people were of all shapes and sizes. It looked as though they sold cigarettes to minors, but that would be hard to prove and would be a waste of their time. Why bother?

Robinson came into his office wearing a shoulder holster with an automatic. She had the look of a marine and the build to be one if she wished.

"You don't need the gun here. Please take it off."

"Okay." He undid the holster and put it all on a table near the door then sat down. "I've been over these several times and they show nothing. The taps on the store phone are equally useless. I'm waiting for the taps on Hamid's cell phone."

"This new the employee. Probably Naib."

Auburn opened a file and they pulled out photos of Naib supplied by the Jordanian army. In the pictures he wore full military dress but was never cleanly shaven. The pictures also showed a man somewhat younger and thinner. The height seemed correct. "We're not 100 percent sure, but we'll proceed as though he is. This sounds bad, but he looks like so many other Arabs that I go from sure to not."

The Jordanian government wanted him too for trying to organize a coup. The file showed that he had been missing for more than three years. It's believed that he went to Syria to join the Islamic State. The pictures would seem to be reasonably current. Auburn wondered whether this

Naib had been fighting for ISIS. There was also an INTERPOL file with information about Naib traveling to Pakistan to purchase weapons for ISIS. The pictures in that file also seemed to match.

Robinson examined the photo carefully. "It looks like him. We can easily confirm it if we get a print. If we can buy a can of soda or something smooth and he touches it, we can make the ID solid. Have we followed him at all?"

"Some. He's hard to follow. It's easiest to watch him when he's at the store. He's staying with Hamid."

"We have to determine if he's a sleeper or hot."

"Hard to tell at this time. He might just be an illegal. We can have ICE go in there and arrest him. They'll print him and he'll just file an asylum claim anyway."

"He'll file an asylum claim. They'll just release him. At least we'll be able to fingerprint him and we'll know for sure. Since we're proceeding under the assumption that Hamid is hot, we'll tag this man as hot too. I doubt he's cheap labor. We need a better ID, but let's proceed that he's hot. If we do more at this time, we'll alert them that we're on to them. Let's just take it slow," Auburn said.

"If we take it too slow he'll kill someone before we act."

"Unfortunately he needs to do something criminal before we can act. You know that. All we have is speculation now. Immigration violations won't do. When we get some facts, we'll get an order to search the place."

"This guy's wanted by INTERPOL. Why can't you pick him up based on that?"

"He's wanted by Jordan for political crimes. Once we pick him up he'll file for political asylum and be out in a few days. In the meantime we'll tip them off and they'll change any plans they have."

"Not good, but we don't know what plans they have."

"We will. Now, the store is open twenty-four seven. We can get in anytime. They get at least six hundred customers a day. We just have to go in and buy something. We can get in undetected. We just can't do much once we're in. When you get the court order, we'll do a walk-in drop. We have a kid for the diversion. He's a local snitch who'll do us a favor."

"If he's a snitch he can't be trusted."

"I believe the NYPD can find one. All we need is a diversion," Auburn said.

"Why?"

"This will allow us to plant a bug in the store. Maybe just a slap-on bug will do."

"If you do a slap-on, we're limited to the life of the battery. Not very helpful. If they find it, well…"

Auburn got up and walked over to a large board with notes and photos and arrows all over it. He placed one of the Jordanian army photos next to others of those being watched. It was his own case investigation board where he followed the action.

"It doesn't seem to be going anywhere, but my gut tells me he's a terrorist. What we don't know is exactly what they have planned. If we act too soon we won't know, and someone else might complete the plan. No. We need to know before we act."

"These guys might be sleepers despite the info coming in. They just don't seem to be doing enough. We have the statement from the informant. The judge accepted it when we got the warrants."

"So? It might be well intentioned and just wrong or even given to us to throw us off the scent. They could have dropped a few red herrings on us. I just feel we're missing a few pieces of the puzzle. Go through Hamid's immigration file. There might be something more there."

"It's a waste, chief. It's all made up. I could pull another twenty immigration files and you'd read exactly the same story. It's like a packaged product. I can't believe the immigration judges don't realize it."

"How are you doing with the wiretaps on the lawyers?"

"It's very hard to go through them. You can't believe the crap that goes on in a law office every day. It's more comedy than crime. We're ignoring everything except Arabic or English. If we listened to the Spanish or Korean, we'd need another dozen agents."

"Have you heard anything useful?"

"Nothing. Just appointments made and discussions about documents. It sounds more like an H & R Block. These guys are always reminding their clients to pay taxes so they can be used to support the case. The next item they talk about is reminding the clients that they owe money. I always thought lawyers had more interesting lives."

When Auburn returned to his office he sent an email to JK. *"Your tip paid off. Thanks."*

* * *

Harold Peters entered the Metropolitan Correctional Facility in New York City with his interpreter. The guards knew that they had come there to see the Imam and gave them a thorough search. They asked them to take everything out of their pockets and Harold's briefcase and put them in a locker, provided for that purpose. Harold had to put his belt and watch in. No cell phones were allowed. Harold could bring in just some papers and one pen. The interpreter could bring in only a dictionary. They allowed them to enter with their shoes only after a thorough hand search.

The interpreter was not searched as carfully.

Harold knew that the purpose was more intimidation than necessity. The prison guards took great pleasure in showing the attorneys who was the boss, at least at the prisons. In this case they took special care because they didn't want the Imam to send any messages to his followers. He had promised that America would regret his arrest and that "punishment was at hand."

Harold also knew that the government was afraid that the Imam would use him to transmit information that might trigger a terrorist act. The Imam had been an outspoken advocate of jihad against the United States and against all Western secular democracies and commonly spoke out against the "decadent behavior" in these countries. Harold wasn't sure if his client was all talk or had also committed the offences he was accused of in the indictment. As an experienced defense attorney, he knew better than to ask his client directly whether the charges were true. Those charges included passing money and introducing would-be terrorists to each other as well as encouraging and making preparations for terrorist attacks in the United States. Several of these would-be terrorists had gone into hiding and were being sought by the government.

Harold knew that the Imam's activities were closely monitored to prevent a terrorist attack but also to provide leads to other conspirators.

After a wait they were allowed to sit in a room and the Imam was brought in. A guard stood in the corner of the room and acted like he was not listening but looked on to ensure that only paper would be passed between them.

"Good morning."

"*Salam Aleichem.*"

"The trial is just a few weeks away and I need to go over a few things with you. You know my interpreter, Farid." The interpreter nodded.

"Yes. Go ahead."

"The U.S. Attorney's office is sure that you have contacts here. They might surprise us with names and details, and I need you to tell me anything that might be important. I can't help you if I'm completely surprised during the trial. If the government knows more than I do about your case, I can't help you."

"You know all."

"They seem to be sure that you have contacts among the supporters and that they are preparing to act. It seems the FBI believes some terrorist activity is imminent and you have knowledge about it."

"I have no information for them. We've already suffered enough. When will they leave me alone? They are trying to create animosity among the believers."

"This is America and even though I am assigned to you by the courts, I assure you that I will represent your interests to the best of my ability. I need you to cooperate."

The Imam whispered to the interpreter at least several sentences and the interpreter said, "Yes."

"Is that everything he just said?" Harold asked the interpreter.

"Yes."

Harold continued. "Okay. The government will present evidence that you passed money, about one hundred thousand, to some unknown persons and that the money has not been seen and is being used for illegal purposes."

"I often get contributions and pass them to the people who run my organizations. The money is to be used for charitable purposes."

"One hundred thousand in cash?"

"I don't usually count the money."

"That doesn't seem believable."

"I am just a bridge between Allah's will and the people who carry out his will."

"That does not sound good at all. The government will present testimony that you knew this money would be used to bring weapons and explosives into the United States. They will show that some of the money went to Pakistan to purchase North Korean-made weapons for ISIS."

"I do the work of Allah."

"They have traced some of the cash to people who smuggle illegals over the Mexican border. They may present wiretaps and witnesses. I cannot put you on the stand to dispute this unless you can provide a credible explanation. Once you're on the stand, they can ask you almost anything. I can't put you on the stand unless I'm sure about everything you will say."

"Allah will protect me."

"Allah has sent *me* to protect you and I need you to cooperate before I can do my job properly. I've listened to the wiretaps and they can be interpreted in different ways. We need to go over the specifics."

"No, we don't. They hear everything we say." He nodded towards the guard. "There is no need for us to talk further. I do not recognize the legitimacy of this court. It is run by nonbelievers. Only Allah can judge. I want to go on the stand and tell the court the truth."

"And what is the truth?"

"That I do the work of Allah. That is all I will say."

"I can't allow it."

"And why not?"

"Because once you are on the stand and answering questions, you will be required to answer all questions or invoke your constitutional rights."

"I will ask the court to proceed anyway. I will tell them that this is a corrupt society and that they are falsely accusing me. I have done nothing wrong to warrant this treatment. Any money I handled was for Allah's purpose. Anyone I spoke to was in furtherance of his kingdom. You are an American and a Christian. You cannot understand what this is about. You may someday come to understand my mission. I believe you are honest and well intentioned within your abilities, but you cannot save me by manipulating my speech and putting false ideas into my head."

"That's not what I'm doing. I can't in good conscience defend you unless you cooperate."

"This is the way it will be. At the last hearing, the judge told you that you could not remove yourself from this case and that you would proceed. That is fine with me too. I trust that you will do your job and I trust in Allah. We may never get to a hearing."

"Oh yes, we will."

"We will see."

"The government is also accusing you of extorting money from Muslim businesses and using that money to support ISIS and world terrorism."

"This is their religious obligation and cannot be called extortion."

"Nevertheless they are accusing you of also running an extortion racket that every Muslim business, food cart and vendor must give you a percentage of their profit. They say you are using this money to support terrorist organizations."

"All good Muslims give this money willingly. ISIS is no more a terrorist organization than your founding fathers were when they broke away from the British Empire."

"I don't think it's the same thing."

"Can I question you?" The Imam bent over and whispered. "You need to contact a Hamid at a tobacco shop on Irving Avenue. Tell him that I need some halal food. The food here is not what I require. Be specific to tell him that the food is not what I require and I need a proper meal before the trial. He will understand."

"I can't do that. If the government thinks I am passing messages, I can be arrested."

"Allah will protect you."

"I won't do that."

"You have to. They will be able to help you to find evidence that will help at the trial. You must trust me."

Harold stared at the Imam for a moment. "What evidence?"

"They will know."

"Humor me. Tell me about this evidence."

"At this time I can only tell you that they have a witness that can explain why I am here and what my plans are."

"Why can't you tell me that?"

"This is what you must do if you want to serve me."

* * *

About two hours later Farid, Harold's interpretor, went to a local branch of the New York Public Library and went to a computer where he logged on to Facebook as Martin Kowalski. The picture on the top of the page was of a blond-haired blue-eyed Eastern European-looking teenager. Farid sent a message to a Thomas Van Buren, another blond Eastern European-looking teenager. "The Imam needs some halal food. The food there isn't what he requires."

Early the next morning at a different library, Hamid logged on to Facebook as Thomas Van Buren and got the message.

* * *

Maria poked her head into Adara's office. "Hamid's here."

Hamid came in and sat opposite her. They spoke in Arabic.

"You called me in today. I think my bill with you is up to date," he said.

"I wanted to discuss other things with you today. Our little talk Saturday upset me. I'm worried that you might do things that will prejudice your case."

"What do you mean?"

"You know what I mean. You might get yourself into trouble."

"Did Sorrelli tell you to talk to me?"

"No, I'm capable of making that decision. It's none of my business what you do but…"

"Forget the but. It's none of your business *but* I'll tell you something. It should be your business. It's bad enough what this country is doing to my country. It's worse what's going on in Iraq and Syria. You should be angry at the United States and how the morals of our people are being polluted by these Westerners."

"It's not your opinions I'm worried about."

"These are not opinions; they are facts. We are in a battle for the survival of a righteous society. You are a Muslim woman and you have adopted their Western ways. The way you dress and the way you live is a departure from your roots. You can never be one of these people and you shouldn't try. They will never accept you."

"Spare me the lecture. I asked you here because I'm afraid you'll do something that will get you into trouble with the law. I want you to play it safe. After seeing you and your friend on Saturday, I was worried. Your friends can get you into trouble."

"Trouble with whom, the American government? They tolerate us because they fear a major war with Islam. I know the way your bosses look at me. Zalmanski only looks at me as a paying customer and Sorrelli likes to feel good thinking that he's helping people. He's one of these people who play with dogs and cats to feel good, and they thinks that that makes them good. They treat us like their pets while at the same time they support a government that suppresses people the world over. They're in it for their own reasons. I'm here doing Allah's work. Trouble? I'm the good guy here."

Adara was sorry she had started the conversation. She had seen men like this before and knew that they could be impossible to control. "I sympathize with you. What I wanted to talk about is the legal consequences of your actions."

"Don't worry. I won't do anything to embarrass your bosses."

"That's not what it's about."

"Yes, it is. Everyone in America worries about how other people look at them."

"And in your country?"

"You mean in *our* society. I worry about how Allah sees me."

"When I saw you that day it looked to me like you were surveying the neighborhood for some reason."

"You don't even trust me. I told you we're looking for a place to open a new store, and you would not even believe me. It's just as reasonable as what you think. But even if I was doing something American society thinks is wrong, as a Muslim you should support me."

"I don't know what to think."

"Just do your job."

"You can be sure I'll do the right thing."

"I'm counting on that. You worry about my political asylum case and about your own moral position. I'll worry about paying my bills." The sneer on Hamid's face grew.

"Your case has been adjourned by the immigration court for six months."

"Good."

"You don't look surprised."

"This country can't seem to finish anything it starts. The wait does not surprise me. I may bring in another friend to start a case next week. I expect you to do the right thing by him. I have brought other cases to you, and I expect you to do the right thing by them."

"You know I will."

"Do not threaten me. You would be very sorry."

"This discussion has nothing to do with threats," Adara assured him.

"I hope so. If I have to take actions, my words will state facts, not threats." Hamid quickly got up and left the office.

Adara went to Bill. He was standing at his desk with the *New York Times* spread over it. She told him what had happened.

Bill looked at the hearing notice. "Do we know why the case was adjourned?"

"No. It could be anything. The judge may have a vacation day planned that day. If we asked for more time, we would have a difficult time getting it."

"He didn't seem surprised or upset?"

"No."

"Did he ask why?"

"No."

"Did you try to explain?"

"No."

"I don't like it. He should want to move it along. Do you think he filed something on his own? Usually they want to get it done as soon as they can unless they think the case is a loser," Bill said.

"Not likely. His case is fifty-fifty. We've seen this before…"

"But his reaction is wrong. He should have at least asked questions." Bill stared out his window. "He may not care what happens with the case."

"I'll keep an eye on it, Bill."

Bill continued reading the paper.

THIRTEEN

Ryan got to the fourth floor at immigration where Ms. Calderon was waiting with her husband Roger Steiger.

"Where's Mr. Sorrelli?"

"He can't make it. Don't worry. You're in good hands. Let's see the evidence that your marriage is real."

Ms. Calderon was there for an interview to prove that her marriage to Roger was bona fide. This was their second interview. It was referred to in the trade as a "Stokes Interview." During a Stokes the parties are usually questioned separately. The answers are compared to see if they match. When they don't, the parties are given a chance to explain the discrepancies.

During the first interview it came out that Ms. Calderon had found her husband Roger on the Bowery in New York where he was a homeless alcoholic. She had a large apartment in Washington Heights in northern Manhattan and she had offered to give him a place to live so long as he stayed sober and helped her with the children and chores. Since he was a United States citizen, he was able to sponsor her once they married.

In order to have a marriage application approved, it's necessary to prove that the parties are legally married and have the intent to reside together as husband and wife. There was no question that they were legally married and that they lived together, but there was a question as to whether they really intended to reside together as a married couple or whether this was a marriage of convenience.

"Did you hand in the appointment notice to the receptionist?"

"Yes," the husband answered. "They already called us once. He said if we weren't ready when he called again he would deny the case. The guy who came out was real nasty."

"Did you get his name?"

"Yes. Officer Baker."

Ryan reviewed the evidence.

They had photos together including some Coney Island beach shots with the children. All the photos were of her family and friends, and there seemed to be only a few with him. They had a joint bank account in both names but when he went through the canceled checks, they showed only her signature. The amount of money seemed realistic. They had a pile of mail and Ryan skimmed over it.

"Remember," Ryan said. "Answer the questions in as few words as possible. Listen to the questions and answer only the questions…"

"Yeah. Yeah. We know the routine," the husband said.

The door opened and Baker came out and called them in.

They sat down and he swore the couple in. He looked at Ryan and turned his head from side to side. "You remember the rules counselor?"

"Yes, sir."

"Don't call me 'sir'. Call me Officer Baker."

"Yes, Officer Baker."

"They sat down and Baker made sure Ryan sat away from his clients.

"Mr. Steiger. Why did you marry this woman?"

"Originally, security and family."

"You're the first person who came before me, ever, that didn't say 'love'."

"You asked me why I married her, not how I feel about her now."

Rose Calderone lightly touched his hand.

Baker looked through the mail and found a letter from AA. "I see you go to Alcoholics Anonymous."

"Yes," Roger said.

"How long you off the wagon?"

"About three years. Since I started living with Rose here."

"Where do you attend the AA meetings?"

"The one near Herald Square."

"Are you still an alcoholic?"

"I'll always be an alcoholic. That's the way it is for all of us. I'm not drinking now."

"How do you get there?"

"The number 1 train to 34th Street and I walk about two avenues east to the address."

"How did you meet your wife?"

"She found me. I was living in the Bowery, homeless but picking up work here and there from the kitchen supply places. She offered me a roof and a hot meal for some work. I had to stop drinking. She made it clear from the get-go, she wouldn't put up with that."

"What was she doing there?"

"She was shopping for some kitchenware and I was helping loading and unloading for tips. We got into a conversation, and I helped her to the apartment with the delivery and installation of her purchases. She tried to tip me and I refused. She invited me for dinner instead. Later she offered me a room to live in."

"Did she do it under the condition that you marry her and sponsor her for a green card?"

"No. She asked me to help with the housework and the children to carry my way. After a few months she said if we're going to live together we should be married."

"Do you know that it's a crime to defraud the government by way of a fake marriage? It's a felony and you can go to prison."

"I know."

"The standard is whether they intend to reside together as husband and wife," Ryan said.

"Don't tell me my job, *counselor*. I've been doing this since you were in grade school." He sat back. "Now, Mr. Steiger. It looks to me like you'll leave her once she gets the green card."

"That's not going to happen. I have a life. The kids look to me as a father."

"Where is the biological father of her children?"

"He is not here," Rose said.

"I wasn't taking to you."

"He's in the Dominican Republic," the husband said. "He was deported on a drug charge years ago. They weren't married. I never met him and he seems to take no interest in the kids. Never calls. Doesn't send money. Doesn't seem to want in. The kids are U.S. citizens and Rose has offered to fly them down, but he doesn't seem to want it. Rose discussed it with his sister a few times, but they're not interested. I don't understand him."

"My notes say that you and your wife reside in separate bedrooms."

"That's right."

Baker turned to the husband. "Do you love this woman?"

"I love having a family and a home and people who care."

"So you don't have sexual relations..."

"Under the Stokes consent agreement my clients don't have to answer intimate questions," Ryan added.

"I told you to shut up, counselor. I know my job." He went back to Roger. "So you sleep separately."

"Yes. She snores and it's better for the kids, but we get some in now and then if you know what I mean."

Baker went through the pictures. "I'm not going to separate you. You'll be notified by mail."

When they left everyone seemed confused.

Rose looked at Ryan. "What happened?"

"I'm not sure. Usually they separate couples and ask them questions to see if the answers match. If he denies the case he has to write a decision detailing each discrepancy. He can't do that without questioning you both and recording it. On the other hand, he might write a decision just based on the way you met and married. We would then have a legal question and it would be a matter to fight on appeal. Either he'll approve the case on the evidence submitted, send it for an investigation or he'll deny it solely on the facts that you gave. He's a tough guy. We'll see. He gave me a hard time on the last case I had with him but approved it."

"How long until we get the decision?" the husband asked.

"Hard to say. It depends on how busy he is. An approval should come quickly. He needs more time to write a decision if he denies it."

* * *

Adara locked the door when the last person left for the day. She pulled Hamid and Naib's files and sat at her deck as she went through them. She noticed that they both had the same address in Brooklyn. No surprise there. She was aware that often several aliens would share a small apartment or house to save money.

There was an envelope attached to a form that Hamid had signed to extend a work card. She noticed that it was mailed from Newark, New Jersey even though it had a Brooklyn return address. She remembered the remark about the warehouse in Newark. It could mean that he had been there for some business and mailed the letter there.

She kept looking deep into the file. She came across an older envelope with a full Newark address. Someone had mailed Hamid some original documents at that address and he had used that envelope when he left the papers at the office. That address was nowhere else to be found. Still not important enough, she thought. If he didn't think it was important, why should she?

Something didn't fit. If they worked there, why didn't they use that address? Adara googled the address and found that it was a warehouse for food and tobacco products distribution. This made sense.

Adara looked at another envelope and saw that it was mailed from Lahore, Pakistan. That got her attention. If they were Jordanian, why would they get papers from Pakistan? It could be nothing but might be more.

Adara pulled both files, made two photocopies of the envelopes and important documents from both cases and put the copies into an envelope. She took the envelope home with her.

She was in a hurry to get to the federal building early before the line to enter really became long. She wanted to be among the first at 7:00 a.m. when the doors opened. There was always a rush of people trying to get into the building each morning. She knew that it would be better to go after lunch for something like filing papers, but that was not her purpose.

As Adara entered the federal building with the papers, she stood directly behind a man with similar papers. He was a middle-aged man dressed casually as he meekly walked up to the metal detector.

A guard stopped the man. "Show me your ID."

The man handed him a green card and a Haitian passport.

"What's your purpose for coming here today, sir?"

"I come to file paper."

"Do you have an appointment, sir?"

"No. I told I have to file paper today. Here is."

"We can't let you in without an appointment."

"But paper says I have to file by today."

"You'll have to file it by mail."

"But I'll miss today."

"Sorry, sir. I can't let you in. It isn't even 7:30. You have time."

"Time for what? How? If I don't file today, my papers for my wife will be denied."

"You should have thought about that before."

"What am I going to do?"

"You'll have to get an infopass online."

"What's a infopass?"

"It's an appointment you can get from your computer."

"But I don't have a computer."

"There's one inside."

"Can I use it?"

"No. You can't get in without an appointment or an infopass."

"Please let me in. I just need to file one paper. It says so on the paper."

"Sorry, sir. You'll have to go."

As he was about to leave, Adara stopped him. "Give me the papers. I will file them for you."

"I don't know you."

"I'm going to do you and the government a favor. Wait across the street in McDonalds and I'll bring you the receipt in about thirty minutes."

"Why should you do this?"

"It's nothing for me."

"Thank you, miss."

"It's nothing."

Adara's turn came a moment later. She leaned over to put her purse, watch and other items into a bin for scanning, being careful to show the guards as much cleavage as possible. She hoped the guard would not ask for an appointment letter or an infopass.

The same guard went over to her with a big smile on his face. "How are you doing this morning?"

She gave him a very big smile. "Good, now that I've seen you."

"Whenever you come here, you make my morning."

"Well. When I see you I feel so safe. Strong men make me feel safe. Men in uniform excite me."

"When I see you I feel so…something."

She laughed. "Don't get fresh now. I'll forget what I came here for."

"What did you come here for?"

"Just to file some papers."

"Go right ahead."

He waved her through.

Adara went directly to the sixth floor cafeteria and bought a coffee. She saw Mark Auburn and went over to him. He was finishing his breakfast and had a stack of small cards with Arabic writing on one side and English on the other. He looked at the cards and seemed to be talking to himself.

"What a surprise to see you," she said.

"I hear you're still working for those bandits?"

"If I thought you were serious, I'd be worried."

"You know I love you guys."

"Need any help with your Arabic?"

"If my wife finds out that I got help from you, she'd kick me out of the house. I'd soon need help from a matrimonial lawyer. Ah. I need it anyway. What are you here for?"

"I came to file some papers, but as long as you're here I have a couple of things to discuss with you. I'm a damsel in distress."

"Do you think I'm a knight in shining armor?"

"Close enough. I think you're someone who will know how to fix my problem."

"Sit. I'm listening."

Adara sat down and put down the papers she was carrying.

"I smell a rat and no one else does."

"Okay."

"I have two or three political asylum applicants that I think are involved in something."

"What something?"

"I don't know. Call it intuition but I think they're casing the area around the courthouse. It could be something about the Imam's trial."

"Why do you say that?"

"I'm guessing."

"Oh."

"But the things they say bother me. They're definitely planning something. They don't care about the result of their cases, just the time they can stay here and work."

"That could make sense financially. They may just want to save some money and return home."

"Strangely enough I believe that one has a real political asylum case. He was a real officer in the Jordanian army. The documents are real or the best forgeries I've ever seen."

With that Auburn sat up.

As they talked, watching from the other end of the cafeteria, Officer Lukens sat with another officer. "Why do the women always get the hot guys like that?"

"Let's go upstairs and talk," Auburn said to Adara.

They went up to his floor. Because he waved her through, no one asked a question and she signed in and got a sticker for her chest with the word "Visitor." Auburn had an office as well organized as her own.

"You have a wonderful office," she said.

He smiled, opened the envelope and started to read through the papers. He took out Naib's preliminary asylum application and was amazed. He did not want to give any information away but thought that she had given them more information than a dozen agents had obtained.

They spoke for a few minutes. Auburn took some notes on a pad and placed them with the papers. Adara explained what she had heard on the intercom.

"You know you can get the boys in trouble for doing this? It's against the code of legal ethics."

"They are not doing it, I am. Anyway, you have handled cases against our clients in the past and I saw your character. You're an honest man and I don't think you would hurt us. As for these clients, I feel that they are planning something very bad. I wish I could be more specific."

"I'll look into it. As for Bill and Tony, I don't think they've done anything actionable here. This is what lawyers do."

Adara took out a business card, wrote a phone number on it and handed it to Auburn. "This is my cell number. Look at what's here and call me if you need help with this. It's better if you call me after work. When we start the new case, I can get you more."

"Bill and Tony should know you're here. Are you afraid for your job?"

"Not yet. They don't know. I don't want to get them into trouble. I wouldn't be doing this if I didn't have a real reason to worry, but I'm not worried about my job."

"Adara, what you are telling me is that you have no specific facts, just their chatter and that's only pieces here and there."

"I grew up with people like this. They will smile at you one moment and slit your throat the next. I couldn't live with myself if I didn't do something."

"I'll look into it, but you have to discuss this with the boys."

"I'll discuss it with Bill first. Tony might go nuts. By the way, I'm sorry to hear that you have problems at home."

"Don't be. Long time coming. Between home and retirement, I may need to reinvent myself."

"We might discuss that too. Call if you need an ear. Just don't become an immigration lawyer."

"Sure."

Adara left, went to the eighth floor and filed the Haitian's papers and then gave the man the receipt on her way back.

* * *

The next evening, Roger Steiger showed up for his AA meeting a bit late and took a seat. From across the room a man got up and walked over, sat next to him and held out his hand. Roger shook it. "Hello. I'm Baker. Remember me?"

"Sure. From immigration."

"Call me Sam." Baker handed Steiger an envelope. As Steiger opened it he saw that it contained an approval of his application for his wife's green card application.

"It's usual to mail it, but I thought you would be here. The card will be in the mail in a couple of months."

"Thank you."

The counselor running the meeting started. He pointed to Baker. "I've never seen you before. Would you start please?"

Baker stood up. "Sure. My name is Sam and I'm an alcoholic…"

163

FOURTEEN

Ryan put on his best pair of laundered blue jeans and a white oxford button-down-collar shirt. He liked the way he looked and put on a blue double-breasted blazer. He was concerned about fitting in.

"You look fine," Rachel said.

"This is the first social event since I've been working there. I want to dress nice but not overdo it."

"Well, you look very…. Republican. Perfect for a Sunday luncheon at the country club."

"Where have I heard that before? Ha. But what about the Sorelli family club?"

Rachel took his arm and gave him the look. "You look fine. Stop this. They need you more than ever. You're doing a great job."

"A need can be filled. I want to earn their trust and respect."

"You earned my father's and that was one hell of a job. Let's go."

Rachel was a cute dark-haired woman in her early twenties with about fifteen extra pounds on her tush, a bit short but just right for Ryan. He had a few extra on his tush, too, and neither seemed to mind.

She was attractive but was not getting any offers for modeling. She wore a loose sweater in an attempt to hide the few extra pounds. It didn't work.

They drove through Queens and stopped to pick up Adara.

As Adara walked to the car in her high heels and skintight dress, Rachel wondered if she could actually get into the car without splitting a seam. Ryan wondered how she could breathe with a blouse that tight.

Ryan introduced them as Adara got into the back.

"Good to meet you," Rachel said as she turned to give Adara a good look-over. "Ryan didn't tell me how attractive you are."

"You have a wonderful man there," Adara said. "Have you been going together long? Ryan doesn't talk much about his personal life."

Rachael wondered whether she had competition. Adara was a woman who it would be hard to compete with, at least figure to figure. She decided she wasn't going to eat anything tonight. She would start her diet there and then.

"Thank you, Adara. Ryan is wonderful. We're so happy together. I've heard a lot about you. Ryan says you make the office run like clockwork and you do a great job."

"He's exaggerating. Everybody does their job and things works well. I just do mine. I understand that you are in law school."

"Yes. I'll be starting second year. I hope to go to work for a nonprofit where I can use my skills to help people."

"That's very noble of you. My advice is to make sure you can pay the bills first. If you make enough, you can use some of your money for good. If you make only enough to live on, you will be able to do much less than you want."

Rachel gave Adara a surprised stare. "You don't value charity work, do you?"

"Oh I do. It's wonderful when someone is secure enough to do charity work. I know what it's like to have nothing. My family lost everything under Saddam Hussein. I never had the luxury to do charity work. It took us years to catch up in America. We got help from the Hebrew Immigrant Aide Society and our cousins here. I couldn't think of helping anyone else until I could stand on my own two feet first."

"We have the luxury of being born here. Our families came a long time ago, and I appreciate the advantages we have. Others should have them too."

"We have to protect what we have before we can help others."

"If we don't help others, we can never be secure."

Ryan interrupted. "So do you think Tony's mother will cook a good dinner?"

"Don't try to change the subject," Rachel said. "Adara and I are having a discussion. How else are we to get to know each other?"

Oh shit, Ryan thought. "I hear that Tony's mother is the best cook in Brooklyn, and that's saying a lot," he said.

"Working for a nonprofit is a noble goal, Rachel. Americans have that luxury."

"Are you meeting your boyfriend at Tony's mother's house?" Rachel asked.

"No. I'm between boyfriends."

"I'm sure you have no trouble meeting men."

"Meeting isn't my problem. But meeting the right man is no easy task."

Rachel smiled a bit too much. "Yes. You're an attractive woman. I'm sure the men would line up for a chance to date you."

"Thank you. So are you, but I don't think I would be interested in anyone who would line up for me. I need a man who would charge in and push the others out of the way. I want a man who'll be there for me when I need him. Not many of those around. Most men want to pay for a dinner and then they expect you to sleep with them. Those men are a dime a dozen."

"I'm sorry Ryan hasn't told you more about us."

"When we work, we work. I haven't been on the job long enough but everyone will meet you tonight," Ryan said. "Tony knows you're coming."

"You know, Adara, Ryan has told me so little about you and Bill and Tony. Ryan needs to be a bit more vocal," Rachel said.

"How did you meet?"

"Blind date."

Ryan wished he had brought some Zantacs.

When they arrived a bit early at Tony's mother's house, the women insisted on staying with Ryan as he looked for a parking space. Neither wanted to be alone with Tony's mother.

The house was an attached house on a street that consisted of row houses in an area known as "Bath Beach." Tony's mother's ancient Ford sedan was in the driveway. It was not easy to find a parking spot, and it took awhile.

As they entered the house Tony stood there in faded jeans, a black tee shirt and an apron that said "Don't expect marriage." The living room was dominated by a French-style couch covered with plastic and Lladro figurines here and there next to pictures of the various saints. One table was filled with photos of the family growing up. Ryan looked around and was reminded of his grandmother's apartment in Brighton Beach Brooklyn when he was a child, minus the saints, of course. He thought about how his grandmother's place was so clean that she wouldn't allow anyone into the living room.

Behind the living room was the dining room where an elaborate table was set up. There were about two chairs too many around it.

"Come on in. You must be Rachel." Tony gave her a hug. Ryan pulled her away.

"It looks like you're prepared for a wedding," Rachel said.

"Don't forget about me," Adara said as she gave Tony a bigger hug and pressed her breasts into his chest. "I hope that apron is suppose to be humorous."

Tony's mother burst into the room. "Hi, I'm Rosa." Rosa was a gregarious woman of about sixty with too much dyed black hair done in a bouffant. She had obviously enjoyed her own cooking a little too much over the years. "Adara! Wonderful to see you." She gave Adara a polite hug. "You must be Ryan." She gave him a polite hug. "I hope you came hungry." And she turned to Rachel. "And who is this?"

"This is my almost fiancée, Rachel."

"Fiancée? Ryan is a lucky man. And what's this 'almost' business? Tell him he's almost going to lose you if he doesn't chuck the almost stuff."

"You're too kind. Ryan is saving for a ring." Rachel took her hand.

"Come. There's all sorts of food and drinks to start. We set up in the backyard," Tony said.

Tony led them outside to the postage stamp-sized backyard that was furnished with a table and some lawn chairs. The table was filled with cheese and crackers, grapes and other small fruits and vegetables. Tony got them all drinks.

Adara sipped her club soda and took a few grapes. "You have such a wonderful place, Rosa. It's always a pleasure to visit. I can see that Tony had a good childhood here."

"Yes. Tony is such a good boy. I'll get some of his pictures to show you."

As Rosa got up Tony said, "Please Mama, maybe another time. Nobody wants to see old photos. Please!"

Adara turned to Ryan and Rachel. "She shows them every year anyway. Tony resists but ends up telling everyone about the pictures."

The albums came out and as Rachel opened one book, Tony explained, "That was my dog Mr. Peabody, named after the cartoon character. He was the smartest dog ever. He understood when my parents talked so they started to talk in Italian to fool him. He figured that out too. He was bilingual."

"I thought bilingual dogs said 'meow'," Ryan said.

"Who was that?" Rachel pointed to a picture of a heavy-set man.

"That was my father. He died while I was in law school. He had diabetes and didn't take proper care of himself. He loved food and ate too much." Tony took a cracker and cut a large piece of cheese and swallowed it in one bite.

Rosa brought Ryan and Rachel glasses of wine and sat down next to Rachel. "So. You're both Jewish. It's so important for a couple to share the same religion. Tony's father and I always had our Catholic faith to support us."

"Mama. Dad wouldn't go to church unless you dragged him by the ear."

"Oh, that's not true. He was a good practicing Catholic."

"Tony has an older brother and sister who both married Protestants," Adara whispered to Rachel. "A big family scandal."

"I heard that. The children will be brought up Catholic," Rosa said as she stood up, straightened her dress, picked up her chin and went in for more food.

"We'll see," Tony said when Rosa was out of the room. "I'm not getting in the middle of that."

The front door bell rang and Rosa went to answer it. "Bill! I'm so glad you could make it."

Bill turned and looked at the taxi as it pulled away and wondered if it was too late to take it home. He leaned over to give Rosa a peck, and Rosa grabbed him and gave him a big hug, stuffing her oversized breasts into his oversized chest. "Oh, come on. Give Rosa a real hug."

Bill tried to comply. "I bet you have the best meal in all of New York."

"Always the best for you, Bill. Can I get you a glass of wine?"

"I think a Jack Daniels on the rocks would be better."

"I don't think I have that."

Bill handed her a bag. "Here. You do now. You didn't last year so I bought a bottle."

As they entered the backyard, everyone said hello and Tony got up to make a place for Bill near the food. Bill started to catch up. Rosa brought him the drink and Bill put half of it away immediately.

Bill leaned towards Rachel and took her hand. "And who is this?" Ryan explained.

"I see why Ryan kept you a secret. He doesn't trust Tony or me." Bill kissed her hand.

"You're sweet," Rachel said.

As they went into the house for dinner, Rosa insisted that Bill sit at the head of the table. "As the head of this family, at least at work, Bill should sit in a place of honor."

"Nah, Rosa. You don't have to butter me up. Tony is great and that's enough for me."

"Sit here!" As she pushed him, he flopped into the head chair. Rosa went into the kitchen.

Adara went into the kitchen after her. "Let me help you, Rosa."

"How wonderful. But it's not necessary."

"Oh yes it is. I would feel terrible if I didn't help in some way."

Bill took out a pill from his pocket and popped it into his mouth.

"Are you feeling all right?" Ryan asked.

"Just a Zantac."

"Can I have one too?"

Rachel asked Ryan and Bill, "What about Tony's siblings?"

"One lives in Boston and the other in Los Angeles. You'll have to wait to meet them," Bill said. "I think they wanted to be as far away as possible but couldn't find work in Antarctica."

Rachel sighed. "I'm so happy that Ryan is working in a field where he's able to help people. Immigration law is so noble."

"I think it's the best area of law," Bill said. "In criminal law you're helping the scum of the earth, and in nineteen out of twenty cases they're guilty and you're just trying to get the best deal. In matrimonial law the marriage is dead and the lawyers are paid to beat up the other spouse. Everyone suffers, even the kids. The lawyers get rich. In accident law the lawyers try to make a mountain out of a molehill."

"Aren't you the cynic?" Rachel replied. "And what about immigration law? It's altruistic and noble of you to help the downtrodden immigrants."

"I don't believe in altruism. That's the way people justify things to themselves when what they're really doing is trying to make themselves feel good. These are people who want to feel superior to those they profess to help. Doing the right thing is different. That takes courage even when you feel shitty at the end."

"You mean if someone is poor it's wrong to help them?"

"That depends what you mean by help. Usually *altruists* expect other people to pay for and do the work of helping other people. If you give someone an opportunity to work or better themselves, it's different. That would be doing the right thing."

"Okay, Bill," Rachel said. "But some people just can't work or got a bad deal in life. Shouldn't society help them?"

"But that's not what happens. Society gives them help and then they get stuck in a bad place. It becomes hard to give up what they get and move to a better place. It holds them back. In the long run, these people are hurt and the tax money that's paid to support these programs holds everyone else back."

Rachel took a raw carrot and passed one to Bill. "But isn't helping people a good in and of itself?"

Bill refused the carrot and took a piece of garlic bread. "People say that, but they're wrong. Usually when you help someone they resent it and you weaken them. Sometimes the right thing is to let them struggle on till they get it right. Sometimes you help. There's no one answer for everyone, but I can assure you if you're doing it for altruistic reasons, you're doing it for your own reasons and not theirs."

"I think it's fine to help people just because they need it," Ryan said.

"I agree," Rachel said.

"Mr. Zalmanski has some unusual ideas," Ryan said.

"The people who come through our office are coming to America not for altruism but for work and opportunity. I love them for it," Bill said. "But if they're coming here to game the system or because they want to bring America down, they can get the fuck out."

"There you go again Bill with the colorful language," Rosa said from the kitchen.

"Surely we have enough compassion to help people come here and start a new life," Rachel said.

"You're waiting for Ryan to save enough for a ring to get engaged. Is that so?" Bill asked.

"Yes. How did you know that?"

"Are you willing to forgo the ring and give that money to the poor? Are you that *altruistic*?"

"I don't see what one thing has to do with the other."

Bill smiled. "When we have this conversation a year from now you will see it differently."

Adara came in. "I heard that. Bill's correct. People confuse altruism with doing the right thing. I'll give you an example. We have some Jordanian asylum applicants. Some in our office want to do the altruistic thing and help them when the correct thing might be to stop them before they do something stupid."

"Do you know that as a fact?" Tony asked.

"No."

"When you say 'correct' do you mean 'politically correct'?" Rachel asked.

Bill laughed. "Political correctness is lying to someone to make them feel better. It should be called 'bullshit'."

"Oh, Bill. There's that colorful language again," Rosa said. "What am I going to do with you?"

"In order to act on your info, I need particularly articulable facts." Tony took a drink of wine. "That's the legal definition. I can't just go to the police on feelings."

"Adara's feelings are usually correct," Bill said. "But Tony's right. It's just not enough."

Rosa and Adara went into the kitchen and brought the food into the dining room. By each place setting they put a bowl of minestrone soup. In the center of the table was a large salad with prosciutto and cheese, a steaming plate of lasagna, several plates of vegetables and more fresh hot Italian garlic bread with olive oil. In front of Rachel, Rosa placed a plate of broiled salmon.

Rachel pecked.

"Is everything okay?" Rose asked Rachel.

"I'm kosher and I'm going to stick with the veggies."

"I made the baked salmon just for you."

"Thank you, Rosa. How thoughtful."

Everyone else dug in, and for a while the talking stopped.

Rosa sat next to Bill. "I bet you aren't use to a good home-cooked meal."

"Rosa. If I ate your cooking every day, I'd gain fifty pounds in no time."

"I'll take that as a compliment. It's so nice having you here. I don't see you enough. I have plenty of recipes. Why don't you come over more often so I can cook for you?"

Underneath the table Tony kicked his mother.

* * *

Hamid and Naib arrived at the warehouse in New Jersey. As they entered several men were working on food carts in the main garage. No one said a word or acknowledged their presence. The men were repairing one cart, cleaning several others and stocking a few. A truck was backed into the garage, and one man was transferring frozen food and dry ice to the carts.

Hamid and Naib went into the basement and over to the box. They spoke in Arabic.

They lifted the box a bit. "This is very heavy. It will be dangerous getting this into Manhattan. Can you read the writing?"

"No. It's in Korean."

"What does it say?"

Naib ran his fingers over the letters. "The top is the name of the facility where it came from and the rest are warnings. I don't really know what it says."

"It's dangerous enough just to move it."

"We already moved it almost all the way from Pakistan. It went on a freighter buried in cheap shoes all the way to Mexico. We trucked it to the border and from the border to here," Naib gloated. "It is fitting that we detonate it in New York on September 11th."

"There is a nuclear power plant north of New York City. We could do it there instead."

"Isn't the whole point to punish America? The world will know what we did," Naib said. "We will punish the American people, but we will

172

especially punish the government. The American people will understand that the government they support is responsible for this punishment. We will not deny responsibility. We will revel in it. It will be difficult for America to retaliate. It is Allah's will. The whole point is to show the world that we won't allow America to rebuild the site. This will show the world that the Islamic State is the caliphate. Fighters from all over the world will flock to join us. We will regain our losses. We should stick with the plan."

You can count on us all," Hamid said.

"Allah has shown us the way. We have a way to bring this into the artery of American government. What better way to make this statement? I may be the one to sacrifice myself. I will decide this matter. I have the know how to detonate this."

"It is dangerous enough to get this through the tunnel into Manhattan. You now want to get it into a highly secured building. For what, to show the world you can?"

"It's no longer dangerous. We have the perfect cover. We can bring this in a food cart and detonate it in the middle of a workday. This is my decision. You know our plan for this."

"We have two months until September 11th. You are in charge, but I will try to talk some sense into you. We should do it sooner. It's too dangerous to wait."

"It will have the most effect then. We can take care of the other thing first."

"You are the boss."

They opened a panel on the side. Naib pointed to an indentation. "The detonator goes here. The wires automatically attach when it snaps in, and then the timer can be set. A baby could do it."

FIFTEEN

Carmen got up and escorted Mr. Patel from the waiting room to her office.

"So, did you bring the paperwork I asked for?"

"I couldn't get everything. Since I work for myself I couldn't get the job letter."

"An accountant's letter will do. Tony explained that to you."

"I didn't understand."

"If your accountant calls me, I'll explain what we need." She handed him a form letter from her drawer. "Show this to him."

"Sure."

"What about the tax transcripts?"

"I don't know how to get them."

"Your accountant can get them for you. We explained this to you."

"Oh. I'll get it."

"You don't show enough money on your taxes to complete your parents' cases. Your lifestyle shows me you make enough. You support a mortgage and a family. You drive a new Cadillac. If you just reported this income, we'd be fine. Did you find a co-sponsor with the taxes to back this up?"

"Not yet."

"I can't send this in unless it's complete."

"Can't we try, Carmen? I would like to bring my parents here soon. They keep asking me why it's taking so long. I'm embarrassed to talk to them about it. In India we show our parents great respect. This is not good."

"It's taking so long because we don't have the papers we need. If I send these in, they'll just be rejected. You own a business. I know you make enough money to do this. All I need are your taxes to prove it. Okay. Let's talk about a co-sponsor." Carmen wrote a list and handed it to Mr. Patel. The list asked for information from a co-sponsor including taxes, a job letter, and proof of savings. "Without a co-sponsor and all these items, we just can't go on."

"Why didn't someone here ask for these things before? You know, my friend brought his parents here in just three months."

"Impossible. These cases are taking about ten months. You're double that already because we don't have the financials to complete it. My notes show we asked you for these papers several times."

"Please help me. You can do it."

"Not without the proper papers."

"Try. Please. You know how important this is to me."

"Listen. I'm not asking for these papers to give you a hard time. It's easier for me to mail this in and wait for a rejection. I need it because the government is asking for it. If they don't get what they want, I can't bring your parents here."

"I need my parents."

"What about your brother? It says here he might be a co-sponsor."

"He drives a taxi and only makes a couple of hundred dollars a week."

"Impossible. He doesn't want to pay the taxes either."

"My friend went to Carlin and Kaminsky, and they say they can do the whole case in three months."

"You can try them but I do a lot of these, and it's impossible."

"But they told my friend they can do this in three months. They are well known. You can see their name all over the subway trains."

Carmen sat back and put her palms behind her head. "I've heard a million stories about friends doing this or that. When I ask for the proof, it's never there. People talk."

"But I trust my friend."

"Trust me. I want to help you, and I want you to tell your friends I did right by you."

"Then bring my parents here."

* * *

Mo showed up at the food cart on time. Naib had already set it up and begun serving customers. Mo took over and Naib went inside and pulled a small curtain to block him from the public as he took a rifle from a cardboard tube. He checked the scope, the ammunition the operating mechanism.

Naib opened a small window at the back of the cart and looked at the angle to the courthouse in Manhattan. He was pleased with the angle.

* * *

In the next office Tony sat down with Mr. and Mrs. Torres.

Maria came in to translate.

Tony opened their file. "In order to complete the case, the U.S. Consulate in Juarez, Mexico has requested a DNA test for Mr. Torres and your son." Tony turned to Mr. Torres. "They want to make sure that you're his biological father. Once that's done he'll get his green card quickly."

Mrs. Torres looked ashen.

"Sure," Mr. Torres said as his wife looked hard at Tony and nodded from side to side. "Just tell me what to do."

Mrs. Torres spoke a bit too loudly. "I don't think Juan can get it done in Mexico. He's only four, and I can't get him to a doctor. He will panic if they have to stick him with a needle."

Tony smiled. "It's easy, Ms. Torres. Just take him to one of the doctors on the list with this letter and some ID for him, and we're good to go. They'll just take a swab from the inside of his cheek. Your husband needs to go to an office in New Jersey for the same thing. Piece of cake."

"I don't think he'll allow blood to be taken."

"Don't be silly," Mr. Torres said. "We'll get it done even if I have to fly down myself."

"We don't live near a big city. Can't we just tell them it's too difficult for me to bring my child to one of these doctors?"

"There not even doctors. These are lab technicians. It really should be no problem for you," Tony said.

"Please, Mr. Sorrelli. Can we find a way around it?"

"I don't think so. Here's the information. See what you can do."

When Mr. and Mrs. Torres left, Maria said to Tony, "Don't you understand? It's not his son. He thinks he is. The DNA test will ruin their marriage."

"Then it won't happen. He won't get the green card."

"We've got to find another way to proceed."

"She just got her green card. If we can pass the blood test, the kid will have his green card in about sixty days. If we file another application through her, there's a three-year waiting list. If we do this as his stepchild… how am I going to tell them that without telling them everything?"

"I'll have her file an I-130 and we won't tell the husband." An I-130 is the form someone files to sponsor a relative.

"Sooner or later he'll ask. We'll have to charge them for this."

"I know the fees and what to do." She shrugged her shoulders and left.

* * *

Carmen and Ryan went down for lunch and walked up two blocks to a salad bar. They lined up and each picked from an array of vegetables and meats in this design-your-own-salad place.

Carmen was in no hurry to get back to the office. "Let's eat at the area in back of the federal building. There are benches there. It's too nice to eat inside."

They went to the area where they found a bench to themselves in the shade of a tree. As they ate and watched people come and go, they saw several reporters join a press conference in front of the federal courthouse. A podium was set up and reporters were waiting in chairs prepared for the event. Photographers with their cameras were waiting in back.

"What time is Hite going to come out and blow his own horn?" Carmen asked.

"Soon, I think. Every few days he makes some statement. I think even the news shows are getting tired of this. I ignore it all. That bastard. All he wants is publicity."

Carmen laughed.

As they sat and ate they noticed Ali walk through the crowd. As he walked slowly, he occasionally took a photo with his cell phone.

"Look, isn't that our client?" Carmen asked.

As Ali saw them he took off his backpack and held it low. He turned his back and walked in such a way that his face could not be seen, but it was too late.

177

"I see him too," Ryan said.

"What's he doing here?"

"He isn't a tourist."

"We should tell the police. He's not taking pictures to send home to mama."

Ryan looked at her. "Tell them what? That our client took some pictures in a public place and left?"

"Yes. You have a duty to tell the authorities if your client is going to commit a crime. What's in the backpack?"

"You're right on that, but we're not sure it's a crime. It's not anything. If you took a picture would you expect me to report it to the police? If they look at the backpack, what are they going to find, lunch? Maybe his jacket."

"I want to say something anyway. Adara listened in on this guy and she thinks he's up to something."

Ryan thought a moment. "Let's follow him and see what happens."

They stayed well away from Ali as he walked around the square. They saw him walk over to a food cart where he spoke to a young man and was handed a pita wrapped around some meat and salad. He took a few bites and threw the food away.

As Ryan and Carmen neared the cart they looked carefully and noticed nothing. From the corner of his eye Ali noticed them. He looked at the cart, caught Mo's eye and shook his head no. Mo nodded agreement.

Ryan and Carmen went over to a policeman. As the policeman tried to ignore her, Carmen went right up to his face. "Officer, I saw someone we know take several pictures around the square."

"So? Is that supposed to be a crime?"

"I see signs all around town that say, 'See something, say something.' Isn't that correct?"

"You haven't told me anything suspicious."

"He's carrying a backpack. That might be. He also bought some food from the halal cart," Carmen said. "It looks to be like he's casing Foley Square."

"I need more than that to take any action. I can't leave my post. Tell the supervisor over there."

"Where?" Ryan asked.

The policeman pointed and they walked over where there were several people waiting.

"Who's in charge of the police?" Ryan asked.

A policeman responded. "The supervisor will be back in a few minutes."

"We saw something that looks suspicious."

"The supervisor will be back in a moment."

"Who's the supervisor?"

"Officer Alders. He went to his office for a few minutes."

"Where is his office?"

"Police plaza. You can't go there."

"We think we saw something serious," Carmen said. "It can't wait."

"It will have to."

"Don't you want to hear about what we saw?"

"Sure I do, but my boss will be back in a few minutes and you should tell him."

Carmen walked up nose to nose with the officer. "If you can't handle this, what the hell are you doing here? Take me to someone who can."

"Don't push me, lady. Wait right there." He pointed to an area on the side where there were some other officers waiting.

Ryan went over to an officer with sergeant stripes. He was talking on a walkie-talkie attached to his shoulder. "We have a suspicious act to report."

"Who sent you here?"

Ryan pointed to the other police officer.

"He shouldn't have sent you here. This is for coordination only. We're busy."

"But we saw something that could be dangerous."

"The boss will be back in a few moments."

"But this might be urgent," Carmen said.

"What do you need to report?"

"I saw someone we know take some pictures of the square and buy some food at one of the food vendors, and I think it's suspicious. He's carrying a backpack."

"That's it?"

"Yeah."

"Listen. You can wait over there." He pointed to a spot about a block away. "And tell it to the boss when he returns or you can leave. You're interfering with security and if you don't leave, I'll have you removed. Can't you see we're busy?"

"You also said we can wait."

"Not right here."

As they walked away, Ryan and Carmen saw Hite walk out and up to the podium. He mingled with several people as several members of the press lined up for a statement. There were several cameras.

A woman with a badge was watching from the side. Carmen approached her. "Are you with the police?"

"No. FBI. What do you want?"

"We saw someone we knew take some pictures and we want to report it. He's got a backpack."

"Are you kidding?"

"No. Something looks really wrong."

"Where did you see him take them?"

Carmen pointed to the spot and the woman started to look around. She spoke to a police officer, who radioed someone.

"Anything else?"

"Yeah. He bought lunch," Carmen said.

Hite got up to the podium to speak as Naib watched through an open vent in the back of the food cart. Naib held his rifle.

"Today," Hite said, "we completed additional indictments of bankers accused of refusing loans to homebuyers in financially depressed areas. This type of discrimination will not be tolerated. You are witnessing the weight of the law used to protect the American people and show the world that evil will not be allowed to proceed unhindered by the law..."

When the woman realized that she was looking at nothing and starting to imagine things, she turned to Ryan and Carmen. "Nothing's happening here. You're making me nervous for no reason. Please leave the area." She turned and ignored them.

From the food cart, Naib sat and surveyed the area. He carefully watched Carmen and Ryan. When he saw them talking to the police and looking in his direction, he moved away from the window, inserted the rifle in the blueprint tube, quietly left the food cart and blended into the crowd.

* * *

When they returned to the office Ryan and Carmen went into Bill's office and told him what they saw. He called Adara in.

Adara stopped them before they finished. "I don't trust these guys. They're up to no good. I think they're going to suicide bomb the courthouse."

Bill put up his hand to stop her. "How did you get from 'I don't like them' to 'suicide bombers'? You may not like these guys, but that's not the same thing as reporting them as criminals. The police want you to state what they term 'specifically articulable facts.' You don't have any yet. All you have is some eavesdropping that is totally without details."

"We heard Ali and Naib talk on the intercom and they sounded like they're planning something," Carmen said.

"Planning what?" Bill asked. "You don't know a word of Arabic. You just know what Adara told you and that you saw some guy taking pictures and eating lunch. Just what people do every day."

"We're not sure."

"And that's what you want to tell the police? Be real."

"I don't trust these three either," Adara said. "I agree that we don't have much, but we could go on record with the police. If something happens I would feel terrible."

"Why isn't Tony here?" Ryan asked.

"Because he will just argue about how wonderful these new immigrants are and give us a history of all the suspected immigrants in the past who turned out to be wonderful Americans," Carmen said.

"He would stop this conversation," Adara added.

"If we're going to do anything more, we'll need more," Bill said. "We'll need to get them in and get some more evidence. Then we might do something. Bad intentions are not the same thing as a crime." He turned to Ryan. "Didn't they teach you this in law school?"

Ryan continued. "Yes, but bad intentions plus an overt act is a conspiracy and conspiracy to commit a crime *is* a crime. If they have plans to commit a crime and they took photos in furtherance of that crime, we have a case we can bring to the police. We need to get the evidence of the intent. The evidence of the overt act is on the phone."

"You paid attention in law school, I see. Phone pictures are not much evidence," Bill said. "If they see it coming, they'll just delete the pictures."

"Impossible. There'll be a record in the cloud and probably on the phone chip. The police can access it," Ryan said. "Hell, I can access it."

"We can't do anything till we have more. Let's drop it for now." With that Bill waved them all back to work.

Adara went over to Maria and asked her to make appointments for Ali, Naib and Hamid.

* * *

That evening as they got off the Path commuter train in Newark, Naib and Ali walked through the business district and looked at the windows until they were certain that they were not being followed. They stopped at a coffee shop and after a few sips doubled back. They walked a bit more towards the warehouse.

"I'm worried. Those two from the law office saw me taking pictures," Ali said.

"If it comes to it, I'll take care of them. There's nothing to worry about. Taking a few cell phone pictures? The police will laugh," Naib said.

"If you kill them now, it will bring a lot of questions. We need to lay low till September 11th."

"I'll make that decision when necessary. It's not necessary now."

They arrived at the house.

Ali opened a drawer and took out a small green plastic electronic device. He turned it on and an electronic number came on. "It's still safe."

They pushed some boxes away from a corner and removed several boards of sheetrock stored against the wall. That uncovered a hole in the wall around some exposed pipes. It took both of them to pull out the box.

"Why are we looking at this?" Ali asked.

"We need to make sure it's here and in good condition. It would be better to use this now. You know, it's always risky to wait. Something could happen," Naib said.

"Not likely. It's more likely that it will get wet down here."

"However unlikely, it's possible and we need to keep on top of things."

"We need to bring this to the store. It would be safer there and we need to take it into New York anyway."

"No!" Naib said. "We'll bring it directly to the site when we're ready. No one will look for it here. The store is not safe at all. We'll bring it directly to the Freedom Tower."

"Leave it here? I'm afraid that too many people use this place."

"That means that it doesn't look suspicious. It's the perfect place. The government doesn't know we have this place. No one else does. Even if they do, the operation here is legitimate."

"It's not close enough to New York," Ali said.

Naib nodded. "We might not be able to wait. We'll see."

They moved the box back.

* * *

The next day Adara called Auburn's office. His secretary picked up.

"Mr. Auburn, please. This is Adara from Zalmanski and Sorrelli."

"One moment please," the receptionist said.

About thirty seconds later she got back on the phone. "Mr. Auburn can't speak to you. He wants you to know he's too busy because of his lunch plans at Mudville at 12:00. This afternoon is too booked up to get back to you."

"Thanks."

SIXTEEN

Charles Hite stood on the steps of the Federal Courthouse as the press gathered. On the sides were young men and women with signs saying *Hite for Senate.*

"I will make this short. Later today I will formally file papers to establish the Charles Hite for Senate Committee. This is probably no surprise to you. I have also handed the president my formal resignation. It would not be fair to the people of New York if I could not concentrate fully on my duties as the United States Attorney for the Southern District of New York, one of the most important jobs in government. My assistant Renee Curtwright will replace me as acting United States Attorney until such time as the president can nominate and the Senate confirms my replacement. Rest assured that the office is in good hands and that the work in progress will be handled in a professional manner."

The press barked questions at Hite as he smiled, waved and walked away.

* * *

Adara handed Zalmanski an envelope and a flash drive as he left for Mudville. He arrived shortly after noon to find Auburn sitting in a corner booth behind a cup of coffee, reading a menu. Bill sat down opposite him and dropped the envelopes by his side.

"This covers the new guy from Jordan. We haven't filed his case yet, but we will soon. It's more comprehensive that what you got before and includes a new case we're starting for these guys. You can print them in the course of business. You never know. Immigration has most of the stuff on the second file, but you might find something extra in mine. There might be an address or an email or something that can turn into a lead. We scanned everything we have for all three. I don't think Adara heard anything specific enough for you to use, but it might be specific enough to get a search warrant."

"We would need to know what they're planning and where. I just need more."

"If I learn anything, you'll know at once."

"Thanks, Bill. I owe you one."

"Just keep it on the QT. You know my ethical position."

"I'm surprised you're doing this at all. I'll protect you, but if it gets out you could lose everything."

"We've known each other a long time and I trust you to be fair. I also trust Adara's instinct on this one. I feel it too. I think they're up to something."

"No problem. That young attorney you hired was there the other day with one of your secretaries. They're all over the surveillance tapes. What did they say?"

"It seems they saw something funny and tried to tell the police but got stonewalled. That should be no surprise. It might be nothing, but my staff is sure the whole thing stinks."

"Adara came to me."

"She doesn't trust government, but she trusts you."

"I don't know why."

"Because Tony does and she trusts Tony. Do you know her story?"

"No. Well some."

"Most people don't. She wants it that way."

"Whatever you tell me is on confidence."

"Well the short story is that she's a refugee from Iraq, while Hussain was in power."

"I knew that."

"Her father was Christian and her mother Muslim. The father converted in name only to please her family. But when the family practiced Christianity after the marriage, the mother's family tried to have them all killed. They used to celebrate Christmas or something like that. They went to some government official for protection who informed her mother's family. It seems that her own family killed her father. The story isn't all that clear. She blames it on Saddam Hussain because she can't deal with the truth. What's clear is that he disappeared. So did her older brother who was politically active. A lot of people disappeared during those years. Her mother was beaten badly. Adara saw and tried to help her, but as a child she couldn't do much. Some uncle beat her too. Adara has a large scar on her left arm to this day because of that. You don't notice it because she always wears long sleeves. Her father's family payed a smuggler to take the mother and an eight-year-old Adara across the desert by camel to Turkey. They were in danger the whole way. She remembers every detail. They came here as refugees. She grew up here, but she has a lot more scars than the one on her arm."

"Wow. I didn't know that. Does Tony?"

"Yeah, but not the rest of the office. Keep it to yourself. Adara wants it that way."

"No problem."

"By the way. I don't want Tony to know I gave this info to you."

"Count on it."

"I'm going to stay for lunch," Bill said.

"I've got to get back to the office. This might be useful. I'll add them to the files Adara gave me. Thanks."

"I'll cover your coffee."

"I will cover your ass on this. Your help will remain between us." Auburn threw down a couple of dollars. "I never want anyone to claim you tried to bribe me with a cup of coffee."

* * *

Several days later after Tony escorted a client to the door he went to the conference room where Bill, Adara and Jeff Pounders were waiting.

"Sit down, Tony." Jeff pulled himself up and brought a container of coffee over to Tony. "Bill and I have been discussing something extensively. You are playing with fire."

"What are you talking about?"

"Adara and I have given the FBI information about Hamid, Ali, Arafat and Naib. Something's rotten," Bill said.

"I'm here to advise you on the ethical problems you are creating," Jeff said.

"Wait a minute." Tony stood up and leaned against the wall. "No one asked me about this."

"Something stinks and we don't want to be responsible if these guys kill someone or blow themselves up in Times Square," Bill said. "We weren't going to tell you, but Jeff says we have a duty to keep you up to date."

Adara stood up next to Tony and put her hand on his shoulder. "Tony, we love you but sometimes you are just too naïve. These guys are definitely planning something. We don't know what, but I am sure it isn't good."

"I'm here to advise you. Bill felt that it might be better if you were left out of this since you don't know the details. I felt that you're a team and should sink or swim as one."

"What have they been doing?"

"You know everything now. We've given Mark Auburn copies of their files and some details about their discussions in the office. I also have been taking notes about what they say when they think we're not listening," Adara said.

"Are you all crazy? Don't you understand about the attorney-client privilege? This is a sacred space for them."

"Not if they're planning an assassination," Jeff said. "In any event, you have to be on board or remove yourself from the picture."

"How can I do that? This office can't operate without me. I'll have to discuss this with Harold Peters. He's my advisor."

"You can't speak to him," Bill said. "Harold represents the Imam and you might alert them about what we're doing and compromise an FBI investigation."

"You need to stop all work on the questionable cases. Bill will reassign them to Ryan until this matter is resolved. He knows nothing about what's been going on here. Keep him out of the loop."

Tony loosened his tie and took a deep breath. "You two have endangered our careers. We could be disbarred for this. Adara, you have less to lose."

"Just because I'm not a lawyer, don't tell me I'm not part of this team. I share in the profits and I work as hard as any of you. This firm would not be where it is without my efforts."

"It's not the same."

They all looked at Pounders quietly as he continued. "I'm here as a legal advisor. There are ethical and criminal issues here. If nothing happens and the clients get wind of what you're doing there could be serious issues. You do not want to deal with it. If I had been asked about it before I would have told you all to do nothing without more evidence. Everything we're discussing must remain in this room. First, I advise that you discuss this with no one until the ramifications of what's going on sink in. Next I advise you, Tony, not to speak to Peters. You'll put him in an ethical situation and that might tip off the Arabs that they're being watched. If that happens, the FBI could call it obstruction of justice and then we're in a new ball game. Third, Adara, you're not a lawyer and your issues are different, but as a woman I think you might need to be very careful if this info comes out. Anything Tony does to expose this might put you all in danger, but especially you."

"So why the hell did you guys tell me?" Tony asked.

Bill let out a belly laugh. "Don't be stupid. We're a team. That means the good with the bad. We have each other's backs. We have no interest in surprising you."

"I'm sure surprised now."

"Tony, we're doing the right thing," Adara said. "Bill and I couldn't live with ourselves if something came off that we could have prevented."

"This goes against everything I learned in law school. It goes against my better instincts."

"You don't know these people like I do. I suffered and you know. I'm lucky to be alive. I'm lucky to be here. These are violent men who convince themselves that they're right and that everybody else is wrong. They will kill in the name of their religion. I've seen what they can do, and I do not want blood on my hands."

"We have an ethical responsibility not to inform on the clients and I think we should ask for an ethical opinion from the bar association."

"Tony, I'm asking you to wait." Bill opened his drawer and took out an army ranger patch. "I fought in Vietnam and I know what violence and killing is. I don't want to allow them to kill and then claim I'm not responsible in the name of attorney-client privilege. This goes way beyond your feelings. I will insist you do nothing. We'll discuss this in a few days again and we'll see where we are."

They sat there for quite a while.

* * *

Mudville was busy but Tony and Adara managed to find a table in a quiet corner. The waitress came over.

"Hello, Claire. I'll have a Basil Hayden on the rocks. A double please."

"For lunch, Tony?"

"Yeah. And Adara will have a white wine spritzer."

"That's very presumptuous of you," Adara said.

"Was I wrong?"

"No."

Piertowsky and Wong were sitting a few feet away at the bar with half-eaten hamburgers and half-drunk Cokes. As they made eye contact with Tony, Piertowsky and Wong looked at the ground. Wong whispered something and they left some cash on the bar and left.

Tony smiled. "I'm having a difficult time of this. I've never been in this position before. They're talking about me."

"You're wrong. Don't get paranoid."

"I feel like we've done something wrong."

"You didn't. You will get use to it and we'll get things back to normal."

"I don't know how I'll function till then."

"Don't blow this up. We didn't commit a crime. We'll get through this. We all will."

"I appreciate it, but it's not fair."

"What's not fair? That we didn't tell you? Don't tell me about fair. I don't want to belittle this, but you know my story. I'm lucky to be alive. I know what it means to be tough. I need you to be tough. You will win but not if you freak out. The system is not fair, but it's fairer than anything my family experienced in Iraq."

"I know, Adara, and I'm lucky to have you here," Tony said. "This is the first time in my life that I did something that might get me into real trouble."

"You're lucky to have all of us behind you. The only question is whether you can man up to this. You did nothing yet. It's all Bill and me. I see you for the first time a little weak and that can be your downfall. You need to man up to the fight. Bill and I are good with it."

"With all due respect, Adara, you don't have a license to worry about. Bill is getting near retirement age. He has less to lose. Just by knowing about it and doing nothing you have put me in a difficult position."

"Wrong. Bill won't retire until they take him out in a body bag. I will be there as long as you need me. You are my family."

"I'm anxious and I can't concentrate on work."

"You will."

"Not so easy. This thing can overpower me."

Claire returned with their drinks and Tony ordered another drink.

"Tony, you should go slow with the drinks," Claire said.

"Not today."

They ordered some lunch and Tony had the second and a third drink.

"We need to get back to the office," Adara said.

"I can't today. I just need a break."

"Are you a man or a mouse? Squeak up."

"Not the time for humor."

"I'll call Bill and tell him we need some time."

Adara hailed a taxi and took Tony to his apartment and got him into bed. She found a pillow and a blanket and made herself at home on his couch.

Tony's cell phone rang and Adara noticed by the caller ID that it was Viviana. She answered. "Hello, Viviana."

"Adara! I think I called the wrong number."

"No. This is Tony's phone. How can I help you?"

"I just wanted to know how Tony was doing."

"He's doing fine." With that Adara hung up.

* * *

The next evening Adara was setting the table in her dining room. She put out two salads and some bread and looked at the casserole in the oven. It needed another half hour. She took out the wine glasses and a cold bottle of Riesling.

The doorbell rang and she pressed the return buzzer. He came in and took off his jacket and put it behind a dining room chair. He then unclipped his holster and put his gun on the table.

"What did you tell your wife?"

"Just that I needed to stay in the city for work. She doesn't care anyway."

Mark Auburn grabbed Adara. "I've been waiting for this for a very long time." He kissed her passionately.

SEVENTEEN

Viviana looked tense. "Why are you dragging me to New Jersey? You can do this yourself."

Adara sighed. "I just want to take a look at what's going on there. I don't want to go alone."

"What do you expect? That I'll karate chop them if you get into trouble?"

"Don't be silly. I just want to see what's at this address."

They entered Penn Station and found the train to Newark, New Jersey. "You don't need to do this. I don't either."

"I'm not holding a gun to your head, but I don't want to do this alone."

"Why not Tony or Bill?"

"They would try to stop me. We'll just take a look to see what's going on there, and I'll buy you lunch."

They sat silently as the train came out of the tunnel and passed the fields and inlets between New York City and Newark. They passed oil storage tanks and railroad tracks. Adara turned to Viviana. "Bill calls this the soft underbelly of America."

"Bill would know about soft underbellies."

They both laughed.

"Tony hasn't called me."

Adara took Viviana's hand. "That is just the way he is. I tried to stop you, but it just got out of hand."

"I thought we had a connection."

"You thought that because you don't know Tony. He has some growing up to do. Like all men he has the maturity of a sixteen-year-old when it comes to women. If he grew up, I might have been interested."

"I'm sorry."

"Don't be. Did you have fun?"

"Yes, but I felt bad afterward."

"Welcome to the world of big girls." Adara took a map she printed from the computer out of her purse and started to read it. When they got to the station they found a taxi and showed it to the driver.

"Wad? You wand to go dis place ladies?"

Adara bent forward. "We just want to ride by and take a look and come right back."

"Okay, but this meter runs till the ride stops."

"Fine. Let's go. Is it far?"

"Fifteen minutes."

"Go."

They rode through downtown Newark, a depressed shopping area and a well-groomed working class neighborhood, then through an area with housing projects to an area with many vacant lots. When they came to the block on the map, they saw row houses. Several here and there had windows boarded up, but some looked lived in and vibrant. There were abandoned lots here and there.

"This is the address. Please drive by slowly," Adara said.

"Sure, lady."

As they drove by there was nothing to see. The three-story brick house looked as though it was once residential but now was outfitted with commercial doors. The main steps went to the second floor. There was no sign indicating that a business was located there. The house went through the block to the other side. There were curtains on the third story windows. The second story had what looked like paper over the windows.

"Please drive around the block."

The driver did.

In the back there was a fire escape, the third floor of which had plants and some clothes hung out to dry. There were steel gates over every window.

Next to the house was a large vacant yard enclosed by a chain link fence where two trucks were parked. There was a man attaching a food cart to one of them. The back of the other truck was open, and she could see boxes of all sizes stacked inside. The building contained an open garage that was easily two cars wide and at least two deep. It was filled with food carts and boxes. In one corner were two men unloading a flat wagon.

"Nothing unusual here," Viviana said.

"I think you're correct."

"Let's go back."

"Not yet." Adara turned to the driver. Please drive around the block again.

"Sure."

As they drove back around to the front Adara took some cell phone photos. Viviana stayed in the car as Adara got out and walked up to the front. She walked up a flight of brick steps to the main entrance. The front door had three mailboxes. The top apartment looked occupied. The mailbox had several pieces of mail and a Spanish-sounding name. The middle apartment had no name on the box and was empty. Adara went over to the window and looked in through a space in the paper covering. The main room was empty and there were paint cans, sheetrock and tools in places. She went to the ground floor and tried to look in. The windows were completely blocked by white plastic. She could see nothing.

"What did you see?" Viviana asked when Adara got back into the taxi.

"Nothing."

They drove around one more time. When they got to the back again, Adara took several more photos with her phone.

One of the men unloading the truck noticed them. "Arafat," he said.

"Yes?"

"There are a couple of women driving around in a taxi taking pictures of us."

Arafat stood behind one of the carts and shielded himself as he watched the car slowly dive by as Adara took pictures.

"Do you know those ladies?" the man asked.

"Yes, I know one. They're trouble. I need to discuss this with Naib."

* * *

When the women got back to the office they went into Adara's office and closed the door. They sat for a few minutes and looked at each other and then laughed.

Viviana leaned back in her chair, whipped back her hair and pointed to Adara. "You're going to make me crazy. You got me so worked up I expected to find an ISIS terrorist base. Are you going to stop this paranoid stuff now?"

"I'm not paranoid."

"Tony and Bill will think you are. Is it over?"

"For now."

"What does that mean?"

"It means I'll watch them."

"Are you going to tell Bill and Tony?"

"I will."

Viviana smiled. "You owe me a lunch. I want to get back to the office. Should I say hello to Tony?"

"Whatever you want."

"I'll pass today."

Adara went into Bill's office. "Don't yell at me. I just went to Newark."

"Go ahead. Tell me. I would never yell at you."

"You might this time."

When she finished talking to Bill, Adara emailed Auburn. *I took a look at that Newark address and there's some sort of food warehouse there. Nothing sinister.*

Mark was sitting with Robinson as he read the email. He turned to him. "Adara Aden just emailed me." He turned the screen for Robinson to read. "Nothing at that address. I won't waste any further resources on it."

"I would check it out antway."

EIGHTEEN

That next evening on her way home from the office, Adara pushed her way out of the train and went down the stairs onto Roosevelt Avenue. She went into the fruit stand and spent a few minutes picking some fruit, salad mixings and some additional groceries. As she felt the pomegranates, Naib walked up behind her and started to feel them too.

"You should not buy these, lady. They're not ripe and will be sour. I know."

"I can see that. Naib? What are you doing here? How do you know where I live?"

"I don't. It's just a coincidence. I was in the neighborhood to scout out a location for another tobacco store and I saw you come here."

"A one-in-a-million occurrence. I've heard that before."

"Coincidences occur more than you know."

"Yes, just when I'm about to buy a pomegranate."

"I came from the Middle East and we know good pomegranates from bad ones. The bad ones are garbage and need to be thrown away, stamped into the ground. The bad ones need to be destroyed. You should know this too."

"You're following me."

"No, I'm protecting you. You have become very American. You need to examine your roots and learn again where you belong. I will help you. It has been too long. As a good Muslim woman, you will understand."

"You are threatening me."

"No, I am informing you of your duty."

"You are planning something bad and I will stop you."

"You know the consequences of your choices. There is nothing I need to tell you."

Adara tried to walk away. Naib walked with her. He grabbed her arm. "I know that you went to the Newark warehouse yesterday. Why did you go there?"

"Let go of me." She pulled her arm from him.

"I need to know what you were looking for and what you found."

"I found nothing. I was just checking out some information in my file."

"Do you always check out information in your files?"

"It is my job to see that you do nothing to endanger your case."

As Adara turned away, Naib squeezed her arm tightly. "What I am doing you should support as a good Muslim. I demand it. It is my obligation to look after you."

"Thank you. I think I can look after myself." With that Adara pulled her arm away from him and made sure not to make eye contact with Naib again. She walked about two blocks to a small apartment building, used her key to get through the security door and went to her apartment.

Naib followed her from afar, noted the surroundings and the time.

As Adara peeked out from her blinds, she could see Naib looking at her building. She called Mark and told him what had happened.

He got back into his car and drove around the neighborhood to check out the scene.

* * *

Mark Auburn read the email and clicked onto the recordings. As he listened to phone conversations between Tony and Adara with the suspected terrorists, he munched on his sandwich and coffee.

Auburn crossed his hands. "We may be spinning our wheels for nothing here. Seems like routine immigration law talk. We're not going to get anything concerning cooperation with the terrorists except routine legal advice. They're cooperating without pressure. We're using up too many resources here. We should stop the taps."

Robinson took a deep breath. "Curtwright wants to keep the taps going. She's determined to find something. It's personal."

"The secretary was threatened. I have an email from her. She's definitely in danger. I asked the NYPD to put some surveillance on her."

"We'll see about that. How much good do you think it will do?"

"They won't do much. They'll notify the local patrol to keep an eye on her building. When I find some time, I'll see what else can be done. I told her to stay with a friend until this matter is resolved."

"Will she listen?"

"Adara? Not likely."

NINETEEN

Adara was all dressed for a Saturday evening out. She wore a short, tight dress, very high heels and a hot pink blouse. The phone rang. It was Viviana.

"I'll be running a bit late. I'm taking the subway. Expect me about eight."

"Don't rush." Adara's nails were wet and she tried to blow them dry. "I'll change the restaurant reservations. We'll still be very early for salsa at the club. Take your time."

"Thanks."

Viviana got off the subway at Roosevelt Avenue. She exited the subway slowly down the steel steps in her high heels and very tight distressed jeans. The matching jacket was too tight to button. She pulled her blouse into place so her breasts wouldn't pop out of her bra just before she stepped onto the street.

The subway in this part of Queens was elevated. Roosevelt Avenue was like a little United Nations with peoples of all colors and backgrounds. These were the people who filled the immigration courtrooms.

There were store signs in at least twenty languages, and it wasn't always clear who was from which country. Some were Chinese, Japanese and Vietnamese. Some people looked Hispanic but could have been from the Middle East. Others were African-American, Haitian or African. There were no chain stores on Roosevelt Avenue, but there was no shortage of food or goods from around the world. A walk down Roosevelt Avenue past the restaurants was like taking a gastronomic olfactory tour of the world.

Roosevelt Avenue is always crowded, but the side streets are quiet and lined with small homes and apartment buildings where the working class people of New York live.

As Viviana turned the corner onto a side street, she took her cell phone and called Adara. "Sorry to be so late. Come down and we'll go right away."

"Wait for me in the lobby. I'll be right down." Adara turned off her cell phone and put it into her purse.

Viviana called her mother in Argentina as she waited in the lobby. Two ladies speaking Spanish passed by with a dog. An elderly Asian lady came by with a small child in a stroller. Across the street there were two dark-skinned men wearing sunglasses and baseball caps sitting in a car, just waiting. They looked Mexican to Viviana.

Adara came out of the elevator in high heels, pulling her short dress down to limit the exposure of her thighs. She buttoned a light jacket as she left the building. Viviana just nodded "hello" as she placed the phone in her bra between her breasts.

As they came out Adara and Viviana turned towards Roosevelt Avenue and began to walk. The car with the two men started and one of the men got out and walked towards the women. With a strong grip he grabbed Adara's arm and dragged her towards the car.

"What the hell do you think you're doing?" she said.

The man didn't reply. He pulled out a knife and cut her jacket a bit and then continued to force her towards the car. "Get in and shut up," he said.

Viviana grabbed her other arm and tried to push the man away, but the man turned around and backhanded her so hard she fell down. Her head hit the pavement and she was stunned. The driver got out of the car, grabbed Viviana's arm, took her purse, forced her into the trunk of the car and closed it as several people watched. He took the purse into the front. No one came to the women's aid.

The first man sat in back next to Adara. "What the hell do you think you and Hamid are doing, Naib?"

Naib slapped her. "Just shut up and we won't hurt you. We're going for a ride." He pushed her to the floor face down, so that she could not see where they were going and so that others could not see her in the car.

Hamid drove the few blocks to a highway and then they took it to the Tri-Borough Bridge towards Manhattan. Naib went through Viviana's purse, could not find a cell phone, and then tossed the bag out of the window and into the river as they passed over the bridge. Naib went through Adara's purse. He then tossed Adara's shoes out. Adara got a small glimpse from the corner of her eye and knew she was going over a bridge.

Naib found a cell phone in her purse and turned it on. "What is your code?"

"Screw you."

Naib took Adara's ear and twisted it hard.

"0-9-1-1," She said.

Naib tried it and it worked. He looked at the saved contacts. There he found the names of many people he didn't know. He read them out to Hamid, and Hamid explained that some were people he knew from the office and that some might be government numbers. Naib turned the phone off and put it in his pocket.

The police were quickly on the scene questioning people. The women walking the dog came over to help and explained that they had gotten the car's license plate number.

One woman spoke. "It was a dark car, maybe green or black. I didn't get the make but maybe a Toyota or a Honda."

"Do you know what model or year?"

"Not a clue. But we got the license," she said. The other handed a piece of newspaper with some numbers and letters and the letters NJ after.

Viviana was stunned but she still had her cell phone in her bra. She knew at once she was locked in a car trunk. She dialed 911 and quietly told them what had happened.

"Please leave your phone turned on, Madam. Do you have the share your location app?" the dispatcher asked.

"Yes."

"How much juice do you have?"

"Almost full."

"We're on it."

Viviana called Tony. "Hello?" she said in a whisper.

"What's going on?"

"I don't know. Adara was kidnapped and they took me too. I'm in the trunk of a car. Two men. I think they're speaking Arabic. Adara knows them. Call the police."

"Talk louder."

"I can't."

"Sure. I'll call the New York Police. You do, too. Tell me everything you can. Where are they taking you?"

"I called 911 already. I don't know. Help me."

Tony was waiting with a date to be seated at the bar at Keen's Steak House in Midtown Manhattan. "Slow down and tell me what happened and where you are. I need details."

"I don't know. Two men…" She filled him in as best she could.

"Who are the men?"

"No idea but they looked Hispanic or Middle Eastern. They must be Arabic."

"I'm on it."

Viviana pushed the phone back into her bra and under a breast.

"Okay?" His date looked stunned. "What happened?"

"My closest friend and her friend were just kidnapped. Gotta go." He tore a hundred-dollar bill from his wallet and dropped it on the bar. "Enjoy dinner."

"That's not enough."

Tony ignored the comment and made a mental note to delete her number from his cell.

He hailed a taxi and knew right where to go. He called Bill, gave him Viviana's phone number and filled him in. Bill insisted that Tony pick him up on the way to the police station.

Bill had Auburn's office number in his phone and got the answering machine. The machine did not state that he had called the FBI, just the phone number reached. The machine told him what he already knew, that the office was closed. Then the message directed him to press several numbers, and by number eight he pressed to report an emergency.

"This is Bill Zalmanski. This is an emergency. The message is for Mark Auburn. My office manager, Adara, has just been kidnapped near her home in Roosevelt, Queens. We need help. Please call me back at…" He left his cell number. Bill was not sure if anyone would listen to the message before Monday morning.

By the time Tony got there, Bill was waiting in front of his building with a Zip car. In the back seat was a duffle bag.

Tony explained what he had heard. "I don't know who would do this. Maybe a disgruntled boyfriend."

Bill gave Tony an incredulous look. "Schmuck. She has no boyfriend. She's been waiting for you to come around. This has nothing to do with that."

"You can't be serious."

"Open your eyes."

"She never once showed any interest."

"Sometimes you're great with the women and sometimes you're clueless. She's been waiting for years for you to come to your senses."

Tony noticed the bag. "What is that for?"

"It's a Mossberg shotgun."

"We're already breaking the rules. You want to show up at the police station with a gun?"

"Don't be stupid. We're not going to the police station. Let's worry about Adara first. I've already put in a call to Auburn. I want him to see if the FBI can use Viviana's cell to find them."

"Can that be done?"

"Evidently. We do it to you all the time. I've put a call in to Ryan. We're picking him up soon."

"And then what?"

"I think they may be taking her to their place in Newark. I don't know the address off hand. Adara found the address in one of their files and went there to take a look. Ryan might track them. We get her back and punish those fucks."

"How can you know that? If you're correct that it's them, they could be going anywhere."

"That's why we need help. I'm not sure. It's a hunch."

'They have Adara's friend Viviana too."

"They'll kill them if someone doesn't stop this. We can't rely on the police."

"I don't know," Tony said. "We should let the police do their jobs."

"*Now* you want the police to do something? You, who never trust them? You who say the police oppress innocent people? The police will make a report and pass the info on. The girls might be dead by that time. We need to take care of this quickly."

"They're dangerous. We're not even sure where they are."

"We're dangerous too and we'll find them." Bill grabbed Tony's arm and looked him directly in the eye. "Before we act, we need to figure out where they are. Once we find them, we'll call the police."

* * *

Adara tried to take a look when they went over a second bridge and could see that now they were going over the George Washington Bridge to New Jersey.

As they drove through the roads of New Jersey and then the streets of Newark, Naib became agitated. "Why are we going this way? It's taking too long."

"I'm avoiding traffic and police. It's better to be careful."

"Ahh."

As they arrived at the safe house in Newark, the garage opened. A man stood there as they drove in. No one else was in sight. He closed the door.

They pulled Adara and Viviana from the car and took them into the house. Naib threw Adara's purse on the floor next to the door and then took them to the basement to a small room.

Adara looked at the man closing the garage. "I should have guessed that you were in on this, Ali."

Ali smiled.

Adara turned to Naib. "What are you going to do with me?"

"First we need you to tell us what you know."

"I don't know anything."

"We can't take a chance. We know you were here. We need to know who you told." Naib closed the door and Adara could hear him locking it.

Adara waited a minute and tried the door, but it was solidly shut. There was a small window, and when she opened it she noticed that it had bars. The window was partially beneath ground level and there was some plywood covering that would make it difficult to be heard if they screamed. She could barely make out some light around the edges. She tried the plywood and the bars and they were solid. She yelled "Hello!" and "Help!" a few times only to realize that no one could hear her at all.

The room looked like a cell with a small bed and a lamp. There was a toilet and a sink in an adjoining small room. There were religious books in Arabic and English on a small bookshelf on the wall. On one wall there were boxes that contained cigarettes. The other wall had a worktable where paint cans, brushes and other supplies were stored.

Viviana was taken to another room. Hamid took a semi-automatic handgun and pointed it at her head.

Naib stopped him. "She might be useful later. Put her into the room with Adara for now."

* * *

Mark Auburn got the call on his cell phone and listened to the recorded message. The clerk asked him what to do.

"This is a local police matter. We should let them proceed."

"I understand, sir."

"Thanks. Can we trace the cell phone?"

"Yes. They're probably in New Jersey."

Auburn called Bill. "Tell me what's going on."

Bill filled him in. "Mark, I need your help here."

"Can't, Bill. First of all it's not my jurisdiction. It belongs to the NYPD and the Newark Police Department. My office says they may be in Newark, New Jersey."

"Fuck jurisdiction. Save Adara."

"I would if I could."

"We know they have a warehouse in Newark. They could be there. I don't have the exact address. It's in a file in the office and will take too long to get there."

"The police should be able to track their cell phones."

"The number you called from was restricted. Can I have your direct line? You know I won't abuse it."

"Can't do it, Bill. It might look bad for me if someone saw that the target of an investigation was calling me directly. I took a chance to go this far."

"What investigation?"

"Oh, sorry. We were tapping your phones and email looking for info on these same people. We have a court order."

"And you left us vulnerable? That sucks. You owe us now. You owe Adara."

"I'll see what I can do."

"Why are you investigating us?"

"You have several clients with ISIS connections."

"And these must be the guys involved."

"Sorry, Bill."

"You knew this and left us vulnerable."

Tony listened with his mouth opened. "We should let the FBI take over."

"I can't. You can get out if you want."

"No, I'm in." Tony looked out the passenger side and stared aimlessly.

Auburn closed his phone and then re-opened it. He dialed the New York police and they filled him in.

Auburn made another call. FBI agent Ralph Donnelly in New Jersey answered. "This better be important, Mark. I'm in a fancy restaurant with my wife and her parents."

"I have the perfect excuse to get out of it. I need your help. It's life or death."

"Shoot."

"I may have an interstate kidnapping in process. The victim's boss is in pursuit. Here's one victim's cell. The NYPD asked her to leave it on. Easy to track and they're trying. I think you can follow it to the scene."

"New Jersey?"

"Yeah, Newark I think. I live in West Orange and I'm heading in that direction right now," Auburn said. "I don't have the Stingray app on my phone."

"Do we know where they're going?"

"Not yet exactly, but with a little luck we'll know real soon. The boss seems to think they're in a warehouse in Newark."

"I have the app. I'll call the cavalry and let you know if I get a locate on them."

Donnelly turned to his father-in-law. "I have a life or death matter and I've got to go. Looks like an interstate kidnapping in the works. Nothing less would take me away." He turned to his wife. "Sorry." He gave her a peck and walked out before he could get a response.

* * *

Bill and Tony were already in the car on 14th Street and 8th Ave in Manhattan when Ryan came up out of the subway with his ipad.

Ryan got in the back. He moved the gun aside. "Cowboy stuff?"

Tony turned to Ryan. "Are you sure that this is going to work?"

"Absolutely. According to this, the phone is already in Newark."

"Let's go." Bill turned to Tony. "In this traffic it could take an hour to get there. I'll need to stop for a piss."

"Ryan shouldn't come with us. If we do something illegal, he shouldn't be an accomplice."

"I'll get him out of it before it becomes an issue. We need him to track the girls," Bill said.

"I'm not going to let you two be heroes without me."

As they exited the Holland Tunnel into New Jersey, Ryan showed Tony his iPad and explained how the app worked while Bill stopped at a gas station to use the men's room. Tony moved to the driver's seat and Ryan came up front.

"You see, it can use the GPS to find out where a phone is. It's called the Stingray app. This is an app I got through a friend whose father is a policeman. It's not supposed to be public, but anyone in the know can get it. Look. See the marker? It follows the GPS. It doesn't matter whether the phone is on or off so long as the GPS hasn't been disabled and there's some electricity in the battery. Even if the phone is completely off it can be found by residual electricity. In this case the phone is on and we have a location. They may have stopped. We should be able to find em quickly."

Bill returned and glanced over at the iPad. "Can you be sure that it's accurate?"

"Should be. I've tried it before and it always seems to work. My friend's father uses it to keep track of him. My friend gets around it by leaving the phone at home or trading phones with a friend. We have a restricted number and call back on another phone, but his parents don't call much because they think they always know where he is."

"Don't you have to have two of these to work?"

"Not any more. It's GPS technology. You guys are still living in the 70s."

"Yeah. The government can use this to track everybody. No one's safe from government intrusion," Tony interjected.

Bill ignored the comment and drove like a maniac. He went on the shoulders of the road and made dangerous passes.

Ryan sat quietly with his iPad. "Adara's phone shows she's at the same location."

Tony took a deep breath. "We should let the police handle this."

"Let's focus, Tony. Ryan will get us there. First go to the PATH train station."

"Why?"

"So Ryan can get the train home. His girlfriend will kill us both if anything happens to him."

"You need me," Ryan said. "Don't think just because I'm the junior member here that I can't help. What if something happens or something changes? They might move. How are you going handle it without me?"

"He comes with us," Bill said. "If it gets hot, we'll dump him with some taxi money."

"No one's dumping me. You need me. I can help," Ryan said.

"Lets keep driving."

Bill called Auburn and tried to leave a message. The receptionist again answered and Bill told her where they were going.

The receptionist assured Bill. "I've got the address. My next call will be Auburn and then the New Jersey State Police. The NYPD should be following one cell phone."

"So are we. We're following both numbers and they're in the same place."

Within two minutes Auburn called Bill. "I've also called the FBI office in Newark. Wait for backup. It might take awhile."

"How much of awhile?" Bill wanted to know.

"Hard to say. I hope minutes. Unless you can convince the police that you are in direct pursuit of a kidnapping, they'll need a warrant to get in and that will take some time. My direct cell number is…"

Ryan put his hand on Tony's shoulder. "Make a left here. I think it's in the middle of the block."

"Are you sure you know what you're doing? If you're wrong, Bill and I are going to be in big trouble."

"Listen. The phone is there. I'm sure of that. This is the place," Ryan said as he pointed with his arm outside of the car.

"Pull that arm in!" Bill snapped.

Tony drove a few blocks away, offered Ryan some cash and forced Ryan out of the car. Ryan refused the money but insisted that they take the iPad.

Once the car drove away Ryan pulled out his iPhone, opened the same app and hopped another taxi to the signal.

"We should wait for the police," Tony said.

"Can't. They could kill them at any time," Bill said.

"It's too dangerous."

"It's too dangerous not to. We don't know what's going on. If these guys are brazen enough to kidnap them in broad daylight, they can easily kill. We can't wait. Adara wasn't grabbed for money."

"That's right. These guys are dangerous. It's not our job to stop them. That's for the police."

"Grow some balls." With that Bill checked the shotgun and placed three shells into it and put several more into his pocket. He went to check the house. A passerby saw this and called 911 to report a man with a gun checking out a house. When Bill saw the man reporting the incident he said, "Thank you. Please call the police right now. Tell them there's a kidnapping going on and we're going to stop it." The man videotaped it on his phone.

* * *

Naib and Hamid opened the door and Adara was startled. They brought Viviana in and shoved her onto the cot. They spoke in Aracic.

"What do you want?" Adara asked.

Naib slammed the door behind him and pulled a chair near her and sat. "Why did you do it?"

"Do what?"

He slapped her hard. "Don't start that with me. I can kill you in a second if I want to."

"So why haven't you? You're a trained killer."

"Shut up, Adara," Viviana said. She turned to Naib. "We'll cooperate."

Naib ignored Viviana. "You know something, and I need to know what you know and who you spoke to."

"I told the FBI that you're planning a terrorist attack at the courthouse if the Imam is convicted."

"So you don't know shit."

"I know you but my friend doesn't. Let my friend go."

"I can't."

"Why not? She knows nothing."

"She knows too much now but *you* don't know what you think you do."

"Who the hell are you?" Adara asked.

"You know almost everything about me. I told you the truth. In this country, you can tell everything and people don't act on it. It amazes me. You can call me Naib. That is my correct name. I was an officer in the Jordanian army. I *was* trained by the British in Sandhurst. Do you know where that is?"

"No."

"It's the British equivalent of West Point. But you see, I'm also a religious man, an honorable man, a righteous man, and for that I was forced out of the military. I wanted to bring Sharia law to my country and the king took that as a sign of disloyalty. I wanted to bring Jordan into the Islamic State. All that I told your office was true. The king has to show his American backers that they are getting their money's worth. People like me are sacrificed so that others can get the large bribes your government calls "foreign aid." I am here to help a cause that my own country would have called me a traitor for supporting."

"Two wrongs don't make a right."

"Stop that American crap. America uses fine words to justify the violence they do to others, but what they really want is for the world to fear them. I don't fear America because I know that my cause is in the name of Allah and is just. I'm not afraid to die for what I believe in."

"Or make others die for your beliefs. Rivers have been filled with blood by people who felt that way."

"Maybe we need a few more rivers of blood to show the world just how empty America is. Those rivers of blood are making a world Islamic caliphate a reality."

"The Islamic State is in retreat. It will soon be defeated."

"Wrong. Once we complete our mission, young jihadists will come from all over the world to join our cause and defeat the West. Our actions will bring new life to the movement. We will be unstoppable."

"I will be rescued, and you will be brought to justice."

"My cause is justice."

"Your cause is evil."

"We'll see about that." He slapped her again. Viviana was crying. "Shut your friend up or I will shut her up for good."

Hamid took out his handgun and pointed it at Viviana's head. She backed up until she came to a worktable covered with paint cans. She could go no further.

Naib pulled up a chair and sat inches away from Adara. "Let's go over this again. What did you hear and who did you tell?"

"Fuck you," Adara said in English.

"Tell him," Viviana screamed.

He got up and slapped Adara again, harder this time.

"I can shoot Viviana at any time. This is a good time. Maybe I'll just shoot her in the knee and cripple her. I know you care about your friend."

"Fuck you again."

"Adara! Please tell them!" Viviana said. "Don't let them shoot me."

Hamid slapped Viviana hard and she bounced off the worktable and fell to the floor. A paint can fell and hit her head. She bled a bit from one ear. The phone slipped from her breast and fell to the ground. Naib picked it up and in English said. "You won't be needing this. Did you call anyone?"

"I called the police and gave them the exact address here and they said they're on the way."

"I don't think so. You don't even know where we are. Where are we?"

Viviana was silent. Adara answered. "New Jersey."

"You don't know anything. You both don't. You think you do, but you're wrong."

"What's the pass number?"

"1,2,3,4."

"Why did you tell them?" Adara asked. Viviana did not answer.

"Smart. She wants to live," Naib replied.

Naib checked the phone and saw the international call and the 911 call and the Tony call. With that Naib pocketed the phone, locked them in the room and left. "I'll be back later. If we don't get some answers when I return, I will shoot Viviana and then torture you. Because of your interference we are going to act now."

"What are you going to do?" Adara asked.

Naib hesitated for a second. "It will be huge."

Naib locked the women in and went upstairs to the garage with Hamid. "I will leave you here to watch the women. I want to execute the plan immediately. I'm afraid that bitch told the police enough to lead them to us. If they check the store, they will find the detonator. I'll remove it from the store and execute the plan now. We can't wait. See what you can get them to tell you, then shoot them."

With that Naib and Ali loaded the box into the tobacco store van and left. Hamid took out his 9mm pistol and checked to make sure it was in good condition and that he had sufficient ammunition.

Naib pulled the van out and into the alley just behind the building and headed for the street. Ali closed the door and got in just as Ryan turned the corner to see them drive away.

Ryan came up the block behind the building still following the signal on his iPhone. He watched as the van left and noticed that the traceable cellular signal left with it.

* * *

Bill went to the front door and up the brick stairs. Tony stayed back by the car. Bill could hear the car and then the garage door close. *Oh shit*, he thought to himself. Bill looked through a window to see that the first floor was empty but that there were ladders, Sheetrock, boxes and paint cans around.

"I have a bad feeling about this. Please wait for the police," Tony asked Bill.

"Shush," Bill said. "Just call the police and be quiet about it."

Bill tried the lock and then used his shoulder to butt in the door. It took three tries until he realized he could not do it. He placed the nose of his shotgun on the lock and fired. The lock blew away and the door opened.

Hamid immediately heard this and called Naib, who told him to shoot the women and get out of there.

Hamid decided to wait. Whoever was there would hear the shots and know where he was. The women might still be useful. He would wait in the dark and listen.

Tony went to the door and said to Bill, "Let's get out of here. We took a gun out of state and we could get into trouble."

"Shut up and wait in the car."

Tony stood by the main door and watched as Bill tried each interior door. He found the door to an interior stairway down and came to the first floor and turned on the lights. Tony followed him. Bill looked around at the food carts and boxes and saw several empty rooms.

Bill came to the steel door to the basement and saw that it was unlocked. As he opened it, the light in the basement went off and he could hear a woman's gasp. As Bill pumped the shotgun, Hamid grabbed Adara, twisted her arm and held her in front of him.

Everyone could hear Tony's cell phone ring. It was Ryan. Tony listened and said a bit too loud to Bill. "Ryan just saw the van leave from the back. Maybe they've gone."

Schmuck, Bill thought.

"There's one here with a gun," Adara yelled. Hamid hit her hard on the side of her head with his gun. He grabbed her just before she could fall. Some blood ran down her neck.

With that Hamid heard a step and fired a shot through the drywall into the stairwell. It missed Bill.

Bill took his key-ring and threw it down the stairs. Hamid fired several shots in the direction of the sound as the keys bounced. The shots missed Bill.

Bill knew Hamid was nervous. He also knew approximately where Hamid was by the shots. Bill came down the stairs, and just as he turned into the room Hamid said, "Put the shotgun down. You can't use it without shooting Adara, and you won't do it."

Bill could see just a bit by the reflected light from the stairwell. "No, you put the gun down. You'll kill her anyway and I'm willing to shoot you both first."

"What do you know about killing?"

"I'm a veteran. More than you think."

"Bullshit."

"When I give the word, drop the gun. If not, I will shoot you anyway."

Viviana barely pulled herself up, grabbed a paint can from the worktable and slammed in into the side of Hamid's head. The hit was not enough to stop him, but it was enough for Adara to grab the gun and point it towards the ceiling. A shot went off. They wrestled him to the ground. Bill could not shoot without hitting the women. Hamid remained in control of the gun and was just about to shoot Adara.

* * *

Ali drove as Naib sat next to him and stared out the window without uttering a word.

Naib's heart pounded as the old white van with the stencil "IRVING AVENUE TOBACCO CO." passed through the Lincoln Tunnel from New Jersey to Manhattan without incident. He wondered if he was likely to be stopped on a Saturday evening driving a commercial vehicle into Manhattan. He picked up a warm, half finished bottle of water because his mouth was so dry. The traffic into Manhattan was not as unmanageable as it was during the week. There were enough other commercial vehicles that his van went unnoticed.

As they approached the store, Ali was able to park just around the corner where the building had a horizontal steel sidewalk door leading to the basement. He left the truck, ran into the store and grabbed the little box from the back where Arafat had been sitting behind the counter.

Arafat stopped Ali. "What's going on?"

"The detonator. Give it to me. I have the bomb in the truck. We're going to detonate it. Get out of here and away from downtown now."

"What about you?"

"I'm not important."

"This bomb will kill people for at least half a mile in diameter. How will you get away? What about Naib?" Arafat said.

"Get away? When was getting away part of the plan? Downtown Manhattan will be unusable for years and the American economy will sink. That is the plan."

"Should I go with you?" Arafat said.

"We can do this alone," Ali said.

Arafat left. He didn't even bother to lock the store.

The policewoman tried not to doze as she sat in the pizza place across from the store, sipping her coffee and reading her newspaper. She noticed nothing.

Ali handed the detonator to Naib. They smiled as Ali drove.

* * *

Viviana and Adara grabbed hold of Hamid's hand and tried to wrestle the gun away from him. He kicked Adara, and she almost lost her grip. As they wrestled on the floor, Hamid got off several shots randomly. No one was hit. Bill kicked the door in, ran over and pointed the gun directly to Hamid's head. "Drop it or I'll kill you."

"Don't," Adara said. "Something's going down and he knows about it."

Hamid elbowed Viviana and seemed to be getting control of the gun and trying to aim it.

Bill put his foot on Hamid's hand and pointed the shotgun at Hamid's left leg. "One more chance to drop it," Bill said.

Hamid jerked his body in an effort to get control of the gun. The two women struggled and began to lose control.

"Drop the gun," Bill said.

When Hamid did not answer Bill blew his right foot off at the ankle. Hamid dropped the gun.

TWENTY

"Don't shoot," Bill yelled out as he slid the Mossberg towards the stairs.

The police entered quickly with armor and guns raised. Tony was at the top of the stairs in handcuffs as the EMS workers ran down to tend to Hamid and the women.

Bill tried to tell the police that something very bad was going to happen as they wrestled him to the ground and handcuffed him. Bill tried to explain that they had to find Naib when the police came down with Ryan.

"I got it on my iPhone. That idiot has Viviana's phone. I tracked the cell phone in his van, and I'm following it. The truck's going to Manhattan," Ryan said.

"Are you with these two?" a policeman asked Ryan.

"Sure."

The police immediately handcuffed Ryan.

"I have to call Auburn," Bill said.

The police would not let Bill call anyone. "We have to take statements and take you all back to the precinct. No one can leave now."

"You don't understand," Adara screamed. "These men are terrorists and they're going to do something bad."

Viviana was being bandaged but sat up. "Please! You have to stop these guys. There's two of them and they're going to do something bad right now. Stop them. Please."

Tony picked up his cuffed hands. "You don't know that for sure and you shouldn't accuse."

"Are you fucking insane?" Adara screamed. She turned to the man in charge. "Call Mark Auburn at the FBI in Federal Plaza in New York. He needs to take action now."

"I need more, lady."

Adara jumped up. "Are you crazy! How much more do you need. They have some guns or a bomb and they're heading for New York. You want it in carved in stone?"

With that Mark Auburn and Ralph Donnelly entered wearing blue jackets with FBI written prominently on the back. They talked to the police and then Adara. "I'm taking charge of you. I need you for identification and help," Auburn said.

"What about the rest?" Donnelly asked.

"This is your jurisdiction. I'm going to fix things in mine," Auburn said.

"By tomorrow you, Bill, Viviana and Ryan will be heroes. Go," Donnelly said.

"Or we'll be dead," Bill said.

"Where are we going?" Adara asked.

"To find Naib and stop him from doing whatever he's doing."

"Why do you need me?"

"To ID Naib and in case I need an Arabic translator."

"We'll need Ryan. He can track Viviana's phone. Naib put it into his pocket."

"The FBI will do that."

"Ryan can do it *right now.*"

"Bring him."

Adara ran after them in her stocking feet.

* * *

Naib took the detonator from the store and opened the back of his truck. He opened the box and carefully placed the detonator into a slot where it fit snuggly. All the writing was in Korean, but Naib had been trained in Pakistan by the manufacturers and quickly got the detonator in place. A lighted panel came on and Naib typed in "1 hour."

The numbers started to countdown immediately: 59:59, 59:58, 59:57......

* * *

Auburn took out a magnetized blinking light and put it on top of his roof. He turned on the siren as Ryan followed the signal and told him where to go. Mark went around cars, over sidewalks and through red lights towards the Holland tunnel. The backup into the tunnel was heavy, but Mark got around it by breaking almost every traffic rule there was. He went on shoulders and ran over a few fences and barricades. On the way he was on his cell phone calling for help.

By the time they got near the tunnel, the police had stopped traffic and the way was clear.

As he exited the tunnel, there were two unmarked cars waiting with several agents in helmets and Kevlar vests marked FBI. Each was carrying a rifle.

They immediately followed him.

* * *

There was more traffic than anticipated as Naib drove south from the store towards the Freedom Tower. He could not afford to attract notice by passing red lights or speeding. He was resolved to leave the car by the Freedom Tower and escape or die trying. Either way he was in Allah's service.

There was some street fair in Chinatown and traffic was diverted. There were thousands of people at the fair. As he was waiting for a light, a man came up to his car and began cleaning his windshield. Naib reached out and grabbed him so hard he ripped his shirtsleeve off. "Get out of here or I'll break your arm."

The man quickly left.

As he passed City Hall, traffic was still slow because there was some construction on Broadway. Cars were again being diverted into one lane. Naib looked at his watch. Even on a Saturday night Manhattan was busy. He was running out of time.

* * *

Ryan studied his cell phone. "He's going south on Broadway and seems to be stuck near City Hall."

"Ryan, I couldn't do this without you," Auburn said.

Traffic was bad for them, too, as they exited the Holland Tunnel. They drove against traffic onto Church Street. Cars veered right and left to let them through. Horns were honking until people saw the blinking lights and the men in helmets, heads sticking out of their car windows, carrying automatic weapons driving past.

* * *

Naib could hear the horns and the sirens and immediately knew they were coming for him. He knew he was getting close to the Freedom Tower. As his car approached the corner of Broadway and Vesey Street, barely a block away from his destination, he pulled over next to St Paul's Church. He placed the cell phones on the floor and closed and locked the van.

Just as he was about to walk away, a policeman came over. "You can't park here, sir. Please move the van."

Naib pulled his automatic and shot him three times. People started to scream and run away in all directions.

Naib threw the car key into the storm sewer and walked calmly away. He was a block from the Freedom Tower, and that would have to be close enough.

As they approached the van Ryan screamed. "That's the van! Stop!"

They did.

There were already other police on the scene and more cars on the way. Auburn and the FBI surrounded the van, and as they came close determined that no one was in it. Auburn tried the door and an agent with a crowbar forced the door open. They immediately saw the lead box.

Auburn yelled orders. "This is no ordinary car bomb. It's a dirty bomb. Get everyone away from here as far as possible. Tell the NYPD to evacuate lower Manhattan." He turned to Adara and Ryan. "Get out of here fast. Run!"

Several people pointed in the direction that Naib had gone. Some had phone videos of Naib walking calmly away. Auburn ordered two agents to look for him.

"We know what he looks like and we'll go with them," Adara said.

Auburn nodded as she ran in her stocking feet. Ryan went with another FBI agent.

One agent came up to Auburn. "I can handle this, sir."

"I hope you can."

Together they opened the box. The display on the detonator read 1:32. "We have a minute and a half to stop this," Auburn said. They were both sweating.

"I've never seen one like this. If we handle it wrong, it will go off immediately. Even if the bomb doesn't go off, the detonator will and will cause significant damage."

"How much damage?"

"It could fry a small building."

"We can't move it and we have to do something."

"I'm afraid to try."

With that Auburn said. "We have nothing to lose."

"*Clear the area! It's a bomb!*" Auburn yelled. The few people left started to run in all directions. This time there was real panic.

Naib walked then ran through the streets towards the South Street Seaport. On Pearl Street he turned north hoping to make it to Chinatown and blend into the large crowd, or better yet get into a subway tunnel where he might survive the blast.

Adara, Ryan and the agents ran, but after a few blocks no one was pointing them in the correct direction any longer. As they got to Pearl Street one of the officers saw the crowd in Chinatown and on a hunch ran to the right with Ryan. Adara and the other agent went left.

Adara's feet were sore and bleeding, but she went on.

Naib saw Adara and the agent following him into the thick crowd. He bent down as though he were fixing his shoe. As the agent came close Naib stood up and shot him in the face. The bullet went through his face and hit a bystander in the head. They both went down and Adara grabbed the agent and tied to stop the bleeding.

Naib shot a large glass storefront close by and the glass shattered all around them as he ran. Adara could not follow.

Auburn grabbed the detonator and yanked it out. The bomb didn't go off, but the clock continued to run. 00:47, 00:46. Auburn ran across the street to the empty church. People were running away from the site. The only person remaining was Auburn, the one agent and a tourist taking pictures.

Auburn threw the detonator onto the cemetery behind the church and ran across the street towards a subway station entrance with the agent. The tourist was close behind.

As Auburn, the tourist and the agent ran towards the subway station, the detonator went off. Ancient gravestones exploded into pieces in the loud blast. The back of the Church blew to smithereens. Auburn, the agent and the tourist all went down with the blast.

In Chinatown a man came out of the crowd and identified himself as a doctor. He felt the bystander's pulse, looked at the pool of blood and then assisted the FBI agent. Adara sat on the ground and cried. The police and the EMS arrived seconds later.

Ryan and the other agent came over and searched through the crowd. A bullet seemed to come out of nowhere and struck Ryan in his shoulder.

The other agents arrived and ran in the direction that Naib went. The crowd was very thick where Naib disappeared. They gave up after a few minutes.

The trail had gone cold.

TWENTY-ONE

The Sunday news was dominated by the story. All the news stations reported nothing but the attempted bombing in lower Manhattan. Every station played the video of Auburn ripping the detonator from the bomb and throwing it into the churchyard. The tourist who shot it sold it for five figures.

CNN had breaking news flashes every ten minutes giving the same information over and over again. They ran a clip from an "expert" who said that there was no need for the FBI to blow up St Paul's Church. He explained that thirty seconds was sufficient to disarm the detonator. Another "expert" criticized the FBI for not training their agents to handle these problems.

Fox News had hero stories about Bill, Tony, Adara, Mark, Ryan and the shot law enforcement officers.

PBS promised a special on the career of Mark Auburn. When they contacted the FBI for information, they were told to file a Freedom of Information Act request and that the FBI would respond within ten months.

It was discovered that Mark Auburn had written a spy novel fifteen years earlier that had sold just three hundred copies. Barnes & Noble discovered that they had a contract to market the book and within twenty-four hours were promoting it in all of their stores.

CNBC ran a story about the unnecessary way Hamid had been brutalized by a former American soldier trained for jungle combat and how Hamid's rights as an American had been violated.

The *New York Post* had a photo of a thin Bill and Oliver in their army uniforms with full heads of hair taken forty-five years earlier in Vietnam. They carried their M21 sniper rifles. The headline read, *HERO AGAIN*.

Al Jazeera had a story about the reasons the bombers were forced to take this drastic action in their desperation to stop U.S. and Israeli aggression. Al Jazeera ran the same Vietnam photo as they talked about how Bill was 'trained to kill'. They mentioned that one of the lawyers in Bill's office was Jewish. They then had an interview with Mohammed Aziz Mohammad Abdul. He took credit for the attempted bombing and announced that others would finish the job.

Farid Zakaria had a segment about immigration lawyer heroes but had to change it at the last moment when he couldn't find any other than this bunch. He interviewed Judge Oliver Totten and discussed whether or not they had been trained for the actions Bill took the previous day and whether Bill should have moderated those actions. Oliver replied, "Moderate! Are you f…king insane?" Zakaria would not run the interview, but somehow it got onto Youtube and within twenty-four hours had more than fifty million views.

The *New York Daily News* had separate articles from a Catholic Priest and an Imam in Queens, both discussing how Adara was a loyal member of their respective congregations. On the next page was a quote from Adara that she had not been in a place of worship for at least ten years except for two weddings and her neighbor's son's bar mitzvah.

The *New York Times* headline read, *DIRTY BOMB FOILED BY LAW FIRM.* In an additional article they presented information that the bomb had been made in Pakistan with North Korean help and that Pakistan claimed that the bomb had gone missing from its arsenal. They had extensive information that INTERPOL and the CIA had been tracking it but that it had gone cold after it was traced to a carpet warehouse in Karachi.

El Diario had a headline *MUJER ARGENTINA DETIENE TERRORISTAS.* On page two Viviana's father was quoted as saying that he would dedicate a special full-bodied wine called the 'Zalmanski Blend' in gratitude for the man who saved his daughter.

The *Village Voice* headline read *IMMIGRATION LAWYER HERO HARBORS ILLEGAL ALIEN SEX SLAVE.*

The *Wall Street Journal* headline had photos of Naib and Adara with the headline TERRORISTS STOPPED BY IRAQI SECRETARY.

The *National Inquirer* had a photo on the cover of Auburn standing with an unusually tall bald man with a bulbous head and very large ears with the headline SPACE ALIENS ASSIST FBI TO FOIL TERROR PLOT. There was a second article that claimed that the firm of Zalmanski and Sorrelli represented space aliens. As Auburn lay in the hospital bed, he was surprised to see that space aliens bought all their clothes with Ralph Lauren logos.

The *Irish Echo* had a headline RYAN FROM ZALMANSKI'S OFFICE BACKS THE HEROES UP.

The *Jewish Press* had a headline JEW AIDS FBI IN SAVING MANHATTAN.

Pictures of Naib were on the front page of every newspaper as a national manhunt commenced.

Mark Auburn was ordered to fly to Washington to explain to his superiors his involvement in foiling the plot and his conflicting role in the investigation of Zalmanski and Sorrelli. He asked if it could wait until he was released from the hospital.

Curtwright was asked to fly to Washington for a meeting with the Attorney General.

Tony phoned the office and left a message for Maria to tell Bill that he needed a few days off.

Hamid died.

* * *

Ali was wearing a straw fedora and a fishing vest with a camera around his neck as he drove along Route 30 past Gettysburg. Arafat was dozing next to him. There was a bang from the trunk of the car, and a few minutes later he pulled over into a forested area. Naib got out of the trunk and took a piss. "How much longer?"

"We'll be in Chambersburg within the hour."

* * *

The next day Bill arrived at Beckman Downtown Hospital, near the site of the blast, and was allowed to pass through the strict security. He held his hand over his face as he plowed through the press. Cameras clicked away as he bumped into reporters and photographers, knocking them this way and that.

Rachel was already in Ryan's room when be arrived.

"You almost killed my fiancé. What were you thinking?" she asked.

"Oh, Rachel. We saved America."

Bill sat on the bed and put a hand on Ryan's shoulder. "You're the hero, son, you and your iPad. I'm sorry you got hurt."

"Ouch. I was shot there. Please grab the other shoulder."

Rachel waved her finger at Bill. "You're lucky, Bill. He will be out of here in two or three days, but he could have been killed. If he was, I would have killed you."

"I know."

Ryan got up, and Bill could see the bandages where he had been shot. "I'm glad you're doing fine. Don't give any interviews to the press unless you're paid first. Ask big bucks."

Bill hugged Ryan and Rachel and went to the next room where Auburn and the FBI agent shot in the face were recuperating. The FBI agent was all bandaged up with tubes going into his nose. All he could do was give them a wink and a thumbs-up every time he heard something he liked. Each time he did, her husband told her to just rest.

Adara was sitting beside Auburn holding his hand.

"This is another fine mess you've gotten me into," Auburn said to Bill.

"Was there a last mess?" They both laughed. "You better not let your wife see Adara holding your hand."

They laughed again.

"She was here earlier when Adara was with Ryan. She filed for divorce a couple of months ago and now she acts sorry. It would have been better for her if I'd died. A lot of water under the bridge. My children are coming later. One's in college and the other two live away. They're coming in to see me."

"Of course they are. You're lucky you weren't killed," Bill said. "Now you can recover and continue your investigation of Tony and me."

"The reason for that is over. It was out of my hands, Bill, but you must know my heart was never in it. You have to admit that it looked like you were *the* ISIS immigration lawyers, though. I think your role in the case is over now. You're the real hero."

"No, you are."

"No, you are."

Adara raised her hands. "No, I am."

"But we saved you," Bill said.

"But without Viviana and me, there would have been no damsels in distress."

"Where's Tony?" Bill asked.

"He's in Brooklyn at Rose's house. He's feeling a bit down and wants to hide from the press," Adara said.

"Better that way. I think he feels that he let me down, but he belongs on the hero list."

"I think so," Adara said.

"Without you boys, the bad guys would have won," Auburn said.

"I don't think Tony thinks of himself as a 'boy'," Bill said. "Where's your friend Viviana?"

* * *

Viviana was locked in her Manhattan apartment trying to avoid the press. She popped her third Valium of the day when her phone rang. The caller ID showed "Sorrelli" and she answered it. "Hello, Tony."

"I'm so glad that you're fine. How are you doing?"

"I need to be alone for a while. I'll call you."

"Are you angry?"

"No. *I'll* call *you*." She pressed the off button. Enough calls for one day.

* * *

Bill took a cab to 32d Street and Fifth Avenue in Manhattan and went into the *Kim Jong Bad* restaurant. As he walked in, he passed a large portrait of Gen. Douglas McArthur. He found Choe at a table hidden in a corner waiting for him. The waiter immediately came over with a beer.

"I ordered it for you."

Bill took a sip. "Everything's different today."

"The owner knows who you are, and they said dinner is on the house."

"I'd rather have it on the table," Bill said.

* * *

Piertowsky called Wong. They discussed Zalmanski and Sorrelli.

"What? Say it again."

"I got a call this morning. The U.S. Attorney's office want us to arrest the woman Zalmanski's living with," Piertowsky said. "They want us to do it because you're Asian and it will look better for the press."

"Who authorized it?"

"Curtwright. She's got a hard on for Sorrelli."

"She's nuts. It's Sunday. We never arrest anyone on Sunday."

"They want us to do it today."

"My in-laws invited us to a barbeque this afternoon. My wife will kill me if I don't go. Can't we pass this off?"

"Believe me. I tried to get out of it."

Wong sighed. "Tell them you couldn't reach me. Call back and leave a message on my voicemail. I'll call you back tonight and we'll play dumb. You'll say you couldn't go alone. Site regulations."

"We'll just have to do it tomorrow then."

"I'll call the press first."

* * *

General Kahn looked out of his window at the dawn coming through the Khyber Mountains to the east. The sun streaked over the bunkers where much of Pakistan's nuclear arsenal was stored. The early morning silence was interrupted by the sounds of helicopters and trucks. Before he could pick up the telephone to ask what was happening there was a knock on his door. A sergeant in full Pakistani uniform was standing with three soldiers, one of whom was an American officer.

"Yes sergeant."

"Sir. I am Sergeant Ayub. We have orders to detain you. We have orders from the president to lock down and take control of this base and all arms nuclear and other."

Kahn looked at the American and then out his window where he could see the helicopters landing and armed soldiers surrounding the compound.

"One moment please. I need to dress." He turned and walked into an adjoining room but before Sergeant Ayub could follow him Kahn opened a drawer, took a revolver and put a bullet through his skull.

TWENTY-TWO

Bill and Adara returned to work a week later. At the end of the day the staff prepared a party with salad, pizza and champagne. Everyone was there, everyone but Tony.

Pounders sat next to Bill and Ryan.

"It's not over until it's over," Bill said. He turned to Ryan. "You're going to take over more of the weight around here till Tony gets his act together."

"Tony's fine. He's just shaken up."

"We'll see."

Viviana sat in a corner with a glass filled with ice and a bottle of vodka. "I'm going home to Argentina. I moved to New York for excitement. I got too much."

"You came to New York for excitement? You got some, and now you want to leave?" Adara said. "Are you a man or a mouse? Squeak up."

"That's not funny. I got enough excitement for a lifetime."

"We have the Bueno deportation case coming up. I need to know if Tony's going to handle this or I will," Ryan asked Bill.

"What's the Bueno case about?" Jeff asked.

"Well, they've brought us a lot of business over the years, repeat customers. The Bueno brothers operate the Bueno Brothers Valet Parking Company. They do weddings or just about any function that needs valet parking. On the side they steal cars to order. For example, if someone wants a red Porsche 911 convertible, they wait till someone parks one with them, steal it, then play dumb when the owner comes for it. After several convictions one of the brothers is having a deportation hearing next week," Ryan said.

"Postpone it," Jeff said.

Maria and Carmen placed several piles of phone messages in front of Bill. "These piles are inquiries from the press. This one is people who want to use us for new cases." Carmen laughed. "We're gonna need some new help if we sign them all up. This pile is congratulation messages, and this message is from a security service that wants to offer us protection."

"We don't need security," Bill said.

"Are you sure?" Carmen asked.

"Naib is heading for the border. Anyone in his right mind would," Bill answered.

"I'm not so sure Naib is on his way to the border," Adara said. "These people are crazy and unpredictable."

Jeff Pounders looked at the pizza. "Are you trying to kill me? I have high cholesterol and about thirty pounds too many."

"Fifty," Bill said.

"You should know. I'll just have the salad and some diet soda. I have work to do." Jeff had a few forkfuls of salad and then took a slice of pizza.

Harold showed up with a bottle of Tullamore Dew Irish whiskey and put it next to the bottles of champagne. "None of that girly stuff. This will get the party going."

"Hey, bud. One of us 'girls' is a hero," Carmen said.

"What do you mean 'us,' kemosabe?" Adara said.

* * *

Naib, Ali and Arafat went into the basement under the gas station in Chambersburg, surveyed the weapons and discussed what they would need. An old TV was on CNN and a reporter was discussing the events in New York the week before. On the side were pictures of Zalmanski and Sorrelli.

"I'm going to kill those motherfuckers," Naib said. "The immigration lawyers, that bitch secretary, and the U.S. attorneys prosecuting the Imam. One at a time I'll get them all. Even that cunt that hit Hamid with the paint can and that Jew with the iPad."

Farzard, the owner of the station, unlocked several steel gun safes. "Let's discuss what you actually need."

"I need it all," Naib said.

"Well, you can't have it all. It's too hard to get. Let's discuss what you need."

In the basement of the garage they went over several guns. He looked at a Springfield M25 sniper rifle, two Israeli Uzis, two Glock 9mm automatics and a box of a dozen hand grenades.

Ali put his hands on the guns. "Don't let your emotions dictate what we do. We'll make a mistake that way."

"Don't worry. One by one we'll take them out."

"With hand grenades?"

"They're for the immigration lawyers. We'll wait a few days till things settle down and then strike."

* * *

Mark Auburn arrived at Union Station at noon. He had an hour to kill before his train home. As he waited, he passed the tourist shops and bought a handful of U.S. flag lapel pins. He stopped at Starbucks and bought a sandwich and a large bold coffee with room for milk.

His mind went over what he was asked and how he had responded.

His cell phone vibrated in his pocket. He had forgotten to turn on the sound. It was a text message. He responded. "*The discussion was not what I expected. I was offered a new job, but it requires my officially changing my address. I'll tell you the details when I see you. Meet me at Penn Station, New York at 5. We'll celebrate.*"

* * *

Rosa brought Tony lunch as he watched TV. The incident was still news and he was recuperating at Rosa's, where he knew he would be catered to and fed the best food anywhere.

There was an additional story about the Imam's trial and lead counsel, Renee Curtwright and Charles Robinson. There was talk about security in lower Manhattan made greater by the incident the previous week.

"I'm going back to work tomorrow, Mama. Time to pull myself out of this funk."

"You should maybe lay low for a while. Someone might try to hurt you. Too much publicity is a bad thing unless you're an entertainer or a politician. I would recommend a trip, a vacation for a bit until this thing is out of the news."

"Not now, Mama."

"Why don't you invite Adara over? I'll make a special dinner."

"Oh, Mama!"

* * *

Ahmed noticed the mess in the basement in his father's gas station in Chambersburg. He asked his father, "What happened?"

"Please straighten up for me. Naib and Ali were here."

"Sure."

A few minutes later, after his father had gone upstairs, Ahmed took out his phone and texted *"Ahmed and Ali were here and took weapons. I believe they're headed back to NYC."*

TWENTY-THREE

Late that afternoon, at the Metropolitan, Croydon and Totten sat in the back with cocktails.

"What am I going to do?" Croydon said. "The prosecutor won't back down. I'd like to postpone the Imam's case till this blows over. I asked her and she refuses. Hite wants the publicity. I have to let her continue."

"Okay. Let's try this. Hite quit to run for the Senate. There's no U.S. Attorney to replace him yet. None has yet been announced. This is not the moment to postpone the Imam's case. You need the publicity too."

"I'm afraid the search order I issued will come back to bite me. These people are heroes. If the order comes out, it could mean that I'll be stuck here."

"Stuck as a federal court judge? Not a bad place to be stuck."

"I want something more."

"Okay. I'll give you more. Mark Auburn is about to be nominated to replace Hite as U.S. Attorney. He's being vetted now, and the announcement will come in a few days once the process is completed. He looks good. Your name was discussed, but the fact that you once employed an illegal to clean your home took your name off the list. The president wants to nominate Auburn. It will make the president look good. The party has other plans for you. Let's talk."

"So what's in it for me?"

* * *

Naib checked into room 14 at the Windmill Motel in New Jersey. He backed his car in so he could quickly open the trunk and take in whatever he needed to. Arafat took a walk and brought back a bag of tacos and some sodas.

They sat in the room as Naib and Ali cleaned and oiled the guns one at a time and tried each and every moving part to be sure they worked smoothly and reliably. Arafat just sat there and watched them without saying a word.

Naib turned to him. What are you looking at?"

"What are you talking about? I'm just sitting here."

"I don't like to be stared at."

"Sorry. I'll take a walk."

Arafat was walking around the area to waste some time when he passed Richard's West End Pub. He walked in and sat at the bar. It was moderately crowded with mostly young people. As he sat, a woman in very short shorts and a bikini top sat next to him.

The bartender was a woman in her fifties with a good but almost plump figure. She wore black tights and a very tight black top as she leaned close to him. "What can I get for you?"

"Beer. Whatever you have on tap."

As the bartender got the beer, the woman in the bikini top and cut-off jeans turned to Ali. "Hi. Wanna buy me a beer?"

"Sure." Arafat held up two fingers and the bartender nodded yes.

"I'm Elise. You're cute. First time here?"

Arafat's unshaven pimpled face let up with a big smile.

"Yes."

"What are you here for?"

"Just here to enjoy the beach."

"You have an accent. Where are you from?"

"You ask a lot of questions."

"Sorry. Just a working girl trying to be friendly. I can make your trip even more fun."

"I'd like that."

"Where are you staying?"

"At the motel near here, but my friend is using the room and I don't think he wants me back for a while."

"For fifty cash I can take care of you right out back."

Arafat looked at her excitedly. "Sure."

"Only head. More will cost you."

"Head's enough."

She took him around the corner to an alley between a synagogue and a deli. It was dark and anyone on the street could see little or nothing.

"Money first."

He gave her a fifty-dollar bill and she got onto her knees and started to take care of him.

"I'm nervous. We can be seen here."

"I know what I'm doing. It's too dark. No one can see and there are no police around here."

A flashlight shone on them both as a police officer said, "Hold it right there."

Arafat zipped himself up quickly and then started to run to the back of the alley to discover another police officer blocking the path. They were both arrested.

The house phone rang in room 14 as Naib answered it. "What! Are you insane? Get you a lawyer? How could you call me here? I'll call you back in a few minutes."

Naib and Ali loaded up the car and left.

* * *

Monday morning, Zalmanski removed Choe's arm from his shoulder, got out of bed and opened the apartment door to pick up his newspaper. There were two headlines. The big one read *TERRORIST CAPTURED WITH PROTITUTE.* Underneath there was a smaller article titled *PRESIDENT TO NOMINATE HERO FOR POSITION OF U.S. ATTORNEY IN MANHATTAN.*

The article explained that at a press conference to be held that afternoon, Mark Auburn would be nominated by the president to replace Charles Hite. There was an article on page three about Hite's difficulties raising funds for his Senate campaign.

Bill immediately called Pounders.

"Yes, I heard about it. It's on the cable news, channel one," Jeff said.

* * *

Jeff brought in two cups of coffee to Bill's office and sat down.

"I may take a vacation if I can get the office on track. We're still shaken up. Adara's mind is elsewhere. Tony isn't Tony," Bill said.

"You? Shook up? Take a vacation? That's not the Bill I know."

The intercom beeped and Adara spoke. "Bill, I'm taking time off from one to three to look at apartments."

"Sure," Bill answered.

TWENTY-FOUR

Adara got off the subway at Columbus Circle and walked two blocks to the apartment building. The concierge allowed her to pass, and she took the elevator to the thirty-fourth floor where the realtor was waiting.

Mark Auburn showed up minutes later. He put his arm around her. "We can be happy here."

Adara looked out over the city. She looked down at Central Park and imagined walking with a child there. She went into the second bedroom. Mark followed.

"This will be our child's room," he said.

Adara kissed him passionately.

* * *

Ali checked out the halal food stand as he attached it to the back of his pickup truck. Naib opened a food storage panel, and behind some packages of bread he placed an automatic handgun, some ammunition and a few hand grenades in a concealed spot behind a storage compartment.

They drove over the Manhattan Bridge to Police Plaza adjacent to the federal courthouse and placed the cart next to a kosher frankfurter stand. Mo was waiting.

"Mo, you're on time. Good. Take over."

"You got it, boss."

Ali unhitched it and drove away.

* * *

Oliver Totten arrived at the Metropolitan and sat next to Croydon. He took a deep breath and said, "Well? Have you been thinking about it?"

"Of course. I want the seat."

"You have to do it now before someone else jumps in. Hite can't raise another dime, and you're the logical challenger. The publicity you've got from this trial is worth tens of millions in campaign contributions you don't have to finish it. The public loves you already."

"Let's get the team together. I'm ready."

* * *

Later that morning Naib showed up at the halal cart and relieved Mo. The street was getting busy with people.

One building away, Charles Robinson took the last sip of his Starbucks coffee as he arranged the evidence along the wall. The Imam's trial was about to begin and he was doing some last-minute touches. Renee and the investigators were all at work. They had worked all morning, and then at noon sharp they had left their offices to buy lunch at the stands in the plaza.

Naib was serving some customers when he noticed Robinson at the kosher frank stand. Curtwright was in line at the Chinese food cart across the plaza. Naib took out a newspaper clip with their photos to make sure they were the correct people. He looked around and noticed two policemen with armor and automatic rifles on the courthouse steps facing away and two more in regular uniform standing behind a column in conversation, a block away in front of another courthouse. He saw that the entrance to the subway station just across the street was clear. He estimated the distances and determined that it would be close but that he had taken this as part of the mission and he would complete it.

He calmly took a 9mm handgun, screwed on a silencer, put several hand grenades into his pocket and left the cart with several people waiting in line. He walked up to Robinson, put the gun to his head and took a shot. Robinson dropped like a brick and blood from his head ran down the pavement. Only a few people seemed to notice at first. As people realized what had happened they ran and screamed, then more and more people started to panic in every direction.

Renee looked around as several people before her in line left and ran. When she noticed a body lying on the ground and saw who it was, she dropped her food as she walked towards him.

Naib walked behind Curtwright, but she realized what was happening at the very last moment and started to run. Naib shot but missed her. She zigzagged. He aimed carefully with both hands as he took a second shot and hit her in the back. She kept running as he took two more shots. One missed and one hit a bystander in the leg. Police from the courthouse ran towards Naib as he ran for the subway entrance across the street. As the police shouted, he ran down into the subway and tossed a grenade up the stairs. The police realized what it was and turned to run as it went off, blowing several bystanders to the ground. Two policemen from the other courthouse ran down another subway entrance and towards Naib in an attempt to flank him. Naib took one shot and a policeman fell. The other policeman ducked behind a pillar.

Naib watched as the train approached. As he jumped aboard, he tossed two grenades into the station without pulling the pins before any one else could come after him. Everyone ducked or ran as the train pulled away.

* * *

Auburn rushed to the scene with Adara at his side. He surveyed the carnage with the police and the FBI. He discussed the human damage with the EMS workers there. They explained to him the details. Three people had died. Several more were injured.

Reporters were everywhere.

He walked up to several of them. "The United States of America will not be intimidated by violence. The prosecution that these two brave people were working on will continue. Their cases may be delayed, but they will be completed. The Imam's trial will continue as soon as practicable. Mr. Robinson and Ms. Curtwright are true heroes. Mr. Robinson will be missed. He was a personal friend and I am deeply grieved. I am told that Ms. Curtwright is expected to recover. One policeman and a bystander were also killed. Another policeman and several bystanders were injured. I am told that two are in serious condition but that they are expected to recover completely. Preliminary reports seem to suggest that the same man who tried to bomb the Freedom Tower committed these crimes. We will bring this man to justice. Of that you can be sure."

Cameras flashed. Every news channel had the video. The next day the newspapers had pictures of Auburn with Adara at his side. As Naib and Ali watched on television Naib said, "Next the lawyers. We'll save her for last."

TWENTY-FIVE

Maria came into Tony's office. "A Mr. Ma here to see you. Here's the info sheet. He paid the consultation fee and wants to discuss political asylum."

"Bring him in."

Tony read the sheet as Mr. Ma sat opposite him.

"So, Mr. Ma. You say here that you are afraid to return to China because of their one child policy. Is that correct?"

"Yes, Mr. Tony."

"It also says that you are married and have two children."

"Yes."

"I see that the children are both in their early twenties."

"That is so."

"Well, if you already have two children, after all these years do you really intend to have more children? Is this really an issue for you at this point in your life?"

"Your office did these cases for my friends. They got permission to work and one of them got a green card. I want the same thing."

"If you lose, this can lead to deportation."

"My wife's brother is an American citizen and filed for us ten years ago. The waiting list is very slow and this will be faster. If this case takes a few years, we may have a green card through her brother by then."

"Maybe, but this is not a good case."

Mr. Ma leaned over to him. "I need the work card. I need to stay in America. I want to file. I have a right to file. This is America."

"If the government decides it's a frivolous case, the law says you can be barred for life from obtaining a green card."

"Isn't it true that I can finish my brother in law's case without returning to China if I file this application?"

"Yes, that might be so."

"I want to do this. My friends all filed frivolous cases and this didn't stop any of them. You did some of them."

"I'm not going to do this one. Sorry, Mr. Ma."

"Why not? These cases are granted by the court every day. I know what you charge and I'm willing to pay the whole fee. I don't believe you can lose a case right now. If you don't take it, I'll open the Chinese paper and find another lawyer. I trust you because you did right by my friends and family. I'm willing to pay more for it if you do it."

"I'm a bit more careful about what cases I take now. I'm sorry, Mr. Ma. This is just not an honest case."

* * *

Maria went to Bill's office. "The police are here."

"Bring them into the conference room and tell Tony and Adara. Tell Ryan too."

As they gathered, a woman and a man entered. The woman was in uniform. "I'm sergeant Malloy. I will be the person in charge of your security. As you know, until the terrorists are caught your office will be assigned a full-time policeman during work hours, and another plain-clothes officer will be either outside the building or in your office much of the time. There's a national manhunt going on. It shouldn't be long before they're caught. This terrorist Naib killed several law enforcement officers in several states and is extremely dangerous. They both are."

"So we're the bait," Bill said.

"Not at all," Malloy said. "You are considered a low priority target for him, but just in case, you need protection. We are setting up cameras across the street, in the lobby and right now I have a man setting one up in your waiting room. If Naib comes here we'll see him."

"Seeing him and stopping him are different," Adara said.

"We do not consider you a likely target," Malloy said.

"Tell that to Charles Robinson," Bill said.

"That was unfortunate," Malloy said. "We were caught by surprise. We thought any rational person would try to escape and head out of the country. We were surprised that he knew Robinson's habits."

"These people are anything but rational," Adara added.

"We were wrong. We don't intend to be wrong again."

"You must know that we tried to warn the police and the FBI that these men were planning something and that we were not listened to," Adara said.

"We're listening to you now. Well in any case," Malloy added, "we won't make the same mistake twice. You are possible targets, especially you, Mr. Zalmanski. We will protect you. This terrorist, Naib, has at least one accomplice and maybe more."

"We know," Adara said. "We know Ali and there are certainly others. Every food cart vender that uses their space is a suspect."

"You can't accuse all Muslims in the food industry of terrorism."

"No, but I would be watching them," Adara said.

"We can't suspect all Muslims. Most are decent citizens."

"I said watch them. If your child's life was at stake, you would be talking very differently."

"The terrorist we caught in New Jersey was with Naib at the time he was arrested but hasn't given us enough information to capture Naib yet. We don't expect Naib to double back to any place he was indentified. We will update you if we have anything."

"Did you waterboard him?" Adara asked.

"You know we don't do things like that," Malloy said.

"If it costs one of us our lives, you may be sorry that you didn't. Arafat might give up a lead or two."

"Thank you," Bill said. "You can't be with each of us all the time."

"We'll try. In any case, he may try to hit the office to make a statement. He might case this building first. It is possible," Malloy said.

"You just said that you don't think we're targets," Adara said.

"Just in case."

As the police left, Bill asked the rest to wait and took them to his office. As he opened his desk, he took out two revolvers. "I have two revolvers. They're loaded. I don't think he'll come here, but it's a good idea to be prepared."

"I'll take one," Tony said.

"Did you ever shoot a gun?" Adara asked Tony.

"No. How hard can it be?"

"It can be very hard. Forget everything you saw in the movies," Bill said. "We have to practice. We'll go to the range near here after work. Adara's right."

"Are these guns legal?" Ryan asked.

"Not the right question," Bill said. "The correct question is how are we going to feel if we can't defend ourselves and this nut job shows up."

"Where did you get the guns?" Ryan asked.

"I picked them up at gun shows when I had a cabin upstate. They were bought legally. They're old but work fine."

"So they're not registered in New York City. This could be a problem for us," Tony said.

Everyone looked at Bill and there was a moment of silence. "Getting killed could be a bigger one. No one has to take one. You'll just rely on that NYPD broad to protect you when you take the trains to work, when you are alone at home. Huh. You think that makes sense? You don't think that leveling the playing field makes more sense?"

Ryan sighed. "I'm nervous around guns."

"Did you ever shoot one?" Bill asked.

"In the Boy Scouts," Ryan answered.

"This will be a wake-up call for you," Bill said.

"I will take one," Adara said.

"Have you ever shot a gun?" Bill asked Adara.

"Yes. Don't ask about the details."

"What about you, Tony? You still want one?"

"I'll take one," Tony said.

"Eighty per cent of the things we worry about never happen. This is almost certainly part of the 80 percent, but just in case it's better to be safe than sorry," Bill said.

"My opinion," Ryan said, "is that it's not likely that we'll be able to use these when we have to. Things like this happen fast when you least expect it."

"You're a Jew. Where would Israel be today if every Jew there thought like that?" Bill said.

"I'll take it."

"Ryan's right. Naib and his friends won't care if you have it or not," Adara said. "When he comes it will be so fast we won't know what hit us. We need to change our schedule every day. While we're here he'll know that the police might stop him."

"The police didn't stop him yesterday," Ryan said.

"I'll leave one in my desk drawer. We'll leave the other in Adara's. We use them only in the worst case."

"The worst case is that we won't have them when we need them," Ryan said.

"Well, we have two. Use your judgment." Bill continued. "Tomorrow we have a contractor coming. We're getting a steel entrance door and a bullet- proof window for the receptionist area. Visitors will have to be buzzed in. It's not perfect but will have to do."

"I wonder if we'll be safe even if this guy is captured," Tony said. "You never know if there's some copy cat who'll try something."

Bill stood up. "We can't fix everything forever. Let's do what we can. Back to work."

When Bill returned to his office, he sat down and looked at Totten. "Thanks for waiting. Well? Did you listen?"

"Yes. You and I are the only ones who would pull the trigger if it comes to it."

"Adara would."

"No one else."

"I hope you're wrong."

* * *

"Stan. Come over here," Gomez said. "Here's the schedule for this week. You and Wong are doing Starbucks from eight to one on Monday and Thursday, then on to your regular duties. Bring your sides. Katz and Leroy will replace you those afternoons."

"Got it. Kevlar?"

"A must."

"Who authorized this?"

"Too many questions."

"We're Homeland Security. Justice Department can't authorize us to do this."

Gomez looked at them directly in the eye. "Just do it."

* * *

As the sun rose, Ali got out of the bed over the gas station in Chambersburg, Pennsylvania. He went into the bathroom and started to shave. Naib got up from the other couch and turned the TV on to CNN.

CNN had a headline about the manhunt for them. The commentator began, "Breaking News, law enforcement teams assure our sources that everything possible is being done to capture the terrorists known as Naib and Ali. There is not an airport or bus terminal in the country that can be used by them to escape. Highway patrols have been alerted and are watching traffic for suspicious vehicles."

"They don't know shit," Ali said.

"Don't believe what you hear. This is what they want the public to know. Maybe they hope to leave a door open as a trap, but that won't get us. We'll take our time. No one knows we're here."

"We should be out of this country," Ali said.

"No. We will punish them."

"Naib, I understand revenge. This whole thing is about revenge. Revenge for what the West is doing to us, for the Imam, but what you are doing is making it personal. This is wrong."

"These people must be punished. The world must know."

"There is a saying that when you plan revenge dig two graves."

"We live by the Koran."

"Don't you see? You are not on the mission anymore. Your ego has taken over. It's become about you."

"You don't understand."

"When people tell me that I don't understand, I know that they don't. I think we should get out and live to fight another day. We'll find another mission."

Naib walked into the bathroom, grabbed Ali by the neck and smashed him against the wall. He squeezed Ali's neck till Ali started turning blue. "We will finish the job, me and you. If I hear you talk like a coward again,

I'll kill you. Do you understand? If we go back as failures, we'll have to charge some Syrian army unit with suicide vests. Got it!"

Ali barely nodded "yes."

"Say it!"

"Yes."

"The Islamic State is in trouble. We can turn things around. We, you and me, can bring hundreds of thousands of jihadists to the cause. Say it again."

"Yes."

* * *

Auburn sat in his office when he texted to his phone. *Naib and friend at the gas station?*

Across the street from the gas station, a man working in the thrift shop read the text and called him back. "Don't think so, Mr. Auburn. I didn't notice any unusual activity. I don't think they're here…..Yes. I'll report to my supervisor at the end of every shift…I promise that I will report anything immediately. I know my job….No, we didn't install the cameras yet…Yes, we will do it soon…as soon as we have an opportunity…Yes, I know how important this is, but someone else is responsible for that…. No, I'm not sure who that is."

Auburn called the FBI office in Harrisburg and asked to speak to the supervisor. He explained that it was urgent and that he knew where the terrorists could be arrested immediately.

The receptionist took the call. "I'm sorry, Mr. Auburn, but my boss is out at just this moment and I do not have authority to act until I speak to him. As we talk I have already sent him a text message to call here immediately."

"No, please. He needs to call *me* at once. The terrorists may be at the gas station in Chambersburg and we need to get every police and FBI agent there at once!"

"I'm sorry, Mr. Auburn, but my instructions are to just text the boss. I'm sure he's at an important meeting just now, and he'll call you back very soon."

"Very soon is no good. They'll be gone. Right now may be too late. Don't you see the urgency?"

"I have my instructions, sir. I will get back to you as soon as I can."

"These bastards tried to nuke New York. We need to drop everything else and get them. Call him right now and tell him I ordered you to do it."

"I'm doing everything I can, Mr. Auburn."

"Okay, let's do it this way. I am ordering you to contact whatever FBI and police units there are in the Chambersburg area and have them converge on that gas station and arrest the terrorists. Got it?"

"I'm sorry sir. You have no jurisdiction here. My boss will get back to you when he can."

"I will do it then."

"With all due respect, sir, this is not your jurisdiction."

Auburn called the Chambersburg police and asked for the supervisor.

"Yes, can I help you?" he answered.

"This is Mark Auburn, FBI New York."

"I know who you are, sir."

"I think the terrorist Naib is at the gas station by you right now. I need a team to get him immediately."

"With all due respect sir, I have orders to take orders only from the FBI office in Harrisburg. I promise you I will call them to get the okay right now."

* * *

Naib was now shaving to see how clean-shaven he could look. He took some makeup and rubbed it onto his face. His constant five o'clock shadow seemed to recede. He opened another bottle and rubbed something into his hair that made his hair go from black to brown. Ali watched the evening news on CNN. There was a breaking news headline. *TWO TERRORISTS STILL AT LARGE, MANHUNT CONTINUES.*

"Every half hour they have the same breaking news headline. You would think people would get tired of this shit," Ali said.

At that moment the CNN displayed photos of the terrorists. "People are stupid," Naib said. "Most Americans will watch this show for hours with the same news and the same photos of us, but when they actually see us they won't even know who we are."

"You can't count on that. It takes just one."

"That's true, but even if they recognize us it will take a minute to sink in. It's our job to act fast enough so that that minute doesn't matter."

"Let's discuss the plan again."

"Simple," Naib said. "We enter the office on a Friday afternoon. Things will be quiet then. We'll take them all hostage and cut their throats one at a time. I want Zalmanski and Adara to go last so they can see everyone else die before them. We then get out quick and go to Bay Ridge, Brooklyn where we will be hidden until we can be taken to safety."

"It is Wednesday evening already. Do you want to wait till Friday?"

Naib waited until it was very dark and peeked out through the blinds. "We'll have to. Let's get out of here now. It's dangerous to stay in this place too long."

"Wait for cover," Ali said.

"I don't think we're being watched."

"Better safe than sorry."

"Okay."

Naib and Ali waited a bit more until the station was busy and there were several tractor-trailers filling up the stalls. They went through the store and out the back of the garage through another building. They carried nothing and walked about a block to a forested area and disappeared into the trees. About thirty minutes later they emerged in a clearing where a car was waiting. Naib checked the trunk and saw that it was filled with weapons, ammo, a suitcase with a change of cloths and some cash. They slept in the car until light and drove down the dirt road to a county road and then north on Highway 81 towards New York City.

Very early the next morning a swat team showed up at the gas station.

Auburn got a call from the chief of operations for the FBI in Harrisburg telling him there was no sign of the terrorists but that they found a treasure of weapons and that the family was arrested.

Auburn asked to have the son Ahmed separated from the family and given special treatment.

TWENTY-SIX

Tony and Harold stood outside the courtroom and looked at the calendar. Tony ran his finger down the list till he found the name *Jose Bueno*. They were number two. Judge McCormick's courtroom was only moderately busy that afternoon—nothing like the usual morning zoo. There were four cases on the list, and each one required more attention than could be given at a master calendar hearing. Two of those cases were scheduled for the afternoon and testimony would be taken.

Tony noticed the two linebackers waiting in the hall and thought to himself *oh shit*.

Sandra Peterson walked by. "Hi, Tony."

"Good morning, Ms. Peterson." Tony smiled a bit too much.

Harold Peters was waiting for the hearings to begin and came over to Tony. "Hey, Tony."

"Glad you're here."

The judge called the first case and a lawyer came up to the respondent's table with his client. After the preliminaries the judge asked the lawyer. "Counselor, your client has a conviction for robbery and obstruction of justice. You admitted this at the master hearing and admitted that he is removable from the United States."

"Yes, your honor," the lawyer said.

"This is a Joseph hearing. You requested this hearing to discuss the respondent's release on bail. His notice says that he is subject to mandatory detention but was released on bond in error. Do you have anything to say to this?"

"He was released on bond and that bond should be continued."

"The officer who determined the bond did so in error and the respondent should have the bond revoked," Peterson said.

"Will my client's money be returned if the bond is revoked?" the lawyer asked.

"Yes," the judge answered.

The lawyer looked at his client and the client nodded yes. "Then we have no objection to the bond being revoked."

"Since there is nothing in disagreement, I will revoke the bond and schedule this matter for April 22 two years hence. Please wait for your hearing notice, counselor."

Tony stood in back with his mouth open and wanted to intervene but couldn't bring himself to. *What an idiot,* he thought.

As the client walked out, the two linebackers handcuffed him as his lawyer stood there stuttering. "B-b-but the judge said the bond was revoked."

"You shouldn't be here if you don't know the system," one of the officers said.

"579," McCormick said.

Tony and Bueno approached the respondent's table. Judge McCormick looked at Bueno and then took a second look.

The judge turned to Tony. "You are a hero, Mr. Sorrelli."

"I can't discuss it right now."

"Understood." The judge pressed a button on his computer to begin recording. "This is Judge McCormick on this day at the Immigration Court in New York City. Will counsel for the respondent introduce himself?"

"Tony Sorrelli for the firm of Zalmanski and Sorrelli, New York City."

"And for the government."

"Sandra Peterson, Assistant District Counsel."

Tony smiled. "Good morning, Judge, and again, good morning, Ms. Peterson."

Sandra smiled at him but didn't answer.

The judge went through the usual preliminaries such as representation and addresses.

"This is a Joseph hearing. The government requested this hearing to discuss the respondent's release on bail. Their notice says that he is subject to mandatory detention but was released on bond in error. Do you have anything to say to this?"

"My client is a legal permanent resident of the United States and is eligible for cancellation of removal. The law is clear that mandatory detention occurs when the respondent is turned over from criminal custody to ICE custody. That was not done here. He was released with bond. He is not subject to mandatory detention."

"This man runs a valet parking company and steals cars to order. He is a danger and deserves to be incarcerated immediately. He was charged with grand theft auto and should be deported," Sandra said. "Last conviction he was charged with stealing a red Porsche 911."

Tony looked around and saw no other deportation officers. "His conviction was for petit larceny, and you have the record of conviction. It is irrelevant what he was charged with. Police often overcharge suspects. It's the conviction that counts. Anyway, just look at him. He couldn't get into a Porsche 911 if he wanted to."

Jose hit him lightly on the arm. "Hey!"

"Please let your lawyer talk until you're asked a question," Judge McCormick said.

"Yes, judge."

The judge picked up some papers. "Let's see." He read for a minute. "It isn't at all clear to me that he's eligible for mandatory detention or not from these papers."

"Then he should be detained until he can prove he is eligible for relief and then we can determine his threat to society and what the terms of his release should be," Peterson said.

"He's innocent until proven guilty. In any event, this is a civil court, not a criminal one. This court is not here to punish Mr. Bueno but to determine if he should be allowed to live in the United States," Tony said.

"That is true, Mr. Sorrelli."

"I have an expert witness available, Mr. Bueno's criminal attorney." Harold Peters waved and the judge nodded in recognition. "He can testify as to the disposition. Then I have a memo of law he prepared on the crime and another one I prepared on his right to a bond based upon that conviction to document this." Tony handed the memos to Sandra first and then to the judge.

The judge read them and looked at Peterson. "Well, Ms. Peterson?"

"We will not oppose the continuation of his parole."

"On the way out, Bueno took out two rolls of hundred dollar bills and gave one to Tony and a smaller one to Peters. "You guys earned it."

"Come to the office soon. Friday might be good. I'll give you a receipt and we have to discuss your case," Tony said.

"I don't need no receipt. See you Friday." Bueno smiled. He may not have needed the receipt but he did need a god dermatologist.

* * *

As Tony returned to the office he noticed a man standing in front of his building selling individual roses. They looked old and withered and Tony wondered who would buy them. As Tony passed the man smiled and flipped his lapel to reveal a police badge. Tony winked back.

As Tony entered the office, workmen were busy installing a new steel door between the waiting area and the rest of the office. Maria was now sitting behind a plastic window two inches thick. Maria handed Tony several messages.

"Can you run down and get me a Starbucks? You know what I want." Maria nodded yes.

As he passed Ryan's door he stuck his head in. "Your memo did the trick. You'll do the next one."

Maria ran down to Starbucks. She looked over her shoulder and was afraid every moment. When she returned, she said to Tony, "I'm very afraid. Can I have some time off till these guys are caught?"

"I don't know. If everyone takes off, we can't function. I need you. Let me discuss this with Bill."

That meant no.

TWENTY-SEVEN

Mario's of Fourteenth Street was busy that night; but isn't it busy every night? Jeff was the first to show up and immediately put away some challah garlic bread and wine. Bill, Tony and Ryan showed up.

Bill sat next to Jeff. "Hey! Leave some for us."

Jack Martin and Harold Peters came next. The waiter had to bring more bread. As usual, Harold was the only one to show up with a briefcase.

Mario came over and announced, that for tonight, wine was on the house in honor of the heroes. Mario put down two more bottles of red wine and they were gone in about three minutes.

Harold Peters pulled out his pad and started the proceedings. "Well, tonight we have to debrief Bill and Tony about their adventure. Since they're heroes, I propose that we pick up their bill for tonight."

"You cheap bastard," Jack said. "Mario has already picked up the wine. What about waiting till we have a more expensive dinner?"

"We can do that another time," Jeff said. "We'll plan the next one at an expensive steakhouse. Let's eat."

"Jeff, I'm taking you to a salad place," Bill said. "Vinaigrette dressing only."

"Look who's calling the kettle black," Jeff replied.

Harold thumbed through his notes. "Our business for tonight is about our heroes. They saved the world and we need to toast them."

They all raised their glasses and Ryan stood up.

Jack stopped him. "What the hell are you toasting for? You are one of the toastees."

"Not me. I just happened to be there."

"That makes no sense. You got shot. How often does that happen? You earned a place on the hero list, but go ahead," Jack said.

"I didn't know what the hell I got myself into when I took this job."

"No shit," Jack said.

"I thought I was working for a meshuganah and a crusader. I thought I would work until I found a real estate job, make a few bucks and move on. I haven't looked back. These guys have taught me a lot, and I found my calling. I thank you personally for that. You really did save the damsels in distress and America. I thank you for that, too. But most of all you both have been mentors to me and have taught me how to be not just a better lawyer but also a better person. For that I toast you both."

"How about a few bucks, kid? This is a good time to ask them for a raise," Jack said.

"That too."

Jack Martin took a sip and turned to Bill. "This kid really knows how to suck up to his bosses."

"I have a toast," Jeff said. "These are true patriots, great Americans." He held up his glass and they all took a sip. Jeff smiled and stuffed a piece of garlic challah into Jack's mouth.

"Well said by a guy born in Jamaica," Jack said.

"I'm an American. Where were your parents born, Jack?"

"The Dominican Republic and I'm proud to be Dominican and American."

"If we're finished, I have other news to get to," Harold said.

"Shut up, Harold," Jack said. "I have a toast. To two lucky bastards. You had the wrong clients, handled them the wrong way, and did the wrong things according to the law. Where did you go right?"

Amid laughs they drank another sip.

Harold stood up. "My turn, and then we'll get to business."

"Screw you," Jack said. "Make your toast and then we'll see what we want to do. I'm here for a good time. I do business all day. Let's celebrate."

Harold cleared his throat. "To my buddies Bill and Tony and to my new buddy Ryan. May you never again have to go through what you did."

"That's it?" Jack asked.

"We have things to discuss."

"Let's vote on it," Jack said. "All in favor of deep sixing Harold's list and having more wine and eating, raise their hands."

They all did except Harold.

"But we have to discuss the new procedure for extending DACA applications and changes in Stokes interviews."

"I won. You lost. Let's eat."

"I want to ask Bill and Tony how they feel after all of this," Harold said.

Everyone looked at Tony. "I'm a bit of a nervous wreck. I need some time to process everything."

"That's all you've got?" Jack said.

"For now."

"And you, Bill?" Jack asked.

"I'm sort of upset that I didn't kill those other bastards. There might be more."

"You got one. You're a real Rambo. It's more than the police did," Jack said.

"He is," Peters said. "He took action and saved the day. How many of us would have done that?"

"Well, three of the six of us participated in this. That's half and that's pretty good," Jack said. "And you, Ryan? How do you feel? You took a bullet for the cause."

"I'm the low man on the totem pole. I was just glad to be of some help."

"Okay, Bill," Jack said. "How's Choe working out for you?"

"I'm gonna be broke if she stays."

"Why? Is she spending a lot of your money?"

"No, I can't afford the Viagra. My insurance won't cover it." Everyone in the surrounding tables looked and listened.

"A little louder, Bill. They can't hear you in Seoul."

People all around laughed.

Jack brought the volume down. "What about the twelve-year-old girls, Bill?"

"After Choe I'm lucky if I can stand up."

They went on for a while. After the tiramisu they split the bill three ways.

At the bar two men were drinking a beer and watching the Yankees play on TV. Once in a while one of them glanced toward the immigration attorneys. As Bill left the bar he walked past them and whispered, "Stan. Wong. Thanks."

They winked.

As Harold and Tony walked down Foureenth Street, Harold asked, "Are you going to visit your friend on this block?"

"No more. I'm looking for more, a friend and an ally."

"Since when do you demand that of a woman? You only look for lovers."

"Things change. People change."

"By ally and friend do you mean Adara?"

"Don't know."

* * *

The next morning Mark Auburn left the Senate office building and on the way to the airport called Adara. "It went well. I think both sides of the aisle like me. I wasn't asked about any political affiliations and they seemed to be fine with my lack of experience as an actual prosecutor."

"You're the perfect man for the job. I can't wait till we're together."

"Soon. The divorce papers have been filed. Once I'm sure that they are signed, we can tell the world."

"Love you," Adara said.

"Me too."

TWENTY-EIGHT

Friday was unusually busy at Zalmanski and Sorrelli.

Maria showed up with her daughter and explained that she didn't have a babysitter for the day and promised that it wouldn't happen again. Adara acted tough and didn't believe her, but within minutes Adara had Pepita were drawing pictures together.

Bill sipped his coffee as he played with his revolver and read the day's newspapers.

Late in the morning Bueno came in with his girlfriend. She was as small as he was large. Blond and boney with messy hair, cowboy boots, and in severe need of a decentmeal she strangely looked the part.

"We're here to see Tony," Bueno told Maria.

"Mr. Sorrelli wants you to see Mr. Goldberg. He's going to work up your case."

"I wanna see my Mr. T just for a moment."

Tony came out. "Mr. Bueno. I wanted my associate to work up the papers for the court. I assure you he knows what he's doing."

"That's okay. I wanted to give you this. Like a tip." Bueno handed Tony another roll of money.

"You already did this. I owe you a receipt for the last one."

"Yeah. Rodriguez's wife is coming later to discuss money. You've got four thousand there. Tell her that you're going to give her a four-thousand-dollar discount. She only has another two thousand for you anyway. You did me a great favor by trying to help them."

"That's my job. And who is this?"

"My girlfriend. If I'm deported, she'll suffer big hardship."

"My associate will start the paperwork with you."

"You got it."

They sat down with Ryan.

Ryan listened to Bueno's explanation about his girlfriend and then responded. "Only if you're married. Hardship to her won't count otherwise. And you have to show you're paying taxes. Without taxes we can't show that there's a loss to your spouse."

"I'll file taxes next year."

"You have to go back two or three years."

"Costs too much."

"You'll need to do it anyway. How long have you been together?"

"We met last week." She smiled.

"We have to document hardship and reformation. There's economic hardship. If you're making money and you're deported to the Dominican Republic, you can't support yourself or your family the same way you can here. To prove you're supporting yourself here, you need taxes. If you don't have taxes, you'll be telling the judge that you're either lying to the IRS or to him. Not a good position to be in."

"I'll work on that," Bueno said.

"There's psychological hardship. If you just met, there isn't much hardship."

"We love each other."

"We'll need a lot more than that. Let's discuss reformation," Ryan said. "We need to show that you're doing the right thing now. Taxes will help show this."

"What's your favorite car?"

"What?"

"What's your favorite car? You know a fun car."

"I guess I might like a Mustang Shelby. A convertible; in orange."

"I know where you can get one, white sedan with black leather interior. Has a racing stripe up the middle. It's easier to get than a color like orange. I'm not sure that model comes in a convertible."

"You're in this mess because of your convictions for auto theft. What are you doing?"

"Don't worry. I've reformed, but I'd like to reward you for doing a good job. I know how to get good deals on cars."

"*You* have to do a good job. If you get arrested on another charge in the middle of this case, kiss America goodbye."

"I'll even fix the paperwork for you."

"What paperwork?"

"On the Shelby."

The blonde just sat there and smiled. Whenever Ryan looked at those misplaced, missing, stained teeth, he cringed. He thought of what the teeth marks on Bueno's penis must look like and he opened his drawer and took a Tums.

"Mr. Bueno, I really want to help you. You have to understand how the system works. We need to present the court with a package of evidence and forms to show certain things. We have to make it hard for the judge to say no to you and easy for him to say yes."

"I get that. I also support my mother."

"Without the taxes it doesn't mean much. Does she work?"

"Sure. She owns a bodega in the Bronx."

"Does she file tax returns?"

"Yeah. I think she shows about eight thousand a year."

Ryan popped another Tums.

"Okay. Now we need to make a list of things in your favor that we can prove. We have to document them. For example, any community activities would be helpful."

"Like what?"

"If you were a member of a church or if you coached a team."

"Oh yeah. I play on a softball team. Every Saturday morning we play softball in Great Neck with some Jewish guys. We play from eight to ten in the morning, the Dominicans against the Jews. We win more than they do. The Jews have to finish by ten to get to shul."

"*Oh boy.* Do you play with a Max Goldberg?"

"Yeah. Short stop."

"He's my father. He bought a used BMW recently. Do you know anything about it?"

"Sure. I found it for him. I gave it to him at a price he couldn't have gotten anywhere else."

"Did he know it was stolen?"

"I don't steal cars. Every car I deal was handed over to me, legal-like."

"'Like' is not the same as legal."

"It's legal."

"The State of New York may have a different opinion about that."

* * *

Mrs. Rodiguez showed up without an appointment and with a large shopping bag full of papers. She walked up to Maria. "I came to see Mr. Sorrelli with the documents he told me to bring."

"You picked a busy day. Mr. Sorrelli asked Mr. Goldberg to see you. He'll be a few minutes. Can you wait?"

"I'm here. I'll wait."

* * *

Adara and Bill went to Mudville for lunch.

The waitress came over and put down some pickles and slaw. "Good afternoon. Is Tony coming?"

Adara refused to look at her. "No, Claire. Just the menus, please."

"Just trying to be friendly. Drinks?"

"Coffee," Bill said. "For both and we'll split a club sandwich and fries."

Bill took a pickle from the table. "When are you going to tell Tony?"

"I'm not telling anyone. It's nobody's business. Tony's not my boyfriend. Mark wants to wait till his divorce is finalized, and I think we should just live together a while to see how it goes."

"I think Tony loves you."

"I don't. He had plenty of chances—years' worth. He never showed it. He wants to play. Let him. He knows that if we have a real relationship his playing days are over. He's played with my friend right in front of me. I need a man who can be serious. I want to come home to a man who appreciates me: who's excited to see me. I want to be excited about him. I want a man who wants to build a life with me. I found that man. I'm not getting any younger and Tony's not growing up. He's still a boy. I need more than he can give."

"He grew up a chunk."

"Doesn't show it. Anyway, I'm ready to sign the lease with Mark. He needs a New York address for the job. He's been staying at my apartment and he's the best thing to happen to me since political asylum. We're exotic for each other. We want the same thing from the relationship."

"You mean sex?"

Claire came with the coffees. "The conversation just got interesting."

Bill smiled at Claire. "Thanks."

They were silent until Claire walked away.

Adara continued. "No. Well, yes if you want to know. That's part of it, plenty of passion. He's very healthy. I guess he's been saving it up for years. So have I. I want to build a life with someone. I want to live like the family on *The Cosby Show*. Time's passing. Mark wants to get it right this time. I can do that for him. I want a child before it's too late. He's good looking, intelligent and serious, and every minute with him is a pleasure for me. When I wake up in the morning, I'm so happy that he's beside me."

"You didn't use the word 'love'."

"Of course I love him, but that word is misplaced."

"What do you mean?"

"Love isn't enough. People also need to want the same thing out of a relationship. We do. Some people want to play. That's fine, but I want more. I can say I love Mark *and* I love our relationship."

"What about Tony? Do you love Tony?"

"Tony may be fun to play with, but when you grow up you need more. Americans can't seem to distinguish between playing and building a real relationship. You don't enter into a relationship to play."

"I ask again. Do you love Tony?"

"Like a brother."

"Does Mark know you want a child?"

"Sure."

"What does that mean?"

"It means I told him I want a family before I'm too old and he understands what that means. He told me he's excited about doing it again."

"Are you sure you're not rushing into this too fast and for the wrong reasons?"

"Too fast? I've known Mark professionally for ten years now. We've been dating for the past couple of months. The only reason I didn't make a move before was because he was married. What's the wrong reason? Love?

Family? Security? What would I get with Tony, a child? Yeah. I would get a child. He's the child."

"If you're so sure about him, why do you want to wait? Are you afraid he's on the rebound?"

"The prudent thing to do. I've known Mark a long time but not like this. I do want to make sure he's not just on the rebound. He's going straight from his marriage to me. I want to be sure he knows what he's doing. Everything he does is honorable and straight. What you see is what you get and I always admired what I saw. His wife's an idiot. I know what's out there. She's going to trade down. Maybe she wants a woman. Anyway, it might be a complication if he married a Muslim right now."

"I never knew you considered yourself a Muslim. You always seem to avoid the subject of religion."

Claire brought the food and they started eating.

"I don't and I do. I grew up between two religions. Religion has been a curse to my family and me my whole life. Did you know I had an older brother?"

"I don't know any details. I only know he died a long time ago."

"I was very young when he disappeared. He was much older. I barely remember him. We think Saddam Hussein's men took him away and we never heard from him again. He was a teenager and we never found out what he did. My mother thought it was because he was a Shiite or a Christian. His friends said he expressed opinions against Hussein. We got it from all sides. You know the rest."

"Mark comes with baggage, an ex and children."

"The children are grown and off on their own or in college. I have my own baggage. It's called Iraq."

"Adara, I love you like a daughter but you can be too businesslike sometimes. This is one time that you should let your feelings lead you."

Adara sighed. "I'm not sure if I ever had the luxury of acting just on my feelings."

"What time are you leaving today?"

"They're throwing Mark a farewell party at the FBI at four. He submitted his resignation contingent on his Senate confirmation. I told him to wait till his appointment was confirmed by the Senate, but everyone seems to think it's a sure thing."

"It probably is."

"He'll pick me up around three-thirty."

"I gotta get back," Bill said.

* * *

Carmen stood in front of the building and took a smoke. She noticed a woman standing across the street in the bank lobby watching the entrance. She noticed the man selling flowers. She noticed Piertowsky stand next to the woman and they began chatting. She caught Piertowsky's eye and they nodded to each other. When Carmen returned to the office and went to Bill.

"The police have someone watching us during the day until the terrorists are caught. Security. Just in case. Piertowsky must be checking things out. Enforcement doesn't do that type of work."

"If immigration has someone there too, they must think we're in danger."

"Better safe than sorry."

At that same moment the woman in the bank called headquarters. "It's very quiet there. Nothing happening this Friday afternoon. Should I report in?"

Malloy thought a moment. "Stay till three-thirty and if it's still really quiet, report in."

The woman looked at Piertowsky. "Everybody goes home early on Friday. Are you staying?"

"For a while."

"It's not your job."

"I'll just watch awhile."

* * *

Tony ran across the street and up to Judge McCormick's courtroom. The court was empty as it usually was on a Friday afternoon. Sandra Peterson was already waiting at her desk with one file in front of her. Tony sat at the respondent's table.

"Good Morning, Sandra. Do we have anything to discuss about this case?"

"It's afternoon and I don't think so. This shouldn't take long. How are you doing? You've been through a lot."

"Pretty good. We have a good team. I consider myself a lucky man." Tony looked at his watch. "Didn't the judge say one thirty? He's already late."

"He'll be here any minute. You could have sent Goldberg to do this conference. Why did you come yourself?"

"He was busy with a client and I know the case. Anyway, he likes to leave a bit early on Fridays to have dinner with his parents on Long Island."

"You're a good boss."

"Our attitude is that if the work gets done well and the clients are happy, the employee is doing a good job. He's doing a good job and we want to keep him happy too."

"Judge McCormick saw him a couple of times and was impressed. He said he reminds him of the way you were as a kid."

Just then the judge came in. "Are you two ready to discuss the Kakamonesis case?"

They both nodded yes.

"Okay, Mr. Sorrelli. Our very own hero."

"Well, I don't think so."

"Were the papers filed in this matter?"

Tony handed a package of papers to Sandra and then to the judge. "The fee has been paid, the government has been served and we're ready to proceed at the court's convenience."

"Have you conferenced to determine if there are any issues we can resolve before trial?"

"Not yet," Sandra said. "We both filed briefs on the charges. There's an issue whether the conviction is for an aggravated felony. You will have to rule on it. In any event, we are ready for a trial on the merits."

"Mr. Sorrelli?"

"Nothing to add, your honor."

"In that case I will schedule this matter for trial on June 25 two years hence. If I decide that the crime was an aggravated felony, I will have to order him removed, and you will have thirty days to file an appeal, Mr. Sorrelli."

Tony nodded.

On the way out, they both got on the elevator. As Sandra got out first, she turned to Tony. "Call anytime."

"Sure," he said as he looked elsewhere.

* * *

Naib and Ali attached the halal cart to the truck and left a warehouse in Brooklyn. They wore beat up overalls, work boots and tool belts. Leather work gloves stuck out of their back pockets. In the back seat were two beat up white construction helmets.

Mo organized the food in the cart. He then pushed the helmets aside and got into the back seat of the truck.

Ali strained as he put a toolbox into the cart. Naib took one last look at the contents of the box to make sure it was in order. He looked at a second toolbox, opened it and looked carefully at the contents. He checked the wires and the cell phone attached to one of several sticks of dynamite in the box. He nodded to Ali.

They said nothing as the drove through the streets of Brooklyn and over the Manhattan Bridge.

They turned south on Broadway and parked the cart directly in front of Bill and Tony's building. Mo unhooked the cart and went inside alone. Ali drove away to park the truck as Naib entered the building. About a block away, Naib left the truck in work clothes and a white helmet, carrying the first toolbox.

Across the street Piertowsky watched as the cart was set up and said to himself, *Shit. It's right in my field of vision.*

* * *

On the way out of the federal building, Tony stopped at the information center on the first floor to pick up some forms. It took only a moment. As he left, he ran into Mark Auburn.

"Tony. How are you doing?"

"Great. And you?"

"Are you in a rush? If not let's get a cup of coffee and kill some time. I'd like to talk."

"Sure."

They went to the Starbucks across the street and got coffee.

Mark poured some cream into his coffee. "You went through a lot you weren't prepared for. I was shaken up. You should've been."

"Me? You were the one that stopped that bomb. I would have peed in my pants."

"You did fine, Tony. Adara and Bill really showed their courage too."

"I would agree."

"It's none of my business and I would not be offended if you told me to mind my own business, but how come you and Adara never got together?"

"Oh boy....It's not a problem....That's not an easy one to answer. I don't know. I guess I was afraid to start something with someone I worked with. You know, if it didn't work out I'd have to deal with it forever, and it wasn't fair to start something with her if I wasn't sure."

"I understand. What weren't you sure about?"

"I just don't think I wanted anything serious, with anyone. She was almost too real. I just wasn't ready."

"Ah hum. Are you ready now?"

"No," Tony continued. "She's a tough woman, maybe too much so. I always felt intimidated by her. And I don't think I want a woman who has to be the boss all the time. She does. Hard to be sure."

"My ex was the reverse—always needy. She used that to manipulate me. It got old fast."

"I run from that," Tony said.

"I do too now."

"That's part of the problem."

"How would you have felt if she had met someone, and he married her out from under you?" Auburn said.

"Adara?"

"Yeh."

"Mark, she deserves a life. I would feel good for her."

"So, I don't understand why you didn't do something about it. You deserve a life too."

"I'm doing fine."

"I always thought you two were an item. I don't understand why it never happened."

"Neither do I. It's probably too late anyway. Even if she threw herself at me, I'm just not in the right place to go for it."

"What about Viviana?"

"You know about Viviana?"

"Now I do."

"Do you know her?"

"No. I just know that she's Adara's friend and you went out with her anyway. She's very sexy."

"She's fun but that's all. What about you? Word is that you're getting a divorce. How will that play during your nomination?"

"Strangely, the Senate staffers didn't ask much about it. They asked me to release a copy of the divorce papers and nothing more. I'm surprised."

"It's not their business."

"Well, they have a different opinion about that."

"What's this really about?"

Auburn took a deep breath. "We need to talk."

"That sounds like a Joan Rivers joke."

"No joke."

"Okay, shoot," Tony said.

"Adara and I have begun a relationship. We're renting an apartment together."

Tony's mouth became dry. He paused a bit. "How could I have missed it?"

Auburn continued. "She's been on my radar for a long time. I care deeply about her."

"O-M-G. But you're still married."

"Only technically. As soon as I agreed to a divorce, my wife started staying with her boyfriend. She's an accountant near where we live and she was having an affair with the maintenance man in the building where she works."

"Ouch!"

"No, it's a relief. The papers are almost done. I'm waiting for the judge to sign. It can't come soon enough. I don't want to step on your toes. I know you've been close to her, but I haven't seen more. Adara seems to think you're not interested. I wouldn't push her for more info. If I had thought I was stepping on your toes…"

Tony was white as rice. "I'm flabbergasted."

"Do you love her?"

"I'll say I love her like a sister."

"Good. I want to be straight with you."

"You don't have to be. It's not my business. Do you love her?"

"I do love her," Auburn said.

"Good."

"It is, Tony. But she also loves the office. It's important to her happiness that we all get along. You and Bill are her family. You're really all that she has, and I don't want to spoil that. We've discussed having a child."

"You really want to do the whole family thing."

"Yes. I loved my children but tolerated my wife for many years. If she had been happy I would have stayed, but now…"

"Now you have Adara."

"Now I have a chance to do it right before I'm too old. I'm forty-seven. In ten years I don't think I'll be able to do this. Adara wants to have a child, and I do too. I'm young enough to do this now. I've always been crazy about her. I remember the first time she came to my office. She dropped off papers on one of your cases. We only spoke for a minute. We argued a bit about whether the papers were complete. I liked her feistiness. Her class really shined. I would see her at the federal cafeteria once in a blue moon and we would chat. She's been to my office filing papers on several other occasions and the way she dealt with us on behalf of your office showed her to be someone very special. Because of the marriage it was impossible. I was always faithful to my wife. I made sure of that so I could leave with a clear conscience. I just assumed that you were the man in Adara's life."

"Did you get divorced because of Adara?"

"Nah. The divorce wasn't my call, but I can tell you at this point…" Mark placed his palms together with fingers up, looked up and whispered, "thank you."

TWENTY-NINE

Everyone was winding down for the weekend.

Bill poured himself a Scotch and discussed Vietnam stories on the telephone with Oliver. Ryan had a file spread out before him while he discussed the law with Bueno. Maria was cleaning her desk for the weekend and arranging photos of her daughter and the statues of the saints while Adara was praising Pepita's art and paying bills.

Viviana walked in. She sat next to Pepita. "And who is this?"

"Hi, I'm Pepita. My mother works here. I'm helping Adara."

"You are the cutest thing. I hope I have a little girl just like you some day."

"You will," Adara winked.

"Not if I keep finding men like Tony. I'm in need of a glass of wine in a nice place."

"I can't leave for an hour or so. Hang out with me."

* * *

Mo organized the cart in front of the building as Ali returned from parking the truck. Piertowsky walked by and paid little attention to Ali when he saw Mo working on the food setup. He wondered why they were starting so late and then he walked away.

Mo opened up the cart as though he was about to sell food.

Ali went into the building, then into the stairwell. He found Naib several seconds later. They went into the basement and quickly found the junction boxes for the telephones. They each reached into the toolbox and took out wire cutters. They reached up and cut every telephone wire they could find. On the way up the stairs they found several more telephone cables and cut each one.

As Bill spoke to Oliver the phone went dead. He called out to Maria. "Are the phones dead?" He took the .22 revolver from his desk and pocketed it.

As they entered the office Ali and Naib took out their hand guns from under their jackets, looked around and saw a green plastic sphere. Ali ripped it out of the ceiling. Naib locked the door. Everyone in the waiting room began to gasp and scream . Maria picked up the telephone to call for help and realized that it was dead. As Maria went into her purse for her cell phone, Naib busted through the second door and took her purse. Ali pointed a gun at the people in the waiting room and ordered them into the conference room.

Naib and Ali ran from room to room and herded everyone into the conference room.

Adara tried to text Auburn an SOS just a millisecond before she was stopped.

Bueno and his girlfriend tried to get up and leave, but Ali saw and waved them into the conference room. Pepita started to cry. The secretaries were all lined up on one wall.

"Bring your cell phones," Naib said. "I want every cell phone turned off and on this table now. If one goes off I will shoot the owner immediately."

One at a time a pile of phones appeared on the conference room table.

"Are you crazy?" Bill asked. "We're being watched. The police will be here in a minute."

Naib bent to within a centimeter of Bill's face. "A minute is all I need. You are the crazy one. You killed my friend and I will punish you for that. He was a righteous man."

"He was a dickhead. He was going to kill two unarmed women. What kind of *warrior* is that?" Bill said.

Naib slapped Bill hard. Bill did not budge.

"I may not make it out of here today," Naib said. "Ali may not either, but today we will make a statement. That statement will tell the world that we remember our enemies. We remember our cause and our values and that the cause and the values are just."

271

"You're just a fucking wacko, and that's the way you'll be remembered," Bill said. "You're not man enough to take me on man to man even though I'm twice your age."

Carmen kicked Bill.

"Shut up, Bill," Adara said.

Naib walked up to Viviana and as they almost touched noses he said, "We will finish today what we failed to finish before. You are here by the will of Allah."

A woman in a hijab spoke up. "I'm a Muslim from Albania. Let me go."

"Prove it," Naib said.

"Take not life, which God hath made sacred, except by way of justice and law: thus doth He command you, that ye may learn wisdom. Six, one fifty one."

"Get out."

She ran.

As she left, Bill reached for Naib's gun. Naib hit Bill on the side with his automatic. Bill fell to the floor and then got up.

"It all doesn't matter. I should kill you now, but I want you to suffer first. I know what you want. You want to be a hero. No. You won't be today. I will punish you by executing the people you love right in front of you: one by one. It will be slow. The police will do nothing because they are confused. They don't believe enough in their cause to take action. I do. I believe in my cause because my cause is just. I am doing God's will. You will be next to last and Adara will be last."

"I repeat. You're a fucking wacko."

Naib shot Bill once in his thigh. It didn't hit a bone and Bill didn't budge. "Now you stand for the last time. Soon you will take your last breath."

There was complete silence in the room. Everyone was afraid to speak or move. Adara took a scarf from Viviana and wrapped it around Bill's leg as she tried to stop the bleeding.

"Very good," Naib said. "You think you're tough. We'll see. I will finish the job very soon."

Adara stepped in front of the crowd. "You want me. Do what you have to, but let the others go. They will tell the world that you took revenge but were merciful at the same time. The others have nothing to do with this. Some are clients just like you."

Naib slapped her hard. "Shut up, woman. You will talk when spoken to. Act like a true Muslim woman. This society has corrupted you. I will end that. I will turn you into a proper Muslim woman if only for a few minutes, and you will be able to die with some dignity."

Naib opened the toolbox and took out two Uzis and gave one to Ali. Naib then took out several hand grenades, put two into his pants pocket and lined up a few on the conference room table.

"Such brave jihadists. You need to carry Israeli guns," Bill said.

"Please shut up, Bill," Adara said. She turned to Naib. "Let the others go, and I will cooperate."

"No. You must suffer first. You must see others die as avenge for your sins. Only then will you be able to grasp the full measure of those sins. Only then will you be able to die honorably."

"What the hell are you talking about?" Bill said. "You sound like you're a character in a B movie."

Naib hit him several times with the butt of his Uzi. Bill fell to the floor. Blood ran down from his head as well as his leg.

"I repeat again. You're a fucking wacko."

Naib kicked him in the stomach.

Piertowsky was watching as the Muslim woman came running out of the building screaming just as Auburn and Sorrelli arrived. A crowd was gathering. He stopped her.

"There are two men with guns upstairs. Do something."

"What's happening?" Piertowsky asked.

"They have guns and they threatened to kill everyone. They asked me if I was a Muslim and then let me go. They say they are going to kill everyone."

A policewoman took charge of her.

Auburn took out a badge on a chain and put it around his neck. Without a word he pulled his gun and ran into the building with Tony right on his tail.

Piertowsky picked up the phone and called his office, but no one answered, not even the voicemail. By four o'clock on a Friday everyone had left. He called Malloy at Police Plaza and asked about the surveillance cameras.

Malloy checked her computer. "The camera in the waiting area is not working." She looked a bit more. "The last thing seems to be a hand reaching up to it."

"Send backup. Pronto. Two or more men with guns at the site."

"Cavalry on the way."

Mrs. Rodriguez stood up and held up two thousand dollars in cash. "I'll give this to you if you let me go."

Naib took her into another room and took out a knife. Without answering, Naib cut her throat. She flew back into the wall and fell to the floor in a pool of blood as the money spilled all over the room. Every woman except Adara was either screaming or crying.

Piertowsky saw Auburn and Sorrelli enter the building, but by before he could do anything they were in the stairwell. Auburn looked at the cut cables running along the wall. He looked at Tony as they realized something was very wrong. As Auburn and Sorrelli got out of the stairwell they heard the woman scream.

Ali turned his back as Bueno pulled a knife and put it to Ali's neck. He grabbed Ali's gun hand and pushed it up as he told Ali to let go of the gun. Ali would not and called out to Naib. "I'm in trouble here."

Naib ran in and pointed his Uzi at Bueno.

"You don't have to do this," Bueno said.

"Why do people always say that just before I shoot them?" Naib said.

He shot Bueno in the shoulder and Bueno collapsed on the floor. Ryan went over and tried to stop his bleeding.

Everyone in the conference room was now screaming. Naib yelled, "Shut up or you're next!" He turned to Ryan. "Don't bother. He will bleed to death. Your turn will come."

Auburn and Sorrelli heard the shots and looked at each other. Auburn just put his forefinger up to his lips.

As they tried to enter the office, Tony noticed the door was locked.

"We can't wait," Tony whispered.

In the conference room there was panic. Naib entered. "Sit down and shut up. I will shoot anyone who gives me a hard time."

A woman raised her hand. In a Russian accent she said, "We're just clients. We have nothing to do with this. You can let us go."

"You're Russian," Naib said. "Your people are killing Muslims in Chechnya. You will be punished too." With that he grabbed her arm and pulled her into the corner. Her boyfriend jumped up and grabbed Naib. Naib easily pushed him away and shot him. The woman jumped on top of him to stop the bleeding. She turned to Naib. "You bastard." He shot her in the head and dropped her next to Bueno. They both lay there in a pool of blood. The boyfriend sat there with his mouth open as he quickly bled out.

Maria and Carmen sat in front of Pepita. The child was crying. Everyone was crying.

"Shut her up, or I'll shoot the child next," Naib said.

Maria hugged and tried to comfort the child as Adara stood up. "Leave the child alone."

"You will get yours very soon."

"You're a coward. Try fighting a man fairly one at a time," Adara said.

"Your country doesn't fight fairly. Why should I?"

"Thank you. You just acknowledged in your own warped way that America is my country."

"You want to be one of these people, you will suffer their fate."

"You are just a murderer looking for an excuse."

As his hands shook Tony took out his key and as quietly as possible unlocked the door. As he entered he saw Ali holding a gun. Mark grabbed Tony's shoulder and pushed him away. Ali shot a blast of bullets as Mark ducked and pulled his own gun. Ali ducked and Tony crawled away.

"The police are on the way," Adara said. "You are about to meet Allah and your seventy-two virgins. I don't think you'll know what to do. You're not man enough for one."

"We have a few surprises for the police." Ali pulled the pin and rolled a hand grenade towards the front door. Auburn slammed the door shut and both Tony and Mark ran for the stairwell. The blast destroyed the front door and the waiting room and blew out some windows in the suite but little else.

As the glass burst from the windows it started to fall onto the growing crowd on Broadway. The police began to surround the building.

"Too late for you." Naib grabbed Maria by the hair and pulled her out of the chair. Pepita was screaming as Adara and Carmen protected her.

Naib ripped the cross off Maria's neck. "You think this will protect you? You think those statues on your desk will protect you?" He threw the cross away. He then pulled out a knife and slit her throat.

"You bastard," Bill said as he pulled the gun from his pocket. As Bill stood up Naib dropped the knife and swung his Uzi. They fired together. Bill was hit once on the side. One bullet hit Ryan on his side. Bill's shot hit Naib. Bill fell and his gun slid away. Naib fell into the corner and was bleeding on one side.

As Naib lay there he pulled a grenade from his pocket and pulled the pin. Bill managed to jump on top of him, grab the grenade and toss it into his empty office where it exploded.

As Bill struggled with Naib, he slowly faded until he was too weak to continue. Naib sat against the wall and pointed his gun at his hostages, "Your boss will bleed to death in just a minute. Just enough time for him to see you die."

Auburn and Sorrelli were on opposite sides of the door opening as Ali fired several more shots. They could hear the explosion and shots from the conference room. Auburn pumped two shots through the open door as Ali put several shots into the walls on either side. The bullets did not penetrate. Auburn quickly leaned in and fired a shot at Ali and missed. Ali fired many shots at them.

"Is he out of bullets?" Tony asked.

"Can't be sure and I can't take a chance. He's got an Uzi and probably more ammunition than I have." Auburn again leaned in and took another quick aim at Ali but saw him replacing a cartridge in his Uzi. He turned to Tony. "He's prepared."

Auburn took a small revolver from his ankle and slid it to Tony, who picked it up.

Tony whispered, "I'll give you a chance to finish him." Before Mark could stop him, Tony stood with his hands up. He held the gun with two fingers on the handle of the gun and said, "I give up. I surrender. Take me. Take my gun."

Ali looked surprised as Tony entered the waiting room. Ali reached for Tony's gun. In a fraction of a second Tony jumped to the side and fell onto the floor. As Ali began to turn to fire at Tony Mark slid along the floor and took one aimed shot and hit Ali in the center of his skull.

"What's happening?" Naib asked Ali.

"Drop the gun," Auburn said. "You're alone."

Naib looked at Adara. "You did not win." He pointed the gun at Adara as Carmen jumped in front of her. Naib shot and Carmen fell.

Auburn went up to the bulletproof window as Naib looked up and fired several shots at him. The window stopped the bullets.

Auburn picked up the other Uzi.

As Naib propped himself against the wall he took out a hand grenade and tossed it into the middle of the conference room filled with people. Ryan calmly picked up the grenade and tossed it across the hall into the secretarial area. It went off and destroyed that room without hurting anyone else. This time glass flew across the street on Broadway as a larger crowd gathered.

Just as Tony was about to go from the waiting area to the offices, someone with a gun came up behind him.

It was Mo. "Put it down. Now!"

Mark sized up the situation in an instant. "You're a kid. You don't want to do this."

Mo took out a cell phone and began to dial. "In a few seconds there will be no police outside to stop us."

Tony quickly pointed his revolver up as Mark raised his hands and offered his gun to Mo. "Let's trade the gun for your cell phone."

"No." Mo misdialed and said under his breath. "Shit!"

They walked into the offices with Mo behind them. "I got them. Ali's dead," Mo said.

"Bring them in." Naib looked at Adara while he grabbed Viviana and put a knife on her neck. "This is good. It seems that Allah has delivered everyone to me to punish together. I will punish you now."

Viviana karate chopped him in the balls. As he doubled over she used the same arm to elbow him in the chin. Naib tightened his grip and dragged Viviana down with him.

With that Mo turned to firing position.

Mo hesitated as Mark jumped onto Naib. He grabbed the knife by the blade and pulled it away from Viviana's neck. As they struggled Tony pulled the small gun and dropped it. Naib tried to push Mark to the side as Tony tried to grab the gun from Mo. Mark took the knife away from Naib and while still holding the blade cut Naib's neck from ear to ear.

"Stop it," Mo yelled as Mark made sure that Naib's neck bled more than his hand.

Tony wrestled with Mo and they struggled for the gun. "Drop it. You're just a kid. I don't want to kill you."

Mo pushed Tony away.

Mo jumped towards Tony and tried to grab his gun. Tony shot him again and again.

* * *

Piertowsky, the police and two EMS ambulances showed up moments later. Ryan and Carmen were being worked on as Bill was coming around. Within minutes there were news trucks around and reporters bullying everyone they could.

As two EMS workers were taking Ryan, Carmen and Bueno out under IVs, one reporter ran up to a worker with the name "Paul" on his shirt. "Paul. Can you tell us what happened?"

Paul pushed him aside. "Can't you see we're trying to save lives here?" He turned to his partner. "What a schmuck."

Viviana ripped the bottom of her skirt and was bandaging Mark's hand. "You saved my life. I don't know how to thank you." He looked surprised as she kissed him passionately.

Adara thought to herself, *not again.*

Bill insisted on walking out and into the ambulance on his own. Just as he entered the ambulance and was out of sight of the cameras, he collapsed. Another team of EMS workers pulled sheets over Maria, Mrs. Rodriguez and the Russians.

* * *

Police were taking pictures of the scene and of the three dead terrorists. Auburn bent down over Mo and turned to Sorrelli. "He couldn't have been over fifteen. How could they bring this kid into this?"

Tony identified the other two terrorists and got the files that contained their photos.

Adara sat and cried as Tony and Mark came over. Tony put out his hands but Adara stood up and would not allow herself to be hugged. Tony turned and went into the other room.

The Mayor of New York and several other politicians came across the street from city hall and tried to take credit for the demise of the terrorists. They wanted to be seen with Auburn and Sorrelli. Mark and Tony walked away.

Piertowsky got a call from Supervisor Gomez congratulating him.

THIRTY

Tony knelt beside Maria's coffin, crossed himself and said a prayer as Adara watched by his side. An old woman came over and thanked Tony for coming to the wake. She handed him a card commemorating the event. Tony said he was sorry that he was unable to save her. He promised that the firm would help Pepita.

Adara ran out of tissues and left the room to get more. Tony followed her and hugged her in the hall. "I'm sorry, Adara."

"You did what you could. No one could expect more."

"No, I'm sorry for many things. I'm sorry that I treated you the way I did for so long. I get it now, but I always knew the truth. I never grew up."

"You are you and that's what I loved. You couldn't love back."

"I guess I always knew that, but I'm sorry that I couldn't return the feelings. It's not that I didn't love you. I did. I guess that it was because the feelings were too real, too much for me to deal with, so I always pushed them away and told myself that I would deal with them at some later time. It was easier to just play. The women I played with didn't matter, so it was easy. I just wasn't ready. Now it's too late."

Adara blotted some tears from her eyes with a clean tissue. "I'm sorry you never said that before. I needed to hear that. Life goes on, Tony. You always knew that. I waited and waited for you to come to your senses. What did you expect?"

As they took the taxi to the office, Tony took a clean tissue from Adara and blotted his eyes. "If I could do it all over again, I would do things differently between us."

"You couldn't. If you could you would have."

"I'm sorry I'm not a better me."

Adara gave Tony a hug. "You are a great person. You are loving and caring to a fault. You just have trouble being that person when things get too close to home."

"A better me wouldn't have lost you."

"Don't tell me I was your only chance at love, Tony. You never had trouble attracting women."

"Getting dates and wanting to build a life with someone are very different things. We had a life together."

"You mean in the office?"

"Sure. That's a life. Now you have a life with Mark."

"That's not what I mean by 'having a life' Tony, and you know it. Much has happened. Yes, Mark and I have moved along very fast. I have a new life now. Having a life together in the office doesn't count for enough. You once said that you like strong take-charge women. Well, I took charge. Surprised?"

As the taxi drove to the office they each looked out of their windows.

"If I had another chance I would do things differently," Tony said.

"You can't do that to me. Right now we're friends. If you dredge up too much dirt, you'll poison what we have. It really is time to move on."

"Well, we're talking."

"Why are you doing this to me now? We've talked enough." She spoke to the driver. "Please stop right here." With that Adara got out of the cab.

"Adara! Get back in. We're not at the office yet."

"I'd rather walk the last few blocks alone."

As the taxi continued on, Tony told the driver to stop and paid him. He waited for Adara to catch up. She did. "Let's walk together."

"Enough," she said.

"Are you having problems with Mark?"

"I said 'enough'."

"Are you sure you're ready?"

"I moved a little fast."

"Can you slow things up?"

"He moved a little fast. I'm not sure what's going to happen."

"What's happening with Viviana?"

"Either she's the worst traitor or the best friend I've ever had."

They quietly walked the last two blocks to the office. The entrance to the office had been hastily boarded up by the insurance company. There was a private security guard.

Tony opened the door as they surveyed the damage. There was damage all around. Yellow police tape, destroyed furniture, files and papers all over, blood, books, broken glass. They went into Bill's office for a look. It was dark. All the windows were boarded up and there was debris everywhere. In one corner was a small frame with broken glass. In it was a medal. Adara picked it up.

"What's that?" Tony asked.

"It's a medal. It says it's a Purple Heart."

"That's for being wounded when he was in the army. I've never seen it."

"It says on the frame *For wounds incurred in defense of the Republic of South Vietnam February 2, 1968.* I never knew this."

"Me neither." Tony took the medal into the light and looked for a while and cried. Adara came over and gave him a hug.

"You will be all right. You stepped up and saved lives. You're a hero too."

"You mean 'too late'."

"No, I don't. You never had to be a hero like this before. No one should have to. I came from a country where people faced these choices every day. Most of them ran away or did the worst things imaginable. I came to America to escape that. You proved yourself and I hope you never have to again."

"This goes to the heart of how I feel about myself."

"You were always a hero in other ways. Now you are a hero in this way too."

THIRTY-ONE

Adara walked over to Auburn's office. The guard recognized her and gave her a visitor's sticker as she signed in.

She found Mark sitting with a pile of files reading with his damaged hand in a sling.

He looked up at her. "The doctor took another look at my hand and says the scar will remain for life."

Adara smiled. "It will always be a reminder of what a hero you are."

He put down a file. "What's on your mind?"

"I need to be assured that you know what you're doing. I don't want you to jump from the frying pan into the fire."

"Not happening."

"Are we moving to fast?"

Mark looked intently at her as he searched for the right words. He took a bit too long to answer.

"We have been moving fast. Too fast," Adara said as a tear rolled down her face. "I want you to be sure that you know what you're doing. I've held my love for a very long time and I can hold it for a bit more. I need to be sure you're not just on the rebound."

"Are you afraid you aren't sure?"

"I would rather take it a bit slow than make a mistake. I saw the way Viviana kissed you. You liked it."

"Well…"

"Don't say anything. You weren't kissed for a long time until I came along. You were starved. You needed that kiss. I know because I needed it too. When she kissed you, I could see that you liked it. You liked it but didn't want to hurt me."

Mark sat there and folded his legs as he looked aside.

Adara continued. "You know, when people are starved, their appetite exceeds the size of their bellies. I know because I have starved. I have starved in Iraq and in the desert. I have also starved other ways in New York. There it was food. Here it was love. I had a taste of you and it was good. I want to be sure it's not because I was starving that you taste so good."

"You're having second thoughts."

"You might say that."

"Do you want to break up?"

"I want to slow up. I want to be sure that we both know what we're doing. Is that wrong?"

"No."

"I'm burying people I deeply cared about and I need some time to get myself through it all. Can you understand that?"

"Sure."

"Can you wait?"

"Of course. Whatever you decide, I will back you up. I'm not going anywhere. Next week I will make a speech at the memorial at Ground Zero to commemorate September 11. I need time to prepare, so let's take a break and we'll talk then. You can tell me yes, no, you need more time or anything else. Whatever you decide, I will love you."

* * *

Adara showed up for the memorial ceremonies and stood on the side with the crowd. As Auburn caught her eye, they both smiled and they both knew what Adara had decided.

THIRTY-TWO

Adara threw up, washed up and returned to her office. Just a bit of morning sickness, she thought.

Bill took off his new Prince of Wales tweed jacket, put it on the back of his chair and stood at his brand new desk. He picked up the *New York Post*. There were ads for Thanksgiving sales at all the major department stores. In the time since 'the incident,' as it was called, things moved back towards normal as much as they could. The Imam's trial was about to start. One article said that Curtwright was lead prosecutor and there was a quote from U.S. Attorney Auburn that under Curtwright's leadership he had the best team possible for the task.

Adara came into Bill's office. She wore a long-sleeved shirt buttoned to her neck and a long, tight skirt. She wasn't yet showing. "How's the new receptionist working out?" he asked.

"I explained to Rachel that she needs to ask questions. She's taking a course in immigration law and she's asking too many questions. I can't shut her up. I didn't think that hiring Ryan's fiancée would work out. I think she might work out too well."

"So you're okay with the part time while she's in school."

"Sure, so long as she switches to evening classes in the spring."

"Don't worry, she won't replace you."

"You don't have to worry either. I won't replace you."

"What about the work out front?"

Adara smiled. "I like the new doors and the sign. They're going in right now. That's the last of it."

"Good."

Rachel walked into Tony's office with Mr. Nagy.

"Thanks, Rachel." He turned to the client. "Good to see you, Mr. Nagy. Before we begin there's a matter of a past due bill."

"You can trust me. I will pay you as soon as I can, but right now things are tight."

"Mr. Nagy, I can't. The hearing is in forty days. You had a year and a half to take care of this bill. If I don't get full payment by Monday, I'm going to file a motion with the court to be relieved."

"But we're friends. You understand."

"I understand that we have an office to run, people expect to get paid and I must put my effort into those clients who pay me for my services. You could have made payments along the way, but you waited until the last moment."

"I'll try to get you the money before the hearing."

"Let's be clear. If I don't have the money in cash and in full by Monday, I will not continue. I will file a motion with the court to be relieved. That motion will be granted. Do you understand?"

Rachel sat at the window as a middle-aged but very fit man came up to her. "Max, good to see you. I'll tell Ryan you're here."

"Tell him to hurry. I'm parked illegally." Max ran into Bill's office. "I love the new sign."

Bill laughed.

As Ryan ran out he poked his head into Adara's office. "My dad's here. I'm going out to buy that item."

"If you think you're getting a good deal, tell my man," she said. "We're also looking for a wedding band. He needs the ring real soon." She put her hand on her belly. "Don't worry. I won't tell anyone that you intend to propose to Rachel at our wedding."

Bill answered the phone. "Hey, Mark! Good to hear from you. I saw the article about the arrests in Chambersburg. I'm glad the kid got a good deal in the witness protection program. No details of course."

As Ryan and Max ran downstairs, Ryan turned to his dad. "How could you park my new car illegally? My new yellow Shelby convertible. My baby."

Max laughed. "The car is fine. Your mother's in it. The jeweler will wait and once we get this matter moving, I can look forward to a real baby from you."

Bill answered the phone again. "Hey, Oliver...Yes....The home study has been approved?...Even though they're not legally married yet?...I really appreciate this....That's right. It's already taken care of....Yes, Maria can rest in peace knowing this....Yes....You'll perform the ceremony....Yes. His mother has insisted in having a priest there....Good. I was afraid it would be a problem for you....You should call Adara and tell her yourself.... It's nice that they'll celebrate their wedding anniversary every year on Christmas eve....Okay, I'll tell her. Sure....Bye."

Bill walked into Adara's office. "It's done. You two will have temporary custody of Pepita before the wedding. Oliver says the adoption will take place in due time. He also agreed to perform the ceremony and will accommodate Rosa's request. He says he must."

Adara got up and hugged Bill as a tear ran down her face. "And you will walk me down the aisle."

"No one better for the job. I always thought of you as my children. You know I love you like my daughter and Tony like a son."

"Viviana and I are going shopping tonight for her maid of honor dress."

"She'll be walking down the aisle with Mark in his best outfit. Can't wait to see that. Are you sure you're okay with that?"

"More than you know."

As Bill left the office, he looked at the new sign. *Zalmanski, Sorrelli and Goldberg P.C.* He smiled.

Tony came out to look and they both smiled. "Wanna go for a quick bite?"

"Sure."

They sat down in Mudville.

"Did you get your car yet?" Bill asked Tony.

"I'll have it Friday. I had to wait till the government's settlement check cleared."

"What color?"

"A white Corvette ragtop with blue leather interior."

"Of course. What else would you drive? You can race Ryan. New?"

"Not brand new. I got a great deal. It's a year old, four thousand miles and I got it at a real discount."

"Nice."

"One of our clients. You know. Bueno found it for me."

"Yeah. He also helped Ryan."

Claire came over and put down menus. "How you doin', boys?" She turned to Tony. "I heard you boys. How long does a girl have to wait for a ride in your new 'vet?"

"I can't promise you that, Claire."

"That's all I'm looking for. Can you promise me a ride?" She slipped him a matchbook. "I just wanna ride...to start." When he opened the matchbook it contained her telephone number. He looked at her and winked.

Tony handed the matchbook back to her. "I'm a one-woman man now. I've already found her."

"Lucky bitch."

CPSIA information can be obtained
at www.ICGtesting.com
Printed in the USA
BVOW03*1345170817
492150BV00002B/2/P